D0328763

A TWIST OF ORCHIDS

ALSO BY MICHELLE WAN

Deadly Slipper

The Orchid Shroud

A TWIST OF ORCHIDS

A Death in the Dordogne Mystery

MICHELLE WAN

MINOTAUR BOOKS

A Thomas Dunne Book
New York

TO DEAR FRIENDS MICHEL, MARIE-SYLVIE,

GARRY, MARIE-PIERRE, AND BOB.

TO TIM, WITH LOVE.

AND ESPECIALLY IN MEMORY OF MARY WOODMAN.

This is a work of fiction. All of the characters, organizations, and events portrayed in this novel are either products of the author's imagination or are used fictitiously.

A THOMAS DUNNE BOOK FOR MINOTAUR BOOKS.
An imprint of St. Martin's Publishing Group.

For information, address St. Martin's Press, 175 Fifth Avenue, New York, N.Y. 10010.

www.thomasdunnebooks.com
www.minotaurbooks.com

Library of Congress Cataloging-in-Publication Data

Wan, Michelle.
A twist of orchids : a death in the Dordogne mystery / Michelle Wan. — 1st U.S. ed.
p. cm.
ISBN 978-0-312-54994-7
1. Wood, Julian (Fictitious character)—Fiction. 2. Dunn, Mara (Fictitious character)—Fiction. 3. Women interior decorators—Fiction. 4. Orchids—Fiction. 5. Dordogne (France)—Fiction. I. Title.
PS3623.A456T95 2010
813'.6—dc22

2009041519

First published in Canada by Doubleday Canada, a division of Random House of Canada

First U.S. Edition: April 2010

10 9 8 7 6 5 4 3 2 1

ACKNOWLEDGMENTS

I am deeply grateful to many people at home and abroad who helped this book become a reality. In France, my heartfelt appreciation to Marie-Pierre Kachintzeff, Patrick Lemesle, and especially Garry Watt and Michel Renard. I cannot thank you enough for your unstinting and timely assistance. Not only did you correct my French, you enabled me to get my police and planning procedures straight and my facts right. I also wish to thank Maryvonne Chaumel, mayor of Carves, for further elucidating French planning regulations. In Canada, my thanks to Rana and Murat Fahrioglu for their help with the Turkish language; Larry Hawkins for his insights into the real world of undercover drug policing; Wayne Hawkins for generously sharing with me his knowledge of motorcycles and air transport; my agents, Frances and Bill Hanna, for their encouragement; my editor, Lara Hinchberger, for helping to make this a better book; and my computer guru, James Lewis, for keeping me up and running. I thank my sister, Grace, for her enthusiastic support, and last but far from least, Tim for his botanical guidance, his critical read of the manuscript, and most of all, his loving and steadfast presence in my life.

Finally, I owe an enormous debt of thanks to Holger Perner for his friendship, for generously sharing with me his tremendous knowledge and love of orchids, and for the choice of *Paphiopedilum sanderianum* as one of the orchids appearing in this book.

AUTHOR'S NOTE

This work of fiction takes place in the Dordogne (dor-DOHN-yuh), a *département* in southwestern France. The characters in this book are fictitious, and the landscape is a mix of real and invented places. The orchids, with the exception of one, exist. Long may they continue to bloom for the pleasure of all.

PROLOGUE

In the pre-dawn light, the ruin of the Temple of Vesunna rose as a shadowy hulk. Relic of a time when France was an outpost of the Roman Empire, it stood in a circle of parkland in the middle of Périgueux, departmental capital of the Dordogne. An empty pop can, wind-driven, skittered along its base. The can bounced and clattered down an incline to land on a walkway where it went careening off again, singing its hollow, tinny song. Tumbling and spinning, it eventually came to rest against a pair of boots.

The boots, badly scuffed, pointed toe-down into the ground. Bare expanses of ankle above the boots showed that their wearer, a man, was without socks. Perhaps he owned no socks, or perhaps he had dressed in a hurry. He wore jeans and a denim jacket and lay on his stomach on the walkway, legs at a slightly higher level than his head. His arms were bent at the elbows, hands cupping, as if protectively, the sides of his face. A careful observer would have noted that the man's clothes were frozen, that water had leaked from his mouth as he lay in this position, and that a small, icy pool of it had collected in a stony depression beneath his chin. An even more careful observer would have seen that the man's nostrils were filled with dark vegetative matter, like soil, as if the very earth had risen up to stop his breath.

At this early hour, the parkland surrounding the temple was still. Pigeons, roosting high in the broken masonry, slept.

The pop can remained, rocking gently against the obstacle against which it had come to lodge. Until another violent gust of wind sent it dancing on its way.

1

The young man was an exoticism, a flamboyant figure against the mid-March backdrop of a small-town street market in southwestern France. He was dressed in an elaborately embroidered saffron-yellow vest worn open over a long white cotton robe. His hips were draped in a wide, colorfully striped sash, his feet clad in bright red shoes with pompoms at the toes. A length of green silk was twisted around his neck and knotted fancifully at the front. A red cap sat like an overturned flowerpot on his black, curly head.

As if his outfit were not remarkable enough, the young man was strapped to a large, chased brass and silver urn. Or rather, in the manner of traditional Turkish salep sellers, it was strapped to him, secured to his back by way of a diagonal sling that passed over his right shoulder and under his left armpit. The urn narrowed at the neck before swelling out again into an oriental cupola that rose behind him like a second head. The spout of the urn, long and curved, was hooked under his right arm. A faint swirl of steam escaped from its ornate beak. A circular metal tray attached to the young man's waist held Styrofoam cups.

"*Hadi oğlum daha canlī bağir, Kazīm. Orda korkuluk gibi duruyorsun* . . ." urged a large, middle-aged, mustachioed man in Turkish. He stood nearby before a bulwark of spices and foodstuffs from Anatolia, homemade baklava and glistening dolmas at two euros fifty each. These articles were equally out of place among the stands filled with the usual offerings: root vegetables, bread, baskets of eggs, loops of sausages, walnuts, farm-cured hams, cheeses, fish, tubs of honey, and bottles of dark fruit wine. Flattened duck carcasses, picturesquely called "overcoats," shared display space with plucked chickens that lay heads dangling, feet crossed. What the man, Osman Ismet, said was: "Put some life into it, Kazim. You're standing there like a scarecrow. How do you expect to get their attention like that? Drum up business, can't you? Do your spiel. A real *salepar*'s got to have a spiel," and so on. The Turk's mustache flowed magnificent as a stallion's mane on his upper lip. Kazim shot Osman, who was his father, a bitter look and muttered something, also in Turkish, the general import of which was: "This was your stupid idea. You do the spiel. I'm freezing my ass off."

It was true. Kazim's face was pinched with cold, despite the fact that under his getup he wore a second set of clothing. The skirt and sleeves of his robe snapped and fluttered in the wind, exposing banal glimpses of frayed sweater cuffs, faded blue jeans, and gray wool socks.

"Watch your tongue," the father reprimanded, prodding the son forward into the path of shoppers who filled the central square of the town. "Show some respect."

It was getting on for noon, and the market was beginning to wind down. People, loaded with purchases, were drifting away. Some of the vendors were already closing up their stalls. Business for the Turks had been slow all morning. Soon it would be time for them to pack up as well.

Sullenly, ironically, and in French, Kazim began to call out: "Okay, folks! Here it is! All the way from Istanbul, the Aphrodisiac of Sultans!" He said it, emphasizing each syllable: "Aff-ro-dee-zee-ack of Sul-taaaans!" His dark eyes flicked glumly over the slowly moving throng, focused momentarily on the buildings on the side of the square opposite his family's stall, took in the steep stairway leading up to the porch of the Two Sisters Restaurant, and swept on.

"Good, good," encouraged Osman Ismet. "Aphrodisiac. That always gets their attention."

And indeed, some shoppers, attracted by the young man's cry, were stopping, willing to be momentarily amused, because street markets in the Dordogne, indeed everywhere in France, were always a form of entertainment as well as commerce. Kazim's eyes continued to roam while his mouth formed a version of the prescribed *salepar*'s pitch:

"Got the wilts? A slurp of Elan will perk you up. Do wonders for the little woman, too. Made with a secret ingredient from a centuries-old formula. You don't think Scheherazade's old man kept it up for a thousand and one nights without a little help, do you? Here it is, folks. Elan, the drink of drinks. Three euros a cup, or buy a pack of powder mix for twelve, make it at home, the Viagra of Sultans . . ."

A quartet of teenage girls gathered around him, giggling. A middle-aged couple, trundling a wire shopping cart laden with vegetables, baguettes, and a spit-roasted chicken, paused. Moving toward him through the thinning crowd, like a galleon in full sail, came a big man in a green-and-brown checked overcoat. He was accompanied by a thin man dressed in black. The thin man's face was as narrow and gleaming as the blade of a knife. A pair of gendarmes strolled up from the opposite direction. Kazim took in the man in the overcoat and his companion as well as the approaching gendarmes. He bent forward swiftly, causing the spout of his urn to give forth a stream of hot, creamy liquid that he caught somewhat inexpertly in a Styrofoam cup.

"*Voilà, monsieur.*" He shoved the cup into the hands of a fat fellow in a black beret and a bulky zip-up sweater who happened to be passing. "Free to you. Special promotional offer."

The fellow, a pig farmer from Saint-Avit-Sénieur, sniffed it suspiciously. "What is it?"

"Something you'll thank me for. Old fart like you could use a stand-up-and-salute," said Kazim the *salepar* very loudly, to the laughter of some bystanders. Jeeringly, he addressed them at large: "You French are all alike. Don't know what you keep in your pants."

"What the hell—" objected the old fart at the same moment that the father, mustache leaping, hissed in Turkish, "Are you crazy? That's no way to talk to customers. What's gotten into you?"

"Watch your mouth, shithead Arab," yelled a tough-looking, acned youth.

"Yeah," yelled a couple of his mates.

Kazim's dark eyes singled out the pockmarked face. "You call me a shithead, you come and talk to me. Or don't you have the guts?"

"I'll send you back where you came from, minus something, *sale bougne,*" offered Pockmarks, surging forward. The crowd, interested in a fight, surged with him. More people hurried over to catch the action. Vendors left their stalls.

Kazim, the erstwhile *salepar,* slipped swiftly out of his harness. The heavy urn dropped with a clang to the ground, rolled, trailing a sudsy stream of Elan, and came to a stop against one of the wooden legs of the table bearing the family's wares.

"Filthy terrorist!" another voice shrilled.

The gendarmes, alerted by the hubbub, pushed through the growing crowd of people.

"Please! Please!" shouted the father, switching to heavily accented French. He stood arms and legs akimbo before his minor international enterprise. "Stop. I beg you. Is no way to talk. We are people of peace—"

At that point, his son crashed into him, propelled by the acned tough and his two mates. The Turk himself was driven backwards onto his stand. It collapsed beneath the combined weight of the five men in a rain of spices, olives, baklava, dolmas, stuffed peppers, and paper packets containing the Aphrodisiac of Sultans.

"Break it up!" yelled the gendarmes, wading in to quell the brawl.

On his back, piled atop his father, Kazim planted a pom-pommed shoe in the stomach of the first gendarme.

Because he was the only one looking up, Kazim alone saw the woman fall from the restaurant porch. She came flying at a slant down the diagonal of the stairway, arms outstretched, mouth straining open like an avenging djinn.

2

Madame Chapoulie, hurrying out of her flower shop to see what the commotion in the square was all about, nearly tripped over the body of the old woman lying at the bottom of the Two Sisters' stairs.

"*Mon Dieu!*" screamed the florist, terrified by the thin sound that came from the woman's gaping mouth, by the staring eyes that already seemed to be taking on an awful vacancy. "*Au secours!*"

Her cries drew people from the fight. By then the gendarmes had things more or less under control anyway. The crowd flowed out of the square toward the hysterical florist. The gendarme who had been kicked came, dragging Kazim with him; the other followed with the pimply-faced youth in tow. The youth's mates had seized the opportunity to run for it. The first gendarme let go of Kazim to check for a pulse in the fallen woman's neck. Kazim obliged the officer by sticking close. The other gendarme held on to his captive. He took in the position of the body, the steepness of the flight of eighteen stone steps that rose above it, and observed: "Must have missed her footing."

It was the general consensus. The restaurant spanned the upper stories of a pair of houses that in former times had been owned by two English sisters, the reason that the restaurant's name was rendered in English rather than French. The houses were separated by a narrow alley and bridged at the top by an elevated porch. In summertime, the porch was a pleasant spot for a meal or a drink. In winter, except for waiters hurrying from one house to the other—that is, one part of the restaurant to the other—or customers crossing to use the toilets located on the right-hand side, it was deserted.

"It's those damned steps," a man muttered, and there were murmurs of agreement. "She must have been distracted by the fight at the Turkish stall and tripped."

"Should have used the cage," someone else said, referring to an old-fashioned elevator that crawled up and down the back exterior of the restaurant. It doubled as a goods lift and a means of conveying those not inclined to use the stairs, which was the majority of customers, since parking was also around the back.

Kazim's gendarme stood up. He looked grave. "I'm afraid she's had it." He pulled out his cellphone and began punching numbers.

•

The death was reported on the eight o'clock news that night: Amélie Gaillard, eighty-five years old, wife of Joseph, resident of the hamlet of Ecoute-la-Pluie. Cause of death: a massive cerebral hemorrhage caused by an accidental fall. There was some discussion of the condition of the Two Sisters' stairs, which were in fact sound and equipped with a sturdy handrail. The restaurant owner was interviewed. "We absolutely urge patrons to use the elevator," he declared.

Amélie's death, however, was overshadowed by the evening's main story. In the early hours of the morning, Périgueux municipal workers had discovered the body of an unidentified male near the Temple of Vesunna. The man was described as of European type, brown hair, blue eyes, 180 centimeters tall, weighing 78 kilograms, and between thirty-five and forty years of age. Needle marks in his arm tagged him as an intravenous drug user and possibly a petty pusher. For these reasons, it was assumed that his was a gangland killing.

· 3 ·

After the service, everyone went to the cemetery, situated a short distance beyond the church. Amélie's coffin was borne by a pair of nephews (the only two who had not left the region), three immediate neighbors—Louis Boyer, Jean-Marie Roche, and Olivier Rafaillac—and another man from elsewhere in the commune. Joseph, Amélie's husband, ten years her junior and suffering from Parkinson's disease, shuffled along behind, supported by Francine Boyer and the *notaire,* Maître Joffre. A small, gray man in his sixties, Maître Joffre had attended to the Gaillards' affairs for nearly thirty years. After them trailed the nephews' wives, followed by the rest of the residents of Ecoute-la-Pluie, where the Gaillards had lived for more than half a century, among them Mara Dunn, *la canadienne,* the couple's closest neighbor. Mara walked with nurse Jacqueline Godet, who provided home care for Joseph. Bringing up the rear were other people from the commune at large.

Because of Joseph, the pace was excruciatingly slow. Already there was a widening gap between the coffin and the mourners. At one point Joseph simply froze in place, causing the procession to come to a halt. But the pallbearers, unaware of this fact, continued down the path so that the gap was now almost unseemly, as if Amélie were bound for a destination unrelated to the knot of people who waited patiently for something to click on again in Joseph's brain, for his feet to resume their laborious forward shuffling.

The walled cemetery was a cluster of sad marble monuments made even more desolate by a litter of faded plastic flowers. Perched on a hillside, it overlooked muddy fields and wooded valleys that in this season stood stripped and bleak. A fine rain had begun to fall, and a raw wind gusted out of an unforgiving sky. The coffin was lowered into the earth. At the graveside, the mourners huddled tightly, perhaps for warmth. Mara was aware of surreptitious glances. It was the artichoke farmer, Olivier Rafaillac, who started it by looking over his shoulder. Other heads turned, eyes met eyes. Their faces said it: she hadn't come. At this late hour, wouldn't come. But whether their expressions held censure, anger, or relief, Mara could not tell.

A latecomer of only nine years' standing in the hamlet, Mara had never met the Gaillards' daughter. All Mara knew was that she had left home years ago, that her name was never mentioned. It was as if Christine Gaillard had somehow ceased to exist. And of course Mara had never thought it proper to ask why.

The priest was reaching the end of the rite of committal when the metal gate of the cemetery clanged. A man and a woman, shielded by a large golf umbrella, came hurrying up. The umbrella, green and white, was the only spot of color in an otherwise somber scene. Their approach was greeted by soft exclamations of surprise.

"Ils sont venus!"

"Que c'est gentil."

"Joseph sera touché . . ."

They came! How kind. Joseph will be touched . . .

The O'Connors had come. All the way from Florida, Monsieur and Madame O'Connor had made the journey to say their last goodbyes, while that heartless daughter . . . There was a flurry of nods, whispered greetings, a quick touching of hands. Mara did not know the couple well, but she was French

Canadian, from Montreal, so they exchanged rapid embraces as fellow North Americans. From Daisy she received air kisses and a quick impression of boniness and sugary perfume; from Donny, the silky feel of expensive Ultrasuede, no doubt weatherproofed, and a waft of his own brand of aftershave. Daisy wore a navy blue Aquascutum raincoat and a clear plastic rain scarf decorated with white polka dots over her ash-blond hair. The O'Connors had been coming to the region for years. They had a house not far away in the village of Grives.

With a display of self-deprecating body language, offers to share the umbrella, Donny and Daisy slipped in between Mara and stout Suzanne Portier, whose walnut orchard adjoined the Gaillards' land.

"Terrible weather," Daisy mouthed at Mara in English with an excessive shaping of red lips. A stick figure of a woman with staring blue eyes, she reminded Mara of a middle-aged Barbie doll. "The flight over was awful. How's Joseph holding up?"

"Not well," Mara answered truthfully. He was standing tremulously near the head of the grave, still supported by Francine Boyer and Maître Joffre, and had not noticed the Americans. It was Francine who took the single red rose from Joseph's hand and dropped it for him into the open grave. Others said their last goodbyes by throwing down small handfuls of damp earth that thudded on the coffin.

"It's so sad," Daisy murmured. "Honestly, they were like family to me. I had to come. For Joseph's sake. Amélie would have wanted it."

A moment later the Barbie doll left the shelter of the umbrella to insert herself in Francine Boyer's place, where she gathered the widower in her arms. Briefly, Mara glimpsed Joseph's face, bobbing dazedly over the Aquascutum shoulder, and felt a tug of the heart. She herself had held back from going to him during the service and the burial, observing the proprieties, deferring to family members and older friends. She felt a sense of minor outrage that the Barbie doll had so simply jumped the queue.

Then it was over, condolences were expressed, the rain fell harder. The mourners hurried as quickly as decorum allowed back to the covered porch of the church and the little square where their cars were parked. For the moment, Mara walked alone. She was a small, slim woman, forty-something, with an oval face ending in a pointed, determined chin. The rain rolled off the black beret she wore pulled down over her dark, short-cropped hair. It dripped off her bangs and clung to her lashes. She blinked and realized that with the rain she was blinking away tears. She dug in her pocket for a tissue and blew her nose.

Jacqueline Godet caught her up. The short, fat nurse's words came out in breathless bursts as she waddled along.

"It's cruel . . . her being the first to go."

"Yes." Mara had assumed—they all had—that Amélie would outlast Joseph. Eighteen steps had made the difference. "Will he be able to manage on his own?"

"Oh, he'll do. He can get . . . extended home care. Until then . . . I'll arrange for daily nursing visits. We'll take it as it comes."

"But"—Mara's dark eyes filled with concern—"he's starting to freeze up. You saw how he was earlier. What if he falls?"

"He's better than he looks," the nurse reassured her. "He's just having a bad day. You can imagine."

Donny O'Connor came alongside. "You talking about Joseph?" Gallantly, he held the golf umbrella over them. He was a big man in his fifties, bareheaded, his iron-gray hair styled in a boyish brush cut. "Daisy thinks he's in pretty bad shape. She's also worried about his heart. Parkinson's may be neurological, but it affects the muscles, and the heart's a muscle. Plus, we've just heard he's starting to hallucinate. Sees things in the room with him, bugs in his food."

"Side effect of the drugs," said Jacqueline. "Nothing serious. They get used to it."

Mara glanced back. Joseph was at the rear of the straggling line, between Maître Joffre and Daisy, who teetered precariously on high heels that dug into the soft ground. She seemed to clutch Joseph's right arm as much for balance as to help the old man along. The notary, trying to make his umbrella do for three, struggled to support both of them.

The nurse shook her head. "It's the day-to-day stuff . . . I'm more concerned about. Amélie . . . used to take care of everything. He was very dependent on her. He'll have to learn . . . to do for himself now. Main thing is . . . his pills. It's important he remembers to take them on time."

Donny's permanently suntanned face—he golfed year-round, Mara knew, had even toured professionally—expressed concern. "Well, if you ask me, he looks worse than when we saw him last fall." The American had a bit of difficulty with his vowels, with the throaty *R,* but his French was serviceable.

Jacqueline shrugged. "Parkinson's is progressive. So his tremors . . . his movement . . . are always going to be 'worse.' He's had it ten years now. But he's a tough old boy. He'll last . . . a good while yet. I've known Parkinsonians . . . to go fifteen, twenty years on their own."

They reached the square. Everyone huddled in awkward little groups under the dripping church porch. By now, Donny's brush cut was heavily beaded with moisture. At last Joseph appeared, led by the notary, with Daisy miming assistance on the side. Daisy detached herself and came to join her husband, Mara, and Jacqueline.

"He's in terrible shape," she almost accused the nurse. Unlike her husband, her *R*s were beautifully formed and her French fluent. "He'll never make it without Amélie."

"It's a bad time for him," said Jacqueline, stiffening. "We'll get him through it."

Daisy shook her head emphatically. Her plastic rain scarf made a faint scratching sound against the collar of her coat while giving off little sprays of water. "It's not a matter of getting him through. I was saying to Donny on the way here, he was fine while Amélie was alive. That woman was a saint. But now he needs round-the-clock, professional care. He needs to be in a proper nursing home."

"We're pretty concerned," said Donny.

Jacqueline's face went stony. "He doesn't want a nursing home. He wants to live out his life in his own house, on his own land. It's his choice . . ." She broke off, laboring for breath.

"Damned right," muttered Mara, and was rewarded by a cool, porcelain stare from Daisy.

"And he'll get good care, if that's what you're worried about," said Jacqueline drily.

"Oh, I didn't meant *that,*" said Daisy.

"Not at all," seconded Donny, anxious to conciliate. "Anyway, Daze, I'm sure the nurse knows best." He knew Jacqueline but always called her "the nurse," as if she had no identity outside of her function.

Mara left the Americans to make their peace with Jacqueline and went to Joseph who, with Maître Joffre, was making his way slowly to the notary's car.

"She's gone," Joseph said as Mara came alongside him and took his free arm. It was what he had said to everyone at the service and graveside, as if repetition would somehow help him to grasp the reality. His gnarled face, made wooden by his affliction, was unable to shape to his emotion, but his eyes shone with the anguish of unshed tears. The sagging lower lids were red and dry. They made Mara think of something desiccated and at the same time newly flayed. A bubble of saliva winked at the corner of his mouth, burst, and began to snail down his chin. She fumbled in her pocket for a tissue, found only the one she had blown her nose on, and used it to wipe away the trail of spit.

"Yes, she's gone," she tried to comfort him, "and we'll all miss her. But you won't be alone, Joseph. You're surrounded by people who care for you, who'll stand by you." Neighbors who themselves were aging, but who would support him out of solidarity. And herself. She was the incomer, the youngest resident of Ecoute-la-Pluie. She would repay every kindness Amélie and Joseph had ever shown her. She turned to the notary.

"Are you coming back with us?" A simple funeral reception was to be held at the Boyers'.

"*Oui,*" Maître Joffre sighed. He opened the car door. "It's a sad day."

Together they backed Joseph onto the passenger's seat. He had been a big man, still was, although today his body felt to Mara like a gathering of bones. His eyes followed the notary as he walked around the front of the car to the driver's side. Urgently, Joseph tugged at her sleeve.

"You've got to find out." His lower jaw trembled, and his voice was barely audible. Mara had to bend forward to catch his words. "They won't tell me. But they might tell you."

"Won't tell you what, Joseph?" she asked gently.

"Why?" Joseph looked at her pleadingly. "Why was she up there?"

4

"Does it exist or not?" demanded the fellow orchid enthusiast, thumping a page of the open book they held between them.

"As I said, it's an uncertain sighting. Not mine, unfortunately," said Julian Wood.

The enthusiast was no fellow but a towering female whose salient bosom nearly struck him in the face as she leaned over to make her point. Above that part of her anatomy he was aware of shrewd blue eyes in a round face and a full head of unnaturally red hair. For the moment he felt dwarfed and a little desperate. Of course, he was sitting and she was standing, which gave her an unfair advantage. A long, lean, middle-aged Englishman with melancholy features obscured by an untidy mustache and beard, he found the little table at which he crouched very uncomfortable. It was positioned just inside the doorway of the Librairie Mazeau, the newest bookstore in the town of Bergerac. The idea was that customers coming and going would stop to purchase an autographed copy of his most recent work, *Les orchidées sauvages de la Dordogne/Wild Orchids of the Dordogne,* a stack of which stood on the floor beside him. With spring around the corner, it was theoretically a good time to promote a book about flowers. But winter still had the land in its grip; people were exhausted and grumpy from months of nasty weather and far from believing in spring. So far, all he had attracted was this woman and cold air every time the door opened.

"Ach! Then why include it?" Her English was stiff but correct.

German, he thought. Or, he modified, picking up a singsong intonation, Swiss.

"Because I think it almost certainly grew in these parts once and hopefully still does." Julian spoke guardedly of an unidentified Lady's Slipper orchid of which he had only artifactual traces. His book, a lovingly annotated bilingual photo-guide of every species of terrestrial orchid known to the region, included a blurry photo and an artist's sketch of a flower he had provisionally named *Cypripedium incognitum,* not known at all. The orchid was a thing of mystery and almost sinister beauty. Its bright pink middle petal, the labellum, was shaped into the characteristic pouch-like slipper that gave the genus its name. Two astoundingly long, twisted, dark purple petals sprang dramatically from the sides of the flower.

Perhaps because it was unknown, *Cypripedium incognitum* drew Julian like a siren's song. *Find me,* the flower seemed to whisper. And from the moment it had thrust itself into his life a couple of years ago, he had been obsessed with doing just that, combing hills, meadows, and woodlands in his search. Ardently he believed that one day this flower, seductive as a phantom bride, would reward his quest by showing him its face. Somewhere it waited, just for him, on a sun-dappled ridge or around the next turning of the path.

The woman, still skeptical, said, "You know, of course, Western Europe has but one indigenous Slipper orchid, *Cypripedium calceolus.* If this"—she thumped the page again—"proves to be a native, it will be two. It will make a sensation for the orchid world."

Good God, she didn't have to tell him! The monumental possibility had long teetered in his mind like a boulder on a slender finger of stone.

"However," she went on, "I think it is more likely an import that has managed somehow to establish itself in the wild."

"Even so, it makes for a remarkable story," Julian countered. The chances of a transplant surviving were slim, which made his *Cypripedium* not only alluring but vulnerable and valiant.

"Hmm. And you are sure about the lateral sepals?" She referred to two blackish purple petal-like structures flanking the labellum; a third of similar hue arched over top, like a canopy. "This, too, I question. As you know, except for the Ram's Head and *Cypripedium plectrochilum,* all other Slipper orchids typically have the lateral sepals fused as one. In your book you show them clearly separated."

"It's what makes this orchid so remarkable."

"But what is your evidence? Ach! A picture taken in situ, not very good, and this drawing of some kind of embroidery." The photograph she referred to had been shot in May 1984 by Mara's twin sister, Bedie; the drawing was an artist's sketch, based on an antique embroidered representation of *Cypripedium incognitum* dating from 1869. Bedie, unfortunately, could not be asked about the orchid; she had taken all knowledge of it with her to the grave. The embroidery, however, told a tale. It was a remarkable piece of needlework done by someone with an eye for detail and was the most complete depiction of the flower Julian had. The photo, blurry and stained, was unreliable and by itself could have shown merely a one-off mutant. However, the embroidery was botanically precise and gave the flower a second, much earlier reference point. The two, taken together, were sufficient to convince Julian that the orchid, native or transplant, was no isolated event.

"Moreover," went on the Swiss, "you give no information on how you came across the photograph or where you found the embroidery."

"No," said Julian firmly. "I don't." That would be to reveal the areas of his ongoing search. The world was full of orchid hunters, most of them, as far as he was concerned, totally unscrupulous.

"Hmm," she said, perhaps divining his motives. "Such an orchid I have never seen, and I would very much like to do so. I am particularly interested in Slipper orchids. This one"—she cocked a shrewd, bright eye at him—"I don't mind telling you, I particularly wish to have." She paused, the eye sizing him up. "I am prepared to pay you extremely well to find it for me."

"You—what?" He gaped, unable to believe what he was hearing. She was proposing to engage him in the same way collectors of past centuries had hired plant hunters to go to the ends of the earth to bring back exotic species. He understood what drove collectors, being prey to some of the same mad forces himself, but really, this Alpine Valkyrie had a nerve. The orchid, if it belonged to anyone, belonged to him. He had no intention of delivering up what could prove to be the greatest orchidological find of the twenty-first century to anyone but the botanical world at large, a world he intended one day to stand on its ear. He struggled to maintain a civil front.

"Well—er—it's been nice talking to you."

"Perhaps I do not make myself clear. I want this orchid."

She had, and he wanted her to leave. She was blocking the entrance and, more importantly, potential buyers. The door opened, admitting another blast of frigid air, and a man squeezed past.

Julian backpedaled. "As I said, it's an uncertain sighting. One can't really be sure of it."

Her gaze narrowed. "So you are now saying you don't know if there really is such a thing?"

"No. Well, yes. I suppose when you get right down to it, that is what I'm saying."

"Ha!" Her wide red mouth opened in a predatory laugh, and

she punched him playfully on the shoulder. The blow rocked him backwards. "You are dodging." She pronounced it *dotching*. "You are afraid I will steal your darling. All right. Simply prove to me *Cypripedium incognitum* exists. I will pay."

Julian heaved himself up. He was taller than she, but not by much. He said briskly, "Well, that's my point, isn't it? In order to prove anything, I first have to find it. So you see, it's sort of a chicken-and-egg thing. And if I find it—*when* I find it—I won't need to be paid." He gave her a ghastly grin. Let her chew on that.

The woman waved chickens and eggs aside. "Monsieur Wood, I am not just an ordinary collector. I am also a botanist and a breeder. I specialize in Slipper orchids. I have a greenhouse full of rare species that people from all over the world beg to see. I am Adelheid Besser. You have heard of me?"

"Ah." He had, and he acknowledged the name with a sinking feeling. She also had a reputation for ferocious acquisitiveness and was exactly the kind of person he needed to shield his orchid from.

She went on grandly: "However, my interest in orchids is more extensive than collecting and breeding. I do also research into the food and medicinal uses of orchids. For example, do you know the European Lady's Slipper has a very interesting phytochemical makeup? It contains cypripedin, an allergenic quinone that gives some people a bad rash."

You give me a bad rash, he thought.

"The plant makes this substance to protect itself from fungal attacks. Now, have you ever thought that perhaps cypripedin has antifungal properties that can be commercially exploited?"

My God. Julian's mind flew protectively to his orchid, and his stomach lurched. *She'll grind it up. Or boil it. To make a cure for athlete's foot.* He stared at her in horror, much as he would have stared at a cannibal about to eat him.

"So," she pursued, impervious to his state of mind, "to get back to *Cypripedium incognitum.* If you can prove to me this orchid exists, as I said, I will pay you well. Call me when you have considered my proposition." She gave him her card.

"Look, I'm really not interested—" He backed away as Adelheid Besser accosted him again with her enormous anatomy.

"I would not," she said ominously, "wait too long."

5

Julian drove back to Ecoute-la-Pluie at the end of the afternoon. His encounter with Adelheid Besser had left him feeling paranoid and helpless. Paranoid because he was desperate to protect his orchid from people like her; helpless because in order to protect it, he first had to find it. It would not come into bloom—if it bloomed at all; orchids could be bloody temperamental—until early May. Until then, there was little he could do. Without its flower, *Cypripedium incognitum* would be hard to spot.

Mara was in the kitchen assembling a *gratin dauphinois* when he came into the house. They alternated cooking nights. Tonight was her shift, and when she cooked she was typically distracted, if not downright cranky. Julian exchanged quick pecks with her and edged between their two dogs to get a beer from the refrigerator.

"How's Joseph bearing up?" He did not know the Gaillards well but had liked Amélie, was sorry his book signing had made him unable to pay his last respects.

"Not well. I passed on your regrets. A nephew and his wife are with him now." She squinted at an opened cookbook through a pair of varifocal glasses that she had never learned to see through, near or far. "But they can only stay for a few more days. After that, until some kind of regular home care is set up for him, Jacqueline and another nurse will rotate to visit him daily, and Francine Boyer, Huguette Roche, Suzanne Portier, and I will work in turns to drop in, see to shopping and his evening meals. I'm taking some of this over to him later."

"Poor old boy. Who'd have thought she'd go first?" Julian echoed everyone's sentiments. He dodged around her, getting a glass, rummaging through drawers. Her kitchen, a model of good design, boasted color-coordinated appliances, strategic track lighting, and a center island table with matching stools that were too low for him. Interiors were Mara's profession, and she had successfully transplanted her Montreal practice to the Dordogne, where her services were much in demand. However, Julian still had not figured out where things like the bottle opener were kept.

"Here." She found it for him in the dishwasher. "Now stop hovering."

So he backed off and stood watching her, sipping his beer and feeling a bit at loose ends.

The problem from Julian's perspective was that the rest of her house was like her kitchen: a showcase.

"You have to understand," Mara had told him when he first moved in, "my home is my shop front, my display window."

"Yes, but the display keeps changing."

This was because she ran a sideline in one-off furniture and accessories. She was forever picking through junk shops and *vide-greniers,* unearthing an old farm cupboard, a fire surround, an antique standing clock, all of which took their places in her dining room or salon or vestibule, waiting to be sold on. Other things would take their places. It was very hard for Julian to feel settled.

However, his grievance with the furniture was nothing compared to the running battle he had with Mara's cleaning woman, Madame Audebert. She was a gaunt person with a rotten temper who had taken a dislike to him from the start. On her days in, she glared at him with eyes as black and sharp as olive pits and went about with a disapproving mouth, puckered like a knot of worms.

"You leave your things everywhere," was a frequent Audebert complaint. "And then there are your plants."

Julian was a lover of growing things. He had brought with him a legion of potted plants that dropped leaves and had to be moved each time the woman wanted to polish the furniture.

"And your dog. I find his hairs everywhere."

Initially, he had tried hard to win the heart of the steely *femme de ménage.* He had bobbed and smiled like an idiot as she drove him inexorably from room to room with thrusts of a vacuum cleaner that roared at him like a windy, Jurassic beast. He had tried conversation. Madame Audebert wanted no part of him. Her grumbles had escalated from the olive-pit looks and the mouth to outright war. Soon Julian gave up trying. He knew that good cleaning women were hard to find and even harder to retain. Sometimes he actually wondered, if push came to shove, whom between them Mara would shove.

That was probably why he felt the need every so often to return for a few days to his poky little cottage outside the village of Grissac—to check up on things, he said, but really to be at his ease, to reassure himself that if things got too bad in Ecoute-la-Pluie he still had somewhere to go. It was a kind of unofficial Time Out during which he reacquainted himself with his books (he had an enormous quantity of them), his old leather armchair (it sagged to the shape of his body), and his smoky fireplace. He did his laundry, puttered, mused about the state of his roof, and checked the garden for winter's damages. Mara seemed to accept these breaks, maybe even welcomed them. It was what made his living situation so peculiar. Neither here nor there. *Like camping out,* he thought sadly.

From Mara's viewpoint, the *ménage à deux* was a necessary experiment. Both of them had survived unhappy past marriages; both of them had become used to their own company. After months of dating, this trying out of each other at close quarters was something she really felt was the logical next step.

"A relationship is like a shark," she often said. "It has to move forward or it drowns."

But there were times when she actually wondered what she and Julian were doing together.

"We have such different approaches to life," she had complained to him more than once.

"Yes," he had agreed. "You like to move things around, rearrange space, even between people."

"I like to make a bad layout better. It's my métier. Nothing wrong with that. But you seem content just going with the flow."

"And I suppose, seen through the shark's eye, that's tantamount to drowning?"

"Well, sometimes it's important to be proactive. Take Madame Audebert, for example."

"You can have her, as far as I'm concerned."

"Please, Julian. I'm serious. I at least tidy up before she comes. I need this place to look good." It staggered her that Julian, with unbelievable nonchalance, simply left his whisker hairs in the bathroom sink, his clothes on the radiators, his reading material everywhere, and always seemed surprised at the consequences.

"Or communication. I happen to think it's important to talk about things, to get down to the real us. Whereas you take everything, even me, at face value."

"Oh, give me strength," he had objected.

He also had an annoying habit of standing about, as he was now, looking long, shaggy, and slightly displaced. And then there were his botanical passions.

Normally, Mara could have off-loaded by email to her best friend and touchstone, Patsy Reicher, formerly resident in the Dordogne, now returned to New York. >*Patsy,* she could have written, *what am I doing with a man who gets more excited about a flower than me?*< And Patsy would have shaken her wise, frizzy, iodine-colored head and written back, as she had done before: >*You're with him because, despite everything, he's a sweetheart, and there's something about him that tells you in the long run he's a keeper. Stick with him, kid.*<

Except that Patsy was not in New York. A gum-chewing psychoanalyst–sometime sculptor with a patchwork history of relationships of her own, Patsy was with a new partner of the heart, a burned-out fellow shrink named Stanley, on a journey of the soul in Nepal. Which was good in a way, because it had allowed Mara to arrive, uncoached, at the conclusion that she really did want a life with Julian. It was just the getting there that was difficult.

So it was that the only ones really comfortable with the living arrangement were the dogs. Bismuth, Julian's bony, sad-faced mongrel, liked the larger space; Jazz, Mara's white and tan pitbull (also Bismuth's sire) welcomed the company.

She was now bringing a liter of salted milk to the boil and grating nutmeg into it. Then she had to do something with 50 centiliters of crème fraîche and 80 grams of butter, but that came later. She had already peeled and sliced the potatoes into rondelles, which lay ready on the cutting board. *Spuds and milk,* she thought. *Can't go far wrong with that.* It was the main problem with having a housemate: she, a rotten cook, felt obliged to come up to some minimal standard where meals were concerned.

"How did the signing go?" she asked.

"Oh, fine."

"Sell many books?"

"Er—no. But I met the most bloody awful woman. Adelheid Besser. Big orchid collector and breeder. She also dabbles in the food and medicinal properties of orchids."

"Oh?" Mara, studying the glossy photograph of the prepared dish, which looked brown and rich and crusty, wrinkled her forehead. "I wonder if I cut the potatoes thin enough."

"She actually had the nerve to try to *commission* me to find *Cypripedium incognitum.* Can you believe it?" From where he stood Julian eyed the photo, too. "That looks good. I'm starving."

"Well, you pretty much put your orchid up for grabs by including it in your book."

"That was in the hope someone might have information on it."

"And if they did, do you think they'd tell you? You know what orchid freaks are like. Obsessive, secretive, and paranoid."

Fleetingly, Julian wondered if she meant to include him. But he said, "Like Géraud, you mean." Géraud Laval was an irascible man and Julian's bitter rival when it came to things botanical.

"And this Adelheid. You were bound to attract kooks."

"She's not just a kook. She's downright scary. I think she'd be capable of reducing the entire population of European orchids to a tincture."

"Yes, well—" Mara gave a small scream as a rapidly forming head of white froth suddenly caught her eye. She snatched the saucepan from the fire, but not before most of the milk had cascaded over the sides.

"*Merde!*" She made an attempt to wipe up the spill before it crusted on the range top. Then she said, "Oh, *flûte!*"

"What now?"

"It says here to cook the potatoes *in* the boiled milk."

Julian considered the great mound of potatoes on the cutting board.

"Your pot seems very small," he ventured.

"I know that," Mara snapped, and lunged into a cupboard from where, with a great deal of clanging, she extracted a larger vessel into which she transferred the milk and the potatoes. She stared at the mixture for a moment, then banged on the lid, adjusted the gas fire, and expelled a gusty sigh.

"Sorry." She turned to him, looking sheepish. "Pour me some

wine, will you? This has to cook for ten minutes."

They went into the dining room where they sat down on flimsy-looking chairs that went with a round table with fluted legs, recent acquisitions from a *brocante* in Villeréal.

"God, what an awful day," Mara said, shoving Bismuth away with her foot. Jazz had gone to sprawl in his usual spot on a costly Aubusson rug of floral design that dominated the front room. "First, the daughter, Christine, didn't come, but then the O'Connors did. All the way from Florida."

"The O'Connors?" Julian started to lean back but stopped; he was never sure if the new chairs would take his weight. He had met the Americans twice. Donny struck him as a decent enough sort of bloke with whom he had nothing in common—the man was in "development," whatever that meant, and golf. As for Daisy, he could not get past her scent. It preceded her into a room and lingered heavily after her departure. Oddly enough, it had a bitter underlay that he could almost taste on his tongue.

Mara took a sip from her glass. "Daisy is very attached to Joseph, you know. In fact, she was all over him with TLC at the reception." She added drily, "Even to the point of feeding him. He kept having to open his mouth so she could cram food in it. And she spent most of the afternoon telling me about Amélie's virtues, as if I didn't know her, too."

Julian caught her tone. "You don't like Daisy much, do you?"

"No, I suppose not." Mara used to think it was because Daisy laughed at her French. Like many *québecois,* Mara was a mix of things (Scottish father, French-Canadian mother) and fully bilingual. Her English was indistinguishable from standard Anglo-Canadian. Her French, however, was pure *montréalais,* where words like *même* came out *mime,* where whole syllables slid precariously together and consonants got strained through the teeth. Daisy, whose French was near to perfect, had thought it necessary to say to Mara, on their first meeting and in English, "Wherever did you get that darling twang?"

Now, however, Mara understood that her dislike had deepened to something more elemental: fear of loss.

"Daisy has a way of taking people over," she said, "of reshaping them according to how she sees them. I don't want that. I want to remember Amélie as she was for me—not a saint, but big and bossy, a real stickler for proprieties. You didn't want her to catch you doing the wrong thing. But she was generous and warm, and I loved her." She reflected wistfully, "You see, Julian, when I first moved here, everyone was nice, but it was the Gaillards who really took me in. Amélie set me up with her butcher, her market vendors, her cheese merchant. At first I didn't know a *cabécou* from a *brebis.* We formed a mutual bond of affection. She was always interested in how I was doing and usually keen to tell me how to do it better. And Joseph, before his Parkinson's got bad, was always ready to help me out."

Mara felt the tears coming again. Sympathetically, Julian took her hand.

"They taught me so much," she mourned. The virtue of patience, the value of local gossip, the many ways of beating a system that often drove you crazy. Best of all, Amélie and Joseph had revealed to her the litany of their quiet but rugged existence built around food and governed by the seasons: the race for morels after a spring rain; the succession of summer vegetables; the autumnal activities of harvest and hunt; the secretive search for cèpes and truffles; the bottling and the canning; and the cracking of walnuts around a neighborly winter fire. In so doing, they had given her a precious gift: they had enabled her to become part of life in Ecoute-la-Pluie.

Whereas—her chin snapped up—Daisy and Donny were visitors. They did not live there year-round but came and went as they pleased, taking the best and discarding the rest. Mara shook her head. She knew she was being petty and unreasonable. Visitors or not, Donny and Daisy had known the Gaillards for years, far longer than she. They had earned their place in the Gaillards' lives.

"Sometimes," she mused, "I wonder if I haven't been more of a daughter to Amélie and Joseph than Christine."

"It really is too bad about her," Julian said. "She should at least have made the effort to attend her own mother's funeral. Was Joseph upset she didn't show?"

Mara considered this. "I don't know. To be honest, I think he was more worried about what Amélie had been doing up on the Two Sisters' porch."

"Good question. It's a godawful place for a restaurant, unless you're a mountain goat. Those stairs are really steep." Julian drained off his beer. "Maybe Amélie was checking it out for lunch."

Mara said doubtfully, "The Two Sisters is a pretty upmarket spot. Not the Gaillards' kind of thing."

"All right. She went up there to meet someone."

"No. They'd gone to Beaumont simply to do their marketing. Anyway, Joseph would have known if it had been anything like that."

Julian stroked his beard. "The way I heard it, Amélie took Joseph to the WC. Then she went off to get her vegetables—"

"Unless it was someone Joseph wasn't supposed to know about," Mara mused. "I wonder if that's what he meant when he said 'they won't tell me'?"

He gazed at her suspiciously. "You're at it again."

"What?"

"Ferreting."

"Ferreting?"

"It's what you do."

"I do not."

"You do. You invent puzzles where none exist."

"I'm not the one asking the question. It's Joseph."

Julian shifted in his chair. "All the same, I think you're making it unnecessarily complicated." He drew on his botanical background. "In plant classification—"

Mara closed her eyes and made a sound between a growl and a groan. Julian heard it but went on.

"In plant classification there's a thing called the tenet of parsimony. It says you should go with the simplest hypothesis that squares with the facts. I'd say"—he broke off to sniff the air—"the most straightforward explanation is that Amélie took Joseph to the gents, lost him in the crowd, and climbed up the stairs to have a squint round for him." He sniffed the air again. "Something's burning."

"*Merde!*" Mara leaped up, knocking her chair over in her rush for the kitchen. When she lifted the casserole lid, she saw that the milk had boiled dry. The potatoes on the bottom were crackling dangerously while those on top still had a raw, slimy look. Smoke rose from the mixture.

"Oh, damn and blast!" she yelled and punched the exhaust fan button. Who said you couldn't go wrong with milk and potatoes?

· 6 ·

The Ismets' Turkish food shop was situated between an ironmonger's and a *tabac* on the main street of the town of Brames. The front was painted green, and the word *Lokum,* Turkish for the gummy, sugared confection known in English as Turkish delight, was lettered in flowing script on the display window. Julian, with his sweet tooth, was a valued customer of Lokum. Whenever he was out that way, he always dropped in to buy squares of Betul Ismet's baklava, which oozed honey beneath the tooth and left telltale shards of pastry on his beard. He treated himself to little tubs of *mulhallebi,* a cold, fragrant milk pudding dusted with ground pistachios, or savory, multi-layered *borek* stuffed with red peppers or eggplant. The latter were sprinkled with sesame seeds that he liked to pop between his teeth. Some of the seeds lodged there, affording (although he would be ashamed to admit this publicly) a delightful reserve for popping later.

That morning he had another reason for stopping by the store. He had heard that the Ismets were selling a drink at their market stall that they promoted as a "health and sexual stimulant." They called it Elan, the Aphrodisiac of Sultans, and claimed it contained a secret ingredient. He had a horrible suspicion the ingredient was salep.

For centuries, Turks had used salep, a starchy powder, to make a popular drink of the same name. It was reputed to be a powerful love potion. Julian had heard that there was some scientific evidence for this, although he did not believe it. Still, at three euros a cup for the ready-made drink or twelve for a packet of the powder, the Ismets' concoction was a lot cheaper than Viagra.

Julian's problem was not truth in advertising. His real concern was that salep was made from orchids. For centuries the Turks had dug up wild orchid tubers, which they dried, ground up, and mixed with hot milk, honey, and cinnamon to make salep drink. Salep was also used in other foods, like Turkish ice cream. The traditional practice had not changed, but demand had increased. He had read that between thirty and fifty million orchids of numerous genera were harvested every year to make salep. Julian was all for tradition, but the relentless collection of tubers in the wild had put many of the source plants on the endangered list. Consequently, the Turkish government had banned the export of all forms of native orchids, whole or in part, chopped up or pulverized. However, large amounts of the product were still consumed domestically. Salep also continued to be internationally traded. Unlike illicit drugs, it was a minor blip that did not register on a customs officer's radar screen.

The long and short of it was that Julian took any threat to orchids almost as a personal attack. By trade he was a landscape gardener, a profession that he practiced in the Dordogne with varying financial success. But his real love was wild terrestrial orchids, wherever they grew. And the last thing he wanted to see was the popularization in his corner of France of a product that encouraged their destruction.

That was what he planned to talk to the Ismets about that morning. He had been debating for a couple of weeks how to put his case: directly (please stop importing the stuff); or edging into it sideways (look, your specialty is Turkish foods, not so-called "health" products. Why not stick to what you do best?). He wasn't sure how either approach would be received. Osman and his wife,

Betul, were hard-working people who had probably never thought about the ecological impact of their commerce. That was the trouble with the world in general, he thought. Too busy. Too unconcerned. As he parked his car and hurried against a biting wind toward the shop, Julian decided to try a blend of direct and indirect. He was disappointed to find Lokum's front door locked and the *Fermé* sign hanging crookedly in the window.

Surprised, too, because he could see lights and activity inside. Osman appeared to be having an energetic conversation with a tall, fair-haired gendarme whom Julian recognized: Sergeant Laurent Naudet. Julian had met the gangling young policeman the previous spring. He knocked on the glass. Osman's arm waved him away peremptorily, but Betul, seeing who it was, came to open the door.

"*Mon Dieu, qu'est-il arrivé?*" Julian stared about him as he stepped inside. Had the place been hit by an earthquake? Everything was off the shelves. Plastic bins of homemade foodstuffs had been overturned, their contents strewn across the floor where they had been stepped on, making a slippery mess. It also seemed unusually cold in the shop.

"It's terrible." Betul shut the door and relocked it. She was a comfortably built woman whose face in youth might have been full and cheerful but with age had taken on the loose-fleshed droop of a bloodhound. Today her large, sad eyes were red and swollen with crying. She wore a coat as well as ankle-high, fleece-lined boots. As usual, a kerchief was tied over her hair. Julian had never seen her without some kind of head covering.

"Thugs! Racist thugs!" Osman exclaimed, turning to Julian with a gesture of despair. His face, with its horse's mane mustache, was both outraged and tragic. Unlike his wife, he wore only a baggy cardigan by way of extra clothing. His big stomach hung over his belt like a sandbag.

Another gendarme, chubby, dark-haired, rosy-cheeked, emerged from the back of the store. Julian recognized him as Albert Batailler, Laurent's partner. Julian exchanged greetings with both men.

"What the hell happened?"

"They broke in through the back," said Albert, pushing his kepi off his forehead.

Osman shouted in his imperfect French, "Is all you can say? I know that! Who do you think sweep glass? Who fix window?"

"Well, you shouldn't have," Albert said severely. "You might have disturbed evidence."

"Evidence? Evidence? Is everywhere. How long you take to come? Meanwhile, is great hole for wind to blow in. My wife, she freeze. Anyway, you think these thugs are nice to leave fingerprints? DNA maybe?"

"We came as soon as you called." Albert was not backing down before the near-hysterical shopkeeper. "And the perp might well have cut himself."

"Cut? I give him cut he remember, *pis haydut!*"

"Was anything taken?" Laurent asked, trying to calm things down.

"Who can tell?" Osman moaned. "They destroy, only destroy. Food they smash. Everything on floor." He turned about him, surveying his devastated shop.

"Any money missing?"

"Money? Maybe."

"How much?"

"I don't know."

Laurent went to the old-fashioned till on the counter and released the cash drawer. It popped open with a clang, revealing perhaps a hundred euros in bills and coins. Not robbery, then, but sheer vandalism.

"You live over the shop?" Laurent asked.

Betul and Osman nodded.

"And yet you heard nothing?"

"I sleep good," said Osman defensively.

"He sleeps like a dead man," said Betul softly. "Our bedroom is two floors up, monsieur. The living room and kitchen are in between. It's impossible to hear." Her French was considerably more fluent than Osman's, and more idiomatic. Although she deferred to her husband in most things, Julian had the impression that Betul was more attuned to the realities around her and was the shrewder of the two.

Julian went to have a look at the rear of the store. A glass pane in the back door had been smashed. An attempt had been made to block it with cardboard, but the cardboard had been pulled away, no doubt by Albert in his search for evidence, and now hung by a strip of masking tape. A fearsome gale blew through the jagged gap. Bags of spices had been slashed open. The air smelled of aniseed and pepper. Pistachio nuts, coffee beans, and dried apricots were scattered all over. A big sack of flour had been upended, its contents driven into little drifts, like snow, by the draft from the broken window. His foot slipped in an oily magma of crushed tomatoes and black olives. The damage was vicious and thorough. Julian understood the Turk's anger.

When he returned to the front, Laurent was asking the Ismets if they had any enemies, anyone who wished them ill, or whom they might have offended. Betul, who had been hovering at the edge of the circle of men, was now openly sobbing. Osman ignored her.

"Racist thugs at market in Beaumont," he answered bitterly. "Three of them, one with pimples. Call bad names. Was big fight. Smash stall. Beat Kazim up for no reason."

Beaumont was outside Laurent and Albert's jurisdiction, but they had heard about the brawl. The gendarme who had received the full force of Kazim's pompommed shoe in his stomach six days earlier might not have agreed with the Turk's account of events. Kazim had given as good as he got, perhaps had even provoked the incident, according to a pig farmer from Saint-Avit-Sénieur. Kazim and one of the youths had been hauled off to the local gendarmerie, where they had been held for a time to cool off. They were later released with a stern warning to stay out of trouble.

"You think they were the ones who did this?" Laurent tugged at one of his oversized ears. His bony wrists stuck well beyond the cuffs of his navy jacket.

"Of course. Is persecution. Because we are Turks. Always we are made to suffer."

"Okay. We'll check it out." Laurent shot a questioning look at his partner. "Although it's funny they didn't touch the cash."

The gendarmes left.

"You see?" Osman fumed after they had gone. "You see how we are treated? Twenty years we are here. Good citizens. Not cheat taxes like everyone else. Work hard. What thanks? They beat us. Break our shop. Spoil everything. Who pays? Who pays for good food thrown on ground?" (Betul's weeping became louder; it was her labor that had gone into all the ruined pastries and dolmas, the sugar-dusted squares of Turkish delight). "Does criminal pay? Does government pay? No. Is poor Turk pay." Osman beat his massive chest and, like his wife, began to cry.

"Come on," Julian said, suggesting the only helpful thing he could think of. "I'll help you clean up."

•

It did not take them long to clear the mess away. Everything was dumped or scooped into plastic bags. Osman taped the cardboard over the broken pane again and closed the door leading to the back part of the building. Fortunately, there was no real damage. The floors and walls just needed a good scrubbing, but the Ismets would have to restock. Julian could see that the loss, much of it imported goods, was considerable for a small enterprise such as Lokum. He wondered if the Ismets carried vandalism insurance.

After Osman and Julian had dragged the last of the garbage bags out to the bin in the alley behind the store, the Ismets invited Julian upstairs for coffee. It was the first time Julian had been in their living quarters. The decor was overwhelmingly red. Red carpets covered the floor. There was a divan upholstered in red plush with chairs to match, a carved buffet with a red runner. They sat at a table covered in a red-fringed cloth. On the walls hung hammered brass trays and photographs of Anatolia, of the Hagia Sophia. Betul made them coffee, hot, strong and sweet, served in little glass cups with wire handles.

"We have nothing but misfortune." Her eyes filled up once more. "First Kazim, now this."

"You mean the fight?" Julian asked.

Osman shook his head. "Not fight. Is worse than fight. Kazim is leave home."

Betul clarified, "After the gendarmes let him go, Kazim came back to the store. I was here alone. Osman was still at the market, cleaning up the mess those hoodlums made. Kazim said, '*Anne,* I have to leave.' I said, 'Leave where?' He just said, 'Don't worry about me. I'll be okay, but I can't stay here.' He'd only come back for his motorcycle, you see. We are his parents, and we are less to him than his *moto.*" She added miserably, "He's always been stubborn, always difficult, always in trouble, ever since he was a little boy."

"He don't let people step him, that's why," said Osman, rousing himself. "He hit back. Kazim is trouble because he got guts. Is how he should be, right?" The father struck his bulging stomach with a clenched fist in a man-to-man appeal directed at Julian.

"What good does it do?" The mother's bloodhound face drooped even more. "A Muslim in France should go softly. It doesn't pay to make waves."

"Well," consoled Julian, "I'm sure he'll be back."

Betul stared into her lap. "No. He's unhappy here. We try, but happiness you cannot make for others. People reject him because we are different. In school, he always felt apart from the other children. He thinks there is no future in the store. After those toughs beat him up, I think he was very angry—with them, with us, with everyone. Maybe he believes going away from home will solve his problems. Maybe he wants to forget he's Turkish. He is our son." She raised her eyes to Julian. "Monsieur Wood, what should we do?"

Julian scratched his head. Up to now, he had only known the Ismets as purveyors of good food. Their private affairs had not entered into his transactions with them. Helping them clear away the vandals' wreckage, entering their upstairs domain, seemed suddenly to have placed him in the position of confidante and counselor. Both husband and wife were looking at him expectantly. He shifted uncomfortably in his chair. "Do you know where he is?"

"With her," Osman said disgustedly. "With bad-influence girl."

Betul was more informative. "Her name is Nadia Beaubois. They were at school together. They went out sometimes. Osman objected because she's not Turkish. We think maybe Kazim is staying with her. But how can he live? He has no money, no job. I'm afraid for him. He's young still. His place is here with us. Out there, he'll fall in with a bad crowd. Monsieur Wood"—she eyed him tentatively—"please, if only you could help us."

"Me?" Julian was dumbfounded. "What can I do?" He had no experience with the young. Moreover, he had never met the lad. Kazim worked at the family's market stall with one or the other of his parents, moving from town to town according to the day of the week, so it was only Betul or Osman whom Julian ever saw at the shop.

"Find him, talk to him, persuade him to come home. He might listen to you."

"But why would Kazim listen to me? He doesn't even know me. Surely there's someone else you can ask? A relative? Someone he respects in the Turkish community?"

Osman shook his head. "Is no community. Not here. In Istanbul is plenty uncles, cousins. But Istanbul is Istanbul. Besides, Kazim does not respect Turkish things. Like Betul says, he want forget he is Turkish. He want," concluded Osman disdainfully, "to be like French riff-raff."

"I'm sorry," Julian continued to resist. "I'd like to help, believe me, but I wouldn't know where to begin."

Betul had a ready answer. "Begin with Nadia Beaubois. She works at the Intermarché in Périgueux. For a girl like her, we're nothing but immigrants. Turks. But you, she might talk to you. If Kazim isn't with her, maybe she will tell you where he is." The mother's plea settled on Julian, heavy as a hairshirt.

Julian pondered, took a gulp of cooling coffee. He fiddled with his cup. He liked the Ismets. He supposed he could give it a try. And maybe . . . His initial dismay now gave way to an idea.

"All right," he said. "I'll do what I can. But I want something from you in return."

"Anything, anything!" cried Osman expansively. "What?"

"Your Aphrodisiac of Sultans. Elan, or whatever you call it. Does it contain salep?"

"Of course," said Osman proudly. "You know what salep

means? Is 'testicle of fox.' Is miracle ingredient. Is first-class product."

"Is illeg—" Julian stopped himself; Osman's speech pattern was catching. "It's illegal." He went on to talk about the ban on Turkish exports of orchid products and the ecological reasons behind it.

"That's crazy." Osman waved aside Julian's explanations. "Is plenty orchids in Turkey. Salep you can buy on Internet. I have supplier in Istanbul. Every month he send one, two kilos. No problem."

"What does he ship it out as?" Julian challenged. "Chickpea flour?"

"Arrowroot," Osman said with apparent ingenuousness. Either he had not thought through the implications of his supplier's mislabeling or he was cannier than he looked. "But is best salep, made from Males Orchid." A variety of *Orchis mascula,* Julian assumed. "Good for man. I mix Elan myself from secret recipe." Osman reached across to poke Julian in the chest. "You drink. Make strong like Turk."

"Regardless, I want you to stop using it."

"But"—Osman looked scandalized—"without salep, Elan is not Elan. You want I cheat customer? Besides, is start to sell good."

Betul rounded on her husband. "Elan is more important than your son? Illegal means nothing?" And she swept on in a torrent of Turkish, the meaning of which Julian easily guessed from the emphatic rise of her voice.

Osman pounded the table, jumped to his feet, put his hand to his breast, and declaimed something, also in Turkish.

"Stop it!" Betul cried out in exasperation. She explained to Julian, "He is saying, 'I am a Turk. I am correct and hard working. I am ready to sacrifice my existence for the existence of Turkey.' It is the pledge of allegiance that we all had to say as schoolchildren. But I ask you, what good is Turkey to us here?"

Osman looked sadly from his wife to Julian. His shoulders drooped. "Okay," he gave in. "Okay. But problem is not me. Problem is Kazim. Elan is first time he is interested in business, in anything Turkish. Why? Because he is smart, like father"—the big man tapped his head—"he knows product got good future. He say, 'Okay, *baba,* now I take more responsibility, handle deliveries, do inventory.' And like I tell you, Elan is success. In market we sell as hot drink for promotion. Also as powder with paper explain how you make at home. People try, they like. They think is good for make love. They like that Kazim dress up like *salepar,* walk around with *güğüm,* salep urn, on his back."

"No," said Betul sharply. "That was your idea. You made him do it. He hated it. He said it made him feel stupid. Maybe it's one of the reasons why he ran away."

"How?" cried Osman, hurt to the core. "Is good publicity. What's wrong with Turkish *salepar?* Is traditional character, is attract attention, show people a little of Turkish culture. But if we stop"—dolefully, Osman returned to his reason for objecting to Julian's proposal—"if Kazim come back, find no more Elan, what will he say? He will be more unhappy."

"Never mind," Betul snapped, losing all patience with her husband. Life had returned to her sad eyes. "Don't worry about Elan, Monsieur Wood. Just find Kazim, make him come home. We'll explain everything. He'll understand."

"And you'll stop importing salep?" Julian pressed.

Reluctantly, Osman nodded.

"Then it's a deal," said Julian. "Although there's just one thing." A critical point of information. "I don't know what your son looks like."

"Like me," said Osman proudly. "But younger. Is nineteen."

"Not like you," Betul cut in bluntly. "Kazim is skinny, not fat like Osman, and without walrus mustache."

"What walrus?" Osman objected.

"A photo would help."

Betul got up and left the room. She returned minutes later with a school photo, taken when Kazim was perhaps fifteen. A round face with dark curly hair, his mother's long nose and large eyes.

"Nothing more recent?"

She shook her head.

"Well, what kind of motorbike does he have?"

"Honda," said the father. "Big shiny red."

"A Bol d'Or," said the mother, ever more practical. "New. He just bought it this year."

"And what was he wearing when he left?"

"Ha!" Osman slapped the table with the flat of his hand. "White robe—what we call *önluk*—long to ground, yellow vest, red shoes, red hat." The man's natural buoyancy came bubbling up as he tried to make a joke. "You cannot mistake. When he left, Kazim is dress like Turkish *salepar!*"

"Don't be foolish," Betul scolded. "Monsieur Wood, when Kazim came for his *moto,* he took some clothes and his leather jacket. He left the *salepar* outfit. I put it away where my husband would not see it. I knew it would only upset him."

Osman's face fell. "You see?" he said miserably to Julian. "You see what I say? Our son is try take off his Turkish skin. But—" The father sat up straight, his head lifted with pride, and he said with conviction, "He cannot. Once you are Turk, you cannot change what is inside."

7

The Brieuxs' commercial empire in Grissac occupied the ground floor of a large house built of honey-colored Périgord limestone. A small, thriving conglomerate, it consisted of a general store, a *dépot de pain,* a *tabac,* and a *marchand de journaux*—that is, it supplied not only groceries, mousetraps, and dish detergent, but daily deliveries of fresh bread, cigarettes, and newspapers as well. It also served as the informal hub of activity and gossip for the surrounding villages and farming population. Most important, it was the site of the Chez Nous Bistro, which offered some of the best cooking in the region. Julian knew the owners, Paul and Mado Brieux, from his bachelor days when he had lived full-time at his cottage, a twenty-minute walk away.

On that Friday night, the bistro was full as usual. Julian, Mara, and another friend, Loulou La Pouge, a retired policeman, sat at their customary table at the front. Bismuth slept at Julian's feet, Jazz near the bar. Friday was their weekly dinner get-together. Loulou did not know it, but Fridays were also becoming the occasion of Julian and Mara's weekly fight: Madame Audebert cleaned on Fridays.

The fight had begun earlier over a little thing. Or, from Julian's viewpoint, not little at all. He had left his English newspapers scattered about. She (la Audebert) had thrown them out. When he had asked her about them, she had retorted that they were old papers. She could read the dates, that much she could do. And she was right, except that they were last

Sunday's editions of *The Independent* and *The Observer.* Although he spoke and read French like a native, these papers were Julian's weekly treat to himself. He liked to stretch the enjoyment of them—the sports, politics, news of home—over the whole week and, well, yes, over the whole house as well. He had retrieved the crumpled pages from the garbage only to find that they were soggy with coffee grounds and vegetable peelings.

Understandably irritated, Julian had pointed out that the newspapers were now unreadable. To which the cleaning woman had declared, "*Pah! C'est la montagne qui accouche d'une souris,*" equating his complaint to a mountain giving birth to a mouse, her way of saying "a tempest in a teapot." At that point, he had lost his temper and told her in future not to touch anything that was his. She had snapped back, in that case she might as well not come at all, since his things were everywhere, and slammed out of the house. Mara, instead of taking his side, had asked him quite testily if he couldn't pick up a bit, as she did, before the woman's weekly visit. He, aggrieved, had replied: "I thought picking up was the whole point of having a *femme de ménage.*"

Then he had made the mistake of adding that he was surprised that Mara, who was afraid of nothing, could be so easily intimidated by a cleaning woman.

That was the spark that had ignited a gunpowder mood that lasted all the way to the bistro and now into dinner.

"*I* ordered the escargots," Mara snapped at Bernard, the weekend waiter, when he mistakenly put a plate of snails sizzling in garlic butter before Julian. She made it sound like an accusation.

"Um, yes," said Julian, with a slight shrug of apology to the young man. Bernard, when he was not waiting tables, served as Julian's heavy labor during the gardening season. "The—er—crayfish in tomato sauce is mine."

"Eat. Be happy," urged Loulou, digging into his platter of aubergine fritters. Fat and cheerful, he looked more like an elderly cherub than an ex-*flic.*

Conversation was strained during the main course. Loulou tried to keep his end up, but eventually fell to mopping up Mado's rich cream and morel sauce with bits of bread. Over dessert, Julian tried to jolly Mara out of her sulk by referring to their lovers' quarrel in a lighthearted way. It was, after all, he told Loulou, a case of the mountain and the mouse.

Loulou chuckled as he cracked open the crust of his crème brûlée with the back of a spoon. "*Eh bien,* which of you is the mouse?"

Mara glared. Julian was reduced to picking his teeth.

Later, they lingered over coffee, staying on as they always did until Paul and Mado could join them. By then, they and the dogs had the restaurant to themselves.

When Paul came out from the kitchen, he, too, looked out of sorts. He shook hands perfunctorily with Julian and Loulou, poked his head at Mara's face in a simulation of the double-sided kiss, hooked a chair over with his foot, and dropped his large frame into it. Bismuth, who had been lying under the chair, shot away. Jazz looked up from his spot by the bar.

"*Bigre!*" uttered Paul. "Some people are never satisfied. There was a *crétin* actually had the nerve to tell me our menu needs variety. 'Variety?' I said. 'I'll give you variety. How would you like a face full of pudding?'"

"You didn't," marveled Loulou, highly entertained.

"I did."

The bead curtain separating the bistro from the other parts of the Brieuxs' enterprise parted noisily. Mado, statuesque and beautiful, came through. She had just been up to check on their young son, Eddie, asleep in the couple's apartment upstairs.

Wearily, she embraced everyone around the table, pulled up another chair and sat down next to her husband.

"*C'est trop,*" she sighed. It's too much.

"Are you all right?" Mara asked, peering at her anxiously.

In fact, Mado looked exhausted. She had miscarried a month ago. Although the couple pointedly refused to talk about it, the loss of the baby had knocked the spirit out of the normally vibrant redhead. Out of Paul, too.

The addition of the Brieuxs did not improve the company. Julian unwittingly started an unpleasant exchange of words by mentioning that he had run into Loulou's grandnephew, Laurent. The conversation began calmly enough.

"Someone broke into the Turkish store in Brames on Sunday night," he said. "Laurent and Albert were there investigating."

"Are you talking about Lokum?" asked Mado. She knew the Ismets slightly, since they were also in the food business. Her golden eyes widened, accentuating the shadows lurking beneath them. "Robbery?"

"No, the money wasn't touched. It was a trash job, and they made a right mess. The Ismets think it was an anti-Muslim statement. Osman and his son were involved in a dust-up at the market in Beaumont last Tuesday. Name-calling ending in bodily contact. Osman thinks it was the same group of *voyous.* And to make matters worse, the son, Kazim, has left home. I'm supposed to get him back. You know about people who go missing, Loulou. This ought to be right up your street."

It was. Loulou had spent part of his career in Missing Persons with the *Police nationale* in Périgueux. In fact, it was with respect to Mara's missing sister Bedie that Julian and Mara had come to know him. Loulou's eyes lit up, and he embarked on what threatened to be a lengthy lecture. He told them that in cases where a person vanished willingly, the key was to understand the background, the psychology behind the subject's wish to vanish. "However," he went on, warming to his subject, "in the case of someone who disappears involuntarily—*ah ça!*—that is another matter. There you have to look at misadventure, kidnap, murder, human trafficking, and all too often"—he hunched forward—"a body."

"I doubt it's anything like that," Julian cut in, stemming the flow. "His parents think he's trying to shake his Muslim roots. Apparently he's fed up with being hassled for being Turkish."

"*Les arabes,*" Paul muttered. Whether he was referring specifically to Turks or to France's six million Muslims jumbled together regardless of national origin was unclear. Then he added, leaving no doubt as to the even broader inclusiveness of his meaning, "Too many damned immigrants in France. They come here, live off the system, drag everything down."

"That justifies a trashing?" Mara bristled. She did not know the Ismets, but she had been combat-ready all evening, and this was as good a cause as any for opening fire.

"I didn't say that," objected Paul, shifting about, making his chair groan.

Mara bore down. "You as good as did. It's a fact that people of color aren't treated well in France. They're stuffed into ghettos. They're poorly educated and can't get work."

"*Bigre!*" Paul stuck his jaw out. "They *won't* work. That's the whole problem."

"You're both generalizing—" Loulou began, but Paul, resentful, cut him off.

"Easy enough for her to talk. Canada's a big country. All that ice and snow. Canada wouldn't survive without immigrants. Needs them, just to stay warm. Well, they can have ours, as far as I'm concerned."

"Oh, come on, Paul." Julian weighed in. "You can't say the Ismets are a drag on the system. They struggle bloody hard to make a living, and they turn out a good product. You should taste some of Betul's pastries." This earned from Mara an almost friendly glance. She did have a personal acquaintance with Betul's baklava.

Paul snorted skeptically. "*Peuh!* Heavy. Doughy. Not like ours."

"Have you tried them?" Mara challenged. "Don't be so chauvinistic."

"Chauvinistic how? No one makes better pastries than the French. It's a recognized fact."

Julian said, "Forget pastries. You'd change your tune if you saw what those *crapauds* did to their store. You wouldn't like it if it happened to you."

"Let them try!" The big man swiveled around fiercely, as if warning off all comers.

"What happened to the Ismets is an isolated incident," Mado said, trying to soothe matters. "We don't have those kinds of problems in the Dordogne."

Loulou shook his bald head. "Ah, that's where you're wrong. It's coming. In fact, it's here. Bigotry knows no home. And what about those break-and-enters in the last few months?" He referred to a string of unsolved house burglaries. The last two had been accompanied by signature poems teasing the police.

Paul said ungraciously, "That's my point. Foreigners come to the Dordogne, buy property, push up the prices, and then live here only a few months of the year. You have all these houses sitting around empty most of the time, asking to be robbed."

"Julian and I are foreigners," Mara snapped.

Paul scowled. "Not you. You live here. You're like us. I mean those others."

"Oh, you mean like Prudence?" Prudence Chang was a mutual friend, a retired Chinese-American advertising executive who maintained a summer residence not far from Mara. She usually spent all or part of her summers there but, like the O'Connors, came and went as she pleased. She was also a very good customer of Paul and Mado. Every fall she hosted a gala eight-course lunch, catered by the Brieuxs, for her large circle of friends. The ticket accounted for a decent percentage of the Chez Nous annual take, to say nothing of the free publicity.

"Not her, either." Paul's face grew very red.

"Well, who then?"

He glowered and shoved away from the table. For a moment it looked as if he would stalk out, but instead he stomped to the bar where he appeared to struggle with his better nature. Eventually he returned with a flask of plum brandy and fresh glasses.

"There's also an increase in drugs on the street," Loulou went on, watching Paul pour out the ruby-colored liqueur. "In the last year there's been a spike in the supply of heroin in the region. I tell you this in confidence. Ton-and-a-Half may be back in business. If he was ever out of it."

"Ton who?" asked Mado.

"Rocco Luca."

"Wop," said Paul.

"French. Local boy. He was born down the road in Bergerac."

Mado asked, "If his name's Rocco Luca, why do they call him Ton-and-a-Half?"

The ex-cop took a sip of plum brandy, rolled it around in his mouth, and swallowed. "Good, this. Some say it's because he packed a big punch. Used to be a heavyweight boxer. But he really got the name because back in the seventies he was caught trying to land a ton and a half of marijuana along the Côte d'Azur. He did time and passes nowadays for a legitimate man of business leading the blameless life in a big house north of Brames."

"Brames? That's Laurent's turf," Julian observed.

Loulou nodded. "And his boss is very well aware of it, let me tell you. Compagnon's had his eye on Luca ever since he moved back to the Dordogne five years ago. He thinks Luca's behind the new action in the region. He thinks drugs are Luca's source of money and business is how he launders it."

"Is he right?" Mara leaned forward with interest. She and Julian personally knew Laurent's brigade commander, Adjudant Jacques Compagnon, a big, prickly man with a reputation for working his gendarmes hard.

Loulou lifted his shoulders. "Who knows? It's not really Luca's style—petty stuff—but Compagnon has a theory that it's leakage from bigger shipments that are being moved on. But if it *is* Luca, how is he bringing it in? Is he reverting to his old MO and landing it on the coast? Trouble is, the drug squad boys don't take Luca seriously anymore. He's pushing seventy, and they think he's past it. They're after new blood like Reynaud in Marseille and Félix Bidart in Bordeaux, who they figure are handling big transshipments to New York. However, Luca has ties with Pascal Goudy in Toulouse, a *type* with known drug connections. Those two go back a long way. He also employs someone named Serge Taussat as a kind of general factotum, and that one's as nasty as he looks. Judge a man by the company he keeps, they say. Except the Ton also has some pretty powerful political pals who owe him favors, which makes him untouchable. So far, only Compagnon is keeping Luca in his peripheral vision, and he's going on nothing more than a hunch."

"Drugs!" Paul seized the point and slammed a hand as big as a ham on the table, making the glassware jump. "That's another thing. Who brings the stuff in? Foreigners. Albanians and Kurds. Turks."

"And the Dutch," added Loulou. "Sure, most of the heroin

that starts out as poppies in Afghanistan is processed in Turkey—"

"They ship it here in boats, trucks, planes, trains, even in dogs' stomachs, *parbleu!*" Paul rumbled on.

"But the fact of the matter is that a lot of it winds up in Holland first, and from there it comes into France."

"Whatever. They're killing our kids with their poison. Look at them. High on something most of the time, shooting stuff into their veins or swallowing Ecstasy. And we're left to clean up the problem. I tell you, it wasn't like this in my day. Everything's going down the drain." Paul had recently turned forty-one. Whatever excesses had defined his youth in *la France profonde*—the depths of the country—things like soft, hard, and designer drugs had completely passed him by.

"We don't have a drug problem here," said Mado.

"Just wait for it!" roared her husband.

Julian shook his head. He had never seen his friend in such a mood. Maybe it was more than Mara's goading, foreigners, and drugs. Maybe it was change itself that was bothering Paul. It bothered him, too. You felt it in the air, saw its imprint on the land, heard it in the way people talked. The old ways, the old ties and courtesies were breaking down. Young people were restless, discontent. Every year there was more traffic on the roads. Fields that had once grown wheat and oats and maize were sprouting houses. Ugly red smudges of raw bricks (waiting to be faced with limestone; that's what everything was nowadays, facing, not the real, solid stuff) were replacing the blaze of poppies on the hillsides. Mara had criticized Julian for always going on about the vulnerability of the stretch of woodland and meadow that abutted her own property. But only last fall he had seen a team of surveyors there. "Just waiting for someone to snap it up," he had predicted grimly. And now a resident drug baron.

"Since the cops know where this Ton-and-a-Half lives," said Mado, "why don't they just pull him in?"

Loulou brought his shoulders to his ears. "On what charge? He's smart, is old Luca, and, like I said, well connected. Compagnon will want to be very sure of his ground before he makes a move."

"That *type* they found in Périgueux have anything to do with this?" asked Julian. They had all read about the sensational gangland-style murder. Chlorinated water had been found in the dead man's lungs, and there were particles of some kind of commercial soil and peat moss mixture embedded in his nostrils. It was as if he had been drowned in a swimming pool and then dragged through a flower bed before being dumped, like an offering, at the foot of Vesunna's temple.

"Ah," said Loulou. "Yvan." He drained his glass, pausing for dramatic impact.

"Yvan—they've identified him, then?" Mara's dark eyes widened.

"Yes." Loulou put the glass down, leaned in, and looked at them each in turn. "But as far as the public is concerned, no. *Alors, mes amis,* this doesn't go any farther."

"Well?" demanded Paul impatiently.

"His name was Yvan Bordas, and he was one of *ours.*"

Mado, Julian, and Mara sat up in surprise.

Paul scratched his chest. "What, you mean *un mouchard?*"

Loulou leaned back, satisfied with his effect. "Not an informer. An undercover narc."

"A narc?" Mado shook her tawny head. "They said he was an addict. He had an arm full of needle marks."

"Nevertheless, he was one of the best we had. He'd been working Marseille for the last three years. Before he died he told his contact he had a lead on a big drug shipment being planned.

So how did he wind up dead 600 kilometers away in Périgueux, eh? There's nothing to link Bordas to Luca, but it makes you wonder if Jacques Compagnon's little idea doesn't have something to it after all."

"*Merde,*" said Paul, deeply impressed.

8

It is the small hours of the morning. A broken moon rides on the backs of clouds that stream across a turbulent sky. Wind batters the house and rattles the shutters. The old man moans and struggles in his bed. He is having a nightmare. The noises, incorporated into his dream, take the form of something that has just broken down the exterior wall and is now pushing through the hole it has made, its dark mass bulging menacingly into the room. He tries to roll away from it, but his body is rigid, heavy, inert.

"No!" Joseph Gaillard tries feebly to fight it off. "Amélie!"

With a rush of relief, he opens his eyes to discover his wife there, bending over him as she often does. Then he sees in the moonlight that in place of her face is a tangle of colorless hair trailing like dead vines over a large, black hole.

His own scream of terror wakes him. In his head, the scream is shattering. In reality, it comes out as a thin, protracted wail.

Joseph often has vivid, frightening dreams. Things reach out to grab him, monsters chase him. He is trapped in rising flood waters, stands helpless in the path of thundering avalanches. Like his hallucinations, the dreams are a side effect of his disease and his medication. When she had been alive, Amélie would wake up, too, whenever he screamed. She would turn on the light and sit forward to check the clock with the big digital display to see if it was time for his pills. He took them every four hours, day and night. If it was, she would shake him fully awake and make him take them. Then she would push the reset button to activate the alarm to the time of his next dosage. Every evening before bedtime, she set out his medication and put a plastic tumbler of water on his bedside table. The tumbler had a lid that was equipped with a drinking spout, like a toddler's cup.

Usually, when she was awakened by him, Amélie would also help him go to the toilet, since he needed to urinate frequently but was usually quite unsteady, getting out of bed like that in the middle of the night. The trip down the hall to the WC was slow, with Joseph shuffling along, taking little steps, and Amélie beside him, gripping his arm. After the equally slow trip back, his wife would settle him down again and tell him rather crossly to go back sleep and not bother her again until morning.

Tonight, he is alone. Henceforth will always be alone, will have to do everything for himself, for as long as he is able. The prospect is daunting and engulfs him like a dark, cold lake. He lies on his back, listening to the gusting of the wind. It drives before it a squall of rain that spatters against the windows, batters the old hornbeam that stands by the corner of the house. The branches creak and groan. They had planted that tree, he and Amélie, fifty-one years ago, on the birth of Christine, their only child. As if in sympathy with his solitude, the house complains around him. A moan of self-pity, a desolate bubble of sound, squeezes from his chest.

His medication. He turns his head, straining to make out the hour. The numbers on the digital clock swim before his eyes: 2:49. Almost time for his 3 a.m. dose. With difficulty, he pulls himself to a sitting position, using a special railing that has been built onto the side of the bed, reaches stiffly for the electrical cord dangling from the wall lamp, and follows it upward until he finds the switch. The lamp sheds a pale circle of light. As usual, the water tumbler and the dispenser that he uses to help him keep track of his medication are on the bedside table. It gives him a sense of minor achievement to know that he has remembered to put them there.

But getting the pills out of the container is not easy. His hands shake badly, and he spills several before he is able to pick out three: two yellow, one white. He makes a messy job of getting them down. He has trouble swallowing. Water leaks from the corners of his mouth, trails down his chin. Parkinson's affects every muscle in his body, including those of his mouth and throat.

Tap-tap. Something is striking the north bedroom window. At first he thinks it is an ivy branch hitting the panes. *Tap-tap-tap.* He listens more carefully. The sound is rhythmical, like ghostly fingers—the fingers of the storm—beating out a code that ought to have some meaning. For a moment he almost thinks, almost lets himself have the fantastic hope, that it is Amélie, blowing about outside, signaling to come in. Is that what the tapping is trying to tell him? He nearly calls out to her.

Rap-rap. The noise is louder, its cadence faster now, and it has shifted to another window farther along the wall, and yet another, the one by the old walnut dresser, as if unknown hands are playing some kind of crazy game, flying from window to window, beating frantically on the panes. *RAP-RAP.* His breath catches in a hiccup of fear. He follows the progress of the noise with terrified eyes. *RAP-RAP-RAP.* The sound seems to fill the entire room, to rock the very house.

"Go away!" he finally manages, but the words come out as a croak. "Leave me alone!" And he waits paralyzed, knowing that at any moment the unnamed horror will burst in on him in an explosion of glass, making a reality of his nightmare.

The buzz of the alarm, sounding three, nearly makes him choke with fear. The sound goes on and on until at last, clumsily, he fumbles for the reset button, depresses it. In the silence that follows, he realizes that the pounding has also stopped. Even the wind seems to have let up. Only the pulsing of his blood rings deafening in his ears. Confused, Joseph wonders if he has been having another nightmare. He is aware of the normalcy of things about him, the aureole of light cast by the wall lamp, the steady reshaping of time by the clock display, the familiar forms of furniture in their accustomed places.

The electricity goes out. This often happens in the countryside when there is a big wind or a rainstorm. Power and phone lines collapse to lie like tangles of black spaghetti across the roads. Joseph sits frozen in the darkness. Then his heart skids as he hears the grating of the back door over the kitchen flagstones. Someone—or something—has come into the house. Sobbing with terror, he wills his hands to move. They grope tremulously over the surface of the bedside table, upsetting the water tumbler, knocking away the flashlight that is always kept there for power outages such as this. It rolls and thuds to the floor. But it is the phone he wants. He finds it, his fingers wrapping gratefully around the familiar shape of the old-fashioned receiver. The phone, too, is dead.

"Who are you?" he calls out into the darkness. "What do you want?"

He hears only silence. After a long moment, the tiny, telltale squeak of a floorboard signals that the intruder has moved into the hallway outside his bedroom.

9

"Is he here?" The nurse's face was wet with rain and pale with anxiety. She had been banging frantically on the front door and now stepped fully into the vestibule, leaving wet footprints on the tiled floor.

Julian, in his pajamas, his hair on end, moved aside to let her by. "Who?"

"Joseph, of course." As always, Jacqueline Godet was breathless and a little impatient.

"No. Why should he be?"

"Because he's gone. I can't find him. It's twenty past ten. He knows I always come at ten." She frowned at Julian, at his purple-and-white striped sleepwear. Her look said he should not have been caught lying abed at this hour, he should have been up and dressed long ago.

Julian looked out at the cold, wet day and shut the door. "Um, wait here, will you?"

A moment later Mara appeared, pulling on her dressing gown. Her hair, too, was tousled.

"I looked everywhere," Jacqueline explained without further preamble. "Inside, outside. He's nowhere to be found."

"But where could he be?"

"I thought you'd know. That's why I'm here."

Mara's forehead crimped sharply in a frown. "Just give us a minute, will you?"

•

Joseph really seemed to have vanished. The Gaillards' house was a rectangular, single-storied structure made of local limestone and roofed with flat tiles that had once been red but were now discolored and furry with lichen and moss. Owing to Joseph's mobility problems, the day room off the kitchen had been made into a bedroom so as to be nearer the WC and bath. Mara and Julian saw that the bed was unmade. A plaid bathrobe hung over the back of a chair. A flashlight, a pillow, and one carpet slipper lay nearby on the floor. The second was near the armoire on the other side of the room.

Jacqueline informed them in a worried tone: "He hasn't taken his 7 a.m. pills." She indicated tablets scattered over the surface of the bedside table. The digital display of the clock was flashing on and off. She picked it up, consulted her watch, and reset the time.

The other rooms were tidy but less informative. Julian clattered down into the cellar, reappeared a moment later, and then went outside to look around, even though Jacqueline had said she had already done all that.

"And I checked up there as well," she called out as Mara started to climb the steep, narrow stairway leading from the living area to the garret.

Mara went up anyway. The garret had once served as a drying area for tobacco and herbs. The wires, now rusted, were still in place. Long-forgotten pieces of furniture—a child's bed, a girlish commode, a dresser, all that remained of the daughter Christine—stood draped in dirty plastic. The rest was dust, spiderwebs, and dark, comma-shaped droppings. *Rats,* she thought.

•

Outside, the rain was beginning to freeze, laying a gray, mushy coating on the ground. Soon everything—trees, bushes, stones—would be encased in ice. Julian pulled the hood of his down-filled parka farther forward and started down a muddy path that led him past a forlorn vegetable garden, where barren tripods recalled last summer's crop of runner beans, and beyond it a chicken house on stilts, its roof caved in, its wire fencing lying rusted on the ground.

The Gaillards, now just Joseph, owned 45 hectares that extended away from the road, most of it open meadow. The land had been put to many uses over the years—tobacco, maize, oats, wheat. Sheep, too, until Joseph had hurt his back. Julian passed a small fruit orchard and beyond it a little vineyard, the gnarled, dormant stumps bespeaking vines probably as old as Joseph himself, sufficient once for the family's needs. The trees now stood unpruned; the vines had been left to run wild; the sheep had been sold long ago, the chickens killed and eaten. The vegetable garden was the only thing that had continued to receive attention, but with Amélie dead, that, too, would go to grass, like the fields. For the last ten years or so, the Gaillards had rented their land to other farmers for grazing cattle.

Julian was overcome with an uneasy feeling the instant he saw the stone well. It looked disused and was covered over with rotten boards. He approached it unwillingly, noting with an icy dread that the boards had been shifted partially aside. He tore them away. His relief was immense when he found that under the boards the well opening was closed off by an intact, if rusty, metal grating.

The path continued down to the end of the property. He crossed a stream, passing the ruin of an old mill that had once operated there, giving the hamlet its name. The mill depended on the rain-fed stream to operate, hence Ecoute-la-Pluie, Listen-to-the-Rain. The way was rough and slippery. How far could the tottery old fellow have got on his own? Julian continued walking, beating back the bushes on left and right.

•

The women stood in the living room, staring about in bafflement.

"*C'est bizarre,*" murmured Jacqueline.

"Maybe he went out with someone. One of the nephews?"

"In his pajamas? His pajamas aren't there, you know. It means he's still in them. I wonder if he had a bad turn in the night and had to be taken to hospital."

Mara said, "One of the other neighbors might know if an ambulance came for him. We wouldn't have seen anything." The Gaillards' was the last house on the left as you went down the lane that ran through the hamlet from the main road. Mara, the closest neighbor, was also at the end of the lane but on the other side and further down. She moved to a phone that stood on a stand. "I'll call around, shall I?"

"You'd have thought someone would have let me know." Jacqueline looked perplexed.

Julian came in through the front door, pushing back his hood and bringing cold, damp air with him. His shoes were wet and muddy, so he stood just inside the doorway. He shook his head. Nothing.

"*Merde,*" said Mara, dropping the receiver back in its cradle. "It's dead."

The nurse seemed to come out of a trance. "Oh. I forgot to tell you. The phone's out. It was the first thing I tried. Then I tried to call on my *portable.* But wouldn't you know, my card's expired. That's why I had to walk over to you."

"I suppose that means everyone else's line is out, too," Mara said, predicting the worst.

"It was the windstorm last night. You should see the trees and wires down everywhere."

Julian brightened. "Then that's probably what happened. He needed to make a call and went out to use someone's cellphone. In fact, I'll bet he's at Suzanne Portier's right now. I'll go check."

Julian pulled his hood up and went out again, shutting the door behind him.

Jacqueline sat down heavily in an armchair. "Let's hope that's it."

"Yes," said Mara. She stood staring out the front window. "Although if he needed a phone, I wonder why he didn't come to us. We're closer." After a few minutes, she saw Julian's van go past. The neighboring houses were spaced far apart, so it made sense for him to drive up the lane. Mara walked across the room to stand at another window, this one giving onto the back of the property. The rain was coming down now as sleet.

The nurse groaned. "When the weather's like this, I really feel it in my knees."

The old house was dim and still, except for the ponderous ticking of a grandfather clock. Mara flicked a switch. It activated a couple of old-fashioned wall sconces shaped like flambeaux that gave faint illumination to an obscure matter.

Mara began to pace the floor. "Maybe we should call the police."

The nurse shook her head. "He won't like us involving the gendarmes." She followed Mara with her eyes. "They would have been married fifty-two years come summer, you know. It's hard . . . losing someone after so long. And he was always so dependent on her. Maybe because she was older than him. You knew she was married before? Her first husband was killed in the war. When she got Joseph, he was a brawny farm lad . . . pretty wet behind the ears. I expect"—the nurse laughed, recollecting something that she did not volunteer to share—"Amélie taught him a thing or two. Did I tell you he wants to restock with sheep?"

"What? How?" Mara looked appalled. She almost said, *He's out of his mind.* Perhaps his mind *was* going.

"He's not crazy, if that's what you're thinking," said Jacqueline.

"Sheep! He'll never manage."

"Of course not. But you have to understand it's his way of coping with loss. Joseph used to love his sheep, gave them all names, even if he did end up selling them for meat. I suppose he thinks if he can get sheep back on the land, he can get a lot of other things back as well. Best to let him believe it will happen." She added with uncharacteristic gentleness, "We all need our dreams, even if the time for dreaming is over."

"Listen," Mara broke in sharply, turning back into the room.

"What?" With an effort the stout nurse pushed forward in her chair. "What is it?"

Mara waved her still. "I thought I heard something." But the only sounds were the ticking of the clock, the wind in the chimney, the patter of sleet against the windowpanes. And then, a muffled thump that Jacqueline heard, too. Their eyes were drawn to a cupboard under the stairs at the far end of the living room. It was the only place they had not looked into. Mara flew to it and yanked the door open. At first, all she could make out was a clutter of broken shutters and fly screens standing on end and leaning against the interior wall. Then, further back, she saw him, folded up on himself, lying like a thing discarded in the darkness and the dust.

•

He looked dead. His skin was cold to the touch. His mouth gaped open, and his body was as rigid as the shutters they had to shift in order to reach him. Only his eyes gave sign of life.

They dragged him out and got him into bed by carrying him between them, Jacqueline hoisting him under the arms, Mara taking his feet. Despite his size, he was surprisingly light. *A shell of a man,* Mara thought. He was unable to swallow his tablets. Jacqueline rummaged in her bag and gave him a nasal spray of apomorphine as a quick-onset therapy to kick-start his system. She laid him back against a stack of pillows and sat on the edge of the mattress, rubbing warmth into his chest, arms, and legs.

The front door banged. "No one's home but Olivier Rafaillac," Julian called. "They're all off doing their marketing." He came into the bedroom. "You found him! Where the hell was he?"

"Cupboard under the stairs," said Mara in a low voice.

"Shouldn't we call a doctor?"

Jacqueline shook her head. "No need. He'll come round in a bit."

Julian stood by, watching her ministrations. Mara went to fill a hot water bottle in the kitchen and brought it to Jacqueline.

"There, *mon vieux,*" said the nurse. "Get that on your feet. Like blocks of ice, they are."

It took Joseph almost forty minutes to recover sufficiently to tell them what had happened. His voice came out in a barely audible croak.

"She was beating on the windows. Trying to get in. Then the lights went out. She came in through the back, right into the room."

"She, who?" Mara looked askance at Jacqueline and Julian. "What's he talking about? Was someone trying to break in?"

"Amélie." Joseph's voice broke into a quavering sob. "She was here. She stood over me, big and black, like a tree." The corners of his mouth pulled down, the muscles of his throat working spasmodically. He might have been crying, but no tears came out. His eyes looked as dry, as red, as flayed as ever. "She said, 'You have to die, Joseph.' She wanted me to join her, you see. I told her, 'I'm not ready to go.' I said, 'Leave me alone.' Then"—his trembling fingers danced on top of the covers as he relived his terror—"she put a pillow over my face. I tried to fight her off. But she was too strong for me. And—and she had no head. *Mon Dieu,* only a big black hole!"

Jacqueline said briskly, "You had a nightmare, Joseph. A bad dream. None of this really happened."

"I swear it's true," he moaned, and his entire body shook in his agitation. "She was here. I felt her. I heard her breathing. Her hands were big. And—and . . ." He struggled to find the words. His extreme mental effort was visible in the way his head writhed, his mouth twisted.

"And what, Joseph?" Mara leaned forward to hear him.

"Her skin . . . was loose and rubbery."

Big hands and loose, rubbery skin? Mara raised doubtful eyes to Jacqueline. The nurse's mouth pursed skeptically. But Joseph was staring at Mara piteously, needing to be believed.

"What happened then?" she asked, taking his hands in hers.

"She went away. She just went away. I heard her go out. But I was afraid she'd come back. I got out of bed. I kept bumping into things and falling down. The lights were out, you see. So I crawled. I crawled into the closet under the stairs and hid there. I hoped she wouldn't find me. Because she can break down walls, you know. She's done it before."

He lay back exhausted. Just before he fell into a deep sleep, he mumbled, "Don't let her come for me."

They left him. In the kitchen, Jacqueline made a strong brew of coffee. The three of them sat drinking it at a scarred wooden table.

The nurse shook her head. "Nightmares and hallucinations. His drugs bring them on, make it hard for him to separate fact from fantasy. He's had a bad few hours, but he'll be fine. In fact, it's actually a good sign that he fought Amélie off in his dream. It means he's not ready to give up living. I wouldn't be surprised if he doesn't remember a thing about this when he wakes up."

Mara said, "But you don't suppose someone really did come

in? He and Amélie never locked their back door, you know. Amélie used to say a locked door kept only friends out."

Jacqueline said, "But the back door *was* locked. I had to unlock it when I went outside to look for him." She drained her cup. "Well, no real harm's been done, *grâce à Dieu.* But one never knows . . . what with those housebreakers about." She poked her chin in Julian's direction. "What did you tell him, Monsieur Rafaillac?"

"That we couldn't find Joseph, of course."

Jacqueline pulled a mouth. "I wish you hadn't. Now it'll be all over the place."

"The others will find out about it anyway," said Mara. "You know how word gets round. How much longer do you think it will be before he gets home care?"

Jacqueline shrugged. "These things take time. Especially out here in the boondocks." She said it with a little sniff. "I just don't want those O'Connors to hear about it. I meant to tell you, I saw *her* at the supermarket the other day. She had another go at me. About putting Joseph in a home. This will just give her fuel to stoke her fire."

"They're still here?" Mara had thought that the Americans had returned to warm, sunny Florida right after the funeral.

"Oh, I think *he* has some business in the area." Just as the O'Connors called Jacqueline "the nurse," she referred to them simply as "he" and "she," usually with wry emphasis.

Julian said, "Well, all the same, old Rafaillac was surprisingly helpful when I told him about Joseph. Offered to go out and look for him. And by the way, *his* phone is working. So the break in the lines must be beyond him. Rafaillac said he'd wander down and check out the wires, give France Telecom a call."

"Joseph needs a cellphone," said Mara. "I'll see about getting him one."

There was a pounding on the front door, and Olivier Rafaillac himself stepped inside when Julian opened it. He was a big man with a red face and a disposition that could sometimes be as prickly as the artichokes he cultivated. Little pellets of ice slid off the surface of his padded nylon jacket onto the floor.

"Did you find him?" he asked, getting straight to the point.

"Yes," laughed Jacqueline. "He was here all the time. We just didn't know where to look."

Olivier looked about him doubtfully. "Where was he, hiding in the *cave?*"

"No, no." Jacqueline brushed aside a direct answer.

"Well, I came to tell you the phone lines are all okay. Except here."

"If it's here, that means us, too," Mara said gloomily. It would be days before France Telecom got around to them. She saw herself having to stand outside in the rain to use her *portable,* since the thick walls of her house impeded mobile reception.

"No." Olivier shook his head. "I'm telling you it's just here. Come out and see for yourself. The feed leading to this house is down. There are a lot of broken branches lying around, so that could be what did it. Although"—he paused to scratch his head—"the wire looks cleanly broken, almost like it's been cut."

"Cut?" Mara echoed. *Now what was that supposed to mean?*

• 10 •

The wind had felled trees everywhere. At the moment, Rocco Luca, alias Ton-and-a-Half, or simply the Ton, resembled any other country property owner cleaning up after a storm. He was dressed in dungarees, an old beret, and a sheepskin jacket that the French called a *canadienne.* Despite the frigid weather he wore it open. The Ton was impervious to the cold. A poplar had fallen across the lane leading to his house, and he was cutting it up with a noisy chainsaw that gave off a smelly blue exhaust as it bit through the soft wood. He had cleared away the branches and now was slicing the trunk into meter-length pieces.

Ton-and-a-Half was a big man, heavy but not fat. His bullet head with its bristling hair, broken nose, and scarred eyebrows rose like a prizefighter's bad dream out of a hefty pair of shoulders with almost no intervening neck. His personality was supersized to match his bulk. He liked grand gestures, loud clothes, large women, and strong drink. In his youth he had pursued a career in boxing until he proved to be a bleeder. Despite his heft, he had thin skin; his head split open like a melon every time it was hit. From the ring it was a quick step into various illicit activities, including drug trafficking, an activity he had successfully conducted for more than five decades behind a cover of various legitimate business enterprises.

A car turned off the main road and came lurching down the rutted lane. Each time it hit a pothole it sent up a spray of muddy water. It braked short of the fallen tree. Serge Taussat got out, placing his feet carefully so as not to dirty his shoes. In sharp contrast to his boss, Serge was a slim man with a quiet manner, and his color of choice was black. His slacks, jacket, overcoat, and shoes were black. His car, a Mercedes CLS, was black with a black leather interior. At night Serge would have passed unperceived. On this raw afternoon, he was a dark stain against a background of rain-soaked trees and raw, sullen earth. Only his pale, narrow face seemed to reflect what little light there was to the day, and that was because Serge's skin was drawn so tightly over brow and cheekbones that his skull had the appearance of being shrink-wrapped. His hair was whitish-blond, and his eyes were large and flat, like two gray mirrors. From some angles he looked like a modernistic sculpture; from others, an alien being.

The chainsaw sputtered to a halt. Ton-and-a-Half set it down on the ground and waited for Serge to pick his way through the scattered branches.

"*Et alors?* What have you got?"

"*Zéro.*"

Bull-like, the big man lowered his head. "Why do I get the feeling Freddy is getting past his sell-by date?" He made clear his displeasure by picking up a section of tree trunk and hurling it onto a pile of cut wood.

Freddy, also known as Deep Freddy because he was always in it up to his neck, was a junkie and small-time pusher whose life predicaments the Ton resolved in exchange for information. He roamed the streets of Périgueux and was a useful source since he lived rough and knew, as the Ton put it, in which direction the gutters ran.

Serge shrugged. "I told him to keep trolling. What goes down has to come up. Sometime or other." He looked past his *patron* to the house at the end of the lane. It was an imposing structure, built of red and yellow stone, with two towers flanking a fake

Gothic entry. Attached to the west end of the house was a conservatory filled with tiered beds of plants of every description. The Ton's current woman, an ample blonde named Lydia, was crazy about flowers. The conservatory also housed a large hot tub, which constantly steamed up the glass panes of the walls and roof.

Luca gestured massively with a meaty hand and said grudgingly, "I'll say this much for *le petit morveux,* whoever he is. He's smart. Moves fast, thinks on his feet."

A crow in a bare tree nearby gave a disheartened caw. It balanced comfortless on a branch, its feathers ruffled by the wind.

Serge's narrow face registered disapproval. "His feet are on your turf, and his action is attracting attention. You don't want that, what with the *flics* already hanging around like a bad smell because of Yvan."

"They have nothing on me that will stick."

"They'd have less if you'd let me deal with him months ago."

The Ton rubbed his nose with a walnut-sized knuckle. "Trouble is, I liked the bastard. That's always been my problem. I take to people. It's my nature. Too soft-hearted."

Unimpressed, Serge gazed expressionlessly at the heavy sky. More rain was on the way.

"As for Freddy," the Ton went on, "tell him I'm not satisfied. Tell him I don't like that he thinks he can roll up like an empty bottle. Tell him I want something by Friday, or he will prove to be a great disappointment to his friends and relations."

"He is already," said Serge. The crow swayed miserably on its perch. Serge hunched inside his coat and shoved gloved hands into his pockets. He, too, felt the cold.

The Ton stuck his lower lip out. He was brooding on something else.

"I heard from Pascal. He thinks the *flics* are on to him."

"*Merde,*" said Serge softly.

"They haven't moved in on him yet. He thinks they're just letting him know he's being watched."

"Yeah, but if the *filière* in Toulouse is compromised, how are we going move the stuff?"

"Find the kid, we may not need Toulouse."

Serge's flat eyes fixed on his boss. "It's a pigeon-shit operation, *patron.*"

The Ton laughed harshly, like a truck backfiring. "Big oaks from little acorns grow."

He glanced into the rear of the Mercedes. Pots of fleshy-looking plants, protected by clear plastic, stood in a large box on the back seat. They did not resemble oak seedlings. Luca picked up the chainsaw.

"Take those damned things on up to the house," he said, jerking his chin at the cargo in the car and yanking the saw to life again. "Make Lydia's day."

11

Mara woke first. She propped herself up on her elbows. Outside, another cold, gray day was breaking. She burrowed back down under the covers and curled against Julian's back. He muttered something and rolled over, enfolding her in his arms. They both slipped back into an early morning doze. A few minutes later, they woke again. He nosed her hair, her neck.

"Sandalwood," he murmured.

She laughed, brushed his cheek with her lips, and blew gently into his ear.

"God, I love it when you do that."

Sleepily, they kissed. Then they made love, wordlessly forgiving each other for their recent irritabilities, seeking to make it linger, not just the physical act but the feeling of intense closeness and the calm, luxurious aftermath. This was, each realized, the two of them at their best. To hell with Madame Audebert.

Later, Mara made tea. She was learning to make a decent brew by Julian's standards. He liked it as strong as coal tar. Because it was Sunday and they could take their time, she carried it into the bedroom where they had it in bed with their croissants. Julian dunked his. She wished he wouldn't. It left drip marks on the sheets.

"What are you up to today?" she asked.

"I'm afraid"—he took a last swallow of tea and set his mug on the nightstand—"it's time I did something about finding Kazim Ismet. I've put it off long enough."

"Oh." She pulled a pout. "I was hoping we could spend some time together."

"Indulging in more close encounters?" He gave her a villainous leer.

She said quite seriously, "Getting back in touch. We hardly seem to have time to talk anymore. I mean, really talk."

"What do you want to talk about?" He sounded wary.

"Nothing in particular. Us." Their relationship. For months, they had been chugging along happily enough, patching over minor skirmishes. But she wondered how he really felt about living together. They never talked about their long-term prospects. Maybe it was time for some kind of stock-taking.

"Ah. Well, if 'us' is nothing in particular, then perhaps it can wait until I get back?" His bantering tone had an annoying hint of evasiveness. He swung his legs over the side of the bed. "Betul thinks Kazim is staying with his girlfriend, Nadia Beaubois. She works at the Intermarché in Périgueux. I expect that's where I'll have to start." He swept his feet over the floor. "Damn! That bloody mutt has taken my slippers again." They were an old sheepskin pair, trodden down at the backs, that the dog liked to carry off and chew. It was the reason he was named Bismuth (pronounced *Beezmoot* in French). His chewing made Julian want to reach for an antacid.

Mara barely knew how to tell him. "Madame Audebert found them all pulled apart and gummy with dog saliva. I think she tossed them."

He jumped up, waving his arms about in the air. "That bloody, bloody woman! When is she going to learn to leave my things alone? First my newspapers, now my slippers."

"For heaven's sake, Julian, don't make such a thing of it. You needed a new pair anyway."

"And that makes it all right?" He stomped barefoot over the cold floor into the bathroom, where he turned on the taps full bore. A moment later, he came back into the bedroom. "Look, I'm sorry. Why not come to Périgueux with me? We can talk on the way."

By now Mara was up, too, and feeling huffy. The heat of their lovemaking had long since dissipated. "With your head full of hunting down Kazim? No thanks."

"All right. Suit yourself." He disappeared to shower and shave.

•

Twenty minutes later Mara, wrapped in her bathrobe, was sitting at the kitchen table squinting over the top of her useless glasses at sheets of notepaper covered with a large, looping script: handwritten recipes sent from Canada by her mother, a very good cook, whose repertoire ran to rich meat pies, hearty soups, and even moose stew. Hers was the culinary expression of Quebec's heartland (*Maman* came from the little town of Saint-Louis-du-Ha!-Ha!, a place name that rivaled Ecoute-la-Pluie for quaintness. Some said "ha! ha!" was from the antique French word for impasse; or a typographical error—"ha! ha!" was actually "ah! ah!" in admiration of the view; or an Indian exclamation of surprise). She did not look up when Julian came into the kitchen.

"Sure you won't come with me?"

She shook her head. "Anyway, it's my day to cook." She scribbled something on the back of an envelope. She softened. "I'm giving you a surprise. But first I have to shop for the ingredients."

He read aloud over her shoulder: "Potatoes." He asked cautiously, "Another *gratin dauphinois?*"

"Never you mind. When will you be back?"

"How long does it take to find a runaway son? Afternoonish, I expect." He planted a kiss on her cheek.

She watched him as he pulled on his jacket, turning up the collar in advance against the cold. "You know, I think the private investigator suits you. You look kind of tough and sexy with your collar up like that."

He paused on his way to the door. "I do?"

"Uh-huh." Her eyes dropped to his middle, bulky in the down-filled parka. "Too bad you don't have a trench coat. That puffy jacket doesn't quite cut it." She grinned. "Too much like the Michelin Man."

He left.

>*Patsy,* Mara composed an email in her head that would never be sent, *what do I do with a man who's as slippery as an egg custard?*<

She imagined Patsy's response: >*Life is short. Eat dessert first.*<

•

Julian started up his van and set out north on the D710. There was very little traffic on the road that morning. He drove past soggy meadows and dark, newly plowed fields. The recent rains had left standing water in the furrows that reflected flashing ribbons of pewter-colored sky.

As he drove, he realized that, despite Mara's little joke, he *was* playing the *limier,* the bloodhound sleuth, on the trail of a missing person. Now that he thought about it, he rather fancied himself in that role. Tough and sexy. The silly part of him wished he *did* have a trench coat. Or was it only spies and dirty postcard sellers who wore them? No, he was sure Humphrey Bogart as Philip Marlowe in *The Big Sleep* had worn a trench coat. He had seen the film on French television not long ago. It was one of his favorites. He looked at himself in the rear-view mirror and tried talking out of the side of his mouth, Bogie-style: "*M'emmerdes pas, connard.*" Don't piss me off, bastard.

Périgueux was situated some 60 kilometers north of Ecoute-la-Pluie on the River Isle. He reached the shambling outskirts of the town in forty minutes and found the Intermarché supermarket easily. To his disappointment, Nadia was not there and none of the

Sunday morning shift knew her. He wandered from the charcuterie counter to the long-life milk section, wishing he hadn't wasted his Sunday and musing on the existence of so many kinds of milk. Cow's milk, goat's milk, milk in soft plastic bottles, milk in cartons, full cream, half cream, different percentages of skimmed, lactose free, fortified. Well, at least he could tell the Ismets he had tried. A kid with dirty blond hair was hunkered down at the end of the aisle, restocking the lower shelves.

"I don't suppose you know where I can find someone named Nadia Beaubois, do you? I was told she worked here."

The kid swiveled his head around to peer up at him sideways. Julian had a view of the dark pit of a nostril and one glaucous eye. He expected another negative. Instead, the kid said, "She used to. What's it to you?"

•

Julian parked along the river and took the steep ramp leading up to Rue Porte-de-Graule. He was in the Quartier Saint-Front, the old quarter whose ancient labyrinth of narrow, cobbled lanes in Renaissance times had been the artisanal and commercial center of the town. Over the centuries, the buildings had fallen into disrepair. One by one they were being restored. Newly renovated, upmarket residences rubbed shoulders with dilapidated structures.

The house he was looking for was set slightly back between two jutting facades. He had to walk around a skip of debris to reach the entrance. To his surprise, the massive wooden front door stood partly ajar. Within, he saw a dim vestibule surrounded by more evidence of reconstruction: a couple of sawhorses, a coil of electrical cable, stacks of tiles. The air was heavy with the smells of raw lumber and new paint underlain by damp stone and mold. His groping hands found a wall switch for the *minuterie,* a timed light that illuminated the vestibule and first landing. Now he could see that a corridor ran off the vestibule all the way to the back of the building. A decrepit but once elegant stairwell wound upward in a dizzying ovoid spiral. The house seemed untenanted, but he could hear rock music coming faintly from above.

He puffed as he made the tortuous climb, his footsteps keeping a lagging counterpoint to the strengthening basso *thump-de-thump* overhead. When he reached the second level, the light went out, plunging him into darkness. He groped along the wall and found another *minuterie* that lit the floors above.

The music came from behind a door, four stories up, at the very top. There was a doorbell, but it had been pulled out of its socket and hung on a wire. He knocked. Then he banged on the door with his fist. The music ceased abruptly. The door cracked opened.

"Wotcherwant?" said a voice in distinctly East End London English. Julian could just make out a head in a blue knit cap, dark curly hair poking out from under it, and a pair of watery eyes.

"Nadia Beaubois? Is she here?"

"Oo're you, then?" The eyes, slightly out of focus, sized him up.

"Friend of a friend. Who're you?"

"Peter," said the young man, surprisingly obliging. He yelled over his shoulder, "Naahd!" and opened the door enough to allow Julian to step inside.

In addition to the cap, Peter wore a heavy pea jacket several sizes too large for him over army fatigues. Julian understood why. The apartment, which proved to be the garret, was freezing. A portable paraffin stove in the middle of the room offered an inadequate source of heat. The ceiling was pitched at an angle and badly stained. Battered pans had been placed on the floor to catch drips from a leaky skylight. It and a pair of grimy dormer windows provided the only illumination. The furnishings were minimal: a plastic table and plastic chairs that looked as if they had been nicked from an outdoor café, a mattress strewn with rumpled bedding in a corner, a lumpy sofa piled with soiled blankets. Orange crates stacked against the wall formed a kind of shelving for a jumble of bottles, magazines, and CDs. There was an alcove with a hot plate and a sink stacked with dirty dishes. Through an open doorway at the far end of the garret Julian glimpsed a bed, unmade, and the corner of a dresser. The place, makeshift and filthy, had the look of a squat. Except for the fact that the occupants seemed to take no pains to hide their presence, the building's owner might not have even known they were there. Julian guessed they were paying some kind of nominal rent to live in space that was probably legally condemned. Not for much longer, though. Once the work of renovation was complete, the likes of Peter and Nadia would be out on the street.

Something moved on the sofa. Julian made out the head of a girl. He had not noticed her earlier because most of her was buried under the blankets. A gold ring pierced the middle of her lower lip; a multitude of rings skewered her earlobes and eyebrows. She raised an arm to take a drag from a joint. The air was heavily sweet with it. She blew smoke toward the ceiling.

"Hey, Naahd!" the young cockney yelled again. He slouched over to the sofa. "Shove over, Brigitte."

"*Va te faire foutre,*" Brigitte muttered. Get stuffed. With an effort she curled her legs to the side. Peter dropped down, as if exhausted, next to her. He reached across for the toke, sucked on it. The two of them regarded Julian dully.

Another woman came out of the bedroom, tugging a comb through her ragged, bicolored hair. Its black and orange streaks reminded Julian of some kind of animal pelt. Her surroundings might be trash, but this one dressed well. She wore a purple angora sweater, leather slacks, and black leather knee-high boots with platform soles that made her look as if she were treading on bricks. What appeared to be a genuine snakeskin fanny pack was strapped around her hips.

"*Quoi?*" Two unnaturally green eyes fixed Julian in an unfriendly stare.

"*Vooz ahvez ang veezeetuhr,*" Peter said in horrible French, pointing unnecessarily at Julian.

Nadia was tall, sallow-complexioned, and older-looking than Julian had expected. He found her emerald stare—tinted contacts, he supposed—unsettling.

"*Qui êtes-vous?*" she demanded, her voice sharp with distrust.

"*Un ami.* I'm looking for Kazim."

"*Pas ici.*" Not here. Her gaze darted to Peter and then past Julian to the door. She seemed extremely jumpy. She fiddled with the comb. It snapped in half, and she threw it on the floor.

"Do you know where he is?"

"No. Why do you want to know?"

"I told you. I'm a friend."

Her upper lip curled unpleasantly. "I don't think so."

"A friend of the family," he modified. "His parents are worried sick about him." Julian did not expect this to get him very far. It didn't.

"Them!" Nadia blew air out her nostrils. "All they want is to keep him in that lousy shop for the rest of his life."

"Yeah, I know," Julian agreed. "They're a bit old-fashioned. They don't realize Kazim's too bright for that. He could go places if he had the chance. That's why I want to talk to him." *Nice touch, that,* he thought, noting her reaction.

"Oh yeah?" Curiosity vied with skepticism. "What about?"

"Well, that's between him and me, isn't it?"

"Look, you're wasting my time. I'm late for work."

"Will you give him a message?"

"Told you. Haven't seen him. Don't know where he is."

"Tell him to contact me. As soon as possible. It's important."

"How important?"

Julian came forward, digging out his wallet. "Treat this as a down payment." He held out twenty euros.

She gave a harsh laugh. "You're joking. You can't want to see him very badly."

Julian laid on another twenty and added his card. Nadia snatched at the money and read the card aloud disbelievingly. "Julian Wood. Landscape gardener? What is this? You're some kind of fucking grass jockey?" She nearly screamed with laughter. She gave the card a backhand toss. It sailed through the air and came to rest on the floor a little way beyond the broken comb. Then she grabbed a cape-like garment from the back of a chair and headed for the door. She was gone in a diminishing clatter of hoofs that echoed down the stairs.

Peter, who had been watching the exchange with eager interest (Julian wondered how much he had understood of the rapid French), got up and retrieved the card. Communication reverted to English.

"Any more where that came from, mate?" He rubbed thumb and forefinger together. "I could really use a few."

"Depends on what you can tell me. I'm looking for Kazim Ismet. You know him?"

The cockney glanced at Brigitte, who was now asleep with her mouth open.

"Yeah."

"Know where I can find him?"

"'E was 'ere for a bit, wasn't 'e? Then 'e took off. Not seen 'im since."

"When was that?"

"Week ago, something like that."

"That's it? That's all you can tell me?"

Peter scratched his left ear. Then he said, "Used to 'ang round the cathedral, didn't 'e?"

"Are you saying that's where I'll find him?"

"Yeah."

"You don't sound very sure."

"No, swear to God. You'll find 'im there. I wouldn't lie to you. C'mon, man, gi'us twenty."

Julian gave him ten. Peter grabbed it.

"There's more if you can produce him for me. You have my card."

He saw himself out. This time he was prepared for the *minuterie* and managed to activate the light for the lower stairs before the top one gave out. In the vestibule, he noticed something on the dirty tiled floor that he had not seen on his way in. He hunkered down for a better look: wavy deposits of mud in broken patches roughly 12 centimeters wide. Tire marks. Something had been parked there, not recently, for the mud was dry and much trodden on. A Honda Bol d'Or? Despite the fact that he had just parted with fifty euros—sixty if he counted the kid in the supermarket—he left feeling quite pleased with himself. He was getting the hang of this detecting business.

•

The cathedral was also undergoing renovation. Scaffolding braced its western face. Kids were skateboarding in the adjoining square. A group of older boys—fifteen- and sixteen-year-olds, Julian reckoned—were doing ollies off the steps leading down to the walkway along the cathedral cloister. They came off the top step at breakneck speed, crouching low on the decks of their boards, and landed in noisy, grating pirouettes at the bottom. A youth, sitting off to one side, was intent on wrapping one end of his skateboard with string. He wore jeans blown out at the knees and a black sweatshirt with a hood pulled up over his head. His trainers were torn, and his socks had collapsed in loose folds around his ankles. His face looked gray with cold. Julian approached him.

"I'm looking for someone named Kazim Ismet. Rides a red Honda Bol d'Or. You seen him around?"

"*Négatif.*"

"But you know him?"

"*Négatif.*"

"You know anyone who does?"

"*Négatif.*" Without ever looking up, the youth continued to bind the front end of his skateboard, the laminations of which were coming apart, with the string.

"Can't you say anything but *négatif?* And anyway, shouldn't you be wearing a helmet?"

"Get lost."

Julian strolled around the cathedral. There was a little garden with leafless trees, grotesquely pollarded, on the south side. It was empty except for an old man and a dog. A cold wind whipped the man's coat and flattened his trousers against bony shanks as he waited for his dog to do its business. The dog, a terrier of some kind, sniffed around the base of a bronze cannon that pointed over the garden parapet in the direction of the river. Then it lifted its leg against the cement mount.

There were a number of cafés and bars in the streets surrounding the cathedral. One, on the corner of Rue Salinière, advertised parimutuel betting and snacks. Its windows were opaque with condensation and plastered with notices of snooker competitions. Julian found the place full of men who sat or stood staring up at a television showing a rugby match in progress. Toulouse against Biarritz. The air was hazy with cigarette smoke, but the warmth from the radiators and the close press of people was welcoming. As Julian made his way to the counter, the room erupted in groans. Toulouse had missed a try. Julian ordered a coffee. He asked the woman serving if she knew Kazim Ismet.

"What's he look like?"

Julian described him as best he could, extrapolating from the school photo and Betul's information. "Rides a red Honda."

The woman shook her head and called the question down to a man drying glasses at the other end of the counter, who also shook his head.

A successful try for Toulouse brought a roar of approval from the crowd. Julian looked around him. He noticed now what he had failed to see when he had entered. The patrons were men in their middle age and or older, intent on one thing: rugby. Not the kind of people who hung around or wanted to hang around with a Turkish tearaway. He finished his coffee and left.

The café a few doors down, Le Select, was not so crowded but attracted a younger, rougher-looking clientele. The television on the wall was also tuned to the rugby game. Men in denim and leather were clustered around the bar looking up at the screen. A thin fellow with the walleyed look of a bolting mule hung around the edge of the group. Julian pushed between unobliging bodies to the bar.

"*Café-crème.*"

When the bartender brought it, Julian put down five euros, told the man to keep the change, leaned across, and said in a conspiratorial tone, "I'm looking for Kazim. You seen him lately?"

"Kazim who?" The bartender, a big, bald fellow, didn't bother lowering his voice.

"Ismet. Young, slim, dark curly hair—"

"Buddy, they all look like that," said the other enigmatically. He gave Julian a baleful glare and moved away.

"What about you?" Julian asked two men who stood immediately next to him drinking pastis and who seemed openly interested in his inquiry. "Kazim Ismet. Turkish fellow. Rides a red Honda?"

"Why d'you want to know?" asked the one nearest him, a fellow with the hulking stance of a wrestler and small, mean eyes.

"Let's just say I need to talk to him."

"About what?" sneered the other. This one had very bad teeth and wore a row of signet rings like a knuckle-duster on his right hand.

"Business."

The first man fixed Julian with a hard stare that made him decide not to give out his card. Instead he scrawled a number on the back of a coaster advertising Kronenbourg beer and left it on the bar. "Just tell him to call me. It could be worth his while."

Neither man touched the coaster. Wordlessly they turned back to their pastis.

After a few more unsuccessful attempts in other cafés and bars, Julian gave up. Maybe his detecting skills, or his detecting persona, needed developing after all. He had reached the conclusion that Kazim, wherever he was, was not going to be found today. Nor was the Ismets' son going to be as easy to track down as Julian had hoped. But his time had not been entirely wasted. He had discovered that the only people who knew Kazim looked like the wrong sort, and they weren't prepared to talk. So why were they being so secretive? Whatever Kazim was up to, Julian was pretty sure the lad wasn't on the side of the angels. How much, he wondered, did a Honda Bol d'Or cost, and how did the son of Turkish immigrant shopkeepers afford such a toy?

He became aware that someone was following him as he made his way down Rue Denfert-Rochereau. In the Place Daumesnil he paused to stare into a shop window. So did his follower, a man, that much he could make out. After a minute or two of intense study of a display of women's lingerie, Julian began to feel conspicuous. Too bad he didn't smoke. It would have been a natural thing to fumble in his pockets for cigarettes, take his time lighting up. He could pretend to shelter his match from the wind and use the moment to turn around, get a look at his follower. Private investigators did that kind of thing. As it was, he felt obliged to move on. So did the man behind him.

Julian strolled slowly across the *place.* He had already decided against returning to the van by way of the narrow, deserted alleys of the old town. It was mid-afternoon, broad daylight, but he preferred to stay where there were people about. He took Avenue Daumesnil all the way to the bottom and then turned left onto Boulevard Georges Saumande. The street was like a wind tunnel. He zipped up his parka. The River Isle running below him looked choppy and cold.

A quick look told Julian that his follower was still there. The other man, who walked with a limp, quickened his pace when he saw Julian opening the door of the Peugeot. Julian counted to twenty, then turned around.

"What do you want?" he demanded.

The man stopped by the rear of the van. Julian recognized the walleyed bloke from Le Select, a sorry, slouching creature who did not inspire fear.

"You were asking about someone named Kazim?" He was extremely twitchy, and he wheezed like a leaky accordion.

"That's right."

"What do you want with him?"

Julian frowned. He should be the one asking questions. Instead, it always seemed to go the other way around. Time to get tough. He slammed the van door shut and strode back to confront Walleyes. Up close, Julian found that he was a good head taller than his tracker. Also that the other man smelled bad.

"Listen, I don't know who you are, but if you've got anything to say, spit it out direct, okay? I'm not in a mood to fool around."

"No need to get nasty." The other man took a few stumbling steps back and wiped his nose on a sleeve streaked with mucus. His hands, Julian noticed, were shaking. "Maybe I can help you. Maybe I know where this Kazim hangs out."

"I'm listening."

"It'll cost."

"Who are you?"

"Freddy. Everybody around here knows me as Freddy."

"Well, Freddy, you come up with Kazim for me and I'll talk money. Nothing up front. Got that?"

Freddy looked sulky. "I could do with thirty. Say, twenty."

"I said nothing up front. You deliver, and I'll make it worth your while. I'll give you a number—"

Julian had started to dig out pen and paper when Freddy, with a greasy smile, showed him the Kronenbourg coaster he had palmed off the Select bar.

• 12 •

"You gave them my cellphone number?" Mara stared at him in disbelief.

"Oh, Freddy probably had it off those two before they even had a chance to look at it." Julian opened a bottle of red and set it aside to breathe.

"I'm reassured."

"You can trace a land line. I didn't want that lot finding out where we live."

"You can do reverse search with a cellphone number, too. So now I'm going to get death threats on my *portable?*"

"Er—I don't think it'll come to that."

"It had better not."

She moved to the stove, driving the dogs before her. They skittered away and regrouped immediately around her. She emptied some kind of powder from a foil pouch into a pot of something liquid and brought the mixture to the boil. As it thickened, it took on the appearance of a brown sauce.

"This has to simmer"—she broke off to read the cooking instructions on the back of the pouch—"for a couple more minutes."

Julian looked about him and sniffed. Something was cooking, but he couldn't tell what. Something she had shoved into the oven the minute he had walked in the door. When he had asked what was for dinner, she had acted rather mysterious.

"So," he went on, "to cut a long story short, I had no luck running Kazim to earth. And I don't know what he's up to, but it seems to me he mixes with some pretty dodgy company."

"Probably selling drugs. Ecstasy. That's what all the kids are doing nowadays."

He supposed she was right. He took glasses down from the cupboard and carried them and the wine out to the dining room. When he gathered up cutlery to set the table, she said, "Just forks."

He hung about watching her, running through in his mind the kinds of things one ate only with forks. She cut the fire under the brown sauce and turned her attention to tossing a simple salad in walnut oil and vinegar. Ten minutes later, she opened the oven door and pulled out a tray of golden-brown potatoes cut into strips.

"Ta-da! *Frites* the easy way," she announced. "Frozen, pre-cut, pre-seasoned. Twenty minutes in the oven. Dead simple."

"Ah," he said, very little enlightened. He wondered what else came with them. Apart from the salad and the sauce, there appeared to be nothing else.

Now she shoveled the sizzling potatoes into two large bowls, sprinkled handfuls of what looked like wet cheese bits on top, and poured on the sauce.

"Hmm," he said cautiously. "Chips au gratin and gravy?"

She shook her head. "Poutine. The ultimate in comfort food, Quebec style."

"Poutine?"

"Fries and cheese curds with *sauce velouté*. I had a hard time finding really fresh curds. Back home we say you know the curds are fresh if they make your teeth squeak. I also found the sauce packaged. You have to let it sit a minute to give everything a chance to sort of soak in. Bring the salad, will you?"

She carried the bowls into the dining room and they sat down. Jazz and Bismuth settled themselves strategically beside their chairs.

"Well, this is a first," said Julian, gazing doubtfully at the rather soggy-looking mixture before him. When he tried it, however, he found it surprisingly good, in that gut-level, satisfying way that only a high octane mix of hot starch, cholesterol, and salty seasoning can be. As she had said, comfort food.

"What I don't get," he said after a few moments of appreciative eating—she was right, the curds did make his teeth squeak—"is why everyone is being so bloody secretive about Kazim. Nadia wasn't prepared to say anything, and the English kid, Peter, I'm sure led me a wild goose chase just for a handout of ten euros. Surely someone selling Ecstasy isn't such a big affair?"

"Well, it *is* illegal."

"They probably thought I was a narc." He grinned at the thought.

Mara stopped chewing. "Don't say that." She looked at him anxiously and added, "You know what happened to the other one."

•

Freddy tried to bum the use of a cellphone, but no one would trust him with anything that was not nailed down. Finally, he put through his call on one of France's last remaining coin pay phones. The phone was situated at the end of the old-fashioned zinc counter in the Café de Paris. Toulouse had won, and the place was crowded and noisy with topers. He had to shout to be understood as well as plug his free ear with a finger in order to hear. The fact that he was cramping and shaking badly did not make the conversation any easier.

"I said, he's looking for your boy. Tall, skinny *anglais.* No, man, he didn't introduce himself, but I got a phone number and a license plate. Peugeot van. White. What? Shit, man, I don't know. He didn't tell me." Freddy's cramps, coming in rapid waves, were nearly doubling him over. He clutched the edge of the counter for support, fought off a rush of nausea, and realized that he was about to mess his pants. Desperately, he broke in: "Look, I got a name. It's yours for a couple of *balles.* It's urgent, man. No, for crap's sake, I can't wait." A moment later he closed his eyes. "Okay. Okay. I'll be there. But hurry."

•

The Ton, surrounded by asparagus ferns and hostas, was playing toesies in the king-sized Jacuzzi with Lydia. A floating tray between them held a mini-bar and an array of health drinks. The phone rang. Lydia stood up, lowering the water level considerably. Full body streaming, she reached for the phone on a nearby wicker stand, flipped it open, punched a button, and listened.

"It's Serge." Lydia passed the phone across.

"Yeah, what?" barked the Ton.

"I've just talked to Freddy. He knows who our boy is. Kid named Kazim Ismet."

The Ton wiped moisture from his chin. "You think he's playing straight? The little *con* would say anything for a fix."

"He seemed sincere."

The Ton laughed. "Sincerely in deep shit."

"There's something more," said Serge. "Someone else is on Kazim's tail."

Ton-and-a-Half frowned. "A narc?"

"Freddy doesn't know. Said he was a tall, skinny guy. English. Freddy got a phone number and a car plate."

"Okay. Find out who this *anglais* is, but go easy until we know what we're dealing with."

"Right," said Serge.

• 13 •

"The trouble with fighting crime," complained Albert, "is you've got to do it everywhere at the same damned time."

Laurent sighed in agreement.

It had grown colder and more uncomfortable for the two gendarmes as the night wore on. Albert was better insulated by his own body fat, but Laurent, long and lean, kept having to rub his arms and stamp his feet to keep from freezing up altogether. He was tempted to start the engine of the Renault just so they could run the heater for a bit, but of course that would have given the whole thing away. The essence of a good stakeout was unobtrusive surveillance. A police car parked in the shrubbery off a country lane with its motor idling and belching exhaust was hard not to notice on a still, frosty night.

Four days ago, an elderly gentleman, resident of Le Vignal, had seen a dusty green van drive slowly through the *bourg* and turn down that lane, at the bottom of which were two houses, both owned by expatriates, both closed up for the winter. Neither house was visible from the village. The van had come back up the road a few minutes later. Three days later, the man had noticed the same vehicle going down the lane again. This time the van had not returned for a good forty-five minutes.

"Now I ask you," the man had said to the Brames duty officer to whom he had reported the event, "what could anyone be up to, apart from skulduggery, for so long down a road where nobody's at home? Especially with all these housebreakings going on." Owing to the van's tinted windows, he had not got a good look at the driver.

The result was two gendarmes sitting in the dark, freezing their butts off (according to Laurent) and wasting taxpayers' money (according to Albert, who was convinced that the appearance of a green van in Le Vignal on two separate occasions was nothing more than coincidence).

A bright moon rode high in the sky, shedding white light on trees and fields. Laurent's watch read 3:03 a.m. They had been in place for four hours. Except for the fact that the car windows frosted up periodically and had to be scraped clear, the gendarmes had an unimpeded view of the dark bulk of the two unoccupied houses. So far the only movement they had seen had been a troupe of *sangliers*—wild boars—out for a night's rooting.

Albert was in the driver's seat, slouched forward, chin on chest. Laurent had his seat pushed back as far as it would go, but there still wasn't enough space for his long legs. They felt cramped, and his right foot was going numb. Also, he had drunk a thermos of coffee since midnight. He needed a stretch and a piss. He opened the passenger door, causing Albert to stir, and got out of the car. His breath hung ghostly in the air. He closed the door quietly behind him and walked off into the bushes.

As he stood listening to the soft patter of his urine against a tree, Laurent wondered why it was that men pissed by preference on upright objects—walls, posts, fences, trees. Was there something deep in the male psyche that needed to leave its mark on more than Mother Earth? Maybe, like dogs claiming territory and status—he'd once seen a scrappy little dachshund nearly upend itself in an effort to outdo a bigger dog—human males had an atavistic need to make their mark vertically. He recalled boyhood competitions in which he and his pals, Albert among them, had tried to outdo each other in how high they could pee.

Albert, the dachshund of the gang, had perfected a technique of leaning back so far that he shot his whiz higher than any of them.

Back in the car, Albert, made of less philosophical stuff, was thinking only that stakeouts were boring and damned inefficient. All uninhabited houses should be wired and linked to a central station monitored by commercial security personnel. It would make the life of a gendarme a lot easier. A mild socialistic streak also inclined him to believe that people who were rich enough to buy second homes that they weren't prepared to live in ought to pay for their own protection.

The problem was that the Dordogne was steadily filling up with Parisian and expatriate homeowners who came for brief snatches of time, leaving their properties locked and shuttered but otherwise unguarded for the rest of the year. This was especially true of the British, who seemed to be arriving in the region by the planeload. Someone had said that, having lost their claim to France in the Hundred Years War, they were now buying it back by the square meter.

Laurent concertinaed himself into the car again, bringing a rush of frigid air with him.

"The bastard better show," Albert muttered through gritted teeth. "Otherwise, I know our adjudant, he'll have us out here every night until hell freezes over. Which it's close to doing."

The cold and the waiting were not the worst of it. For everyone attached to the Brames Gendarmerie, on whose patch the last two burglaries had taken place, and especially for brigade chief Jacques Compagnon, the main problem, the real indignity, was the doggerel.

In the space of six months there had been five burglaries in different communities in the Dordogne, all targeting houses closed up for the winter. The thief had been selective; only portable antiques and objets d'art had been taken. Paintings had not been touched. Nor had easily disposed-of electronic equipment. The first three break-ins, involving gendarme units of other jurisdictions, could have been isolated events. The fourth, a house on the outskirts of Brames, could also have been an unrelated crime. However, in this case, the thief's sense of humor, perhaps excited by his success, had got the better of him. The burglar had left behind a piece of poetry, the translation of which was:

Tweedledum and Tweedledee
Got into a battle
One fell and broke his arse
The other lost his rattle

The words had been scrawled in magic marker on a wall about a meter from the floor, leaving one to conclude that the author was either very short or had written the piece while kneeling. Adjudant Compagnon's protuberant eyes had bulged with annoyance at this piece of crude whimsy, the meaning of which was not entirely clear. The reference to *Alice in Wonderland* gave rise to brief speculation that the burglar was English. However, Lewis Carroll's fat twins were so well known in France that such a conclusion could not be sustained.

A billet-doux found at the fifth site—it had been typed on the homeowner's old-fashioned typewriter and left in the roller for police to discover—had removed all doubt as to the writer's intent and had caused Compagnon's eyes to stand out even farther from his head:

Two little blue birds
Sitting on a rail
Up comes Bad Boy
To grab them by the tail

Obviously, "blue birds" referred to the gendarmes, who wore blue uniforms and worked in pairs. By extension, Tweedledum and Tweedledee must be taken to refer to the police as well—the Brames brigade specifically, since that robbery had also occurred on their turf—who couldn't get it together and who went ass over rattle in their attempt to enforce law and order. Bad Boy, of course, was the thief himself, who outwitted the police, yanked their tail feathers, as it were.

Adjudant Compagnon was outraged. He took law and order and the *Gendarmerie nationale* very seriously. But mostly he felt personally teased. He expressed himself strongly and publicly on the mentality of criminals who thought they could get away with taunting the police with silly verses. He was widely quoted in the media as promising that the burglar would shortly be singing a different ditty. In confidence, he told his officers and the examining magistrate assigned to the case that Bad Boy had very stupidly given himself away: they now knew they were looking for an educated male perpetrator who worked alone and fancied himself a poet.

Although, the disloyal thought had flitted across Laurent's mind, it might as easily have been a very subtle female heading up a gang of literate dwarves.

Laurent did not like the prospect of continued below-zero stakeouts any more than his partner. But their boss's pride had been piqued, and he, like Albert, knew that until the burglar was caught, all suspicious behavior on their territory would have to be investigated thoroughly.

Laurent said, "We need more bodies. We can't be doing this and keep our eye on Luca as well."

He referred to the fact that their brigade was also carrying out an informal, low-level surveillance on Rocco Luca, alias Ton-and-a-Half, under the rubric of maintaining public order. Like waiting for a housebreaker to turn up, the Luca case was very much hit and miss, and it took up personnel time with nothing to show for it so far. Apart from occasional visits from Serge Taussat, Ton-and-a-Half seemed to lead an exemplary existence. You couldn't arrest someone on the strength of his associates, and up to now the Brames Gendarmerie had no case for launching even a preliminary investigation, or for requesting reinforcements.

Albert grumbled, "A fat zero, if you ask me, our adjudant's hunch. Even if Luca is running a pipeline through the Dordogne as big as the N21, we have nothing on him. Or that extraterrestrial sidekick of his. Everyone else, including the cops in Périgueux, thinks Yvan Bordas's death links to Marseille. So how does Compagnon figure the Ton is back in business and using the region as a transshipment point? Personally, I think Compagnon's dreaming of making a big bust. But he's going down a dead-end road if you ask me."

Laurent, stiff with cold, shifted about. In his experience, drugs were a problem mainly in the rougher suburbs of Paris and other big cities. Here in rural Dordogne, kids went in more for grass and E, when they weren't getting plain drunk, and you had to go all the way to Bordeaux, Toulouse, or Marseille for supplies of the heavy. However—and this was what worried him—things were changing. Now foreigners and Parisians moving into the region were bringing with them their big-city habits, and this was reflected in the stepped-up availability of heroin in modest centers like Sarlat, Bergerac, and Périgueux. You could get a *balle* of shit-quality brown—say, less than 5 percent purity, cut with pepper, talc, or God knew what—on the street for as little as twenty-five euros a gram. Better-quality white sold for a hundred and up.

Heroin—it had other names: *héro, rabla, came, poudre, cheval,* or simply H—was also taking on a new face. Junkies still mainlined, but nowadays users tended to snort or smoke it because of the fear of dirty needles and AIDS. They often took it with pot, Ecstasy, and prescription drugs, or as a day-after soother to calm the crash landing from cocaine and amphetamines. The damned stuff, Laurent thought grimly, had become the recreational user's adjunct drug of choice.

However, unlike Albert, Laurent did not think their brigade chief was necessarily heading down a cul-de-sac. He said, "Supposing Compagnon's right? You've got to ask, why did Luca choose to retire here?"

"The *canaille*'s from Bergerac," Albert pointed out.

"I know. But, I mean, is he really retired? Or is he behind the new action?" Laurent beat his arms to get feeling back in them. "Don't forget, Bordas was found in Périgueux. The word is he was killed because he got wind of a shipment coming in. So maybe Luca is routing the stuff through his buddy, Pascal Goudy, and then moving it on, and that's what Bordas found out."

Albert snorted, "Then the Ton's got a problem. You know the cops in Toulouse are sitting on Goudy's tails. The only reason they haven't brought him in is because they want him nervous to see which side he jumps."

"Sure. They think he's working with Bidart or Reynaud. But if Compagnon's right and Pascal's really bringing the stuff in for Luca, then the fact that the cops in Toulouse are on to Goudy is going to make the Ton nervous, too. Nervous enough to make a mistake." Laurent rubbed his chin thoughtfully. "Maybe that's why he's got Serge Taussat nosing around Périgueux."

Albert's laugh, sharp like a fox's bark, hung frozen in the air. "What, you think Luca's looking to set up there? He'd be crazy to do that. Périgueux's too hot after Yvan, and the Ton is smart enough to know it. If it's him, more likely Périgueux is just a blind. He makes us *think* it's his base, but his real center of activity is somewhere else." Albert added cynically, "Like Narbonne

Plage." Albert's parents had just retired to the small Mediterranean town, some distance away. In recent years it had mushroomed into a popular family holiday destination. Rental condos crowded the beachfront. People walked their dogs in the sunshine, little kids played with their spades and buckets in the sand. "*Merde!*" he uttered a moment later. "You know, Narbonne Plage is exactly the kind of spot a *crapule* like Rocco Luca would choose!"

Laurent sighed. It was pointless, this shooting in the dark. He changed the subject. "By the way, Roussel said Monsieur Ismet called again."

Albert groaned. "Complaining we're not doing enough to catch whoever trashed his shop? I told him just the other day that we'd checked out the toughs his son fought with at the market, but they had an alibi for the night in question."

"Not much of one, though." Laurent pulled his jacket tighter and tried to draw his head in, turtle-like, below the level of his collar. "It's easy to say you were raising hell at a rave in Brives, with a dozen buddies willing to vouch for you, for what their word is worth. Still, I'm inclined to believe them. Or at least I believe they didn't do the trashing. I can't see *voyous* like that leaving cash in the till."

"Yeah. Probably just someone who has it in for Turks."

"Then you'd think whoever it was would have left a message. Racial insults spray-painted on the walls." Laurent recalled the mess of spoiled food. "Or scrawled in tomato paste."

Albert shrugged. "Maybe it's someone who has a grudge against the Ismets personally. I can see the father getting up your nose. And the son. Sounds like the hot-headed type. Maybe that drink they sell gave a customer the trots. Or maybe it was just a random B and E."

Laurent was not so sure. There were a lot of things about the case that bothered him, not least the fact that the son seemed not to be around and the parents were keeping very tight-lipped about his whereabouts. He and Albert had speculated that the trashing might have been some kind of insurance scam, but when they checked it out they had learned that the Ismets carried only basic fire, water, and theft. Nothing had been stolen. The Ismets' losses had been ruined foodstuffs and unrecoverable labor, for which they could not claim. A torching would have been more to the point.

The two men fell silent. The windows were frosting up again. Albert scraped them clear. Eventually, he said, "How's Stéphanie?"

"Oh, fine," said Laurent, trying to sound casual. He had been dating Stéphanie Pujol for nine months now, and he was glad the darkness covered the blush that mottled his fair skin every time he thought of her. She was blond, freckled, and had a forthright manner and well-muscled legs that the young gendarme greatly admired.

"You seeing a lot of her?" Albert, knowing Laurent from boyhood, could sense if not see the blush.

"A bit." Every chance he got. To cover his embarrassment, Laurent slapped his arms again. He didn't like talking about it with Albert. His friend had gone from dachshund status to Lothario of the force. No one knew how he did it, but women fell over stout, curly-haired Albert Batailler. Laurent, by contrast, had remained shy and awkward around girls. Stéphanie was the first he'd really been serious about, and he didn't want his partner's expert advice on how to get her into bed, or what to do with her after.

Albert grinned, teeth flashing in the moonlight. "Sounds like you two are getting it on."

"Mind your own onions," Laurent snapped.

"*Oh là! là!*" hooted Albert.

The next time Laurent looked at his watch, it was going on for five. They had been at their post for nearly six hours.

"Doesn't look like the bastard is going to show," he said wearily.

By six-thirty, the horizon began to lift above a thin wash of gray. By seven o'clock the sky had taken on a uniformly steely aspect. In the harsh morning light, Laurent's normally round, cheerful face looked white and drawn with cold and fatigue. He was also starving.

Albert phoned headquarters.

"Nothing," he reported. "Do we stick with it?"

"I'll get back," said the gendarme on duty.

Five minutes later, the man called them. His tone was ironic. "You can come on home, lads. This just came through. Bad Boy pulled a job all right, but over Belvès way."

"*Merde,*" swore Albert. "At least it's not our patch. Maybe he's moving on."

"Don't celebrate yet," said the duty officer. "He left another calling card. Something about friends and companions. It's a play on 'Compagnon,' and the adjudant is furious."

· 14 ·

Mara's work at the moment was not the kind of thing she really enjoyed. Increasingly, it seemed to be overseeing the rejigging of ancient plumbing and the shifting of walls. In fact, she was becoming a valued *intermédiare* between expatriates in need of structural renovation and a network of skilled artisans to whom she regularly subcontracted work. The finer points of layout and decor, which Mara did enjoy, were usually left until the end, by which time the client was either exhausted or out of money, or both.

At the moment, she sat at her desk trying to focus through her glasses on a fanciful floor plan that a prospective client wanted but that the reality of his recently purchased farm cottage would not allow without major deconstruction. And expense. She looked up when Julian walked into her studio behind the house.

"What?" she asked.

"Nothing," he said, throwing himself into an old armchair where he slouched, staring moodily out a window, his long legs stretched before him.

She watched him. He had been like this every spring since she had known him. He bore stoically with the cold, dormant winter (when his work was at a standstill), but come spring—it was almost April—he was filled with a kind of anticipatory anxiety that made him a poor housemate.

"It won't bloom for another month, you know," she said.

He made no reply.

She yanked off her glasses. "It really *is* all you think about, isn't it?"

He turned to her, eyebrows hovering. "What is?"

"Your orchid."

He still looked puzzled. "Not at all. Why do you say that?"

"Because it's true. You spend far more time worrying about *Cypripedium incognitum* than—than you do about us."

"Us?" He sat up. "What's wrong with us?"

"Nothing. It's just that we never seem to talk."

"You want to talk now? You're working."

She threw down her pencil. "I *was* working. And I mean *really* talk, Julian."

He stirred uneasily. "I never know quite what you mean when you say things like that. *Really* talk. Sounds ominous. All right. What do you want to talk about?"

"Well"—her mouth tightened in exasperation—"how we're doing, for example. We've been living together for six months now. We did it as an experiment. Is it working out? Are you happy with the way things are? I get the impression sometimes that you'd rather be back in Grissac."

He looked at her doubtfully. "This isn't about sharks by any chance, is it?"

"Of course not." She looked scandalized.

"Oh." He settled back with a grin. "That's all right then."

She stared at him, at a loss for a reply. A moment later, he said, "If you really want to know, I was thinking about Kazim."

"Kazim?"

"I'm worried about him. I think he's fallen in with a bad crowd. I have a feeling he's running, not just from his parents, but from something a lot nastier. Betul and Osman aren't at all happy that I haven't been able to find him."

"You've done all you can."

"Have I, though?"

She blew out a lungful of air, pushed away from her desk, and stood up. "Why don't we go for a walk?"

•

Ecoute-la-Pluie lay in a valley bordered on the north end, past Mara's house, by a wooded ridge. Its only road, more a lane really, was roughly surfaced in *castine,* crushed limestone, that did little to prevent a deeply eroded trough from forming, like a gravel riverbed, down the middle of it. At the foot of the ridge, the lane dwindled to an overgrown path.

They followed the path up the forested slope, the dogs racing ahead of them. It was an old deciduous forest that had not seen the axe for nearly a century. Few people, apart from themselves, mushroom gatherers, or hunters in season, came this way. Owls and wood doves nested there. Deer and wild boar fed in its shadows. It was a place dear to Mara and Julian. She in particular had laid claim to it in her heart since the day she had first come to Ecoute-la-Pluie. It was her little island of calm away from a world of obsolete plumbing, eccentric flooring, and failed walls.

As for Julian, he loved trees wherever he met them. Orchids in need of finding might make him jittery, but trees always had a calming effect on him. The thought of their strong roots delving silent and deep gave him a sense of stability; their upward presence helped him get things into perspective. They towered above them now, old oaks, chestnuts, and ancient hornbeams, their branches lightly furred in green. Sunlight was breaking through a sky of shifting clouds. The path they trod gave off a smell of wet earth and leaf mold. Julian breathed deeply, stopped, turned, and took Mara by the shoulders.

"I'm only orchid-crazy a small part of the year, you know," he said earnestly. "The rest of the time I'm a normal, everyday sort of bloke. Please believe me."

"I'd like to," Mara said with equal earnestness. "But I dread to think what will happen when you do find your orchid."

He dropped his hands. "Eh? How's that?"

"You'll have to mount guard on it twenty-four-seven, won't you? Protect it from poachers. I'll never see you, unless I camp out with you. One way or the other I'm destined to play second fiddle to a flower."

He frowned. "I hadn't really thought of that."

"That I could be jealous of a flower? It costs me to admit it, Julian Wood, but I am." She gave him a despondent smile.

"Don't be silly. I meant round-the-clock protection. I've been so focused on the search, I haven't really thought about the after-I-find-it bit. They're doing it in England, you know. The wild yellow European Lady's Slipper used to be fairly common. It's now down to one native plant because of bloody pickers and poachers. The site is now strictly wardened and off limits to visitors."

"Surrounded by armed guards with orders to shoot to kill, no doubt?" She broke out resentfully, "What is it about orchids that makes people go freaky? Yes, yes, I know, they're beautiful and clever. They mimic bees and wasps and put out pheromone smell-alikes to attract pollinators. But is that enough to make normal individuals turn into obsessives?"

He replied a little defensively, "It's much more than that, Mara. Orchids aren't just any plant. They go back a hundred million years or more. They're delicate, tough, and highly evolved. They've managed to spread and survive on every continent except Antarctica under the most extreme conditions. You've got to admire them. But more and more they're coming under threat."

"As is every living thing on this frigging planet. Well, if orchids are so highly evolved, I'm sure they'll find a way of beating the odds."

He shook his head. "If only you were right. Although, I suppose if any family of plants has a chance of surviving, it's the *orchidaceae.* They *are* clever. I don't exactly mean intelligent, but, well, purposeful almost to the point of intelligence."

"Julian, they're a plant."

"No. I'm serious. Take resupination, for example."

"Take what?"

"Resupination. Twisting. You see, if an insect is to pollinate a flower, it's important that it can enter the flower easily. With a lot of orchids, the sexual organs start out in a position that would make a fly, for example, have to crawl in upside down to reach them. So the orchid, as it begins to open up, simply twists around 180 degrees on its stalk to create a nice, horizontal landing platform for the fly. Now, other plants do this, too, but the orchid goes one better. There's an orchid that grows in China in an environment where it can't rely on wind or insects for pollination. Luckily, it's hermaphroditic, so it simply twists its male parts 360 degrees around so it can insert pollen into the female cavity. Now that's smart."

"No," said Mara severely, "it's downright sneaky."

They resumed walking.

It was hard going uphill. The recent storm had done little damage on the south face of the ridge, apart from gullying out the path and leaving a loose deposit of stones washed down from higher up. However, on the north side, several trees had fallen. Julian and Mara saw with a keen sense of loss that one of them was a venerable elm that they had thought of as their special tree. They had picnicked under its great branches, had sought protection from rain beneath its generous canopy.

"*Requiescat in pace,*" Julian murmured, deeply moved by the impressive wreck of its uprooted base, wider across than he was tall. Sadly he stared into the murky pool of rainwater that had collected in the crater left by its fall.

When they came out of the woods into a sloping meadow, they saw in the distance two men, carrying surveying equipment, walking toward a truck parked on the roadside below.

"Oi!" yelled Julian, starting to run after them.

Before he could get close enough to ask what they were surveying for, they had loaded their equipment and driven away.

•

Mara spent the rest of the day trying to find an electrician to rewire a house. Rats had chewed through the wiring over the past five months while the power was off. This happened every spring with places that were closed up during the winter. The only way of preventing a repeat was to sheathe the wires in metal sleeving. It was a big house and a big job, and the English owners, who had just arrived to find no electricity in the main rooms, had left an urgent message asking Mara to have something done about it *tout de suite.* So far, she had not been successful. Jose Texeira, the electrician she normally used, was still in Portugal with his family. Remy Richard, with his bad back, could not be coaxed out of retirement. Nobody else wanted to take on the job. Finding people to do things was increasingly becoming a problem in the Dordogne, a region where out-migration was the norm for young people seeking jobs and where the existing workforce just grew older every year. At the end of the day she called the Hurleys to say that the matter was in hand and she would keep them informed. It was not the truth, but it was not a lie either. Her time in the region had impressed upon Mara the importance of never letting her customers, especially her foreign clients, see the rough side of things, the last-minute scrambles, the near crises. It only made them anxious.

The phone rang. Mara answered it, dreading more unhappy property owners with problems that needed fixing. She was relieved to hear the voice of Prudence Chang, calling from

California where she wintered. Her summer residence in the Dordogne, a picturesque *périgourdin* cottage, was Mara and Julian's particular favorite. The house, for reasons governed by its evolution from stable and piggery, had an ambling structure, thirteen doors, and a wonderful walled courtyard that Julian had landscaped to perfection.

"I heard from my neighbors this morning." Prudence's voice sounded a little shrill. "Would you believe? I've been burgled!"

· 15 ·

The news left Mara feeling sick. She had recently redone much of the interior of Prudence's house, painting and in some places resurfacing the walls. Now her mind reeled at the thought of the malicious vandalism that so often accompanied a break-in.

"Mara? Are you there?"

"Yes. Prudence, this is awful. I'm so sorry. Was there—was there a lot of damage?"

"Apparently not, apart from a shutter they worked loose and a broken pane of glass."

Mara found that she could breathe again.

"I wish they'd wrecked that awful wall in the dining room instead," Prudence's voice was saying in her ear. "Then I could submit a claim to have it put right."

The wall had been a point of contention between them. The bottom half of it stuck out while the top half sloped backwards and was full of irregular planes. Its surface was chipped and marked. Prudence thought the wall was ugly and wanted it built flat and vertical, like a wall should be. Mara had argued for leaving it as it was—the Awful Wall, part of the original stable, had character—and had undertaken to plaster it. Few people knew that Mara was a skilled plasterer. It was a demanding art requiring speed and skill that she had learned during an unhappy time when her marriage to a brilliant but alcoholic architect was coming apart. Then, it had symbolized her need for a new beginning, a clean surface on which to lay the imprint of a different life.

Lately, because it was time-consuming work, she only plastered for special clients.

Prudence had said, when Mara had finished the wall, that she supposed she could find some kind of large, decorative object to put over it.

"What's the point of my refinishing it if you're just going to cover it up?" Mara had been really hurt.

"If you'd done what I asked, I wouldn't have to cover it up," Prudence had responded.

And now, a burglary.

"My problem," Prudence went on, "is that I don't know what they took. You have a key. Can you do me a huge favor and check things out? I need a list of what's missing, and you know the interior as well as anyone. My insurance agent has a record of the really big-ticket items that you can use. His name is Sébastien Arnaud. He's with Assurimax, and if you call him in advance, he can meet you there. You'll like him. He's cuddly, like a teddy bear. Oh, and I also need the shutter and pane repaired."

"I'll deal with it."

"Thanks," said Prudence. "You're a treat."

•

Sébastien Arnaud arrived late at Prudence's house the following day. He was a tall, stooping, slightly overweight man whose umber hair stood up in tough little bunches that curled in opposing directions, giving him more the air of a rough-coated terrier than a teddy bear. An Airedale, Mara decided. He even had round, laughing doggy eyes.

"Sorry to keep you waiting," he said, pumping Mara's hand cheerfully. "I'm always running behind schedule. It's my kids, you see. I have six of them. All boys, and they give me no peace. Today my youngest fell in the duck pond. I had to fish him out. Then I had to change my clothes." Sébastien's broad face pleated into a grin. "*C'est la vie.* I expect you understand."

There was something about Sébastien, a shaggy, ambling, good-humored likableness, that made it easy for one always to understand, Mara thought, as she followed him around to the side of the house where he studied the shutter that had been pulled loose and the broken door pane it was supposed to protect.

"Hmm," he said.

They went inside.

It was a neat, selective job. No trashing. The burglar had simply entered and taken what he wanted. And he had known what to choose. All of the valuable antiques were gone: Prudence's entire collection of eighteenth-century bronze *animalier*, including a wonderfully wrought little greyhound that Mara loved and secretly coveted. The thief had also taken a pair of Lalique lamps worth a few thousand and, most treasured of all, a statuette of a dancer attributed to Degas. True to form, no paintings had been touched, nor had a state-of-the-art espresso maker, the television, the DVD player, or the CD–tape deck. Sébastien told Mara that it was just as well. Appliances were easily disposed of and notoriously hard to recover. However, the objets d'art might be found if an attempt were made to sell them to straight dealers. More likely—he gave a chuckle, half apologetic, half amused—they would find their way to not-so-fussy intermediaries or even private purchasers in London, Paris, Brussels, Amsterdam, New York, Tokyo. The burglar was probably working in league with someone in the antiques trade who acted as a ready fence. It was clever thievery. Small, highly collectable items that would sell quickly for sums hefty enough to provide a good return on effort but not so extraordinary as to attract attention.

•

Mara only learned that another piece of doggerel had been left on site through the following day's *Sud Ouest. Number Six and*

Counting, the headline read. The poem, reproduced in toto, was seen as a nose-thumbing riposte to Adjudant Compagnon's dire prediction about the burglar's career. In French it read:

Cher compagnon, mon vieil ami
Tu sais, c'est pas encore fini

Which translated in English as:

Dear companion, my old friend
You know, it's not yet at an end

It was easy to understand why Adjudant Compagnon, even though the burglary had not occurred on his turf, took the latest billet-doux as a personal challenge and affront. Easier still to sympathize with his indignation over the fact that the burglar had had the insolence to use the familiar *tu*.

16

The wind wakes him, and he sees that the clock has gone mad. Its digital display winks crazily: 9:13, 5:47, 3:25, 11:50. The red numbers frighten him a little. They flash like dragons' eyes, without logic, without mercy, telling him the power has gone off and then on again, as it is wont to do in heavy weather, leaving the clock to scroll through its senseless hours.

The wind buffets the house as it has done for nearly two hundred years. Is it the same wind, Joseph wonders, that goes and comes, bringing with it the smells of all the places it has been? Or a new wind, born each night somewhere high up in the sky? He does not know how long the power has been out. A minute? An hour? He will have to reset the time by the grandfather clock in the living room. He is learning to do things for himself: to boil an egg, to pay the bills (although the nurse Jacqueline Godet helps him a bit with that), to reset the time when the power goes out. He knows that his life is controlled by the clock, by the yellow and white pills that he must take every so many hours.

It is hard work, turning over on his side. His body feels as if it were filled with sand. But he succeeds, using the bedside railing for support, stretches out his arm, fumbles for the light cord behind his head. Slow fingers close on the familiar bulb of the switch. He draws comfort nowadays from the familiarity of things. As quickly as it comes on, the light goes out.

The eyes go out, too. Joseph is now in complete darkness, without even the red glow of the dragon that, smiling, simulates sleep. He lies rigid in the bed, a prickle of fear telling him that this time it is not the wind that has blown the power lines down, for he has heard the light scraping of the kitchen door over flagstones.

The last time, they had tried to tell him it was a nightmare, that it was not his dead wife in her rubbery shroud, wet hair hanging over the void of her face. But if not Amélie, who? Or what? Now he hears again the telltale creaking of the floorboard in the hall and knows he is not dreaming, was not dreaming the time before. The thing has returned. It has chosen its moment with cruel delay.

In his mind he outruns even the wind, legs spinning, bare feet skimming the ground. His heart is the only thing about him that races. It pounds so hard he thinks it will explode. Dimly, he remembers that he has taken precautions against this moment. His fingers grope, seeking the hard little slab of plastic with its confusing array of buttons. He can't find it. In a panic, he realizes it isn't there. With another effort he manages to roll onto his side, to push himself up on one elbow, to extend a shaking hand over the surface of the bedside table. It meets with objects that his crazed fingers can make no sense of. But the thing is gathering shape in the breach of the doorway. It seems to swell up blackly before his eyes. His wail of terror is choked off in his throat.

And now it shrinks upon itself, becomes a dark form writhing slowly across the floor, low to the ground, until suddenly it is rearing over him and reaching out to strangle him in its heavy embrace. As before, it has no face. Joseph sinks down dizzily onto the bed, preparing himself for what is to come. Something touches his head lightly, almost like a caress. The pressure grows stronger, pushing him face down into the pillow. His nose and mouth are full of pillow. Joseph struggles, driven by a tardy autonomic sparking of the brain that triggers a feeble self-defense.

Only now do the fingers of his right hand, in spasms, make contact with the numbered buttons of the cellphone buried beneath the confusion of the bedclothes.

•

The ringing woke Mara first. She swept her hand around on the nightstand for the phone, found the receiver.

"*Allo?*" she mumbled in a pasty voice. "*Allo? Allo?*" She groped for the lamp and switched it on.

By now, Julian was awake. He sat up, eyes puffy with sleep. "Who is it?"

Mara blinked stupidly at the number display.

"Shit!" she cried and grabbed her coat from the closet. "It's Joseph!"

•

They found him lying face down. The light over the bed was on, enabling them to appreciate fully the frightening twist of his body and the twitching of his legs. In his struggles, he had somehow managed to hit the automatic dial for Mara's number. His fingers still clutched the cellphone that she had bought and programmed for him. They had to pry it from his grip.

The only thing to suggest that Joseph had not been hallucinating was the clock. Its flashing random display indicated that the electricity had indeed gone off and come back on. As for the rest of his ordeal, which he recounted in a broken, quavering voice—the faceless form, the attempt to smother him—he had to have been dreaming. Mara and Julian exchanged worried looks. He had told a similar story the last time. Joseph stubbornly refused to let them call the doctor. Or the gendarmes.

Mara left Joseph with Julian and went into the kitchen to make a pot of chamomile tea. As she stood waiting for the water to boil, she noticed how soiled everything had come to look, even though she and the other neighbor women made sure the dishes were washed and put away every day, the counters wiped down. It was as if, while Amélie lived, her presence had stood between the viewer's eyes and the walls discolored with age, the range top and counter tiles chipped with use, the worn upholstery of the chairs only partly concealed by flat, loose cushions—*cache-misères,* "hide shabbiness," Amélie had jokingly called them. Mara was beginning to doubt seriously Jacqueline's assertion that Joseph would be fine on his own, even with the promise of additional home care. Besides, his condition would only worsen with time. She wondered whether the shock of Amélie's death had not accelerated the progress of his disease, causing him to muddle nightmares with reality the way he did. Someone ultimately had to take responsibility for him. It puzzled Mara that no one seemed to consider Christine Gaillard a viable option, perhaps because at the funeral she had fulfilled everyone's expectations: she had not come. What would it take, Mara wondered, to persuade the daughter to show some interest in her ailing father? Did anyone even know how to get in contact with her?

She sat down heavily on a chair. The *cache-misère* not quite doing its job, she felt the stab of the broken wicker seat even through the coat she had flung over her pajamas. It was possible, she supposed, that someone could have come in. After all, there was a rhyming housebreaker about. As a precaution, she got up and tried the back door. The mechanism was a typical deadbolt affair that one engaged by raising the handle and double-turning the key. She was relieved to find it locked.

Then she saw the leaf.

It lay pressed flat on the floor just inside the doorsill: a hazelnut leaf, one of last year's litter, brown, partially decomposed and glistening with moisture. She crouched to inspect it more closely. From that perspective, she also saw faint patches of moisture tracked across the flags. Her mind suddenly went very still, overwhelmed by a silence as heavy as a stone in free fall. It took her a moment to realize what she was seeing. Someone had come in through the back door, had tracked footprints and a telltale leaf into the house. Very recently. The leaf was still wet, the traces on the floor still damp. That person had not broken in. That person had had a key.

The scream of the kettle caused her to jump. She made the tea and carried three mugs on a tray into the room next to the kitchen.

"Drink it slowly, Joseph." Mara steadied the mug for him. Jacqueline had warned her that he had trouble swallowing. His hands shook badly, his jaw jumped up and down. "It's just past two. Is it time for your pills?"

"Not till three," he managed to say.

She continued to help him sip his tea. She asked, "Joseph, where's your fuse box?"

He raised his head from the mug and appeared to think. Then he told her that it was at the back of the house, in the hangar built onto the kitchen, where the wood was kept. Mara nodded. Hers was outside, too. It was an arrangement that allowed tampering by anyone. She remembered the last time Joseph had claimed someone had come into the house. The power had gone off then, as well, and come back on. She and Jacqueline had found the clock flashing. The nurse had had to reset the time. And Joseph's phone line had been down. Or had it been cut? Olivier had said that the wire had been broken cleanly. Maybe Joseph was not hallucinating after all.

•

Mara said, "Everyone here has a key. You, me, the Roches, the Boyers, Suzanne Portier, and probably Olivier Rafaillac for all I know, even though he's not doing meals for Joseph. And who else but the neighbors would know that his fuse box is in the woodshed?"

Julian's eyebrows lifted to the top of his head. "Are you saying it's one of us? And you'll have to include Jacqueline and that other nurse who rotates days with her."

Mara did not reply but climbed back into bed and huddled under the duvet.

"It may not be as suspicious as it looks," said Julian, getting in as well. "Who did his dinner last night?"

"Francine Boyer. Look, whoever it was could have cut the power at the fuse box and let himself—or herself—in, and then turned the power back on when he or she left. But they forgot about the digital clock, and they didn't spot the leaf or their tracks on the floor."

"See sense, Mara. There could be a reasonable explanation for everything. There might have been a real power break. It's always going out here, you know that. And the leaf and the tracks could have been made when Francine came."

"Our power didn't go off. Our clocks weren't flashing. And the leaf and the footprints would have dried out by now if it was Francine."

"Okay. Maybe she came back much later for something. Just let herself in without disturbing him. Or Joseph could have gone outside himself."

"But suppose someone really has it in for him?"

"And what? Is trying to give him a scare? Why? You know he suffers from nightmares and hallucinations. All of this is in Joseph's head."

Mara hunched back into the pillows. It was not unheard of for bad blood between neighbors to fester quietly beneath the skin of everyday appearances for a long time until some event—Amélie's death?—caused the rot to erupt like a suppurating boil.

She was checked by Julian's reminder that Joseph's grasp of reality was unreliable and the fact that she really couldn't see anyone wishing him harm. Perhaps Joseph was having more trouble adjusting to the loss of Amélie than any of them realized. Perhaps he was making things up to get attention. Either way, he needed help. She made a decision: the daughter, Christine, had to be found.

• 17 •

Mara thought that Christine was more of a missing person than Kazim. She had dropped out of sight and stayed that way for far longer than the Ismets' son. Mara was more than a little resentful, therefore, when Julian laughed dismissively at her intention to trace the Gaillards' daughter. They were having breakfast.

"Good luck," he said in a way that struck Mara as irritatingly know-it-all. "I think you'll find it's not as easy as it sounds."

"Who said it would be easy? She might be living in Timbuktu for all I know. I just think Joseph needs his family around him. Whatever happened in the past, she's still his daughter. Someone's got to make the effort."

"And that someone is you? Maybe you should find out how Joseph feels about it first before you launch Project Christine."

Her head snapped up. "What about Project Kazim?"

"Kazim is a runaway kid who has his parents very worried."

"Christine is also a runaway who's made her parents unhappy for a lot longer."

"Betul and Osman asked me to find their son."

"You haven't done a very good job of it, have you?"

"Give me strength! I'm only trying to tell you it's not that simple finding someone who doesn't want to be found." Then he said it: the F word.

Mara swung around on him, eyes blazing. "For your information, *to ferret* means to search out diligently. I looked it up. And a ferret is a smart, active animal with a hell of a lot more energy and initiative than you seem to show."

Julian avoided another fight by jumping up and declaring that he had things to do.

•

For the rest of the morning Mara stewed over Julian's condescension toward her "project." However, she did decide to take his advice about asking Joseph first. She opened the subject obliquely that evening when she brought the old man his dinner. It was an adaptation of her mother's meatloaf recipe. Mara's last attempt at it had come out dry and rubbery, according to Julian. This time, she did not try to prepare it as a loaf. Instead, she simply scrambled all of the ingredients together in a kind of hash. It turned out rather well, she thought, nicely browned and bubbling in its own juices. Joseph received the offering doubtfully. He belonged to a generation of people who were accustomed to eating solid cuts of meat, who associated ground beef with dog food.

"Joseph," Mara said, sitting down beside him at the kitchen table while he ate. "These nightmares you've been having."

"They're not nightmares," he said stubbornly. He frowned and poked his fork into the unformed mass on his plate.

"You think the thing without a head was real?"

"It's what I've been saying."

"Then it can only mean that somebody is coming in dressed up as a monster to try to frighten you." She hoped to force him to come to grips with the reality of the situation.

He looked puzzled, not making the connection. "Who'd want to do that?"

"You tell me. Look, has there ever been any trouble between you and any of the neighbors? Say, a dispute or some kind of quarrel that was never settled?"

Joseph took his time, pushing food onto his fork with his

thumb, moving the fork in a wobbling trajectory to his mouth, chewing, swallowing. He had to swallow several times, with visible effort, before the food went down. The mask of his face registered neither pleasure nor displeasure. Eventually he said, "Old Rafaillac didn't like it much when I told him he looked like one of his own artichokes." He cackled softly. "The choke part. That was before he lost his hair."

"I mean, something serious enough for a person to play nasty tricks on you as a way of getting back?"

The fork resumed its exploration of the hash. "What is this, anyway?"

Mara stifled her frustration and became more direct. "Listen, Joseph, the fact is I'm worried about you. I'm afraid you're not managing very well by yourself."

"I'll be all right soon as I get a home helper. I'm trying to get someone to live in full-time." The old man added ungraciously, "You lot won't have to bring me my meals anymore."

"You also have a daughter. Christine, isn't it?"

He was silent for a moment. Then: "She didn't come to the funeral."

"Maybe she didn't know. I'd like to think she'd be concerned if she realized you're living here on your own."

Joseph made a noise in his throat that could have been a comment or a swallow.

"When is the last time you were in contact with Christine, Joseph?"

The old man took in another load of hash.

"Do you know where she is?"

He rolled the food around in his mouth. "It needs more salt."

Mara knew that her questions had registered with him and that they had upset him. His right hand descended in a shaky arc and came to rest with an accelerated trembling that made the fork rattle noisily against the rim of his plate. She decided not to press the matter. *Find out the background and the psychology of the case,* Loulou had said. *Ask around.* That should have been her first step.

•

In a hamlet such as Ecoute-la-Pluie, everyone knew everyone else's business. They knew the state of their neighbor's health like the weather. They knew if someone had a drinking problem; if a husband beat his wife; if a wife made her husband's life a misery; if a cow was sick. Any major expenditure—repairs to the roof, a new car or piece of farming equipment—was immediately remarked upon, discussed as to value for money, and generally pronounced to be daylight robbery. The history of a place was archived in the collective memory of its residents.

So the neighbor women were Mara's other line of inquiry. She thought at first to bring them all together over coffee and cake (since she didn't bake, she would buy something at the fancy *pâtisserie* in Belvès). That way she could sound them out on her idea and hopefully enlist their help. She could also explore—delicately, of course—the possibility that someone was acting out an old grudge against Joseph. Then it occurred to her that talking to each individually might produce franker disclosures. She was quite pleased with her decision. Julian should not be allowed to flatter himself that he was the only sleuth on the street.

She tackled Francine Boyer first. Louis Boyer had been one of Amélie's pallbearers. The Boyers had held the funeral reception. That had to count for something.

As she sat in the Boyers' dim, unheated salon, Mara reflected that the reception was the only other time she had been in their house. Then, the space had been filled with people. Now, Mara saw it for what it was: a long, severe room filled with dark upright furniture squarely placed. It matched Francine, a tall, no-nonsense woman with bushy, iron-gray hair. A former teacher, Francine still had something of the schoolmistress about her.

"Bad blood between the Gaillards and one of the neighbors? You won't find any of that here," she answered stiffly, making Mara sorry she had asked. "Joseph's monster, as you call it, is in his head. On Tuesday night I took him his meal, and I went back the next morning to clean up and collect my dishes. I'm quite sure"—she drew herself up—"I never tracked a leaf into his house. As for Christine, yes, I knew her. She was a disciplinary problem at school, but then her life wasn't easy. I don't know why you're asking questions about her, but I think you'll find people here don't like raking up old matters. You're a newcomer, so perhaps you see things differently. However, if I were you, I'd leave Christine where she belongs: in the past."

Mara went away feeling very much that she had been put in her place and told firmly to let the matter drop.

•

Huguette Roche, pink and plump as a pillow, was more forthcoming. She served Mara coffee in the parlor and knitted while they talked. A wood stove gave off a blast of heat. It was funny, Mara reflected as she pulled off her coat, then her cardigan, how people's environments matched the people themselves. Francine's house had been cold and forbidding. Huguette's house was stifling and filled with overstuffed chairs, crocheted antimacassars, and lamps with beaded shades. A budgerigar hopped about in a cage by the window. Like her bird, Huguette fluttered when she spoke.

"But the Gaillards have always gotten along well with their neighbors. Except"—Huguette paused to think—"maybe Olivier Rafaillac. He and Joseph rowed over silly things. Olivier's dog, and then there was some problem over the sale of a tractor. Of course," she added coyly, "I always thought Olivier was rather sweet on Amélie and hoped to marry her after her first husband was killed. She came with quite a bit of land, after all. But then she married Joseph, who didn't bring a bean with him. In any case, Olivier might hold a grudge, but—*grand Dieu!*—he's not one to play nasty jokes on people. You surely can't be thinking that?"

Mara's questions about Christine elicited a bosomy heave.

"That poor, unfortunate child." Huguette said it as if Christine, who must be in her fifties by now, had never grown up. Perhaps for Huguette she had not.

Mara put her coffee cup down. "Unfortunate? How?"

"She was so unhappy, you see." Huguette stopped knitting and leaned forward, unintentionally hiking her skirt up to expose a stout thigh above a woolen stocking that ended at the knee. "She ran off young with a man. The relationship ended badly, as these things always do, and it started her on the wrong track. I always suspected there'd been a baby, although Amélie and Joseph kept very tight-lipped about the matter. They brought her home, but she made life very difficult for them. She kept running off, you see. They couldn't control her. One day she simply stayed away for good."

"But why was she so unhappy?" Mara asked. "Surely Amélie and Joseph were good and loving parents?"

"Oh." Huguette exclaimed softly. "I thought you knew. She—she was terribly deformed. She had a harelip."

Mara sat back, surprised. "Couldn't they operate?"

"Well, yes. They did. But it was badly done, and it gave her a complex. In my opinion, that's been the root of all her problems."

"Listen, Huguette," Mara said, taking the plunge. "Maybe it's none of my business, but Joseph needs help. Whatever happened in the past, I think it's time Christine was reunited with her father. Do you have any idea how to get in touch with her?"

Huguette went quite pale. "Oh dear." She fidgeted. "Get in touch? No, I don't. And I—I don't think that's such a good idea.

Not a good idea at all." She stood up, clutching her knitting to her like a woolly shield. "And now, if you don't mind, I really don't think I ought to say any more about the matter."

•

It was down to Suzanne Portier. Mara sat in her spacious kitchen. The big woman, sweater sleeves pushed up to the elbows, was making bread at a table in the middle of the room. Suzanne believed in bread, the kind of bread with body that lasted a full week, not those degenerate baguettes that went stale as soon as you got them home. She was often heard to say that the pap being turned out by today's *boulangeries* heralded the downfall of France, the French people, French culture. Mara watched in fascination as Suzanne turned the dough out onto a floured board where it sat like a fat body, lightly blistered over its entire surface. She began to knead it, leaning her weight into it, pressing down with the heels of her hands, turning and folding the heavy mass. Suzanne's bare forearms were powerful, like a man's.

"There's no one around here who would even think of trying to frighten Joseph, if that's what you've come about," she said sharply, letting Mara know that the news of her visits with Francine and Huguette had run ahead of her. "As for your idea of reuniting Joseph with Christine, have you asked him how he feels about it?"

"Ye-es." Mara took a deep breath. "I honestly think it's worth a try. I don't suppose you know where I can find her?"

"What if she doesn't want to be found?" Suzanne's hands continued to work swiftly, as if they were somehow more intimately bound to the shiny, elastic mass they were kneading than to herself.

"She might if she knew how much her father needs her. These hallucinations of his. They're getting serious. And after all, how many years have passed? People change, you know."

"Then why hasn't she come forward? She could have turned up at her mother's funeral."

It was what Joseph had said.

"Maybe she didn't know."

"Oh, she knew all right."

Mara caught her breath. It was the first real break in the mystery that surrounded Christine Gaillard. She waited for the other woman to say more. Suzanne lifted the dough, placed it in a large bowl, and left it to rise under a cloth. She went to the sink to wash her hands. With her back still to her visitor, she said in an almost resigned tone: "Look, before you go stirring things up, you should know that it might be for the best for everyone if Christine didn't come back."

"But why?"

Suzanne turned around, holding her wet hands before her. "Christine had her own ideas about things, and she had a violent temper. It's something no one here likes to talk about. When she was a kid, she stabbed a schoolmate in the back with a pair of scissors. Created an awful fuss, although the other child wasn't badly hurt. And then"—Suzanne dried her hands on her apron—"she tried to kill her mother."

Mara started. "Tried to kill Amélie?"

Suzanne's eyes glinted. *Got you there,* they seemed to say. "She pushed her down the garret stairs."

Mara sat speechless, thinking of the dark, narrow stairway leading up to the Gaillards' dusty attic. She recalled the looks exchanged at Amélie's funeral, Joseph's unanswered question (*Why was she up there?*), and understood the conspiracy of silence that only Suzanne was bold enough to break. Amélie's death had been caused by a fall down another flight of stairs. Had the Gaillards' daughter tried again and succeeded?

Suzanne stood watching her, hands on hips, her face impassive. "So now you know. If you want my advice, you'll leave well enough alone. But if you're really determined to get in touch with Christine, last I heard she was living somewhere outside Les Faux. I'm sure anyone there could tell you where to find her."

• 18 •

Adelheid Besser waited almost two weeks for Julian to fall in with her plans. When he did not, she contacted the other best-known wild orchid expert in the region, Géraud Laval. A retired pharmacist and Julian's botanical bête noire, Géraud was a troll-like man with hair in his ears and an unpredictable temper. Géraud, too, had been searching for *Cypripedium incognitum* ever since the day Julian had shown him a badly deteriorated photo of a Lady's Slipper orchid, purportedly found growing in the Dordogne.

The orchid was a point of bitter contention and rivalry between the two men. Publicly, Géraud denied it existed at all. Privately, like Julian, he was obsessed with finding it. Géraud had been hunting orchids in the Dordogne for most of his considerable lifetime (compared with Julian, who had been in the region a measly twenty-seven years) and was deeply committed to the belief that the honor of discovering a second indigenous species of *Cypripedium* for Western Europe rightly belonged to him.

At the moment, Géraud was as near as he ever got to speechless. He was the proud possessor of a host of tropical orchids that he tended lovingly in a glassed-in area attached to the back of his house. The greenhouse he now stood in was five times bigger than his. The space was broken up into different environments, each providing controlled amounts of light, moisture, and temperature. Ceiling fans turned slowly above their heads.

In a separate glassed-in laboratory, a woman in overalls was moving between shelves filled with flasks of germinating seeds.

"I don't let just anyone see my darlings." Adelheid addressed him in French; Géraud spoke nothing else.

They grew in pots on rolling metal tables or hung from overhead baskets, ranks of them, orchids he would have killed to own, or at least would have stolen (Géraud acquired his orchids any way he could). However, Adelheid's great breasts were trained on him like torpedoes, and he decided thievery might not be such a good idea after all. They were all of the Slipper type. She had acquired them from all over the world, she said, and often went in person on collecting forays. She had *Cypripediums* from China; *Paphiopedilums* from Borneo; *Selenipediums* from Brazil. Grudgingly, Géraud acknowledged the honor she was doing him. The woman had a reputation for secrecy, terrific orchid snobbery, and, if you were looking to buy, exorbitant price tags. One did not view if one did not have world-class credentials. And deep pockets.

He stared hard at a plant with three remarkable blooms on a single stalk. The labellum of each flower was maroon with yellow markings, the dorsal sepal yellow with maroon stripes. The lateral petals tumbled in spectacular falls, like twisted ribbons, as long as his arm.

"This *Paphiopedilum sanderianum* seems to be doing well." He tried to sound casual, but the words nearly choked him. The orchid was rare. Months ago, he had fought desperately to save a juvenile representative of the species in his collection from some kind of brown rot. It had died.

"Ah," said Adelheid knowingly. "You have tried to grow it?"

"Susceptible to bacterial infections," Géraud muttered.

"Nonsense. Overwatering. That, *mon cher monsieur,* is the most common cause of orchid death."

He glared at her furiously. That this female should accuse *him* of overwatering!

To change the subject, he pointed at three young plants, nothing more than clusters of narrow leaves, on a stand by themselves. "And what are those?"

A cagey expression flitted across her face.

"Guess."

He frowned, trying to appear knowledgeable. While he struggled she grinned at him, seeming to take an amused interest in his hairy ears.

"Give up," she laughed and socked him on the arm, hard. "They are nothing less than plantlets of the fabulous *Phragmapedium kovachii!*"

"*Phrag*—!" His eyes bulged. It was the most sensational find of the twenty-first century, a magnificent Peruvian orchid with a flower as big as a man's hand. Its discovery and subsequent importation into the U.S. had been the focus of intense controversy. He said nastily, "I heard it had been poached to extinction right after it was found. How did *you* come by it?"

"Ach, I bought it legally." She waved dismissively. "As a flasked seedling, of course."

"Hanh." He made the sound through his nose, conveying his utter disbelief.

"So," she said, steering him out of the greenhouse. "You have seen enough?"

She conducted him into her house, where she pushed him into an overstuffed armchair in her front room. "Sit. Let's talk business."

"Business?"

"Mmm-um. I have need of you."

"You do?" He felt absurdly pleased.

What she said next, however, nearly caused him to explode:

"I approached someone else first, you know. But he did not respond. Julian Wood. You know him?"

"That amateur!"

"I don't agree. I have seen his book. It is very comprehensive. In it he has an orchid."

"You're talking about *Cypripedium incognitum,* I suppose," Géraud said sneeringly.

"Mmm-um."

"It's a shameful piece of botanical trickery. This Wood fellow is crazy. He has no evidence—no evidence whatever—that this orchid exists. An absolute dog's breakfast of a photograph. I've seen it. Yet he has the gall to include it in a book. That alone should tell you what kind of an orchidologist he is. Anyway, what do you want with him? Or with me, for that matter?"

"That is the business we will discuss. This *Cypripedium incognitum.* I wish to have it."

"Ha! Good luck."

"I want to hire you to find it for me."

"Me?"

"*Mais oui.*"

"You're mad. I told you. The thing doesn't exist."

"Julian Wood thinks it does. So do I."

"Then look for it yourself. You're an experienced orchid hunter."

"I have no time. I have a very busy schedule with my darlings. I make collecting safaris all over the world. I do research. I attend conferences where my presence is demanded. I will pay you well."

Géraud, who had been on the point of heaving himself up from his chair, paused.

"How much?"

Adelheid said cannily, "First we must talk terms."

"What terms?"

"The attribution. I will, of course, share the glory of the discovery with you. You will take your place beside me in the orchid hall of fame. However, I want it named after me."

Géraud sank back into his seat. Share the fame? Name it after her? He almost laughed aloud. If he found the orchid—*when* he found it—the credit of discovery would be all his, nomenclature and all. He knew her type to the core. She was as violently possessive, as bitterly jealous, as nastily competitive as any he had ever met. But she had fired his ambition and his greed, and the thought of besting Julian at his own game was too tempting.

"However," she went on, "you will have to hurry. It is now April. *Cypripedium incognitum* is said to flower in May. Monsieur Wood has been looking for it already several years. Now that he knows I am after it as well, he will redouble his efforts. Don't underestimate him. I think Julian Wood will give you a run for your money."

"That clown couldn't spot a daisy in an open field," Géraud said with more certainty than he felt. He leaned forward. "Madame Besser—"

"Call me Heidi." She invested the words with heavy innuendo.

Géraud looked at her more closely. Her face was round, her small blue eyes were shrewd, and her scarlet mouth looked positively rapacious. She had alarmingly hennaed hair to match her mouth. Why was it, he thought with annoyance, that so many women of a certain age opted for the red look?

"Very well, Heidi. We share the fame. And now, before we go any further, how much?"

"A thousand euros. That includes expenses."

"You're joking! You might pay that for an unusual specimen. For a new discovery, the limit, as you very well know, is what the market will bear. Seven thousand. And a seedling of

Phragmapedium kovachii," he added. It was time Heidi learned with whom she was dealing.

•

"How will you go about it?" asked Adelheid a little later.

They were seated at her table, having (after considerable wrangling) settled on a price. She had knocked him down to five thousand plus a *Paphiopedilum sanderianum* in good condition (*Phragmapedium kovachii* was off limits). Now they were drinking to their new partnership. Géraud eyed the straw-colored liquid in his glass, swirled it, sniffed, and took a mouthful. He couldn't fault her choice of wine. It came, he noted, ready-chilled. Had she been so sure of success?

He shook his head. "Can't divulge. I have my methods." He could see that she looked doubtful. "But one thing I can say is that I have a way of keeping tabs on where Julian Wood is in his search."

"Oh, yes?"

He took another sip of wine. "My wife, you see, is a friend of his." He referred to Julian's artist, Iris Potter, with whom Géraud lived not in a state of matrimony but in a long-term, on-off relationship. That is, Iris periodically left when her cranky lover became too hard to bear and returned when his temper improved. Julian had once said to Iris within Géraud's hearing that he did not know how a nice woman like her could stand living with a *chameau* like him. That was another score the squat orchidologist had to settle. "She's a very good artist," Géraud went on. "In fact, it was she who did the drawing in Julian's book."

"Your wife did the drawing? Did she see the embroidery he claims it is based on?" Adelheid pushed a plate of cheese puffs toward her guest.

"No. That's the scandal of it. He simply told her what to draw. I'm convinced this embroidery is an invention. Even she felt he was pulling a fast one."

"Hmm. So how can she help you?"

"*Eh bien*"—Géraud's fat fingers dipped into the cheese puffs—"Julian tells her things, and she tells me."

The bright lips shaped into a predatory smile. "So! You ask *her* to ask *him* how he plans to go about looking for *Cypripedium incognitum*. Where he will search. *Et voilà*, you get there first. What if he beats you to it?"

Géraud frowned in annoyance. "Let's get something straight, Heidi. When I search for orchids, I do things my own way. I don't answer questions, and I don't give out information. I want your absolute assurance that I will have no interference from you. Is that clear?"

He expected her to object. However, the woman took it surprisingly well. She cocked her head at him and gave him what passed for a coquettish grin.

"Mmm-um."

Géraud absolutely knew that he could not trust her.

• 19 •

It was a little past ten on April Fools' night, or as they said in French, *poisson d'avril,* April Fish. Kazim was taking fifty euros off a runny-nosed junkie when he spotted the Mercedes parked in the shadows of Place de la Claustre. A man dressed in black slid out of it and moved swiftly toward them, throwing a wedge of darkness before him as he passed under the lamps of the empty square. Kazim recognized the man, the one they called Serge, at once. It was hard to mistake a face like that, the skin pulled tight and as reflective of light as the steel blade of a knife.

"*Merde!*" Kazim uttered. He swung around. The junkie, who had said his name was Freddy, was gone. For a *con* with a limp, he had vanished into the darkness surrounding the cathedral with surprising speed.

Kazim was even faster, vaulting onto the seat of his Honda, roaring off in the opposite direction down Rue Taillefer. A moment later he became aware that the Merc was on his tail. He laughed. With its speed and on city streets, the Honda could outrun anything on four wheels. He led the car on a crazy chase, purposely heading west across the city, three times around the great circle of Boulevard des Arènes, the scream of his 1300cc engine splitting open the night. It amused him that the *flics,* who were normally out in force at this hour on a Friday night and who should have been all over him by now for speeding, excessive noise, riding without a helmet (it was still locked to the rear of his bike, where it bounced wildly), were nowhere in sight. He had used the cops as an escape hatch once already, when he had provoked the punch-up with that zitty *merdeux* and his mates at the market. *Allah askina!* Tonight he could ride his bike through the plate-glass window of a shop and no one would blink. But he wasn't worried. The fourth time around the circle, he slowed. The Merc came up on him like a train. He accelerated suddenly and made a hard right, leaning at 45 degrees, into a narrow street. The Merc attempted the unforeseen turn, fishtailed, and described a 180 in a shriek of rubber.

"Eat smoke, bastard," the young Turk shouted over the roar of his engine. He threw back his head in triumph, feeling the sharpness of the wind cutting through his hair. He was now heading north. Another hard right down a narrow road brought him roaring into a major intersection. He swung back in the direction he had come, down the broad expanse of Rue Président Wilson.

The Merc was waiting for him on one of the side streets. It gave Kazim his first real jolt of fear to see it slipping smoothly, like a barracuda, behind him into the thin, late-night traffic. He accelerated and swung away, first right and then left. He saw the car again on his tail as he hit the bottom of Rue Romaine. It followed as he entered another traffic circle and stayed with him this time as he shot out of the roundabout past the tall ruin of the Temple of Vesunna. For an instant he thought about peeling off into the dark parkland surrounding the temple, but remembered that not so long ago a body had been found there. He kept going.

As he raced along the deserted straightaway, he realized he had underestimated the Mercedes. It was gaining on him, and this, he sensed, was where it would happen. Another surge of fear brought a taste of bile to his mouth. But the Merc merely hung on his ass like a fart, making no attempt to overtake, to drive him off the road, or to send him flying headfirst into its path, where it could finish the job by running him over. Kazim found that he was drenched with sweat under his leather jacket. The bastard was playing with him, like a cat with a mouse.

It was the Honda's turn to fishtail dangerously as Kazim took a squealing right into a narrow lane. And so he went, dodging and weaving through the network of tiny streets. By now he had lost sight of the Merc, but the throaty roar of his *moto,* bouncing off the stone faces of the darkened buildings, announced his presence as effectively as a beacon. He eased the engine back to a soft purr and regained the city center. He knew with certainty that he had shaken Serge when he found himself alone in Place St-Louis. Gently, he nosed the Honda into a cobbled passage leading through the old quarter. From there it was a short run to safety.

•

"Blimey, where you been, mate? They're all over lookin' for you," Peter said in an awed voice when Kazim burst into the garret. "*Eels voo shersh par-too,*" he translated in his execrable French. "*Say vray, Naahd?*"

Nadia, who was sitting at the plastic table eating a takeout, almost choked on her food. She stood up, knocking over a cardboard container. Greasy *pommes frites* spilled onto the floor. She ran to the door and slammed it shut.

"Did anyone follow you?"

Kazim postured, unzipping his leather jacket. "Not a chance. I left him swallowing my dust."

She turned on him, fists clenched. "Well, you can't stay here."

"Hey, what's with you?"

"I said, not here."

"Look, just the night," Kazim pleaded. Stripped of all his swagger, he looked young, scared, and dazed.

Nadia shook her head vehemently. Her black and orange hair stuck up in angry spikes. Her green eyes darted about, her lips, black-lined, in-filled with purple, were pulled back in a grimace of fear. Peter stood behind her, rubbing his nose. Despite his linguistic handicap, he seemed very much a part of the conversation. Brigitte was stretched out on the sofa, blankets pulled up to her chin. She appeared to be the only one enjoying the scene.

"Sling your gear and go," insisted Nadia. "Now."

"Like where?" Kazim's voice was shrill. "Home is off limits. I told you, I don't want to land my parents in it."

"What about us? If they find you here, you'll land *us* in it. We'll all be hyper in the *merde*."

"Yeah," Peter said, not bothering with French. "Be a good boy and push off."

"Three of them," Brigitte spoke up for the first time. She fingered her gold nose ring. "All looking for little Kazim."

"Three?" Kazim swung around and stared about him wildly, as if all of his pursuers were somewhere hidden in the flat.

Brigitte grinned. "A guy with a limp. That skinny, weird-looking guy they call Serge. And a tall one."

"Serge," croaked Kazim. "He came here?"

Peter said, "Nah. Just the tall bloke. Left this." He dug Julian's card from one of his voluminous pockets and flipped it to Kazim. "Check 'im out, mate. Maybe 'e can 'elp you." Kazim, who spoke no English, stared at Peter uncomprehendingly but caught the card.

"He knows your parents," said Brigitte.

"Look," Kazim swung back to Nadia. "I got a couple of caps left. High-grade white. Just let me put down here for the night and they're yours." He dug out the heroin-filled capsules, two of the four that he had remaining.

Nadia gave him a nasty sneer. Reluctantly, he added another capsule. She snatched them from him.

"'Course they're mine!" she screamed. "You owe me that for back rent. Now get going." She gave him a shove.

Kazim shoved back. "You owe *me,* bitch!" he yelled. "Who's your pipeline? Who keeps you in *came?* Where's your supply going to come from tomorrow? The next day? And the day after? You think of that?" He squared off, looking both desperate and furious.

Nadia laughed. "You *nul.* You *double zéro.* You don't know the first thing. Without me you'd have *given* the stuff away. Besides," she added sullenly, "you haven't got a pipeline. Not anymore."

"Save your breath," Brigitte advised him over the top of her sleeping bag. "You're finished."

Kazim looked stunned. Then he advanced on Nadia, his face working in fury. "You sold me! You piece of garbage, you sold me!"

"Get out!" cried Nadia, retreating. Beneath her wild makeup she looked terrified. "We don't know you. We never heard of you."

"C'mon, mate. Use your loaf. We don't want trouble." Peter stepped in to intercept the Turk. The two men struggled briefly, but Nadia jerked the door open and then flew in with a crazed strength to help Peter push Kazim out it.

"I'll make you bleed for this!" Kazim yelled as he stumbled into the blackness of the landing. The door slammed. He heard the bolt click.

The rush of events left him feeling weak and dizzy. After a moment he gathered his wits and what courage remained to him and groped along the wall until he found the *minuterie.* He still clutched the card Peter had given him. He blinked at it in the sudden illumination of the timed light. Slowly, he reached into his jacket for his cellphone.

•

The telephone in Julian's cottage sounded. After five rings, the *répondeur* kicked on with its bilingual message: "*Bonjour. Vous avez rejoint le numéro de Julian Wood* . . . Hello, you've reached the number for Julian Wood. Sorry I'm not here to take your call, but I do check my messages frequently . . ."

Kazim did not comprehend English, but he understood the recorded greeting in French. He wasn't talking to any *fichu* answering machine. He killed the connection. Then he changed his mind. Brigitte said the man knew his parents. He redialed. This time he left a message: "This is Kazim. Look, if anything happens, I want you to know a *gars* named Serge is after me. Nix on the cops. I don't want my parents mixed up in this." He paused to think. "Tell them . . . just tell them I'm okay . . ." He switched off but continued hanging on to the phone as if it were a tenuous lifeline.

The light went out. He punched the *minuterie* again and headed down the stairs. As he went, he tried the doors giving onto the landings. They were locked, as he knew they would be. His *moto* was parked at the bottom of the stairwell. Predictably, the light gave out again just as he was wheeling it out the door. The street outside was deep in shadow, lit only by a distant lamp. He had to negotiate his way around the big skip of debris that seemed to be a permanent annex to the front of the house. A slight noise, coming from his right behind the skip, startled him. He whirled around. A cat slid away. He was almost sick with relief.

Then a voice spoke softly in his left ear.

"*Poisson d'avril,* Kazim. Going somewhere?"

To Kazim, the April Fools' greeting sounded as sharp as the snap of a switchblade.

20

"Frequently," for Julian, meant whenever he stopped by his cottage to collect his mail and check up on things. That was when he also listened to his phone messages. One of these days he would have to break down and get a cellphone. He hated the things, considered them an unnecessary disturbance of his life, which was already unsettled enough. For now, all of his existing clients knew to reach him at Mara's, but prospective new business did not. Perhaps that was why no prospective new business had come his way.

He did not pick up Kazim's message until Monday morning: " . . . if anything happens, I want you to know a *gars* named Serge is after me. Nix on the cops. I don't want my parents mixed up in this . . ." Julian could almost smell the fear in the young man's voice.

Kazim had not left a number, but Julian was able to retrieve it and put in a return call. There was no reply. He left a message: "Kazim, this is Julian Wood. Look, whatever you're up to, you sound like you're in over your head. Don't be stupid. Go to the police. Far better they deal with you than Serge. And call me or at least get in touch with your parents as soon as you get this. They're worried sick about you."

Then he phoned the Ismets, but they weren't answering either, so he left a message for them as well: "It's Julian. Call me. Right away." He hung up, glumly imagining a futuristic world in which telephones that no one answered faithfully recorded urgent messages that no one listened to.

Kazim had said no cops. Just the kind of stupid thing a nineteen-year-old kid in trouble would say. As a compromise, Julian called the Brames Gendarmerie and asked to speak particularly with Sergeant Laurent Naudet. Laurent was not there, but at least there was a live person at the other end of the line. Briefly, Julian considered raising an alarm about Kazim but decided against it. He was probably overreacting, and he didn't know what fallout there could be for Betul and Osman. Besides, he'd rather talk to Laurent, whose discretion he trusted. He left his name and number and asked that Laurent get in touch with him as soon as possible.

Tired of leaving messages, Julian opted for direct action. He decided to drive to Périgueux. He phoned Mara.

"This sounds serious," she said after he had repeated Kazim's words. She put aside being sniffy that he had not taken her attempt to trace Christine Gaillard seriously; also, she was fed up with waiting for a response from any electrician willing to take on rewiring the Hurleys' house. "I'll go with you. You need backup."

•

"Where exactly are we going?" she asked when Julian picked her up at the house in Ecoute-la-Pluie. Jazz and Bismuth, desperate not to be left behind, shoved ahead of her into the van.

"Nadia's place. I'm pretty sure Kazim's been staying there."

They started off. Jazz assumed his favorite position, forelegs planted on the tool box behind Julian's seat, big head resting on Julian's left shoulder. That way he got a comfortable place for his chin and a view of the passing countryside through the driver's window. Bismuth, less interested in the journey than the arrival, curled up between two bags of potting soil and went to sleep.

"Serge," Mara said. "Didn't Loulou mention someone by that name? Rocco Luca's henchman?"

"Not necessarily the same bloke," said Julian, not liking the thought. "It's a common enough name, and it could just be someone Kazim's fallen out with. He seems to run with a tough crowd." He braked at a stop sign. "You'll enjoy meeting Nadia. Hair like a wolverine and a personality to match."

"It has to be drugs. That's probably how he financed his bike. Maybe Kazim pushes for Luca. Kazim held out on him, and Serge was sent in to settle the score."

Julian hated to admit it, but what she said made sense. Jazz snorted gustily, blasting him with a dose of dog breath.

•

The bells of the city had finished pounding out their noon symphony. Now they were followed by a coda of metal grilles being dragged across shop fronts. People hurried out of buildings and down the sidewalks. All had the purposeful tread of those with a serious mission: the quest for lunch. The cafés and restaurants filled up. The day was warm and bright, with that delightful playfulness of spring that is so quickly replaced by rain squalls. The outdoor tables were quickly taken. People were hungry for sun and sat soaking it up, faces raised to a limitless blue sky. Waiters and waitresses, harried, balletic, ran their mini-marathons, dodging, weaving among the tables.

"The shrimp omelet? Who's it for?"

"Two Kronenbourg!"

They delivered up plates of sandwiches and pizzas for fast snackers; four-course meals for those intent on digging in for the longer haul. Conversations took place among the clatter of cutlery, the clink of glassware, the rumble of passing traffic. People chatted into cellphones. A woman drew deeply on a cigarette, draped her arm over the back of her chair, closed her eyes, and let a cloud of smoke drift slowly from her mouth.

Julian parked below the cathedral in the only patch of shade they could find and rolled the windows halfway down for the dogs, who remained in the van. They walked up Avenue Daumesnil. Julian helped an elderly woman carry her little wire shopping cart down the steps leading into Rue Porte-de-Graule. Nadia's building was at the lower end of the narrow road. The skip that had stood in front of it was gone. In its place was a van. A couple of workmen were sitting in the open rear of the van eating their lunch. They paid no attention to Julian and Mara as they entered the house. They appeared to be used to people coming and going.

As they trudged up the spiral staircase, Julian noticed that the *minuterie* had been overridden. The stair lights were on and stayed on. The men were now working on the second floor. Open doors gave glimpses of newly painted walls, tiles being laid. Somewhere in the back of the house someone was using a power drill. This time there was no rock music coming from the flat at the top of the house.

There was no answer to Julian's knock, either. He rattled the doorknob. The door swung open.

The flat looked to have been vacated in a hurry. The plastic furniture was scattered and overturned, the wooden crates empty of all belongings, the pans placed to catch rainwater kicked aside, and the mattress on the floor stripped, displaying impressive aureoles of stains.

"They've done a bunk," he said, stating the obvious.

Mara moved quickly through the flat, turning over old newspapers with the toe of her shoe, peering into the sink.

"Ugh."

Julian looked into the bedroom. The bed there had also been stripped. The dresser drawers hung open and empty.

They went back down.

Julian asked the workmen, "Either of you know where the people who lived at the top went?"

"More like where our skip went," grumbled one of the men. In its absence, the renovators were dumping rotten planks and torn linoleum in a messy heap on the ground.

The other man, a big blond fellow, his cheeks bulging with food, shrugged. He swallowed and wiped his mouth with the back of his hand. The hairs on his forearm stood out, white and fuzzy with sawdust.

"They're gone? Good riddance, if you ask me. Owner probably told them to shift it. They'd have had to get out by next week anyway."

"Do you know how I can contact the owner?"

Blondie could only give them the name of the firm of architects who had hired them: Chauvin et Fils.

Mara and Julian left.

"How about lunch?" suggested Julian gloomily.

•

At about the same time that Julian and Mara were having lunch, a worker at a dump site outside town spotted a blue and white trainer poking out from a pile of rubble. The shoe looked in good condition, and the worker wondered if it came with a mate. He clambered up the hill of debris. The shoe was an Adidas, almost new. He shook his head. People threw away anything nowadays. It wasn't like that when he was a kid growing up after the war. You counted every *centime,* hung on to things until they were of no possible further use. Steadying himself with one hand on the shifting scree, the man reached out with the other to push aside a broken plank to grab the shoe. It resisted his pull. He tugged harder. It came away, revealing a human foot.

•

The story on the eight o'clock news hit Julian like a blow: the body of a young man, identified as Kazim Ismet, nineteen years old, of Brames, had been found at a dump site outside Périgueux.

It had lain in a skip, covered by building debris, until the skip had been taken on Monday morning to be emptied. The body, tumbled out with the contents of the skip, might not have been noticed even then, except that an alert worker, spotting a shoe, had become suspicious. Upon investigating the matter, he had made his grisly discovery.

A preliminary report gave the cause of death as a drug overdose, making this the second drug-related death in Périgueux in three weeks. A hypodermic needle had been found with the body. Documentation in a wallet had led to a positive identification by the youth's father, Osman Ismet. A shaken Osman appeared briefly on the screen. He denied that Kazim had ever taken drugs and blamed bad influences and poor policing for his son's death. Osman appeared to have shrunk substantially. His words carried the conviction of a deflated balloon. At one point only did he give a glimpse of his old spirit. "Who is protect our children?" he raged. "When they are young, stupid, who protects?" Arms outstretched to the television audience, he communicated his anger and pain to every viewing parent like a knife to the heart.

Mutely, Julian stared at the television screen. He imagined Betul's grief. Osman's anguish was plain to see. Julian was furious with himself that he had delayed searching for the Ismets' boy, then overwhelmed by an awful sense of guilt. He had promised. A day might have made all the difference.

Mara reached for his hand. "Don't blame yourself, Julian. You did all you could."

He shook his head and pulled away. He should have done more. And a hell of a lot sooner. He felt a stress headache coming on. Thumpers, he called them. They started with a pressure behind the eyes that quickly became the assault of a manic percussionist beating a bass drum inside his skull.

She tried to hold him. Her voice reached him distantly. "Listen to me. This is not your fault."

He stood up. "Leave it, will you?"

"For God's sake, don't shut down like this. Talk to me!" She had risen, too, and was following him out of the room.

"Talk?" he turned and almost shouted at her. "That's my problem, isn't it? I'm going to have to go to the shop, look Betul and Osman in the face, and say what? How terribly sorry I am that I absolutely fucked up? Frankly, I don't have the sodding bottle to do it."

However, Laurent Naudet was another matter. Ignoring his pounding head, Julian did not wait for the gendarme to call him back.

•

Two hours later, Julian and Mara sat in the office of Commissaire Boutot of the *Police judiciaire* in Périgueux. They had met the Commissaire a few years earlier when Mara was trying to find her missing sister. He was a melancholy man with baggy eyes, a drooping mustache, and a habit of rolling a pencil between his hands. Julian told his story. He repeated Kazim's exact words. Yes, the boy had mentioned a man named Serge. The recorded message was saved on his *répondeur*. Yes, he and Mara had gone to Périgueux to find Kazim. Betul Ismet thought her son had been staying with a former classmate, a young woman named Nadia Beaubois. However, the flat had been vacated by the time they arrived. Of the other occupants—an English kid named Peter and a French girl named Brigitte—Julian knew nothing. Mara corroborated what she could of Julian's statements.

Julian listened to the soft rasping of the pencil rubbing against the dry skin of Commissaire Boutot's palms and admitted that it was a bit odd that the Ismets had asked someone who was not of their faith, who didn't even know their son, to find him, to persuade him to come home. He tried to explain the deal he had struck with respect to the importation of Turkish salep, the marketing of Elan, but his words sounded so meaningless in the face of Kazim's tragic finish that he trailed off and never mentioned orchids again.

The next day, Adjudant Compagnon requested to see them. The brigade commander, a tall, carrot-haired man with pock-marked skin, shook their hands warily but at the same time with an air of suppressed excitement, and invited them to sit down.

"We meet again," he said, and if his eyes held a memory of a past, harrowing experience involving a mummified baby and other corpses, he made no mention of it. "This case is out of my hands jurisdictionally. However, I've asked you here because the Lokum trashing is still unresolved, and there are a few minor details you may be able to help us with since you have some knowledge of the Ismet family."

Laurent sat nearby, ready to take notes on a laptop.

Oddly enough, Compagnon spent more time talking about Kazim's death than about the Ismets' shop. Unusually expansive, the brigade head offered them coffee and was even willing to give out information. The conclusion drawn by the Périgueux police was that Kazim had died in the early hours of Sunday morning of a self-administered overdose of heroin. He was obviously an intravenous user. His arms were covered in needle marks, and the hypodermic found with him was covered with his prints. The speculation was either that he had shot up in the skip and died there, or that Nadia and company had found him dead in the garret, panicked, and dumped the body and needle there themselves.

"Frankly, I don't like it." The adjudant looked like a man scenting a bad odor. "It's easy to knock off a junkie with a fatal injection and make it appear like an overdose."

"Are you saying someone killed him?" Mara asked.

Julian stirred uncomfortably beside her. "I think the Ismets have been through enough without having to deal with the proposition that their son was murdered."

"Ah," Compagnon rose to the challenge like a leaping trout. "But let's look at it logically. Kazim's pals find him dead. If their intention was simply to distance themselves, wouldn't they have been better off leaving the body in the garret and simply taking off? It might have been days before the renovators worked their way up to the top level of the building. By putting Kazim in the skip, which was emptied on Monday morning, they ensured his body would be discovered quickly."

He went on to point out that tracing the body back to the address on Rue Porte-de-Graule had been simple. Only two skips had been emptied that day, and the renovators had been easily able to identify the surrounding debris. Anonymity could not have been the objective. A health card had been found with the body. Plus thirty euros and change. Scum like Nadia would have taken the cash. Whoever was responsible for putting Kazim in the skip hadn't panicked and wasn't interested in money. That person wanted Kazim's death to be discovered and had been making a statement.

"Well, is anyone trying to find Nadia?" Julian asked. "Or Peter or Brigitte? What do they have to say? And what about Kazim's bike? He had a red Honda Bol d'Or."

Compagnon shook his head. "The owner of the building has been questioned. He admits giving Nadia free accommodation in return for her acting as a kind of caretaker. He was probably taking unreported rent off her. But apart from that, he claims to know nothing about her and doesn't know where she's gone. I think we can rely on the police in Périgueux to round up her and her pals. We will also let them look for the missing *moto*. I and my men have more important work to do."

By this, Compagnon gave them to understand that Julian had provided him with the first promising link leading back to Rocco Luca: Kazim had been running from a man named Serge before he died. Serge Taussat was a known associate of Luca. Kazim was a user and probably a small-time pusher who had worked for Luca. Maybe he had tried to hold out on the Ton. *Et voilà.* It was a typical drug scenario. It also explained the trashing of Kazim's parents' shop, which could now be interpreted as a warning. Everything was falling into place, and the Brames Gendarmerie was bang in the epicenter of the action. Luca lived in the jurisdiction of Brames. Kazim's body may have been discovered on the outskirts of Périgueux, but the roots of the case were right here, beginning with the vandalism of Lokum. Jacques Compagnon virtually hugged himself. The cheeky rhyming housebreaker was almost forgotten, if not forgiven.

21

The *femme de ménage* from hell, as Julian had taken to calling her, was now leaving notes. She put them on the dining table where they could be plainly seen the moment one entered the front room. Previous missives had read: "There is a stain on small table from something wet left on it." And, "Ask *him* to buy more Destop! Downstairs drain is plugged *again!*"

Madame Audebert's direction that *he* should buy the French equivalent of Liquid Plumber clearly stated whom she held responsible for the frequent slow evacuation of the bathroom basin.

That day Julian was the first back, tired from an afternoon's hard labor planting a hedge with only the aid of Bernard, the Chez Nous weekend waiter, as his digger. The sight of yet another of those odious slips of paper irritated him beyond belief. He wanted to tear it up, burn it, stamp on it, and yet he felt compelled to read it: "Vacuum not working because of sock (man's) under bed."

The vacuum had been left, also prominently in view, in the middle of the room.

He gathered that the vacuum had sucked up a sock (his) that had jammed the works. He was cursing and struggling to extricate the sock from the power head when Mara came in.

"What's wrong with the vacuum?" she asked.

"Nothing," he said. In the next breath, he burst out resentfully, "Can't you tell her to stop leaving those bloody notes?"

"How else is she to communicate with us if we're not here?"

"It's *how* she does it that's offensive."

"Well, if you'd only make some effort to be a bit less messy, maybe all this unpleasantness could be avoided."

"Look here, don't you think all this behavior modification for the cleaning woman is a bit over the top?" He had hold of the sock now and ripped it violently from the roller. "Frankly, it smacks of middle-class angst to me."

Mara stalked out of the room. Julian, ashamed of his outburst, stood up, threw the sock on the floor, and went after her.

"I'm sorry." He took her in his arms. She pressed into him.

"No, I'm sorry. I know you're still getting over Kazim."

They held on to each other as if they were both treading water in a deep and treacherous sea.

•

It was a slow night at Chez Nous, and Mado and Paul, with the aid of Bernard, had a relatively easy time of it for a change. Julian, Mara, and Loulou arrived together, greeted the room with the customary "*messieurs, dames*" as they came in, and took their usual table. The dogs settled down, hopeful of handouts.

Paul came out to greet them. "The usual *apéros?* What do you want for starters?"

Mara and Loulou chose the baked oysters, Julian the lamb's sweetbreads.

"So, I hear that kid Kazim died of an overdose," Paul said to Julian, waiting pen in hand for their main course orders.

"I don't really want to talk about it," said Julian. "I'll have the rabbit pie."

"That's how the lads in Périgueux are treating it," said Loulou. "But our good friend Jacques Compagnon thinks Kazim was pushing for Ton-and-a-Half, and he called in the kid's account. It would explain why Kazim was running away. And why his parents' store was trashed." He broke off to inquire, "The *blanquette* of veal. Is the meat local?"

"Old Michaud down the road."

"*Ça va.*"

Paul wrote: 1 rabbit, 1 *blanquette.* He grinned. "Speaking of *blanquettes,* see that *anglais* over there?" He thumbed over his shoulder at a hefty Brit wearing a Newcastle United sweatshirt. "He told me he went to a store to buy what he calls a 'blanket.' They told him to try a restaurant. So he went to a restaurant, and when he asked for a blanket there, they told him they didn't do veal. You get it?"

Julian closed his eyes.

Mara said, "I'll have the roast pheasant with chestnuts."

"Trouble is," Loulou went on, sniffing the air appreciatively as Bernard hurried by with a platter of potato croquettes, "a death like that leaves no trademark. A lethal dose of *l'héro,* then *paf!* Lights out, and no one's the wiser."

"Bastards." Julian was moved to speak up. "He was just a kid. And what about Betul and Osman? If Luca really is behind it, their lives could be in danger, too."

"It's what you get for messing around with drugs," rumbled Paul.

Mara, anticipating sticky ground, turned to Loulou. "Anything new on the rhyming burglar? I spoke with Sébastien Arnaud today. Assurimax will have to pay up. They doubt the police will be able to trace Prudence's things."

"*Ah, ça!*" the ex-*flic* drew his shoulders around his ears and held his hands palms up in a true Gallic shrug.

Paul sniggered, "I'll bet old Compagnon's sitting on tacks waiting for the next jingle. I'm no literary man myself, but I like the poetic touch. The Tweedledee one was really good. You have to hand it to him, the *mec* is smart. He's laughing in everyone's face and getting away with it. They'll never catch him."

Loulou semaphored his disagreement with a stubby forefinger. "*Non, non, non, mon ami!*" he exclaimed. "That, in my experience, is why they *will* catch him. Our burglar is laughing, as you say. He feels sure enough of himself to play games with the police. But it will be what trips him up, ultimately. In all my years as a policeman, I have found that the criminal who's too sure of himself inevitably gives himself away, and I have learned that there is one infallible way of spotting him."

Loulou's eyes danced as he paused, making them wait for it.

"What?" they all demanded.

"The walk," declared Loulou, slapping both palms on the table. "It is in the walk, my friends. When a guilty person thinks he or she is about to escape undetected, watch how he walks, not coming toward you but going away from you. It is what I call the guilty waggle."

"The guilty what?" queried Mado, coming out from the kitchen for a brief break. She exchanged embraces all around.

"The guilty waggle," Loulou reprised. "A certain hastening of the steps, the buttocks tucked under just so." He wriggled in his seat to demonstrate. "An almost—how to describe it?—conceited swagger of the hips that says, ha ha, you have not caught me out. All the same, I must hurry off before you do."

"That's just your excuse for watching bums," snorted Paul.

Mado rolled her eyes. She turned to Mara. "I came to ask you how your neighbor is, the one whose wife died. I ran into the nurse, Jacqueline Godet, the other day." She paused. "Is it true you're making his meals?"

"Just for now," Mara demurred. Everyone knew she did not cook. At least, did not cook well. "The other women and I are taking it in turns."

"What d'you feed him? Hot dogs?" jested Paul.

Mado punched him. "He has Parkinson's, doesn't he? I had an

uncle with Parkinson's. He went funny toward the end. Saw things that weren't there."

"So does Joseph." Mara told them about Joseph's nighttime episodes.

"A monster without a head?" Mado marveled. "*Zut alors!* My uncle only saw cats."

"I know it sounds crazy, but I don't think these are just hallucinations. I really think someone is trying to frighten him."

"Why would anyone do that?" Paul looked skeptical.

"I don't know. If I knew, maybe then some people would take me seriously." Mara aimed this remark at Julian, who pretended not to hear.

Mado asked, "Doesn't he have any family who can take care of him?"

"Just a daughter. Estranged, I'm afraid. I'm trying to trace her. I thought she ought to know about her father. Only . . ." she paused unhappily. "Now I'm not so sure Christine's the right person to be looking after him."

"Why not?"

"She . . . she once tried to push her mother down some stairs."

Julian sat up at this. "Christine tried to push Amélie—you didn't tell me that."

Mado, Paul, and Loulou stared at her.

"The same woman who fell off the Two Sisters' porch?" Mado gaped. "The daughter tried to push her down some stairs?"

"It was a long time ago," Mara said miserably.

"So maybe," said Paul with his usual bluntness, "she tried it again. And maybe you're right. Your old boy's not hallucinating after all. This Christine's an only child, right? Once her father's gone, she'll stand to inherit everything. You should check her out, Mara. You're good at these things. Stop her before—" He broke off.

"Before what?" Loulou leaned forward, a professional glint in his eye.

"Well, before she takes it any further," said Paul with uncharacteristic restraint.

22

The village of Les Faux was roughly a hundred kilometers north of Ecoute-la-Pluie. As she set out, Mara pondered the irony that Christine should be so lost to her parents and yet live scarcely two hours away. Somehow she had expected the daughter to have emigrated to the far side of the moon. But then, as she negotiated the network of small roads, going ever deeper into the rough north country of the Dordogne, she realized that Les Faux might just as well have been in another galaxy. The farms and hamlets all had a stopped, stranded look, as if caught in an ancient landscape that had escaped the stream of time. Only an occasional, jarringly new construction, some city dweller's secondary residence-to-be, suggested that the booming real estate market would drag things into the twenty-first century soon enough.

It had been easy finding the listing in the phone book once she knew the place-name to look under. Christine still went by Gaillard. Perhaps she had never married. Mara had thought about calling first, but decided a direct approach was best. She also decided that this was a journey she wanted to make without Julian. He was poor company nowadays, and he strongly disagreed with her desire to find the Gaillards' daughter. Meddling in other people's business was a bad idea generally. Look where trying to fix things for the Ismets had got him. Water should be left to find its own level, he said.

"But suppose Christine did push her mother down the Two

Sisters' stairs and is now trying to kill her father?" Mara had protested. She hated his passive-defeatist philosophy.

"For pity's sake, Mara," he had replied, "Amélie's death was an accident. And Joseph's midnight visitors are imaginary. The man is subject to hallucinations."

"All right, maybe you're right about Amélie, but that doesn't mean Christine isn't trying to capitalize on the chance to shortcut her way to her inheritance. Her father is, after all, sitting on a lot of land. The property market at the moment is hot. She could make a killing. In more ways than one."

"Then why in God's name would you want to get them together?"

"I don't. I wouldn't. Not if that's what she's up to. But don't you think it would be a good idea to let her know in no uncertain terms that we're on to her, and that she'd better leave her father alone?"

"And what if she's innocent? It's the most likely scenario, you know."

"In that case, what's wrong with bringing father and daughter together?"

"*Et voilà,*" Julian had finished, with brittle cynicism. "Problem solved either way."

Mara downshifted into a turn. She had read somewhere that a relationship had four stages: forming (during which a couple, seeking to impress, were on their best behavior); storming (when the gloves came off); norming (when, exhausted with fighting, they decided to lay down some basic ground rules); and performing (when they had worked out the kinks and everything went tickety-boo). She and Julian were past forming. They had gone through storming—at least, she hoped they had. That brought them to norming, but they definitely seemed to be having trouble getting their ground rules right.

"Take fair play, for example," she complained to Jazz, who occupied the front passenger seat. "It's a fundamental issue, wouldn't you agree? I went with him to Périgueux to help him find Kazim. Okay, the outcome wasn't what we'd hoped for, but shouldn't Julian now be helping me to check out Christine? Instead, he's sniping at me. It's like he's saying, 'If I couldn't bring Kazim home, how can you expect to do any better with Christine?'"

Jazz gazed avidly out the window.

"Then there's the issue of communication. Oh, I know Julian's still depressed over Kazim, and I understand his dread of facing Betul and Osman. But it hurts to think he can't trust me enough to open up about how he feels. His way, when things get rough, is to shut me out."

Jazz jammed his nose against the glass, marking it with long, wet smears.

Mara sighed and switched to composing another phantom email to Patsy in her head:

>*The trouble is, things are going to get worse, not better. May is around the corner, and then I'll lose him to his damned seasonal hunt for his orchid. In fact, it'll probably give him a reason to withdraw even farther. Oh, he might ask for my help—tramping through fields and woodlands goes faster with two than one—but he walks around in a kind of mystical world of his own. That is, when he's not being downright overbearing, barking instructions at me and telling me to mind where I put my feet. Orchid season, as I've told you before, Patsy, can be a very lonely time for yours truly.*<

Les Faux stood amid rough, heavily wooded countryside broken up here and there by meadows where sheep and cattle grazed on the new spring grass. She stopped at the *mairie* to ask directions to Christine Gaillard's house. The mayor, a fat, genial man, gazed at her with undisguised curiosity. Then, with a knowing smile she did not quite understand, he told her it was a farm and gave her directions. When she thanked him, he waved a hand.

"Think nothing of it. I have nothing better to do. How much nicer to give foreigners directions than to worry about road repairs." He had picked up her accent. "Oh, and I also have to find the money from God knows where to do something about our eleventh-century church, which is falling to bits. I'd much rather not be mayor, you know, but no one else wants the job. If you need to use the toilet, there's one at the back of the building."

The farmhouse was situated near the road. It had a dilapidated look, its roof badly patched, its shutters in need of paint. Mara parked in the shade of a crumbling stone barn and got out of her car. Jazz moaned his disapproval of her departure through the open car window.

In the distance, sheep were being brought in from pasture. They were a breed Mara had not seen before, with neat black faces, curling horns, and small, almost delicate feet. A tall, slim woman in a straw hat was driving them. She moved with an almost reckless grace as she skipped from side to side, heading off wayward animals, her high voice carrying on the wind like the cry of a bird. She secured a gate and herded the sheep toward the barn. Yellow hair fell loosely about an oval face that, even at a distance, projected a kind of pre-Raphaelite beauty. Mara could see no trace of a harelip. If this was Christine Gaillard, she was not at all what Mara had expected.

The truth was, she did not know what to expect. Everyone had their own way of describing the Gaillards' daughter. She had been a disciplinary problem in school, Francine had said. To Huguette she was a deformed unfortunate. Suzanne was of the opinion that she was violent. The matter of the stairs weighed heavily on Mara's mind.

"*Oui?*" A voice behind her made her jump. A large woman stood watching her from the doorway of the house. She was of an age when features began to lose their definition, but Mara recognized at once Amélie's gray eyes, Joseph's hefty build and square-cut jaw. Her nose was flattened and twisted where it joined the thick scarring of a badly repaired harelip. It gave her mouth a circular, gaping look, like a landed fish gasping in a hostile environment. This, not the fey creature dancing over the meadow, was Christine.

"Mademoiselle Gaillard?" Or should it be madame? Nowadays one never knew.

"Who are you?" Christine's voice was flat, her articulation made nasal by her deformity.

Mara approached. "My name is Mara Dunn. I've come—I've come to talk to you about your father." No point in beating around the bush.

Christine stared at her in surprise.

"Maybe you'd better come in," she said.

Despite its exterior shabbiness, the interior of the house spoke of care and simple comfort, and Mara liked it immediately. The kitchen into which Christine admitted her was large and bright. The whitewashed walls were clean, the windows garlanded with plants. Cooking vessels hung in order of size from hooks driven into a ceiling beam. There was a large table in the middle of the room. Its scarred surface showed the effects of use and repeated scrubbing; the straight-backed wooden chairs surrounding it were in good repair. None of Amélie and Joseph's *cache-misères.* Christine waved her into one of them. Mara sat down. At the far end of the kitchen she noticed a large standing loom. A weaving of rust and ocher wool was in progress.

"Is the wool from your own sheep?" Mara hazarded, trying to strike up some rapport with this marred, wary female.

"Partly," said Christine. She did not sit herself. Instead, she stood, towering over her visitor.

"Are you the weaver?"

"No. Look, if you don't mind, I have a lot to do. What is this all about?"

Mara cast about for a way to begin. "I live in Ecoute-la-Pluie. I'm a neighbor of your father."

Christine studied her. "You're a new one."

"I've been there nine years, if that counts as new. My house is across the road from your parents.'"

"Joubert's old place." Christine regarded her curiously. "But you're not from around here."

"Quebec." Mara forced a laugh. "I'm French Canadian. My Montreal accent always gives me away, I'm afraid."

Christine ignored her attempt at pleasantry. "I suppose Suzanne Portier told you how to find me. I expect she told you a few other things about me as well?"

Her bluntness threw Mara, who scrambled for her next line. "Well, yes—I mean, no. I mean, have your parents always known where you are?"

A shrug. "I made no effort to inform them. Word gets around. And before you ask, I know my mother's dead. I didn't come to the funeral because there was no point."

"It's your father I'm concerned about."

"What about him?"

"He has Parkinson's. Maybe you know that?"

Another shrug. Mara took that to mean yes. So some exchange of information had taken place.

"His condition is getting worse," Mara went on. "He's on his own, and he needs you, Mademoiselle Gaillard."

The woman scowled. "He needs me? After all these years? I hope you haven't come here to suggest I go back home like the dutiful daughter to look after him?"

"No. But you *are* his daughter. I just think it would mean a lot to him to be reunited with you. He's suffering greatly from the loss of your mother. He was very dependent on her."

"You're telling me? He couldn't move a finger without her approval. *Maman* was like that."

Mara sensed that she was getting nowhere with Christine. Nevertheless, she pushed on gamely. "When you're old and ailing, family is everything. In your father's case, you're all he has left."

Christine said bitterly, "He should have thought of that a long time ago."

"At least consider getting back in touch with him."

The daughter tipped her head back to study Mara. A look of faint amusement came over her face. "You're really worried about the old man, aren't you?"

"Yes, I am. He's not managing well on his own. He wants more than anything to stay where he is, and he can, but he needs help. He has visiting nurses, and he's applied for home care. However, he's had some problems lately. There have been . . . incidents." Mara, raising only now what should have been her starting point, dwelled on the last word. "He claims someone—or something—has been coming into the house at night to frighten him."

Christine regarded her blankly. "Who'd want to do that?"

"I thought you might know."

"Me?" The surprise, which was perhaps authentic, quickly shifted to hostility. "Why should I know anything about it?"

"No reason. Just that it's happened twice. If it continues, I intend to call the police." She realized she was handling it badly, but at least Christine had been warned. If a warning were indeed warranted. She could not make up her mind about the woman.

She softened her tone. "It's why I wanted to talk to you. It's possible that he's imagining things, or even making them up because he's unhappy. Being back in contact with you might make all the difference."

"I doubt that." Christine's face took on a surly look. "Let me tell you something. It wasn't easy for me, growing up with them. My father was always under my mother's thumb, and she could be a misery to live with. Oh, I know she was highly thought of, but you don't know what she was really like. Religious, controlling, always worried about doing the proper thing, what the neighbors would think. Anything different was shameful. You hid a deformity, bullied sinfulness into line. I admit I wasn't an easy child. For one, I had a lot of problems because of my—this." She touched her mouth. "Kids used to tease me. There was a boy who really used to give me a hard time. I'm sure the neighbors told you about it. One day, I couldn't take it anymore, so I stuck a pair of scissors in him. That earned me a bad reputation. I was only ten, *bon sang!* No one, not that pig of a teacher Francine Boyer, not even my parents, could see that I had no other way of defending myself. My life was hell until I met someone who was able to see past my face, who encouraged me to be myself in ways my parents could never accept. I ran away to be with this person when I was fifteen. My mother was furious. She found me and dragged me back. I was a minor then, so I had no choice but to come home. One day I got some rope and told my mother that if she didn't let me live my life as I wanted, I was going to hang myself in the garret. She told me she'd rather see me dead than have a daughter who only brought shame on her head. She even followed me up to make sure I did a good job of it. That's when I pushed her. For God's sake, I couldn't even hang myself without her telling me how to do it. I wasn't trying to kill her. I just wanted her to leave me alone, to give me some space."

Christine broke off, breathing raggedly, as if she had just run a long-distance race.

"I'm sorry," said Mara, feeling deeply shaken. Christine's disclosure brought to light a side to Amélie she had not known. "I—I had no idea."

"No, you wouldn't have, would you?" The daughter's eyes were bright and hard, and her voice was flooded with bitterness. She turned away to look out a window. Mara's eyes followed her gaze. The slim woman with the hat had secured another gate and was crossing the muddy courtyard.

"You see," Christine went on, "by the time I was in my teens, I understood my own sexuality better than most people do in their lifetimes. That's what my parents couldn't handle. I was their hidden daughter, not because I had a harelip, but because, as they put it, I was unnatural. *I went with other women.* So now do you get it? They preferred to let everyone think I ran after men, even that I'd had an illegitimate kid, because it was easier for them, particularly her, that way. That's what I can't forgive them for: they couldn't be honest. They made me out to be a slut, when all I wanted was my right to *be.* Oh, I know that kind of thing was hard for them to deal with back then, living in a rural backwater. But times change. Not them. She never accepted me for what I am, and he won't either. And I'll tell you something else, Madame Nose-in-Other-People's-Business. You've got the wrong end of the stick. My parents broke with me, not the other way around. So now I just want to be left alone. My father doesn't want me back, except maybe as a skivvy. As for the neighbors"—her scarred mouth twisted—"they've never approved of me, and I'm sure they all continue to think the worst."

"The worst?" Mara echoed as the door swung open and the other woman stepped into the kitchen. She pulled off her hat, revealing her fey shepherdess's face, finely etched with laugh lines.

Her expression as she took Mara in was avid and mischievous. *What fun,* it seemed to say. *A visitor.*

Christine nearly shouted, "Oh come on. You're not that dense. I'm sure they told you, and I can see it's what you're thinking. I pushed my mother down some stairs before. Who's to say I didn't try it again?"

Mara rose to the challenge in Christine's voice. "And did you?"

Christine laughed harshly as she reached out to draw the other woman to her with a gesture that was both proud and possessive. "You don't give up, do you? For what it's worth, I have a witness who'll swear that at the time my mother fell, I was here with her. My unshakable alibi. Isn't that so, *chérie?* Meet my friend, my lover, Alice. We've been together seventeen years, and I don't intend to let anything, certainly not my father, come between us."

Alice stepped forward, tucking a strand of fly-away hair behind her ear and extending a slender, somewhat grubby hand. "Alice Lescuras. *Enchantée.*" Her voice was slightly mocking.

"Mara Dunn," Mara responded faintly and took the hand.

Alice tightened her grip and pulled Mara toward her, laughing as she did so. "What Christine says is true, you know." Her face was almost in Mara's face. "We were here together."

Mara tried to draw back, but Alice held her with surprising strength. Up close her long-boned body projected an almost feverish energy. Her mouth widened in a malicious grin.

"Her unshakable alibi," she crowed triumphantly. "Beat that if you can!"

23

Mara returned home to find Julian in an even bleaker mood than when she had left him. He was sprawled on an ebony and bronze art deco sofa, the most uncomfortable piece of furniture in her front room. One of last year's acquisitions, the sofa was shaped like a boat and was the only thing big enough for him to sprawl on. However, its contours, as everyone who sat on it discovered, were unsuited to the human body. Not surprisingly, she had not been able to offload it on anyone. It sat in her living room, looking interesting and taking up space.

"Christine's gay," she said.

He gazed at her dully. She wondered if he was having another of his Thumpers. But no, he didn't have that bruised look around the eyes that usually went with his headaches.

She pulled off her jacket. "That's what drove her and her parents apart. For Amélie and Joseph, for their generation, living in a closed rural community, having a lesbian daughter wasn't something either of them could handle." Forty years on, judging from the mayor's reaction, she thought it still might be a problem for some.

Julian made no reply.

"So they covered it up and let the neighbors think Christine was the local Lolita. I think only Suzanne Portier knew the truth, but she never talked about it. Christine hated her parents, especially her mother, for forcing her to stay in the closet."

She had to shove his legs over in order to sit down.

"She lives with a woman named Alice Lescuras on a sheep farm. I'm sure they're barely scratching out an existence. In fact, that's probably the only thing Christine has ever had in common with her parents: an unprofitable propensity for raising sheep."

He frowned. "You're saying they're hard up and could do with money?"

"Well, yes."

"So I suppose the verdict is Christine pushed her mother down the stairs and is now trying to do away with her father so she can pay her bills?"

Mara reddened. "I'm *not* saying that. I mean, it's a pretty monstrous accusation."

He sat up and regarded her with surprise. "You didn't seem to think so a few hours ago. 'Let her know we're on to her,' you said. What changed your mind?"

She crossed her arms and leaned back against the hard sofa cushions. "The problem is, I liked her. Them." She saw again the homey interior of the kitchen, full of warmth and color. Christine's side of the story had awakened her sympathy. The two women were struggling to make a life for themselves against a lot of lingering, unspoken prejudice. "I mean, you said yourself Amélie's death was an accident. And so far Joseph has come to no real harm."

"Ah. Sweet reason riseth like the morning sun."

"No need to be sarcastic. Anyway, if Christine really wanted to bump her father off, why hasn't she done it? Why just be content with terrorizing him? It's more like someone is simply trying to give Joseph a good scare."

The thought rested with Julian. He tugged at his beard. "Maybe that's the intention."

She stared at him. "You mean frighten him to death?" It was a clean, cunning way to kill. And hadn't there been mention of Joseph having a weak heart? The heart was, after all, a muscle.

Julian shook his head. “Your mind is on murder. I’m saying, perhaps all Christine wants to do is gain control of things. She doesn’t have to do away with Joseph, just have him legally declared incompetent. Then she can make a case for taking over his affairs.”

It was a powerful idea, not quite as nasty as murder, but Mara was very sorry to follow out its implications. *Oh, Christine,* she thought. “Well, if that’s her game, let’s hope my visit warned her off. I told her pretty clearly that I’d call the gendarmes if these nighttime apparitions continued. If she’s smart, she’ll realize she can’t get away with it.” She paused uneasily. “Although Alice might be another matter.”

“Alice? I thought you said you liked her.”

“I do. I like them both. But that one bothers me, Julian. There’s something wild about her. And a little crazy. I definitely got the impression she’s the moving force behind the two. And then—” She paused, reluctant to make the admission. “Oh, I may as well tell you. At one point, Christine said that in case I thought she had killed her mother, Alice would alibi her for the time Amélie died.”

“Good God, Mara, you didn’t accuse her of pushing her mother down the Two Sisters’ stairs?”

“Of course not. What do you take me for? Christine just came out with it. But then Alice virtually dared me to make something of it if I could. She was laughing at me, Julian. It was almost as if she were baiting me, as if she wanted the challenge.”

She shifted around to face him more directly. “Having met Christine, I’m not so sure she’s the murdering kind. Oh, I know she had a go at her mother when she was young, but she was acting out of childish anger and frustration. However, I wouldn’t put it past Alice to have done some more recent shoving.”

Julian gave her a long look. “You won’t be able to prove a thing, you know. If Alice can alibi Christine, then Christine can alibi Alice. That's probably what Alice was really telling you. And it makes Christine equally complicit."

"I suppose," she admitted unhappily. She went on, "What I don't understand is, if they wanted to kill Amélie, why they would choose such a public spot as the Two Sisters?"

He offered no answer.

Mara chewed a lip. "Okay. Let's say Christine and Alice are in desperate need of money. They stand to lose their farm, everything they've worked for. They decide to ask Amélie and Joseph for a loan. It's up to Alice to do the asking because Christine has cut all ties with her parents. So Alice arranges to meet Amélie at the restaurant since she knows the Gaillards do their marketing in Beaumont. But Amélie is no fool. She knows what Alice is after and has no intention of giving them a solitary *centime.* She leaves Joseph in the gents, goes to Two Sisters, intercepts Alice on the porch, and says no straight off. That would have been very much Amélie's way. Maybe Alice didn't set out to commit murder, but when Amélie turned her down flat, Alice saw red or simply saw an opportunity. As Loulou would say, *paf!*"

24

Julian could put it off no longer. The following day he went to Lokum. He had sent flowers and a card, of course, but had delayed this moment for as long as he could. The time Betul and Osman needed to bury their son and grieve, he told himself, the time he needed to gather the courage to face them. He was prepared for a poor welcome, but not for the heat of Osman's anger that hit him like a palpable force as soon as he set foot in the shop.

"I don't talk to you!" roared the big Turk.

"I'm sorry about your son," Julian said. "I want you to know I tried. I'll never forgive myself that I failed to find him in time."

"Ha." Osman's chest swelled as if to block Julian from stepping further into his domain. "What try? Too late. Is finish for my boy. And I tell you something, Mister Worry-about-Orchids. I continue to import salep. For memory of Kazim, I make Elan big success. Orchids be damned!"

Betul came out from the back room. She stared at Julian, haggard with grief.

"I'm sorry," Julian repeated. "But please understand that I was working against the odds. Kazim was dealing drugs. He was an addict."

"No! No drugs!" Osman's luxuriant mustache seemed to rear up in a denial of its own. "Never drugs."

"He died of an overdose." Julian pressed home the unwelcome truth. "But I promise you one thing. Adjudant Compagnon isn't satisfied that the Périgueux police have the full story on what happened to your son. If it turns out he's right, I swear I'll do everything in my power to help him find out the truth."

Julian was not prepared for the father's reaction.

"You keep nose out!" screamed Osman. His entire body went rigid. His face turned the color of chalk. "Go away and keep nose out. No one ask your help. Get out. Don't come back!"

Betul burst into tears and fled to the rear of the shop.

Julian left. He stood outside on the sidewalk, shaken by the torrent of raw emotions he had just witnessed. Betul's tears wrenched his heart. But it was the image of Osman's face that troubled him more. He knew the man. Something had happened to frighten him badly. In fact, to Julian he had seemed more terrified than grieving.

•

Later that week, Jacques Compagnon held a briefing with his gendarmes at the Brames brigade headquarters.

"You all know my view on the Ismet case. Luca is running drugs again. So far, he's kept it underground and out of sight. Kazim Ismet worked for Luca, ran afoul of him, and was killed on Luca's orders. Now, Kazim's death might just be Luca's first mistake, and it may be the link we're looking for, provided we can make it stretch far enough." Hands clasped behind his back, the brigade head walked back and forth across the front of the meeting room. The fact that the space was very cramped meant that he had to turn every two or three strides, which was a little dizzying for him and his audience.

"The problem is, all we have is a voice recording possibly implicating Luca's sidekick, Serge Taussat, and that's tenuous. As you know, the police in Périgueux have found nothing to tie Taussat to Kazim or to that skip. You're also aware that, as far as they're concerned, the boy died of a self-administered OD. His pals dumped his body and took off. Case closed. However"—Compagnon paused to face the room squarely—"not for us. I don't need to remind you that I've never believed Luca to be as clean as he looks. So"—the adjudant pivoted and walked in the other direction—"we continue to keep our ears to the ground. Just in case something breaks."

"Sir," asked a female gendarme named Lucie Sauret, "where does Monsieur Wood fit in all of this?"

Compagnon scowled. "Wood's relationship with the case is limited to the fact that he's a friend of the deceased's parents, and they asked him to find their son and persuade him to return home." The adjudant puffed out his cheeks and expelled a lungful of air. "I've never liked this picture. In the first place, they should have come to us about Kazim."

Sauret ventured, "It's the way with a lot of foreigners, *mon adjudant*. They distrust the police, and they're afraid, so they try to handle things their own way."

"If they had come to us," Compagnon said bitterly, "their son might be alive today. He might also have given us the information we need to put Luca away."

"Do you think that's why he was disposed of, sir?" Sauret asked. "I mean, not because he was cheating Luca but because Luca thought he represented a liability?"

"It's a distinct possibility. Which means"—the adjudant's nostrils flared—"our Monsieur Wood's amateur, bungling questions about the kid's whereabouts could have put a draft up Luca's backside and may be what got Kazim killed."

"Now—" Compagnon paused to refer to a white board covered in point-form notes. His face went from a scowl to a ferocious grimace. "Any updates on our rhyming burglar?"

Someone else spoke up: "No trace of any of the stolen items, sir. And no new activity."

The adjudant nodded. "However, there has been an interesting development." He set off on another brief journey across the front of the room and pivoted around. "But before I fill you in, let me put the question to you. Is there anything in particular that strikes you about the burglaries?"

Fifteen faces regarded him intently.

Lucie Sauret said, "There's seems to be no geographical pattern to the break-ins, *mon adjudant.* There were the three around Brames, but the rest were scattered all over the place."

"All of the houses broken into so far have been insured by the same company, Assurimax," offered Albert.

"*Bon,*" said Compagnon. "Both good points. Although the fact that Assurimax"—he began his return trip—"is the insurer is not necessarily remarkable in itself. Assurimax is the largest company in the region."

Laurent stirred. "*Mon adjudant,* the burglar is selective, and he always seems to know which houses to hit."

Compagnon paused mid-stride, rocking back slightly on his heels. "Good thinking, Naudet. So what does that tell you?"

Laurent frowned. "Well, it wouldn't be hard to figure out which houses are closed up for the winter. But how does the burglar know which ones have things worth stealing?"

"That," said Compagnon, looking pleased, "is the question. And the new development. If all of the houses were insured by Assurimax, and if someone were able somehow to access the client files of the different company branches, then wouldn't this person be in a good position to pick and choose?" He looked about him. "So who are we talking about?"

"An Assurimax employee?" someone said.

"An agent?"

"A temp who moves from branch to branch?"

"An IT technician?"

"A hacker?"

"Excellent," nodded the adjudant. "As we speak, a specialized team is looking into it, and it may be just the thing to crack this case wide open! Meantime, our task is to concentrate on the jobs pulled in our jurisdiction, to stay alert to any possible further attempts, and to work in concert with other units. Our man may have moved out of our territory, but I don't need to tell you how important it is to hammer this joker's ass. He can't be left to think he can poke fun at the *Gendarmerie nationale* and get away with it." Compagnon did not refer to the specifically personal content of the last poem. He did not need to.

25

Mara was delighted to discover maple syrup at the supermarket in Siorac. It came in a little plastic jug with a red maple leaf insignia. For a moment, she was overcome by this small symbol of home found so unexpectedly on European soil. She held the jug to her, plunged into a childhood memory of her mother's pancakes, light as angels, she and her sister Bedie as little girls, carefully pouring on the thick, sweet, shining syrup until the soft sponge of each pancake could absorb no more. It brought a lump to her throat.

That was how Daisy found her.

"Are you having a private moment in Sauces and Condiments, or can anyone shop here?"

Mara jumped and nearly dropped the jug.

Daisy wore a beige silk culotte-suit under the Aquascutum raincoat. A Hermès scarf that might easily have been tagged at three hundred euros was thrown casually over one shoulder. Her sugary perfume rode on the air. As much as ever, she reminded Mara of a superannuated Barbie doll.

"Oh," said Mara, burying the maple syrup in the bottom of her shopping cart. Obscurely, she felt that if Daisy saw the precious little jug she would somehow take it over, too. "I thought you'd gone back to Florida."

"We come and go," Daisy responded breezily. "My work takes me back and forth. Donny's, too. I've been meaning to get in touch, so I'm glad I've run into you. We'd like you to come over for dinner. You and—I forget his name."

"Julian."

"Julian. Of course. Will sometime this week do? I'll give you a buzz."

•

And that was how Mara and Julian found themselves a few days later in the O'Connors' expensively reconstructed (not by Mara) house in Grives, sitting at right angles to each other on adjoining sections of a low-slung, moss-green leather sofa. Their knees almost touched. They had been given champagne and strips of smoked salmon skewered around little slabs of brie. The champagne, which stood in a ceramic cooler on a glass-topped table before them, bore a very good label.

"*Sláinte,*" said Donny, flourishing his Irish heritage. He was all welcome and bonhomie, a big man eager to please.

"*Chin-chin,*" said Daisy, her red mouth pulling wide around the words.

Mara raised her glass. "*Santé.*" She was unable to match Daisy's elastic smile.

Julian said, "Cheers."

Neither of them had particularly wanted to accept the invitation. But Daisy had followed up with frightening efficiency, and Loulou had had to cancel their normal Friday dinner at Chez Nous. So there they were.

Through the windows Julian could see a seven o'clock sky that held the sun like a golden seine. He would have much preferred to be outside, breathing air that everywhere held the sweetness of lilacs. Instead, he was stuck indoors with a man who bored him slightly and a woman who couldn't remember his name, whose heavy scent gave him a headache, drinking pricey champagne and about to eat a meal that Donny, who did the cooking, assured them would be "easy." Easy to make, or easy to eat? Julian wondered. Maybe it meant something you didn't have to chew. Donny wore an apron with big red letters that read "Keep Out. Danger Zone" on the bib.

Dinner turned out to be slices of fresh foie gras pan-fried in butter.

"You know," Donny said, as he dished out at the table, "all this talk about the cruelty of force-feeding is way exaggerated, far as I can see. In the first place, it's no worse than the way we keep battery hens back home. At least the ducks and geese here get to walk around a bit before they're slaughtered. And then they only use migratory birds that gorge naturally. Just building on what nature set up in the first place. Heck, a lot of people argue foie gras is part of France's cultural heritage, like the Louvre."

Julian said he couldn't imagine any animal, migratory or not, liking food funneled down its gullet until its liver swelled to obscene proportions. Mara kicked him under the table.

"Hey," Donny offered, half rising, anxious to conciliate. "If you're not okay with this, no hard feelings. I'd be glad to do you an omelet."

"No, no. I'm fine," Julian backed down, feeling the moral coward. He went through this struggle every time. The foie gras, meltingly delicious, was served with bread and chubby spears of white asparagus, another abnormality as far as Julian was concerned: white asparagus was grown in the dark. A normal green salad followed. Donny put everything on the table at once, North American style.

"Now, I know," their host said apologetically, "the French like all these different courses. Back and forth from the kitchen with clean plates and new knives and forks. Never could get into it myself. I like my food out where I can see it."

A little later he held up his glass and said, "What do you think of this Sauternes? Isn't it a beaut?"

Donny talked about property deals he had going in the States, the Caribbean, the Gulf Coast. "Land speculation's all a question of timing," he told them seriously. "And patience. The trick is buy low, hold, sell high. I've even got a sweetheart of a project on simmer in Buttonville, Ontario. That's near Toronto. Your neck of the woods, Mara."

"I'm from Quebec," she said with her mouth full. She had no trouble with foie gras, indeed was wiping up the rich remains with bread.

"Ah well, it's all one big, snowy country."

Donny omitted the cheese course and cut straight to dessert, large squares of baklava, oozing honey, that Julian recognized immediately.

"Now these are great," said Donny, breaking into his with a fork. Paper-thin bits of pastry shot everywhere. "Buy 'em at the market in Saint-Cyprien. There's a Turkish stall there. Woman and her son. She makes everything fresh." He chewed, swallowed, and frowned. "Though to tell you the truth"—he poked the baklava critically with his fork—"I think she's losing her touch. This is definitely not as good as I usually get."

Donny was clearly unaware that the son's market days were finished. Julian thought of Betul in mourning. Another surge of guilt made him put down his fork.

"Listen," Daisy addressed her guests once the preliminaries of the meal were over. "I need to cut to the chase. The reason I asked you two over is that I wanted to talk to you about Joseph." She was completely candid, taking no pains to disguise the fact that she had an agenda independent of the pleasure of Mara and What's-His-Name's company. "I want to know how he's doing, and I can't get a straight answer from that nurse."

"As well as can be expected," Mara said cautiously. She knew Daisy was still pressuring Jacqueline Godet to recommend that Joseph be bundled into a nursing home.

Daisy tossed her head. "Oh, boy. What does that mean?"

"He has good and bad days."

"Listen," Daisy said a little aggressively, "my father had Parkinson's. I know what the disease is like. He was a wonderful man, my daddy. Successful, outgoing, active. Parkinson's changed all that. He had private nursing care, of course, but I visited him every day until his death. I'm not happy about poor old Joseph all on his own with no one to look after him. We go back a long way with the Gaillards: 1975. They were running a kind of bed and breakfast on their farm then. Donny and I wanted a rural experience, and we stayed with them the first time we came to the Dordogne. Their house wasn't exactly comfortable—you know what it's like—but they needed the cash, and the cooking was terrific, so we came back year after year until they closed the B and B and we bought our place here. That's how we became friends. I happen to care a lot about what happens to Joseph."

"But it's really not your call," Mara told her bluntly. "Or anyone's but his. You'll have to let him make his own decisions. And right now he wants to remain in his own home, on his own land. As soon as extended home care is arranged for him, he'll be fine."

"When's that going to happen? It's been a month now."

"This kind of thing takes time."

"Anyway, he needs more than a caretaker, you know. He needs trained nursing supervision. My daddy had three nurses working shifts round the clock."

"Don't push it, honey," said Donny. "Leave the old guy where he is."

Mara looked at Donny in surprise. She expected him to fall into line with his wife on everything, at least publicly.

"You don't know the first thing about it," Daisy said, annoyed.

"She said he's okay, Daze." Donny turned to Mara. "He's coping, right? No bad spells? Daisy's dad was pretty up and down in his final years. Needed constant attention. 'Course, he could afford it." There was just a hint of sarcasm in his voice.

"Joseph's not nearly there yet," Mara said firmly.

"Glad to hear it." Donny rose to clear the table. Daisy glared at his retreating back.

"So," said Julian to Daisy, filling an awkward gap. "When are you two leaving?" Again, the pointed toe of Mara's shoe found his shin.

"What?" Daisy looked momentarily blank. "Oh. Donny's around for a while. He's closing a deal. He's always closing a deal. Or trying to. With my money." That was to get back at him for spiking her argument for getting Joseph into care.

Donny stuck his head back through the kitchen doorway and said, "Now, now, honey," before disappearing again.

"As for me," Daisy went on, "I'm off next week. New York and Philadelphia. London and Paris after that. Then back here. It's the life of a freelance buyer, I'm afraid. I go where the sales are."

"A buyer?" Mara asked. "A buyer of what?"

"Antiques," replied Daisy. "I specialize in nineteenth- and early twentieth-century European furniture and art."

Julian glanced across the table at Mara. She was looking at Daisy with a new interest.

"Really?" she said thoughtfully. Then she asked, "You wouldn't like to acquire an art deco sofa in excellent condition, would you?"

•

Daisy came to look at the sofa the next day. She was all business. Her keen eye picked out a repair to one of the legs. The upholstery was not original. These made the piece less desirable. While she spoke, she scanned the other objects in Mara's front room and quickly dismissed them. She went away saying she would consider it, but Mara knew that this in Barbie doll speak translated as no.

"Damn," uttered Mara as she watched Daisy drive away from the house. She herself had not noticed the repaired leg or the upholstery.

"Worth a try," murmured Julian.

Mara leaned her head against the window. It was a breezy April day. She watched a buzzard spiral up, riding a thermal high above the treetops.

"You know," she muttered, "I really wonder about the O'Connors. They're in and out, spend like money's no object. The stuff on her back costs more than my entire wardrobe. Does land speculation pay that well? And how much do you earn as a buyer in the antiques trade?"

"A damned sight more than I do, at a guess." It had been a long, slow winter financially for Julian. "Maybe," he suggested, "she inherited a pile from her daddy. Whom she visited every day until he died."

•

That night the rhyming burglar struck again, making off once again with a small treasury in portable art objects. As usual, he did not touch easy-to-dispose-of electronic equipment. Nor did he bother with two large abstract paintings of some value, a modernistic tapestry, and an antique but very heavy cast iron wall plaque. The poem he left behind was a real provocation. Like the others, it had been written in French, but strongly suggested the influence of the Baroness Orczy. In English, it went like this:

They seek him here, they seek him there
Those gendarmes seek him everywhere
But none can say
And none can know
where next his cunning hand will show.

Again, the allusion to an English literary work raised questions about the burglar's nationality, and again it was concluded that this was probably a red herring. The Baroness's taunting lines were well enough known that anyone could have cribbed them. However, it was thought that the choice of the Scarlet Pimpernel as a role model suggested an older man with a definite flair for the dramatic.

Adjudant Compagnon was delighted that the robbery had happened in Quinsac, well away from his territory, and vastly relieved that the doggerel had made no mention of him.

• 26 •

Mara and Julian climbed the eighteen steps leading up to the Two Sisters' porch. According to Julian's tenet of parsimony, the best explanation for Amélie's going up there was the simplest: she had used it as a vantage point to pick out Joseph in the throng of market-goers. Mara's suspicions of Christine and Alice had made her want to see the spot for herself, and she was very pleased that Julian had agreed to accompany her.

"Hmm," she said, stopping at the top. From the stair head they had a full view of the *place,* where the market was held every Tuesday and Saturday. It was, in fact, a good spot to look for someone in a crowd. Today, Sunday, there was no market. The square was empty, apart from a few parked cars.

Mara studied the restaurant porch. It ran the depth of the two houses it joined and was roofed with a trellis that showed new growth among last year's withered vines. Chairs and tables had been set out, but the weather that day was too unpredictable—warm, almost hot one minute, showery the next—for drinks or food alfresco. The front of the porch, masked by an ornamental wrought-iron grille, protruded slightly over the street. The gnarled branches of an ancient wisteria—growing up from street level and more tree than vine—were wired to the grille. The wisteria was fully in leaf and setting cascades of little buds.

It was twenty to twelve. The Two Sisters was not yet open for lunch. There was no one in the right-hand part of the restaurant, but they could see movement through the double glass doors leading into the left-hand side.

"So what is it you plan to say?" Julian asked.

Mara repeated her prepared speech: "I'm here on behalf of Joseph Gaillard"—she wasn't, but it sounded better that way—"the husband of the woman who fell down your stairs last month. I'd like to ask you a few—"

"For heaven's sake, Mara, you can't say that. You sound like a insurance investigator."

"Don't be silly. Joseph isn't suing them."

"You'll make them think he is. You'll put the wind up them good and proper. Why don't you just ask if Madame Gaillard came to the restaurant on the fifteenth of March? Better still, if anyone named Gaillard—that covers both her and Christine—or—what's the girlfriend's last name?"

"Lescuras. Alice Lescuras."

"Or Lescuras made a reservation for that date?"

Mara almost said, "I wish you'd stop telling me how to run my investigation," but caught herself, realizing how ridiculous it sounded. His suggestion was a good one. Anyone eating at the Two Sisters would have needed a reservation. It was a popular place, especially with the lunchtime crowd. Even in the off-season it was a good idea to book in advance. Business people who still believed in the lengthy working lunch congregated there. They oiled the pump of good will with aperitifs; sounded each other out over starters; got into the meat of the deal during the main course; hammered home the details with the cheese tray; and sat back to enjoy the sweetness of concluding a mutually beneficial accord over dessert, coffee, and liqueurs.

Mara just hoped the management would not prove sticky about the confidentiality of patron names. If they did, her subterfuge, no matter how cleverly worded, was not going to work.

As it turned out, the only person available for Mara to give her spiel to was a young waiter who was busy setting tables. He hardly listened to her reason, pointed to a little table by the door, and told her to look for herself.

Reservations were recorded in a fat spiral notebook, the pages of which were dated. Mara flipped back to March 15. She and Julian scanned the handwritten entries together. There was no Gaillard or Lescuras.

"Hello," murmured Julian. "Here's a name. Luca." Next to it was a time, 12:30, the number 3, and an X.

"Rocco Luca?" Mara wondered. Had Ton-and-a-Half been at the restaurant at the time of Amélie's fall?

Quickly, they scanned all of the pages, going back through March and then January (the restaurant appeared to have been closed for the entire month of February). There was no entry for Gaillard or Lescuras. The name Luca appeared three times.

Mara thumbed forward again to March 15. "Can you tell me," she called across to the waiter, "anything about this person?"

The waiter set down a stack of napkins and came over to read the name she indicated.

"*Ah, oui.* Monsieur Luca," he said. His expression became animated. "Eats here a lot. Business lunches. Everyone always wants to get his table because he's a tremendous tipper. Looks like he booked for three at half past twelve on the fifteenth. In fact"—he tapped the entry—"I made this one. See this little E? It's for Emile, which is me. We put our initials beside the reservations we make. But it must have been a no-show. That's what the X means. We always put an X beside a no-show. So I guess he didn't turn up."

"What about the other people in his party? Did they come?" Mara asked.

Emile frowned. "Let me see. I think someone did—no, I can't

be sure." He broke off to screw up his face more tightly. "Wasn't that the day that old woman fell down the stairs? *C'est ça.* Everyone was crowding around the windows and going out on the porch to see what was happening. There were cops and paramedics everywhere. Sorry, I can't remember. There was so much going on. Is it important?"

"It might be," said Mara.

"Well, I'll think about it. Maybe it'll come back to me."

They thanked Emile and turned to go.

"He's coming in today," the waiter volunteered as they headed toward the double glass doors. "Monsieur Luca. Twelve-thirty on the dot, as usual. Corner table, by the window. It's where he always sits. If you want to meet him."

Julian looked at Mara. "You don't happen to have space for two today, do you?" he inquired.

•

Their table—the only one left—was tucked into the right of the passageway that led back to the kitchen and the little elevator at the rear of the building. They got the noise and the cooking smells, the bustle of staff who created sudden rushes of air each time they hurried by, and occasionally the rattle of the old-fashioned elevator door admitting patrons who did not want to use the stairs. Which was how they got their first close look at a large man and a thin man dressed in black. Emile, on his way from the kitchen, stepped back to let the pair pass and cocked his head to indicate to Mara and Julian that the large man was Monsieur Luca. The man in black they took to be his sidekick, Serge Taussat. Ton-and-a-Half impressed Mara with his solid bulk. His small, round, bear-like eyes had a dissatisfied, slightly congested look. She noted that he dyed his thinning hair. She could see the discolored roots. Serge, with his narrow, shrink-wrapped face, made her shiver.

"I think I know why Luca didn't keep his lunch date," Julian said as the two men took the window table at the other end of the room. "Emile said the place was crawling with gendarmes and ambulance crew. Not his kind of scene at all."

"Yes. However, the reservation was for three," said Mara. "If Luca and Serge make two, who was number three?"

"The Third Man," Julian grinned, and then his attention was diverted by the arrival of lunch.

In summer, the Two Sisters catered to the trendier expectations of the tourist market, with prices to match. In the off-season, although the prices were still enough to make you raise your eyebrows, you could enjoy traditional fare that was becoming harder to find. Julian had chosen *mique,* served with a hotpot of salt pork and winter vegetables. Usually the *mique,* a large dumpling simmered in the juices of the hotpot, was regarded as the accompaniment. In this case, it had star billing as one of the restaurant's specialties. It was served sliced, revealing an interior studded with diced bacon, chives, and—a Two Sisters innovation—black olives, and came to him steaming smugly in the center of a platter surrounded by the rest of his meal.

Mara had ordered one of her favorites: stuffed goose neck. It was made by deboning the neck of a goose and filling the skin with a mixture of sausage, goose meat, Armagnac, foie gras, and truffles. Then the neck was sewn up and slowly roasted in goose fat. It could be eaten hot, cold, or conserved as a *confit*—submerged in more goose fat in an airtight container—the old way of preserving things before refrigeration.

Mara's dish arrived sizzling hot, like a delicate sausage. She found, as she slid her knife through it, that even the textures added to the experience: the slightly puckered outer casing giving way to a dense interior rich with flavors. She closed her eyes and swallowed. It was remarkable, she thought as she went in for another mouthful. Goose or duck fat was used with everything. She couldn't understand why people in this part of the world didn't all have cholesterol readings off the chart. Also, although many attained a kind of happy stoutness, there were few really obese people around. Everyone looked healthy and seemed to live a very long time. Probably because they were all so well lubricated with red wine and walnut oil.

"What?" She became aware that Julian had said something.

"I said it's odd how often Luca's name seems to pop up. This whole drug business. The death of that narc Yvan Bordas, Kazim, the trashing of Lokum. And now he has a table booked at the time and place where Amélie takes a tumble. I find it damned peculiar."

Mara stopped chewing. "You're not saying Amélie was the third person? What would she have being doing consorting with someone like Luca?"

"Keep your voice down."

"He can't hear us. And why would Luca want to bump her off? It's Christine and Alice who have the motive."

They returned to their meal.

After a long moment, Mara put her fork down. "Okay. Let's go down that road. If there's some kind of link between Amélie and Luca—forget what for the moment—then we have to assume it also involves Joseph. And if it does, then his nighttime monsters, which you don't believe in, take on a much more sinister meaning."

"Then we're back to why would a drug baron want to kill an old woman or terrorize her husband?"

"Maybe it's not Luca. Serge is the hit man. Maybe he does commissions on the side."

"You think Christine and Alice hired Serge to lure Amélie up to the porch and push her off, and now they're paying him to get rid of Joseph?" Julian seemed to find this funny.

"It's one way of reconciling things," Mara said a little defensively. Her eyes, sweeping the crowded room, narrowed.

"Someone's joining them," she said, ducking her head low over her plate. "For heaven's sake, Julian, don't turn around."

"Can you see who it is?"

"It's a man. Now he's sitting down." She stood up suddenly. "I'm going to the toilet."

Before he could react she was gone, taking a circuitous route around the edge of the room. Near the window table where a small man with the look of a startled hare was talking rapidly and Luca was spitting olive pits into an ashtray, she stopped suddenly to dig into her purse.

"I'll need another week," Mara heard the hare squeak. He could be, she thought, a schoolteacher, a government functionary, a minor businessman. "I'm sure I can come up with it, but I'll need another week."

With an exclamation of annoyance, Mara dropped her purse, scattering keys, a comb, wads of paper tissues, her wallet.

Serge was the only one who took any notice of her. His expression was cold and alert, and he did not take his eyes off Mara until she had gathered her belongings and moved on.

She followed through by going out of the room, crossing the porch, and making her way to the other side of the restaurant where the bar and the toilets were located. That half of the restaurant was full as well. On her return, she retraced her roundabout path but this time did not linger. She was back with Julian within ten minutes.

"That was the most transparent piece of play-acting I've ever seen," Julian hissed. "What the hell were you doing?"

"Eavesdropping."

"Yes, I could see that."

"I heard that rabbity-looking man ask for more time to come

up with something. You know, in addition to drugs, I wouldn't be surprised if our Monsieur Ton-and-a-Half isn't also into loan-sharking. If Christine and Alice are hard up for cash, maybe that's the link we're looking for. They took a loan from Luca, and now they have to find some way to pay the devil."

27

There was a thunderstorm in the middle of the week. The rain struck the windows in big, heavy drops. Every now and then the sky fizzled with vertical lightning. Jazz slept unconcerned on the Aubusson rug. Bismuth, who was terrified of storms, crept under the art deco sofa where Julian sprawled, reading a week-old copy of the *Daily Mail* that Madame Audebert had not yet managed to destroy.

The phone rang three times before Julian remembered that Mara was outside in her studio behind the house. He tossed aside the paper and hurried to pick up before the *répondeur* kicked in.

"Julian?" It was Iris Potter, Julian's artist and Géraud's live-in partner. Her voice sounded a little breathless. "He's up to something. He's got that look about him. You know what I mean, that smug, sneaky look he has whenever he thinks he's going to get the better of someone, especially you."

She obviously meant Géraud. Julian stiffened as he always did at the mention of the man.

"He's been seeing someone named Adelheid Besser," she went on. "Do you know her?"

"Er—yes." Julian had the sensation of his stomach dropping into his boots. It was the last thing he wanted to hear. He had forgotten about Adelheid, indeed had hoped she would simply vanish from the landscape. Obviously she had not lost any time getting on to Géraud, and his being "up to something" with her could mean only one thing.

Iris spelled it out for him: "I think they're after your *Cypripedium* thingummy." Iris was bad with taxonomic names but accepted entirely that *Cypripedium incognitum* belonged to Julian. "Apparently this Besser woman—Géraud calls her Heidi, makes me think of yodeling and goats—is a big collector. She travels all over the world in search of orchids, and she has a greenhouse filled with plants that has Géraud lime-green with envy. He said she's promised him a Something *sanderianum.* Since Géraud hates to pay for anything, it can only mean an exchange. Well, the way I see it, there's only one thing Géraud can offer her that she hasn't got, and that's your orchid." For someone whom Julian regarded as beautifully innocent, Iris could be surprisingly astute.

"Damn!" swore Julian, beginning to hyperventilate.

"So I'd watch my back if I were you, ducks," said Iris. "And there's something else I ought to tell you. I've just seen a brochure. You know all that land next to Mara's house? Woods and fields and so on? Apparently it's going to be developed as some kind of big, fancy golf course."

Julian had thought that nothing could have been worse than the news that Géraud and Adelheid had joined forces. Now he found he needed to sit down.

•

"It's a multinational consortium called Montfort-Izawa," Julian said in disgust. It was the next day, and he had just returned from the *mairie,* where the mayor, Madame Marty, had proved extremely helpful. "I can't get any details on who or what Montfort-Izawa is, but they own all the land adjoining your north side, including the woods and the fields beyond. Apparently have done for years. They've just released promotional material on an eighteen-hole international-standard golf course, construction to start next year. Plus clubhouse, pro shop, restaurant, parking, and access road. This is the bumph Iris saw."

He tossed two shiny brochures onto a table. One was in English, the other in French, both showing a happy golfing couple at the height of their swings, superimposed on an emerald expanse of turf. In the foreground, a triangular flag bore the monogram M-I.

Julian disliked golf courses, not because he had anything against the game, but because of the way golfing greens were managed. First, they took up a helluva lot of land. Goodbye to the forest bordering Mara's property. Goodbye to the rough meadow beyond the trees. In springtime it was thick with orchids: purple *Orchis morio,* deep-throated *Serapias lingua,* and brilliant waves of pink Pyramidals.

Second, golf courses used huge amounts of water. At a time when water rationing in summer was becoming the norm, he was amazed that the scheme had been permitted to go through. Madame Marty had assured him that golf courses in France were now required to abide by strict watering regulations, but it still added up to a drain on a scarce resource. Third, golf courses used chemicals like crazy because anything that wasn't grass was regarded as a weed. That included orchids.

"And that's just Phase I," he went on. "Phase II is luxury condos scattered about, plus parking, two swimming pools, plus more access roads. A kind of golf holiday village. You can buy shares in the scheme, or a package deal: leasehold on a condo and all the golf you want. Maintenance, landscaping, and security looked after by the consortium. If you're looking for income property, you can rent out your condo and your golfing privileges. Montfort-Izawa will advertise it on their website and manage the rental for you. For a fee, of course. As a sweetener, if you buy before December 31—this is before they even break ground, mind you—you can benefit from time-share privileges for as long as you own your condo that'll get you accommodation and golf in Florida and the

Dominican Republic. Plus there's a lot of hype about taking advantage of this early-bird offer because in the New Year they expect prices to be much, much higher owing to demand. It seems any number of Japanese corporations are keen to invest in real estate and golfing privileges for their executives, who will come out in fortnightly rotations. The Japanese are golf-crazy."

Mara took this in with growing anger. She, too, had just returned to the house, having talked to all of her immediate neighbors that morning and having picked up some of the same information. She said: "In Ecoute-la-Pluie, Joseph and I are the ones directly affected because the development will abut our properties, but I'm not sure Joseph really understood me when I tried to explain to him what was happening. Everyone else in the hamlet is in favor of the scheme, and it seems to have the support of the whole commune as well. When I talked to Olivier Rafaillac, he said application for the project was made several years ago, not long after I moved here. I had a chance to voice my objection then, but I was so busy trying to get my business going, I don't think I was even aware of it. And anyway, Olivier said I would have been outvoted. Everyone feels the golf course will bring income to the area and increase the value of their land. I'm the only one dead set against it."

"And me," said Julian.

"And you." She sat down miserably in a straight-backed chair. Her expression was desolate. "Oh, Julian. They'll destroy the wood. We'll have idiots yelling 'Fore!' and '*Gare!*' on our back terrace. What will we do?" She picked up the English brochure and stared at it, looking as if she were about to cry.

"There's nothing we can do to stop it," said Julian. "Montfort-Izawa have met all the departmental requirements. Its plans conform to structural, safety, health, and access regulations. The project is very much a go. You—we'll—have to live with it."

"It's so crass!" Mara cried, disgusted.

"It could be worse."

"I mean this." She flapped the brochure in his face. "The whole approach. The hype, the all-inclusive package, the early-bird deal. It sounds so North American, so—" she broke off to stare in disbelief at the open tri-fold in her hand. "Golf? Time-shares in Florida and the Dominican Republic? Julian, who do we know who's into land speculation, who's a former pro golfer, who has development interests all over the place? Who do we know who's been closing a deal in the Dordogne? This sounds like frigging Donny O'Connor!"

· 28 ·

It was Friday again, Madame Audebert's day to clean. Julian took himself off early and did not return until she had gone. So it was not until the end of the afternoon that he and Mara took the dogs and walked to the end of the road and into the forest to take the measure of what they were about to lose. Jazz and Bismuth bounded ahead and soon disappeared into the undergrowth. The air was warm and damp, dusty with the smell of coming rain.

"It's all of this," said Julian as they crested the ridge and came down through the trees on the other side to enter the meadow below.

A wave of sadness swept over Mara. There had been too much loss of late. Amélie, Kazim, Joseph, who was losing his daily battle with Parkinson's. And now the impending destruction of a piece of wilderness that was somehow so essential to her happiness. *What did you expect?* a tough, practical voice spoke up in her head. *The frame to freeze just because you came and thought you'd found your little piece of paradise?* Things change, people leave, or they die. Land was now a highly marketable commodity.

"Plus all of that over there." Julian pointed to a long, fallow field that lay along the road farther to the west. In it stood the ruins of a house that had once been part of a working farm, a legacy to a generation unwilling or unable to remain on the land. Often such parcels were locked in endless sibling battles over what was to be done with a shared inheritance. Fields that had been cultivated were left to the creeping stranglehold of brambles that claimed a bit more of the open space each year. So much of the Dordogne was like that, Mara thought, a melancholy testimony to times past. Unless it was being bought up by the Montfort-Izawas.

"I wonder if there's any way we can find out if Donny is behind this," Julian said. Mara had looked up Montfort-Izawa on the Internet, had found a website but no principal names, and Madame Marty had not been able to give Julian any more information than she had already provided. "Maybe we should just come right out and ask him."

"I'm sure it's him," Mara burst out irritably. "This scheme has Donny O'Connor stamped all over it."

Julian agreed. And yet something puzzled him mightily. Surely this could not be all of it? By his reckoning, the fields and the forest all told were at most 40 hectares, less than 100 acres. An impossible squeeze for a course that was supposed to come up to international standards, let alone accommodate the necessary facilities and the proposed condominiums. A lot depended on layout, but he knew that any decent eighteen-hole course required at least 60 hectares, 150 acres, give or take. Glancing back at the woods above them, he also realized that the topography here was terrible. Everything was on a slope, running uphill or downhill to a departmental road that snaked along the bottom of the land. He imagined a great deal of reconstruction, heard the whine of saws as they toppled trees, the rumble of earthmovers slicing off the top of the high ground and using the earth to fill in the lower levels. It would require expensive cut and fill, or terracing, to create playable space. The cost would be prohibitive.

Finally, the configuration of the land was bad, the meadow and fallow field lying in long strips along the road. In his early days of landscaping, Julian had done golf course maintenance. He remembered one fairway so narrow that golfers had had to hold up play for passing cars in case a stray shot smashed into a windscreen. The space here was like that. How could an experienced golfer like Donny O'Connor get it so wrong?

"You know," he said, with a faint flicker of optimism. "I wonder if Montfort-Izawa—Donny—will really be able to carry this off."

Mara, who had been lost in thought, stirred. "How do you mean?"

He explained his doubts about space and layout. "And there are the condos and the swimming pools to come, don't forget. Where's it all going to go?"

"Are you saying it's a scam?" Hope, like a timid banner, unfurled in Mara's heart.

"Er—no." Donny was a bore, a blowhard, but Julian really didn't think he had the bottle to try skulduggery of this magnitude. "Just a highly speculative venture. Maybe Donny's launching Phase I as a kind of trial balloon to see how many investors he can pull in. That would give him cash up front to set things in motion for the golf course. But I wouldn't be surprised if he's a long time delivering Phase II. If ever."

"Phase I is bad enough," said Mara hotly. "And my land will still be affected. Don't forget, this damned putting green is going to run right along the entire length of my north property line. Joseph's, too." Mara shook her head. "But he doesn't understand. Or care."

Julian contemplated this. "Maybe he does. Just not in the way you want."

"What do you mean?"

"Look, there's no way the consortium can make good on all their promises with what we're seeing here. But Joseph is sitting on a whacking great parcel of cleared, level land that's bang up against the proposed development. Maybe he's planning to sell out to them." Julian stood very still. "Bloody hell. In fact, that's got to be it. In order for Montfort-Izawa to go ahead with their project, they must have secured more adjacent land. What's the betting they have some kind of private understanding to buy Joseph out? His verbal agreement to sell is all it would take at this stage. Nothing formal, nothing on record, but there you have another 45 hectares, enough to make the project feasible."

Mara stared at him in horror. "You're telling me I'll not only have a fairway and condos down one side of my property, but across from me, too?" She shook her head. "No. I can't believe Joseph would do this. He wants to live out his days in his own home, remember?"

"Nothing easier. Montfort-Izawa strikes a deal with him. He stays put in the house, but the rest of the property changes hands. You must see that a piece of land as big as the Gaillards' is key to this whole scheme. It's contiguous to the development, and it definitely offers the necessary space and layout. And there's another thing. Have you stopped to ask yourself why, if the consortium has owned the land for all these years, it hasn't done something with it sooner?"

"The market hasn't been right until now?"

"Or they've been waiting to acquire the final piece. Gaillards' property."

Mara shook her head vigorously. "It's out of character. I told you, Joseph's rooted to the soil. He'd never sell. Neither would Amélie, and even dead her word still rules."

"Maybe he needs money."

"He doesn't. He spends very little. And Jacqueline told me he gets some kind of monthly stipend, plus a bit from the farmers who graze their cattle in his fields. Besides, there's something you're overlooking. No matter how bad their relationship is, I'm sure Joseph would want to hang on to the property for Christine, not sell it if he doesn't need to, just to pump up his bank account. You know how sentimental the French are about land and passing it on to their children."

Julian paced a patch of ground, arms crossed, hands tucked under his armpits. "Then Montfort-Izawa must be getting another parcel of land from someone else. I can't see it proceeding otherwise. Unless . . ."

Mara, who was staring at the tops of her shoes, looked up. Julian stopped pacing, stuffed his hands in his pockets and stared out over the landscape. A dark bank of clouds was building up in the west, blotting out the last angry rays of the sun.

"Christine," they both said at the same time.

Julian took a deep breath. "Apart from Joseph, she's the only one in a position to negotiate with Montfort-Izawa. If they're already distributing brochures, they must be pretty damned confident they have the space they need. You said Joseph would never sell, but Christine might, if she can get power of attorney over Joseph's affairs. And if he's deemed unfit mentally—"

"Or if he dies . . ." Mara cut in. "And if Montfort-Izawa is steaming ahead with the development now, it can only mean that Christine intends to get Joseph out of her road, one way or the other, and very soon."

29

Huguette Roche is early with Joseph's meal today. She brings it in a basket.

"You've heard there's another big storm coming in?" She looks a little windblown, like a precursor of the storm itself. She sets his supper out on the counter: potato soup in a jar with a rubber bung; a hearty pot-au-feu, boiled beef with vegetables, in a covered earthenware casserole; a wedge of prune tart between two plates. It's the kind of food Joseph is used to, not that *steak haché* Mara gives him.

"If you don't want it now, you can heat it up yourself later, can't you?" she asks. "I have to get back and help Jean-Marie tie things down. The last big storm we had, it blew our wheelbarrow right into the next field." She tells him to leave the dishes in the sink. She'll return in the morning to take care of everything.

"You'll be all right?"

"*Oui, oui.*"

"*Bon.* Is there anything else I can do before I go?"

Joseph shakes his head.

"*Okay. A demain.*" Huguette hurries out, relieved to be away.

Joseph is glad Huguette does not have time to visit with him. He does not want to hear any more about the weather, or the local gossip, and Mara has already talked to him about golf courses and condominiums. She was there earlier in the day, sitting forward in her chair, making short, sharp gestures with her hands, filling his kitchen with words. So many words make it difficult to think, and he needs more than anything to think. It will be dark soon, and he knows he has very little time. He looks about him to see what he can use, what he will be physically able to move. He already fears that whatever he can do will not be enough to keep out the coming storm or the headless monster that will arrive, riding like a bird of carrion on its back.

•

"We have to find a way to protect Joseph," Mara said as she and Julian hurried back to the house. Their weekly get-together with Loulou at Chez Nous was at eight that evening, and it was already a quarter to seven.

"Protection is a job for the gendarmes, Mara," Julian said severely. He looked over his shoulder. The livid stain that passed for a sunset was bleeding quickly from the sky. A gusting wind flattened the grasses at the sides of the road. The predicted storm was on its way.

Mara shook her head. "They wouldn't believe us. To the police he'd just be a sick old man suffering from hallucinations."

"Well," said Julian, "there is always the possibility that Joseph really is imagining things. Look, you've warned Christine off. If she did have designs on her father's life, I doubt she'll try anything now."

"We can't be sure of that. There could be a lot at stake for her. And Donny O'Connor, for that matter. Maybe that's why Daisy's been pushing to get Joseph into a nursing home."

"Donny, maybe. But I honestly get the impression that Daisy is genuinely attached to Joseph. In her own way, I think she wants what's best for him."

Mara looked unconvinced. "Why do I have this awful feeling that Joseph's life is hanging by a thread and I'm the only one worried?"

"You have a hypersuspicious mind."

The phone was ringing as they opened the door. Mara shot a look of foreboding at Julian.

He raised a reassuring hand. "Probably just Iris," he muttered, pushing past her. "With more bad news, I don't doubt."

Mara kicked off her shoes and unzipped her jacket.

"*Comment?*" She heard Julian say. He continued in French, "Well, can't you tell me now? All right. I'll be right there." He slammed the receiver down.

"It's Joseph, isn't it?" she cried out.

"No, it's Osman," he shouted, going for his car keys. "That was Betul. Something has happened. She won't tell me on the phone, but she sounds really frightened. She's asking for my help."

•

The dogs shot out of the house ahead of them and into the van as soon as Julian yanked open the driver's door. Mara, one arm in her jacket and struggling to insert the other, climbed in on the other side.

"This is crazy," she yelled as the van roared up the road. "Christine is a job for the gendarmes, but the Ismets aren't? Their son was up to his eyeballs in drugs, probably murdered by Ton-and-a-Half or his hatchet man, don't forget."

"I'm not likely to, am I?" Julian retorted grimly. Irritably, he shoved Jazz's head away from its accustomed position on his shoulder. An exploratory nose, cold and wet, probed the back of his neck before the head, heavy and persistent, returned. He shoved again, harder. Grumbling, Jazz retreated and lay down on the bed of the van. A slash of lightning split the sky, followed by a great crack of thunder. Bismuth, shaking so hard that his teeth chattered, tried to burrow under the bags of potting soil.

"Julian, you're speeding. Slow down."

They drove into the leading edge of the storm, which arrived in heavy spatters against the windscreen. By the time they reached

Brames, ragged sheets of rain were blowing down the main street of the town. They parked in front of Lokum and raced for the entrance. Betul was watching for them at the door, her face a circle of white within her head scarf, her eyes terrified.

"Are you all right?" Julian asked as they pushed inside, dripping water on the floor.

"Yes, yes. It's Osman." Betul hardly took Mara in, accepting her presence without question. "I didn't want to say on the phone. He's been beaten up."

"Beaten up? By whom?"

"He won't talk. Just that it was two men. I think it has something to do with drugs. Please reason with him, Monsieur Wood. He's upstairs. Make him see sense. Make him go to the police."

She led them up the narrow stairs into their red sitting room. Osman sprawled on the divan. His eyes and nose were swollen. The front of his shirt was bloody and torn.

"Who did this to you?" Julian confronted the Turk.

"Go away," Osman said, refusing to look at Julian.

"Was it Rocco Luca and his men? Was it Serge Taussat?"

"I don't talk to you."

"What did they want?"

"I am Turk," Osman recited in a cracked voice. "I am correct, hard-working—"

Julian lost all patience with the man. "You're a fool. Osman, you've got to take this to the police."

"No. No gendarmes," said Osman, looking directly at Julian for the first time.

"At least tell us what happened," Mara urged, stepping forward.

"Who's she?" Osman demanded suspiciously.

"A friend," said Julian. He made a tardy introduction that neither husband nor wife acknowledged.

Betul went into the kitchen and reappeared a minute later with a cloth in a basin of steaming water. She moved a small table near the divan, set the bowl on it, and wrung out the cloth.

"Stupid," Betul muttered as she bent to wipe her husband's face. He flinched and pulled away. She flung the cloth into the basin. "Stupid, stubborn man. They will kill you. Then where will I be? No son, no husband. How will I live?"

"Is nothing!" Osman shouted with sham courage. "Is only fight. Racist thugs."

Julian's temper flared. "You've tried that racist line before, and see where it's got you. Betul's right. If this is about drugs, Osman, these people won't hesitate to step up the violence. You got a couple of black eyes and a punch in the nose this time. You were lucky. Next time, you'll end up in hospital, or—or worse." He almost said: "In a garbage skip, like your son."

Osman maintained a sullen silence.

"I've had enough of this," Julian said. "Give me your phone, Mara. I'm calling the police."

Osman lurched off the divan, knocking Betul and the bowl of water aside. He lunged at Julian but tripped on the fringed edge of the rug. Julian caught him as he went down.

"Why don't you want the police?" he shouted over the Turk's roar of pain. "What is it you're hiding?"

Osman sagged. Julian let him drop the rest of the way to the floor. Betul was crying. Osman shoved himself up on his elbows and shouted something at her in Turkish. She shouted back. Osman groaned and slumped down again.

Betul turned to Julian. "He says he doesn't know who the men are who beat him up, but they said they will finish him if he speaks to you."

"If he speaks to me? Why me?" Julian exclaimed, startled.

"They think you are under cop," moaned Osman.

"Undercover police," Betul translated.

Julian and Mara exchanged shocked glances.

"They know you were looking for Kazim, and now they threaten to kill Osman if he talks to you. Then they will also kill you."

30

Joseph has gathered logs, one by one, from the woodshed. He has found a large, empty feedsack and a length of rope, and now he is pushing the wooden table across the kitchen floor. The table is heavy and difficult for him to move, even though it is set on wheels. They roll with a screeching sound and catch on the uneven flagstones. Sometimes he has to shuffle around to the front of the table to lift it over slight impediments. His breath squeezes out of him in shallow gasps, his legs feel as if they are filled with wet cement.

The table is too wide to go through the doorway. He bends stiffly to tip it back so that it balances on two legs. The table's weight nearly pulls him over with it. However, he lets go just in time. The table crashes onto its side. He leans against it, stooped and shaking and momentarily stunned.

By angling the table back and forth, he maneuvers the forward legs through the doorway. The wheels, adding length to the legs, make the job harder. Then, as laboriously, he angles the table the other way to accommodate the back legs. Now he is in the hallway, which stretches like an endless tunnel before him. He has to stop to rest. It is a mistake. Disastrously, his brain switches off, and his body freezes.

The freezing has happened to him several times in the last few months. He knows the name of this inability to move—akinesia—and it is one of the many indignities of his disease. He can go neither forward nor backward, and in this wavering limbo his balance deserts him. He falls sideways, toppling like a drunkard to the floor where he lies unmoving, face down.

He is still lying on the floor when the storm hits. Rain slashes against the windows. The wind rattles the shutters. He flinches, and the house, as if in sympathy, seems to recoil as well. Somehow, the sounds galvanize him, and miraculously he is able to move again. He pushes himself to his hands and knees, uses the table to haul himself up. Then, with tremendous effort and by bracing his shoulder against the wall, he cants the table forward until he has righted it. He rests a moment, trying to dominate the wild inner choreography of his body, and then, step by step, he resumes his journey, pushing the table, wheels complaining, down the hall.

He is almost to the end of the hall when he remembers there is a second door to negotiate. He must repeat the whole terrible, exhausting process of tipping and angling and righting to get the table into the bedroom, where he will make his stand against the monster of the storm. And then it happens to him again. His feet freeze in place, leaving him wedged helplessly between the table and the wall. Long minutes pass. The wind is roaming like a beast of prey outside the house, and still his legs remain locked. He knows now that he won't make it. He has been beaten. An ocean of despair floods his chest, fills his eyes. And for the first time since Amélie's death, Joseph is able to shed tears, not only for the wife who left him but for the helpless thing he has become.

Time was when he could have picked up and tossed aside something like a table with ease. A young Hercules, people round about had called him. It was what Amélie had liked about him. "You're the back," she had often said. "I'm the head. A strong back doesn't need a good brain." He had left the thinking to her.

Now he must think for himself. His thoughts drift out on a dark tide. What was it he had to do? And how was he to do it? Yet even as he stands there stranded, five hundred years of peasant stubbornness, bred in the marrow, come to his aid. With great effort, he remembers one of the kick-starting techniques that Jacqueline has taught him, slapping his leg. It is a feeble motion, as if he is brushing at a drowsy fly, but it is enough to get him moving again. With a broken sob of relief he finds that he is able to force his will once more to the task he must accomplish before the monster comes. For it will arrive with the darkness. It will come in the door, and down the hall, making the floorboards squeal. And if he cannot secure himself against it, it will bend over him. Then it will push his face into the pillow and hold him fast until the brain that Amélie had always said he did not need goes dark.

•

The road before them was a dancing sheet of water. Their headlights and wipers were totally ineffectual in the downpour. Rain hammered loudly on the roof of the van. Julian drove slowly, hunched forward over the steering wheel in a misery of wordlessness that was more deafening than the rain.

"Julian!" Mara had to yell to be heard. "You can't go on blaming yourself. Drugs are a violent business. What happened to Kazim and Osman may have had nothing to do with you."

"It has everything to do with me." He slammed his hand against the steering wheel. "If I hadn't been nosing around after Kazim, Luca wouldn't have killed him. He wouldn't be threatening Osman. You heard what Betul said. Luca thinks I'm an undercover cop."

"But the Ismets asked you to find their son."

Julian made no reply.

Mara cried out in exasperation, "For heaven's sake, you might as well say none of this would have happened in the first place if you hadn't tried to do a deal with Osman about salep to save your damned orchids!" In the semi-darkness, she saw him stiffen immediately, and she regretted the words even as they came out of her mouth.

"That was a low blow."

"I'm sorry. I didn't mean it that way. But isn't it true? Doesn't it always somehow boil down to orchids with you?"

"If that's what you think, you really don't understand me."

"Then tell me." Mara braced herself against the dashboard as the van lurched over unseen potholes. "What is it I don't get?"

He just shook his head and concentrated on steering.

Mara threw up her hands. "I despair of you. Of us. Why do you always close down on me? How do you think it makes me feel? How can we make any headway in our relationship if you won't talk to me?"

"Why do you always have to bring our relationship into it? And where the bloody hell are we supposed to be going?"

"Nowhere," she shouted, "if you constantly shut me out. That's my whole point!"

"For pity's sake," he exploded, "what is it you want? A dissection of my feelings? Okay. I confess. I'm not good at talking about the things you want to talk about. I've got a thing about orchids. I'm not—what's the word you like to use? Proactive. I go with the flow. I let things slide. In fact, if you want me to lay it out for you, I've a bloody lifetime behind me of things left undone or done too late that somehow add up to one dead nineteen-year-old kid. Is that good enough for you? And now, if you don't mind, I think I've had enough soul-searching, and I'd like to concentrate on getting us out of this."

He fell into a deafening silence.

"All right," Mara said, more quietly. "It's all your fault, if that's how you want it. So what do you plan to do about it?"

Julian stared bleakly through the frantic rise and fall of the windshield wipers. "The only thing I *can* do. If Osman won't go to the police, I'll have to do it for him."

"And what if Ton-and-a-Half decides to make good on his threat?"

"It'll be up to the gendarmes to give the Ismets protection."

"I assumed that. I was talking about you."

"Luca and his boys may know I was asking around after Kazim, but they don't know who I am."

"I think they do. You said you gave Nadia your card. If Kazim called you, it probably means she gave it to him. If Serge killed Kazim, he probably took your card off Kazim's body. Commissaire Boutot said nothing about finding your business card among Kazim's effects, did he?"

"Er—" said Julian, "no." He had to swing wide suddenly to avoid a torrent rushing off a hillside that brought with it a wash of mud and stones.

"Julian," Mara shouted, "we can't drive through this! Pull over."

"Pull over where? I can't see a thing. We'll end up in a ditch."

A few hundred meters later they had no choice but to stop. A whole section of road had washed away. Mara saw the crater, like a mini Niagara Falls, just in time and screamed. Julian slammed on the brakes. The van slithered to a halt.

"That was bloody close," said Julian. "We'll have to go back." He craned his head around and began reversing. After a minute or two, he gave up. "It's no good. We'll have to stay put until it stops raining. Or until daylight."

"We can't just sit in the middle of the road," Mara objected. "Someone will come along and smash into us. At least put your flashers on."

"They won't be able to *see* our flashers. Besides, who in their right mind would be out on a night like this?"

"People like us, trying to get home."

His eye caught the glow of Mara's cellphone.

"If you're calling out for pizza, I don't think they'll deliver."

"Very funny. I can't get a signal. I'm trying to get Joseph. I'm worried about him."

"Joseph? For pity's sake, Mara, you ought to be worried about *us.*"

She put the phone away. Then she cried out, "Oh no! It's Friday night. We completely forgot about Loulou."

"Christ," Julian muttered. "I doubt he bothered."

Above the din of the rain, they heard a tearing, crashing sound. A discharge of lightning gave them the awesome vision of a tree in the process of sliding from the steep hillside on their left down into the crater. It seemed to make its descent in slow motion, like a gargantuan grande dame going into a seismic faint. It came to rest on the road not far in front of them, bringing with it a huge amount of debris.

"Hell's bells," said Julian, shaken.

Mara was clutching the edge of her seat, too overawed to speak.

Another flash of lightning gave them a brief glimpse of their position. They were awash in an inland sea. The tree, a massive pine, would have crushed them if Julian had not moved the van just moments before. The lightning was followed by a bone-cracking crash of thunder.

A hair-raising wail coming out of the darkness behind them made both of them nearly scream with fright.

"What the hell was that?" Julian choked out.

"I think," said Mara once she had recovered herself, "it was your dog."

31

They spent a cold, uncomfortable night in the back of the van with two bags of potting soil as pillows and each other and the dogs for warmth. Mara thought she must have slept, because she was suddenly aware of pale light and an eerie stillness. She sat up and crawled over Julian's legs to look out the back window.

The roadbed was visible, but it was covered in detritus, and the ditches ran high with water. The field on one side of them was flooded. The trees at its margin had the appearance of floating on a lake. On the high embankment on the other side of them, more pines had been toppled. They lay criss-crossed and seemed to cling to the hillside by sheer inertia. Fortunately, none had slid down on them, and none blocked their rear. It was ten past seven. Mara got out her cellphone. This time she got a signal. She tried calling Joseph's land line, and when there was no answer, his cellphone. It was not switched on.

Julian stirred.

"I'm sure he's all right," he said once he was awake enough to realize what she was doing. "At any rate, he's a bloody sight better off than we are. God, what a night."

He sat up, worked his way to the back door of the van, and pushed it open. The dogs jumped out, and so did he. It took him a moment to get his bearings. They were no more than three kilometers from home.

Nevertheless, it took them more than an hour to reach Ecoute-la-Pluie. They could have walked there in less time. By then, the sun was shining brilliantly and road workers with noisy, heavy equipment were everywhere, sawing downed trees, feeding the sections into chippers, or shifting them from the roads. France Telecom and electricity repair crews would soon follow. If it had been later in the year and warmer, mushroom gatherers would have been out in force as well. Morels loved nothing so much as a good rain.

The *castine* road leading through the hamlet had been nearly washed away. They bumped down it, avoiding as much as possible the deep channels that had been gouged out by the escaping water. They pulled up in front of Joseph's house. The first thing they saw was that a large branch of the Gaillards' hornbeam had come down. Fortunately, it had fallen away from the house.

They let themselves in the back door with Mara's key.

"Joseph?" Mara called. She noticed with a sharp stab of alarm that his dinner sat untouched in the covered dishes on the counter. The table was missing, giving the kitchen an empty look.

"Joseph?"

The house was silent.

They went down the hallway to the bedroom. The door was closed. It resisted when Julian pushed it. As worried as Mara now, he backed off and ran at it. The door gave suddenly as whatever had been jamming it on the other side gave way. He was propelled into the room by his own momentum and immediately struck forcefully on the back of the head. Hard, heavy objects rained down on him. He gave a yell of shock and pain and stumbled forward onto the missing kitchen table, which shot away, leaving him sprawling on the floor.

Joseph was sitting upright in his bed, arms jerking with excitement, taking in the spectacle with glee.

"*Et tak!*" he crowed hoarsely, his normally rigid face split by a rictus grin of triumph. "Got you!"

•

He had rigged up an ingenious system using a hook that he had somehow managed to screw into an exposed beam just over the doorway and a feedsack filled with logs that he had hung by a rope from the hook. He had attached one end of another piece of rope to the bottom of the bag and the other end to a leg of the table. When Julian had pushed the table forward, the bag had tipped, spilling its load of logs on him.

Julian sat on the floor nursing a cut lip from his collision with the table's edge and a very sore head from the falling logs. It did not help matters that Mara was laughing hysterically.

"That's it," he said, rising with as much dignity as he could muster. "I've had it. I've been threatened by a gangster, I've come close to being crushed by a tree, I've spent an absolutely filthy night in a storm, and now I've just been sandbagged by a hallucinating maniac. If someone is terrorizing this man, Mara, I'd say they're welcome to him. He's perfectly capable of looking after himself. Now if you don't mind, I'm going home, and by home I mean my own house in Grissac, to have a shower, some breakfast, and a little bit of peace and quiet, in that order."

· 32 ·

It took Julian another hour to drive the few kilometers to Grissac over flooded roads. He stopped off at Chez Nous and persuaded Paul to power down his saw—he was clearing fallen branches from the front of the bistro—long enough to sell him some groceries. When he reached his cottage, the first things he did were to switch on the water heater and throw open the doors and windows—the air outside was warm, but inside the house was cold and damp, with a moldy smell of old stone. Then he checked for storm damage (more fallen branches, one or two smashed tiles). He had a shower and a shave. The water was only lukewarm, but he emerged feeling better. He was home.

He was now in his kitchen making a three-egg-and-bacon fry-up. Unlike Mara's kitchen, his was not color-coordinated. His refrigerator gurgled, and his stove was an old, hybrid cooker. Two of its burners ran off butane, for when the electricity kicked out; a third ran on electricity, for when he ran out of butane. A fourth did not work at all. He turned the eggs and threw in some bread slices to fry in the bacon fat.

As he sat down to eat his breakfast—on a sturdy chair that took his weight—he thought about the fight he and Mara had had in the van.

"It wasn't nice," he said to his dog, who moaned and laid a mournful head in his lap. "I'd say a few home truths were exchanged, wouldn't you? That remark about orchids was really below the belt." Bismuth followed the rise and fall of the fork between the plate and Julian's mouth with rapt attention. The mutt had already had his breakfast, but Julian gave in anyway and slid a remaining egg into Bismuth's feed dish.

He poured himself a refill of well-sweetened tea and went to stand in the open doorway giving onto his back garden, enjoying the warmth of the sunshine on his face. The light covered everything—trees, leaves, grass—in a mantle of distilled gold.

The phone rang. He suspected it was Mara, and for some reason, perhaps because the sun was also dancing in his head, he let it go on ringing until his answering machine cut in.

"Julian"—her disembodied voice rang through the cottage—"look, I'm sorry I laughed. Nerves, I expect. And Joseph apologizes, too. He said the booby trap was for the monster. Are you all right? . . ."

"I am now," he told Bismuth, who joined him in the sun. Julian poured himself a third mug of tea and sat down on his back stoop, awash with a sense of utter contentment.

But the moment did not last. Gradually, an awkward realization began to thump, like a bumblebee, against the window of his mind: now that he was home, he did not want to leave. *Merde,* it wasn't just death threats, falling objects, the Furniture Polish Gestapo, or even the lack of a decent chair to fit his body that had made him seek refuge in Grissac. It was—and this was the awkward and disturbing part—Mara herself.

Why this should be was a bit complicated to work out. He cared deeply for her, wanted, curiously enough, her pushy presence in his life. Unbidden, a scent of sandalwood rose in his nostrils. But her constant talk about moving forward was making him uneasy.

"What's wrong with staying as we are?" he asked Bismuth, and since the dog was on his back, belly in the air, with his eyes closed, he addressed the fig tree by his door. "I hope to God she isn't expecting marriage."

It was something they didn't discuss, as if they had a tacit understanding that marriage was a thing neither of them favored. But holy Christ, was she starting to get ideas? The thought put him in a cold funk and almost made him spill his tea.

"You don't repeat a bad experience," he told the grass. "And it's damned hard to make yourself over after more than a quarter-century of living on your own, give or take a few short-lived affairs."

But it was more than that, he knew. It was a question of privacy.

"I suppose"—he addressed his feet now—"I'm what you'd call a deeply private person. I have my secrets—who doesn't?—and I'd like to keep them that way."

He gazed off into the middle distance. "But she always wants to talk. About us. Our relationship. It makes her nervous when I don't open up. Bloody hell, it's just a matter of time, isn't it? She's a ferret. They nose things out." Proximity forced disclosure. He pictured those clever paws of hers at work, picking apart the padlocks of his entangled heart.

"No," he concluded unhappily. "Staying as we are isn't an option anymore. We've reached a point where I'm either going to have to back out or throw open the bloody door and let her in." He found himself thinking wistfully of a time, not that long ago, when he and Mara had merely dated.

Sadly he tickled Bismuth's belly. "Maybe I should just stick to what I do best. Landscaping and, now that spring is finally here, beating the bushes for *Cypripedium incognitum.*"

But he did remember a little later to phone the gendarmerie in Brames to tell the duty officer that Osman had been beaten up, that Betul thought drugs were involved, that Ismet's life had been threatened, as had his own, and that Adjudant Compagnon ought to do something about it.

•

The storm had one benefit. The night had passed without another housebreaking. In any case, Jacques Compagnon's mind was not on the rhyming burglar. He stood before his gendarmes in the cramped meeting room, hands behind his back, rocking slowly back and forth, toe to heel, which meant that he had something important to say. His eyes glinted with suppressed excitement.

"The situation is coming to a head. At last we have a case. We've been informed by Monsieur Wood"—he shook his head irritably, as if chasing off a pesky fly; the Englishman was too much in the picture for his liking—"that Osman Ismet was roughed up yesterday by two unidentified thugs. Ismet claims it was another racist attack and refused to report the incident. However, his wife told Monsieur Wood that the perpetrators threatened her husband's life and that of Monsieur Wood as well. She thinks the attack has something to do with drugs. I'm betting Luca was behind it."

"And Serge Taussat, sir?" asked Albert.

"No. Ton-and-a-Half wouldn't have used Serge for this job. Not yet, anyway. This was just a warning. Goons' work. Punching someone in the head and leaving him to walk away isn't Taussat's trademark."

Compagnon did his three strides across the front of the room and swung about to face his team.

"All this tells us what we should have realized from the beginning: Osman Ismet is a player in Luca's network. The Ismets import foodstuffs from Turkey all the time. Lokum is a natural cover for bringing in drugs." He gave a bitter laugh. "You have to hand it to the old fox. He kept us focusing on Toulouse while the hot spot was right under our very noses."

Albert dug Laurent in the ribs. "Like Narbonne Plage. What did I tell you?"

Compagnon went on, "So now the break-in at the store and the death of the son take on a different perspective. As I've always suspected, Kazim was working for Luca and failed to deliver. But the Lokum trashing wasn't a warning as I originally thought. It was Luca looking for a shipment. Kazim's death was the warning. To Osman Ismet. Do as you're told or else."

Laurent shifted in his chair. His body was too long and gangly for most furniture. He sat with his knees poking up, but physical discomfort was not his problem at the moment. He spoke out unhappily: "*Mon adjudant,* when we went to the store after the trashing, I had the impression the parents really didn't know what was going on. I think only the son was in on it."

Compagnon shook his head. "Maybe Kazim was the point man here. But if he was involved, there's a good chance the parents were as well. At least the father. And we have to go with the odds. The question is, what's happened to precipitate the roughing up?" Compagnon scanned the row of intent faces before him.

Lucie Sauret spoke up. "Maybe Ismet has turned uncooperative, sir. If Luca had Kazim eliminated, Ismet will want revenge. Say he refuses to let his shop be used any longer as a front. But Luca needs Lokum to remain intact. So he sends in his heavies."

Compagnon nodded his approval. "Right. Next question: why now?"

Lucie again: "Because Ton-and-a-Half is expecting another delivery of goods?"

"*Et voilà!*" beamed the brigade commander, rising up on the balls of his feet. He set off striding in the other direction. "I don't have to tell you this is just the development we've been waiting for. We're in business. I've got authorization to tap Ismet's and Luca's phones. Customs and the drug squad are also being put in the loop. We don't know when or where the delivery will arrive, or by what means. It could be a clandestine coastal drop or smuggled in by truck, train, or air. Hopefully the phone taps will give us a heads-up. My guess is that Luca will somehow involve Lokum, so anything coming in for the shop at any port of entry will be screened by sniffer dogs. If drugs are detected, the shipment will be allowed to go through. Then it will be a matter of tracking what happens to it from there. Unfortunately, from that point, the action will be out of our hands. Luca's men will undoubtedly receive the delivery, and it will be up to the drug squad to catch them at it. Our job will be to keep Luca himself and the Ismets and their shop under surveillance and act on anything suspicious."

The adjudant's chest rose and fell heavily. He would have liked nothing more than to be in on a major drug bust that would nail Rocco Luca, but as usual, he and his officers were assigned the backup jobs.

Laurent spoke up: "You say we'll have Ismet under surveillance, sir, but what about Monsieur Wood? His life's been threatened, too. Shouldn't we—er—be offering some kind of protection?"

Compagnon shook his head. "Done, Laurent, but he declined. Just as well, since I don't have any gendarmes to spare. However, he's agreed to steer clear of the shop and to keep a low profile. As long as he stays down, I doubt Luca will jeopardize his operation to silence Julian Wood. Now, before I go any further, are there any questions?"

A couple of hands shot up.

"Let's just hope Ton-and-a-Half sees it that way," Laurent muttered to Albert.

33

Tuesday morning found Julian, rucksack slung over his shoulder, walking down a woodland path. He had spent the last couple of days cleaning up the detritus of the storm on his own and several clients' properties. Today was the first free time he'd had. The earth was still soggy underfoot, but the rain, followed by plentiful sunshine, had unleashed a riot of greenery. Grasses and wildflowers grew lush in meadows and roadsides. Vines put out sturdy tendrils. Bismuth ran happy circles around him, now appearing ahead of him, now thundering up from behind.

There were only so many ways of finding a flower, he reflected. First, you had to look at the right time of year. Mara's sister Bedie had photographed *Cypripedium incognitum* in early May. It was now the twenty-sixth of April, a little soon for his orchid, perhaps, but the past few weeks of warmth and plentiful rain had brought things on rapidly.

Second, you had to look in the right places. He had two leads. One was the grounds of the Château of Les Colombes, where Bedie had taken her photograph. He had already searched the area thoroughly with no results, but would search it again this spring, just in case he had missed something on the last pass or in case his orchid chose to bloom sporadically. The other was here on Aurillac Ridge, a wooded spine rising above the Sigoulane Valley. The orchid embroidery that he had mentioned in his book had come from nearby Aurillac Manor. Very few people knew this, and Julian had sworn to secrecy those who did. He prayed that Géraud had not yet got wind of Aurillac Ridge.

The problem was that both locations represented extensive stretches of woodland, forest, and meadow. One could, if one had unlimited time and willing bodies, superimpose a grid over these areas and send out an army of people to scour each square of the grid. At the moment, Julian had only himself and sometimes Mara, if she were in the mood and not busy tearing down walls.

Third, if you didn't know specific places to search, you could focus on likely growing environments. Some orchids required wetlands. Others liked fields, or open woods, or rough, elevated scree. Julian had no information on the kind of habitat *Cypripedium incognitum* preferred, but he guessed cool, partial shade and higher ground. That was why he was concentrating on this north-facing section of Aurillac Ridge.

Of course, the easiest way to find a flower was to draw on local knowledge, ask someone to take you to it. But it was not that simple. Julian had asked and been told that a plant resembling his orchid called Devil's Clog had once grown in the environs. Unfortunately, those who knew where to find it were long dead. However, he did have one puzzling but useful piece of information: years ago people had dug up Devil's Clog wherever they encountered it and planted Aconite in its place. Despite the horrible possibility that all the Devil's Clog in the area had been destroyed in this way, it at least gave Julian two things to look for: the orchid itself and either of two species of Aconite, Monkshood or Wolfsbane, to use their common names.

Finally, there was luck. When you weren't particularly looking for something, or when you least expected to find it, there it was, poking up between your feet. So far, he had not been lucky.

Bismuth, who had been gone a long time, reappeared looking muddy.

"Digging for moles again?" Julian grumbled.

As he walked, scanning either side of him, he was aware that his attention was not fully on his search. The Ismets kept surfacing like a murky bubble of doubt. Although he did not know it, he was slowly arriving at the same conclusions as Adjudant Compagnon. Or rather, he was asking himself the questions that could lead to those conclusions. Was there more to Osman than Elan and baklava? Julian didn't want to credit it, but the father, like the son, could be in the drug trade. Although salep was not of the same order of criminality as heroin, Osman had no scruples about bringing in the former, so why not the latter? Turkey was the drug gateway into Europe, after all. And what of Betul? Had she known, or suspected, all along what her husband and Kazim were up to? Was that why she had wanted him, rather than the police, to find Kazim? Had even she been using him?

All these possibilities left him feeling flat. He realized how futile and puny even his best efforts were against the might of drug trafficking and organized crime. Like that oak over there, so heavily smothered in ivy that its true form could not be distinguished. A few branches reached weakly for sunlight out of the creeping mass, but it was a struggle the oak would not win. Julian took out his Swiss Army knife and began hacking away at the ivy, tearing it down with his hands. That, too, was futile. The lifeline of the vine was as thick as his wrist and ferocious in its stranglehold on the tree. He needed an axe. He had not been able to help Kazim, and he could do nothing for this tree. *C'est la vie.* Apologetically, Julian closed his knife and continued on his way.

There were other things on his mind as well. Mara, of course. And he still had Géraud and Adelheid to deal with. Only the night before he had spoken with Iris, who had told him that Géraud had asked her to pump him on where and how he intended to resume his search. Julian had thought for a moment and said that he had found an orchid-rich site up in the north of the region near Cercles that he thought looked extremely promising. It was a poor ruse, but he hoped it would keep the old poacher out of his way for the next month.

He was hunkering down in a clearing to have a better look at a splendid specimen of a yellow Cowslip, one of his favorite spring flowers, when he was alerted by a sharp crackle of movement. He looked up. It was not his dog. Bismuth was nosing about at the far end of the clearing. Slowly he turned his head. The telltale noise had come from a tangle of bushes behind him and off to his right. Nor was it a bird, a lizard, or any of the numerous small animals that inhabited a wood. This was something big. He waited. The innocent landscape wrapped him in its quiet embrace. Abruptly he rose, waving his arms and calling loudly for Bismuth. The dog came running. He knew then that it was not a deer, which would have bounded away by now.

He took his time, digging his camera out of his backpack, fiddling with the settings, clicking off a few shots of the Cowslip, and stowing his camera again. Then he slung his backpack casually over one shoulder and walked out of the clearing and into the trees. Quickly and quietly he circled around to approach from behind the spot he had identified. Parting a screen of leaves, he nearly ran head-on into Géraud.

"What the hell are you doing here?" Julian demanded furiously.

"Enjoying nature." Géraud, clearly amused by the encounter, held his ground.

"You bastard, you've been following me!"

"*Bien sur*," the squat man agreed. "I've been tailing you ever since you left your house this morning, and I must say you're very inattentive. You never even saw me. You didn't think I'd fall for that cock-and-bull story about Cercles, did you?" He looked about him. "Well, well, well. Aurillac Ridge. I should have guessed."

"That woman hired you, didn't she?" was all Julian could manage to choke out.

"Ah. I see I have a leak close to home. Yes, Heidi and I are conjoined in a kind of loose, mutually beneficial partnership. She has an amazing collection of Slipper orchids, by the way, including a *Paphiopedilum sanderianum* for me. But it's contingent on my finding a certain flower. A fair trade, don't you think?"

"*Pirate!*"

"No good calling names, *mon vieux*. Bad manners. Anyway, it was an offer I couldn't refuse. I'm sure you would have done the same thing in my place. So why not be a good fellow and let a serious orchid hunter get on with the job for a change? You're never going to find it on your own, you know. I promise to credit you. In a footnote."

Julian nearly punched him.

34

Julian still had Adelheid's card in his wallet. She lived not far away outside a place called Queyssac. He loaded Bismuth in his van, checked his map, and drove there at reckless speed. His way led past a progression of vineyards, forests, and newly seeded fields of maize. There was little traffic about. He noticed, but was too angry to pay much attention to, a dark car that swung onto the main road behind him just as he branched off in the direction of Queyssac. He rattled through the village in a cloud of dust. A few kilometers farther on he saw a signpost with the word *Besser* on it, directing him onto a tree-lined lane that led up a hill. The car following him pulled onto the verge of the main road and stopped.

Her property was at the top of the lane, surrounded by a high stone wall. There was a wrought-iron gate with an intercom. He pressed the button. A female voice with a strong local accent squawked at him. He identified himself and said he was here to see Madame Besser.

"She's busy," said the voice. "I'll ask if she's seeing visitors."

He waited, simmering dangerously.

Eventually the voice screeched at him, "*Ça va.* Drive in. She'll meet you." The gate swung slowly inward. He drove through and parked beside a beige Renault Kangoo. As he climbed out of his van, he spotted Adleheid coming toward him around the side of the house. She wore mud-stained overalls, Wellington boots, and a floppy hat.

"I want a word with you," Julian barked, striding up to her.

"Ah. You have changed your mind?"

"I haven't, but you are going to change yours."

"Mmm-um?" Her tone was disarmingly mild, but her little blue eyes narrowed, and her scarlet mouth stretched upward in a not altogether pleasant smile.

"You, Madame Besser, are going decide you don't want *Cypripedium incognitum* after all. You are going to call Géraud Laval off. You are going to restrict your interests to your phytochemistry and your already considerable collection and leave my orchid alone."

"But," she said reasonably, "it is not your orchid. You said you are not so sure even that it exists."

"It doesn't exist for you," Julian snapped. He stopped, his attention captured by the impressive greenhouse that extended off the back of her house. Through the glass walls, he could see that it was crammed with orchids. It left him momentarily speechless.

"Impressive, no?" she asked, reading him aright. "Would you like to see inside? I can show you *Paphiopedilum besseri,* one of my most famous hybrids."

He pulled himself up. "I haven't come for that."

"No? Unfortunately, you are too early for the *Cypripediums.*" She indicated ranks of outdoor beds in a park-like setting at the side of her property. "I have them here, from China, North America, Japan, all in specially designed habitats. My collection"—Adelheid waved an encompassing hand—"is extensive. But," she added significantly, "not complete."

He bristled. "And to round it off, you want *Cypripedium incognitum.*"

"Exactly. It is fitting, don't you think?"

"Anything but," he retorted. "*Cypripedium incognitum* may be down to one representative. It needs protection in situ. It doesn't need you, or anyone else, digging it up."

"Who said I will dig it up?" she asked mildly. "Perhaps all I wish to do is gather seeds from it and germinate them. That would be far better, would it not?"

"It would. But that villain you've hired to find it won't do that. He'll take the seeds *and* the plant itself to make sure he has a monopoly." In fact, Julian decided, that was probably what Adelheid would do, too. She, like Géraud, would want sole rights.

"Mmm-um. You know, you should really reconsider my offer. It is still open. And already I have told you I will pay very well whoever brings me *Cypripedium incognitum.*"

"Oh, that's your game, is it? You want to play Géraud and me off against one another. I suppose this is your idea of fun?"

"But isn't it sensible? Why have only one person looking for a thing when you can have two? And since you are looking for it anyway, why not get paid to do it? Look, tomorrow I go on a little trip. I will be away some days. You have time to think it over."

"Off to plunder more orchids?"

She was unperturbed. "Not at all. Everything I do according to regulations. In fact, I am going to Turkey for a conference where we will consider the plight of Anatolian orchids, ground up for the Turkish drink and ice cream industries."

He stared at her in surprise. "Salep?" The thought that she, too, might be a proponent of the ban on salep stunned him.

"Ah. You know it? Salep drink is very popular, and ice cream in Turkey is not ice cream without salep. Personally, I find it makes too thick and ropy the texture, but the Turks have always made their ice cream with it, and they love it. So I will listen to them talk about starch substitutes and better ways of harvesting orchids and so on. Then I will make a little field trip, and I will bring back many dozens of plants—"

"You're digging them up?" Julian inquired hostilely.

"*Nein.* A research colleague supplies them. Don't worry. It is in the name of science, and they will have the best of care. I have my own specially adapted vehicle for transporting the darlings."

He stared at her, incredulous. "You're driving all the way to Turkey?"

She gave him a look that told him he was being silly and went on: "This colleague asks me to run experimental trials on root damage recovery in *Ophrys* and *Orchis* genera. Maybe you know the country people in Turkey harvest orchids for salep by taking the fattest root of each plant they dig up? If the orchid is properly handled, it can regenerate."

Julian was momentarily without reply. Adelheid Besser, champion of sustainability? It was a side to her he had not suspected and did not quite believe.

"I return on May 6. Give me your answer then. Unless, of course, you want to accept now." She added with playful malice, "Or perhaps you are afraid of being beaten at your own game? Géraud is sure he will find the orchid first, you know."

"Géraud?" Julian scoffed. "That robber couldn't find his own two feet on a bright day. But I told you already. I'm not interested. And if I were you, I wouldn't put my faith in Géraud Laval. You can't trust him, you know. He's absolutely unscrupulous."

"And you?" She regarded him blandly. "He says you are a fraud. So tell me, Monsieur Wood, who should I choose between you, the robber or the charlatan?"

It was the second time that day that Julian nearly hit someone. He turned on his heel and stomped away. When he reached his van, he glowered at the Kangoo parked beside it. He could see that the cargo area inside was fitted out with shelves and what looked like growth lights. Undoubtedly, it was also equipped with some wizard system of climatization as well. Adelheid's sodding specially adapted vehicle.

By the time he had started up his engine and was roaring out the gate, his anger had dissipated and he was overcome with a feeling of sheer desperation. Against those two, his orchid was in real jeopardy. He saw them bearing down on it with shovel and spade and cursed himself that the only way he could see to prevent this awful outcome was to kill both of them, or at least break Géraud's legs.

Julian was still seriously plotting some degree of incapacitation to the man when he turned onto the main road. A black Mercedes was parked ahead of him on the verge. He slowed, glancing at the driver as he went past. It gave him an unpleasant shock to realize that the remarkable face that stared back at him belonged to none other than Ton-and-a-Half's hit man Serge.

The recognition triggered a vague memory of a dark vehicle falling in behind him at some point on his way to Adelheid's house. With a prickling of fear, Julian stamped on the accelerator, causing the van to lunge clumsily forward. A few minutes later, after he had passed through Queyssac, and with nothing but a clear stretch of road behind him, he was puzzled to conclude that Serge was not following him after all. But he still did not feel entirely safe.

35

"Me?" Donny put two large fingers to his chest and looked surprised.

"Just give me a straight answer," said Mara.

She had found Donny home alone, Daisy having left for New York a few days earlier. The big man waved her toward the sofa and sat down on it himself. The leather seat sighed audibly as it received his weight.

"Look, what's this all about? You want a drink?"

"No thanks. It's about this"—Mara waved a brochure at him—"and the fact that it's happening in my face. Are you Montfort-Izawa? Are you behind this golf course?"

The look of surprise now had a bland quality to it. She knew that she had guessed correctly, and that he was about to lie.

"Me?" he said again. He did not even glance at the brochure. "Montfort-Izawa? You gotta be kidding. Mara, I'm small fry. M-I's a big outfit. It's got French and Japanese backing up the yingyang. And, don't tell anyone I said so"—he leaned forward and lowered his voice, even though there was no one else to hear—"maybe some serious Hong Kong money as well."

"For someone who's not involved, you know a lot about it," Mara accused. Away from Daisy, he had lost his anxious, conciliatory air. He was more himself, more relaxed, certainly sneakier, she thought.

"We-ell"—he writhed a little, and the leather squeaked—"maybe I had something to do with getting them interested in the idea. I mean, I used to pro golf. I know the game, I know the courses, I know the market. So maybe I give them a piece of advice every now and then. Technical stuff. Most people don't know squat about green layout. But that's as far as I go."

"In other words, you're designing the course for them."

"Did I say that? Call me a consultant. A kind of golf course architect. That's your field, isn't it, architecture? Look, it was bound to happen sooner or later. They're golf crazy, those Japanese. Do you know the minute they break ground here, there'll be planeloads of Tokyo corporate execs ready to fly out here for a week of golf? It's cheaper than trying to join a club in Japan. Even if you can ante up for the membership, you still can't get green time. And it's not just them. You've got the Germans and the Brits, to say nothing of Americans. The Dordogne is crying out for a top-notch, championship-standard course."

"Top-notch how? Julian says there's no way you can build eighteen holes on so little land. He says the configuration of it is all wrong."

Donny laughed and threw his hands up. "I can tell neither one of you is a golfer. Mara, it's amazing what you can do with smart design. A little cut and fill here, the use of double fairways like at St. Andrews—"

"You're actually planning to build the entire course on 40 hectares?"

"We-ell. Look, take the case of Japan. Nobody's shorter on space than the Japanese. So what do they do? They build vertical. They have escalators taking you up and down to different levels. You gotta hand it to them. Smart." He tapped his forehead.

"Listen." He put his hands on his knees. "I can see you're upset about this. And jeez, the last thing I'd want to do is lose a friend—"

Hah! Mara almost interjected aloud.

"But let me tell you, it'll do wonders for the value of your property. How many folks can say they overlook the eighteenth hole?"

"I don't want to overlook the damned eighteenth hole," Mara cried out angrily.

"Well, think of the bigger picture. A scheme like this'll pump up the regional economy. Provide jobs, generate income. It's supply meeting demand, know what I mean? I should tell you, the project has a lot of local backing. A whole bunch of people like the idea. You gotta go as the world turns, Mara. You can't stop progress."

"I don't call it progress to have a commercial development bang in my sightline."

"Whoa, Mara, this isn't some strip mall we're talking about. This is a world-class course. Golfers aren't hoodlums. They're good people, they dress great, the kind of folks you'd be proud to have over for dinner. But if it's your privacy you're worried about, tell you what. I can have a word. Maybe suggest they leave a little tree screen between you and the action."

She nearly screamed at him. "That's supposed to make me happy? You're clear-cutting the entire forest, and a little tree screen is supposed to make it all right?"

"No way." He was offended. "The trees stay. Only they'll be thinned a bit to make way for the condos. After all, it's the wooded setting that makes them attractive."

"Thinned? How reassuring. And there's another thing. Golf courses are environmentally unfriendly."

"Who says?"

"Julian."

"Well, there I gotta tell you, Julian is way behind the times. The Big E is very much on the radar screen for golf courses nowadays, and this one will use environmentally friendly everything: drought- and pest-resistant grass, recycled glass instead of sand bunkers, minimal chemicals, and minimal use of water. Besides, we got our own water source. That reassure you?"

"Not at all. Anyway, it's not just the golf course. It's the condos. Where are you going to put them?"

"We-ell"—again he writhed a little—"that's down the road a ways. Phase II, if I remember rightly."

"But they'll be going on sale in the New Year. You can get a two-bedroom condo for an early-bird price of 350,000 euros, plus time-share privileges." She played her trump card. "It's the Gaillards' land, isn't it?"

He blinked. "Not following you."

"Donny, don't play dumb. I think you—Montfort-Izawa—are angling to get it. Do they have some kind of agreement to buy Joseph's land?"

He shook his head. "Look, Mara, I'm just their golf consultant. I'm not privy, so to speak, to their business plan." He looked absolutely sincere and segued into another subject. "Speaking of which, how is old Joseph? Daisy and I were talking about him just the other night. Doing okay?"

"Very," she said stiffly, recalling uncomfortably the old man's self-congratulatory cackle at Julian's debacle. "He's found a very nice live-in caregiver. She starts on Saturday."

"Well, that's just great. Daisy, as you know, worries about him a lot. Overly, I think, but that's just Daze. Underneath the spit and polish, she's a real marshmallow. Say"—he rose—"you sure I can't get you something? How about a nice glass of muscat?"

This time she accepted. She still had one more thing on her agenda. He bustled off into the kitchen.

"I want to talk to you about Christine Gaillard," she said when he returned with a chilled bottle and two large goblets.

"Who?"

"You know very well who. Joseph's daughter."

"Oh," he said. "Sure." He poured and sat down again. "What about her?"

"Does Montfort-Izawa have some kind of understanding with her?"

"What do you mean?" He set the bottle directly on the glass table. No ceramic cooler this time.

"I want to know if Montfort-Izawa has entered into an agreement with Christine to buy her father's land."

"With Christine?" He looked taken aback. Then he shrugged and showed her a pair of upheld palms. "Can't help you there. If I knew, I'd tell you. But I honestly don't know. And that's really all I got to say on the matter." He took a gulp of wine and slid off in another direction. "By the way, did you hear that rhyming burglar hit another house?" He grinned. "You gotta credit the guy. He's got a real sense of humor. I mean, it's pretty damned funny when you think about it."

Mara glared at him. "Prudence Chang doesn't think so. You know Prudence, don't you?"

"Who doesn't know Prudence?"

"Her house was one of the ones hit."

He paused, mid-sip. "Shit. I didn't know. That's too bad." His expression was properly regretful. "I didn't mean to imply I condone housebreaking, don't get me wrong. Besides, one thing leads to another. People get too confident, they tend to up the action. So far, this guy has B and E'd empty houses. There's been no violence. But what's to stop him from getting careless, going in where someone's at home? No telling what might happen then." He drained his goblet and put it down with a little chatter of glass on glass.

"What I say is everybody needs good security." He looked around him. "I'm thinking of wiring this place. And you ought to think about it, too. Back home we got Armed Response. Anyone so much as touches a window, the whole shebang goes up in noise and lights, the heavy artillery comes roaring in. We take that kind of thing seriously, let me tell you. If you're interested, I can probably get you a 30 percent discount on a damned good alarm system. Say, you want a top-up?"

It was a pointless question since she had hardly touched her wine. He was not thinking of refills or house alarms, however. Mara saw his eyes stray to her bare legs. A speculative look came over his face. It was furtive, like the shadow of something whisking around a corner.

"You know," he said, moving slightly closer to her on the sofa. "I'm really glad we had this little talk. Gives us a chance to iron out our little differences, get to know each other better."

She set her glass down and rose abruptly.

"No thanks, Donny. I'm on my way."

As the French put it, *When the cat's away, the mice will dance.*

•

One down, one to go, she thought as she drove out of Grives in the direction of Les Faux. Donny had not told her much that she did not already know or suspect. Now she was off to try her luck with Christine. Take the matter back to its source.

As she made her way cross-country, her mind shifted to Julian, and she composed another mental email:

>*I'm worried, Patsy. He's been gone four days. Our Time Outs never last this long, a couple of days at most, whatever he needs to work in his garden, catch up on his affairs. I mean, I've always understood his need for space. But what gets me is his silence. You'd think at least he could have returned my call.*<

She remembered the way they had parted—she laughing hysterically, he leaving Joseph's house, indignant and with a sore head. Had he gone back to Grissac simply to nurse his bruises? To be alone so he could continue beating himself up for things he could not help? To escape Madame Audebert? It really was a shame he couldn't get on with the woman.

>*No way, kid!* Patsy's image rose up before her, knuckles on hips, hair fairly crackling from her head. *You can't slide past on that one. Be honest. For months now you've been using old Audebert's complaints to cover your own gripes with Julian's mess. Heck, instead of standing up to the* femme de ménage *from hell, which you should have done, you ducked. Shame on you.*<

Mara threw a hand up.

>*Okay, okay. You're right. I'll give you that. But a relationship needs intimacy, and we both know that kind of thing is definitely not Julian's long suit. He has a lot of good qualities. He's kind, he's a good friend and a great lover. But he keeps me at arm's length. For example, he says, "I want to be with you." But he's never said those three little words: I love you. And of course, we never talk about marriage. What is it about him that lets me in so far but no farther?*<

To this, Patsy made no reply.

"Face it." Mara turned to her dog since Patsy was no longer answering. "Julian's passion is orchids. He lives to find his *Cypripedium.* His feelings for me are of another order. That's how it is. I should have learned by now not to try to rush an orchid hunter or compete with a flower." Jazz, dozing on the passenger seat, opened a bleary eye.

"It's like we're at a crossroad," she went on, and saw that she had come to one literally. She braked to let a tractor bounce past.

Jazz roused himself enough to let out a sleepy *woof.*

"I can't see my way forward, and I don't want to go sideways. So what does that leave?" The disheartening thought assailed her: could this Time Out be Julian's way of going back, a withdrawal into an old routine that had worked for them once, Friday-night dinners at Chez Nous, weekends together but weekdays apart, each living his or her own separate life?

"Well, maybe that's what it's come to," she addressed the back of Jazz's broad head sadly. "Just you and me again, boy."

•

Christine was working in the courtyard when Mara arrived. Alice, Mara assumed, was off with the sheep. There was no invitation to go inside this time. They stood in the angle formed by the house and the barn, and Mara got straight to the point.

"I've just come to tell you that I know what you're up to, Christine. I won't go to the police, but only on condition that you agree to two things. First, there must be no more attempts on your father's life or his sanity. Leave him alone. If I ever see you near the house, I'll report you. Second, end all negotiations with Montfort-Izawa. You father wants to live out his days where he is, and the land isn't yours to sell. Not yet anyway, and not for a long time if I have anything to do with it."

Christine, who had been thinning out a mass of lilies of the valley, stood up. She drove the pitchfork she had been using into the ground and stared at Mara. "What Montfort-Izawa? What land are you talking about? And why would I want to harm my father?" She sounded angry but also genuinely puzzled.

"Oh, come on," Mara burst out. "I know Montfort-Izawa is the consortium that's developing the golf course adjoining my and your father's properties. I know they need land, and you need money. I expect you and Alice are hip deep in debt. Your father is sitting on 45 hectares that become yours when he dies. How much has Montfort-Izawa offered you for it if you can complete a sale to them in a timely manner?"

Again there was silence, but only long enough for Christine to gather breath and expel it in a hearty laugh.

"*Vous êtes folle, non?* You don't know what you're talking about. I have no claim on my parents' property. I already told you, *they* broke with *me,* not the other way around. If you want it spelled out, they not only rejected what I am, they cut the final tie. They disinherited me."

It was Mara's turn to laugh. "Don't bullshit me, Christine. I'm familiar enough with French law to know they couldn't have. People can't disinherit their children of property."

"They can if they sell out. My parents sold their land years ago. In 1985. It's no different from disinheriting me. I have nothing to gain from my father's death, except maybe a few sticks of furniture he might choose to leave me, certainly not enough to pay our debts here. If you don't believe me, ask his *notaire,* Maître Joffre. He handles all of my father's business."

•

Mara could not get an appointment to see Maître Joffre until the end of the week. He received her at his ancient mahogany desk in a gloomy, high-ceilinged office. He looked as dry and dusty as the files and other paraphernalia around him. However, his computer equipment was disjunctively in the twenty-first century: an ergonomic keyboard and a slim, wide-screen monitor more up-to-date than Mara's own. She wondered if it had been forced on him by his pleasant, efficient daughter who acted as the cabinet's secretary-cum-receptionist. The new technology could not have been his idea; he was obviously uncomfortable with it and typed with only two fingers.

"I found Christine Gaillard," she told him.

Maître Joffre raised eyebrows that reminded Mara of pale,

shaggy caterpillars. The look in his eyes, however, told her that he had known all along where Christine was.

"And she told me her parents' land was sold in 1985. She said I could check with you if I wanted confirmation."

At first he was absolutely unwilling to discuss another client's affairs. Probably the only reason he did not ask her to leave directly was that she was also his client.

"Just tell me if it's true," Mara pressed. She did not explain her reasons for asking. "Yes or no."

In the end, he gave her a surprising piece of information. The Gaillards' house and property had not been sold outright but *en viager,* that is, a sale in which the balance of the price, after a down payment, was computed as a monthly installment to be paid out during the seller's lifetime. Maître Joffre, moving quickly from the particular to the general, became more communicative. *Viagers,* he explained, typically involved elderly property owners, often a couple in need of cash, who sold their property but retained the right of continued occupancy and usufruct. Theirs were the lives named in the contract, and the installments were receivable on a joint life and survivor basis. In such cases, the sale was deemed to be complete only upon the death of both spouses. A critical aspect of a sale *en viager,* Maître Joffre said with a wintry smile, was that it necessarily involved an element of risk. In short, it was a bit of a crapshoot. Purchasers gambled that the sellers would die sooner rather than later, thus ending the installments. Sellers gambled that they would live a long time to enjoy the income from *la rente viagère* at the expense of the buyer and in the comfort of their own home. The only way a buyer could get out of his obligations or terminate the *viager* was to sell it to someone else or to include a clause, called a *rachat de la rente,* in the original sales contract. This allowed the buyer to pay a certain capital sum and force the seller out. Without such a clause, the buyer had to wait until the seller's death.

But who had bought the Gaillards' property *en viager,* the *notaire* would not disclose.

"I think, Madame Dunn, I have said more than enough," he murmured with a fine pursing of the lips. He fidgeted, signaling that he wanted her to go.

Mara did some quick thinking. If not Christine, there was one other person who had an interest in the Gaillards' land; who had admitted an involvement with Montfort-Izawa; who, if he were the purchaser, would now have an interest in Joseph's quick demise; and who, she remembered, believed that Joseph had a weak heart.

She took a deep breath. "At least tell me this. Was the buyer Donny O'Connor?"

Maître Joffre drew himself up. He gave her a stony look.

"No," he said severely. "It was not."

•

Mara left weighed down by the realization that nothing was as it seemed. Christine had no motive to kill her father because she had no claim to the land. Donny's tie with Montfort-Izawa might have given him a motive, but he was not the purchaser of the Gaillards' *viager.* No one had pushed Amélie down the Two Sisters' stairs, and the monster was in Joseph's head after all. So where did this leave her?

In need of a hot bath, a stiff drink, and some decent food.

That night she made a simple omelet with fresh chives harvested from the kitchen garden that Julian had started below the terrace. To her surprise, it did not burn or go rubbery, as her omelets were inclined to do. It rose plump and light in the pan, crisping slightly at the edges. She ate it with a slab of dense country bread and quite a bit of wine. Jazz got a portion. The first food Julian had ever cooked for her had been an omelet. It really was too bad, she thought with a pang, that he wasn't around to share this one with her.

• 36 •

Mara parked outside Chez Nous that Friday evening in a high state of expectation. She had not seen or heard from Julian for nearly a week. She felt immeasurably let down as she pushed through the bead curtain of the bistro to see that he was not there, that she was, in fact, the first to arrive.

>*Stop worrying, kid,* Patsy's voice spoke up in her head. *He's never on time, and you know it.*<

She sat down at their usual table, exchanged brief pecks with Paul, ordered a kir royal, and settled down to wait. Jazz walked around, greeting the other diners, then flopped down in his usual spot in front of the bar.

Loulou turned up a few minutes later. They embraced, and she could see right away that he was primed with news.

"I've heard via the grapevine," he said confidentially, lowering an eyelid. "The lads may have a lead on the rhyming burglar. In fact, they may be closing in on him even as we speak."

Paul reappeared. The men shook hands, and Loulou ordered a pastis. He said no more until it arrived. Mara knew better than to hurry him. The chubby ex-cop liked to keep his audience dangling.

"You know, I have always thought from the beginning"—he smacked his lips around his first sip—"that there had to be some common element to these burglaries. Now what do you suppose it is?"

Mara drained her drink. "I would have thought the MO was enough. Unoccupied houses, objets d'art, the poems."

Loulou shook his head. "Turns out all of the burgled houses are insured by the same agency, Assurimax."

"Oh?"

"The thinking is, the burglar is an employee, someone able to access the company's client databases. That explains how he was always able to select houses worth hitting, and it explains the scattered pattern of the break-ins."

"An inside job?" Unwillingly, Mara thought of Sébastien Arnaud, his puppy dog eyes and Airedale hair, his immense likableness, his six children. Did he also have an aptitude for doggerel and computers? She fiddled with her empty glass. "Do they have a suspect?"

Loulou grinned and sat back in his chair. "Oh, I wouldn't be surprised if the gendarmes know exactly who it is and are just playing the fellow out to catch him in flagrante. And now," he demanded jovially. "What about you? What new *criminalité* have you discovered this week?" His tone was not entirely teasing. He had come to expect nothing less of her and Julian. He signaled to Paul for another round of drinks.

"If you really want to know," she said, and went on to tell him about Montfort-Izawa, the Gaillards' land, the *viager,* and Joseph's night visitors.

Loulou rubbed his nose with a knuckle. "Tricky things, *viagers.* You've surely heard about the case of Jeanne Calmont? Made national headlines a few years ago. She lasted to 126, outliving the buyer, and the buyer's heirs were stuck with continuing the payments. And there was another case right here in the Dordogne. Fellow bought *en viager* from a widow in her seventies. Well, the purchaser is now a widower himself in his eighties, and the old dear is 103, still going strong and likely to outlast him. Fortunately, the two get on like a house on fire. He visits every Sunday and brings her flowers."

"Sweet," Mara murmured absently.

"Speaking of flowers, where's Julian? He's very late."

Six days late, by Mara's count, with no attempt to contact her. Nor had she tried calling him again. It was as if they had entered into some kind of non-communication agreement. Mara felt a knot of anxiety tighten in her gut.

"Um, I'm sure he's just been held up," she said.

Paul placed another pastis before Loulou, and a second kir royal in front of Mara. He asked if Julian was planning to show. It was going on for nine.

"Maybe you could order now," he said bluntly. "Mado wants to close the kitchen pretty soon."

They both chose the thirty-seven euro menu. Mara glanced out the window. A fog was gathering. No van came rocking to a halt outside the restaurant, no figure hurried toward the door. Julian had never failed to appear for their Friday nights at the bistro, except on the night of the storm, of course, and she had been with him then. Even if he were coming from a job at the other end of the region, even if he had sometimes turned up looking a little soiled because he'd had no time to run home and clean up, he still made it. Could he have forgotten? She was almost certain he was staying away purposely. But how could he just do that, without a word of explanation to her? She dug in her bag for her phone and then thought better of it. Julian absolutely must not think she was hounding him.

Loulou was studying her.

"Is everything all right?" he asked. "Between the two of you?" His voice had a kindly solicitousness to it that made Mara's reply catch in her throat. Loulou reached across to take her hand. She burst into tears.

•

Julian woke with a start in the old leather armchair in which he had fallen asleep. *Merde,* it was past nine o'clock, and he should have been at Chez Nous more than an hour ago. There was no time to change, no time to shave. He had meant to arrive on time—in fact, early, to have a few moments alone with Mara to say whatever it took to put his unexplained absence right. "Look, I'm sorry I haven't been in touch. Awfully busy." It would have sounded lame, he knew. She wouldn't have been convinced, but he had hoped it would do for the moment. Now, he wasn't sure she would even still be there for him to sound lame to. He gave a sharp whistle for Bismuth and ran for the van.

•

Mara's tears were drying up, but she occasionally hiccuped into the capacious handkerchief Loulou had gallantly offered her.

"Maybe it's my imagination. Maybe Kazim's death is what's still getting him down. But somehow I think it's more than that. The problem is, he won't talk. I'm afraid . . ." she trailed off.

"You're afraid . . . ?" prompted Loulou in a fatherly way.

"I—I don't know how well this living together is working out. I think"—the tears welled up again—"I'm afraid Julian wants to break things off."

"Ah, *non*," Loulou assured her vigorously. "Julian cares very much for you. He would never do that."

"I think he would. He's essentially a loner."

"He is lonely," said Loulou wisely. "As are you. There is a difference, you know."

Was that all that bound them, Mara wondered, their common sense of isolation? How did the song go? Two lonely people together? France, for all that it was the land of *amour*, could be an unnerving place for a single expatriate.

Just then Bismuth bounded in the door. He was followed a moment later by his owner.

"About time, *mec*." Paul slapped forearms together with Julian in a kind of wrestling hold.

"Sorry, I fell asleep."

Hugging, Mara had read somewhere, was good for you. It released oxytocin into the system and gave you a feeling of well-being. Hastily, she blew her nose, stood up, and hugged Julian hard, taking in his familiar smell, the aura of dampness that he brought with him from outside. A great sense of relief filled her. He had fallen asleep. It was as simple as that. It was almost as if the past anxious week had not really happened.

Julian, who had been braced for testy comments about tardiness and poor communication, was pleasantly surprised at the warmth of Mara's embrace. He returned it enthusiastically. She seemed so happy to see him. But why was she crying? They both held on, enjoying their arms around one another. The Time Out, their bodies said, was over, even though their minds puzzled over how they had got there.

Loulou cleared his throat. The two of them sat down. Mara's eyes were still a little moist, and her face had gone quite pink. Julian looked both pleased and slightly flustered. His right cheek bore the impression of whatever he had been sleeping on. He waved aside an aperitif and ordered straight away. He was starving. And exhausted. Gobbling a piece of bread, he told them about his run-in with Géraud. As a result, he had been getting up early to put in a few hours searching out likely habitats for his orchid before proceeding with the less interesting but equally pressing business of earning a living. And then continuing with the search after work until the light failed. It was like holding down two full-time jobs, and the orchid search part of it, as Mara well knew, involved leagues of walking.

"I don't suppose you could help me?" he turned to her. "I hate to ask, but now that Géraud knows I'm looking around Aurillac, the orchid will be at his mercy if he finds it before I do. It would go a lot faster with two."

Mara's chin went up. A small voice, aggrieved, rang out in her head. While she had anguished, he had not communicated with her because he was too busy searching for his orchid? She took a deep breath to expel the "no" that was already forming in her mouth. And then she saw his face, boyish with hope and yet doubtful. They both knew that the last time she had gone on an orchid hunt with him she had been charged by a wild boar. She brushed aside remembrances of past searches, opted for generosity, and said, "I wouldn't think of letting you out on your own."

His look of amazed delight made her feel pleasantly heady. Or maybe it was the champagne cocktails. They agreed on a hunt the next day.

Then Julian told them about his encounters with Adelheid and Serge.

Loulou raised his head sharply. "You're sure it was Serge following you?"

"Positive," Julian said with his mouth full with bread. "I was on my way to Adelheid's house, and this car was behind me. I didn't pay any attention to it then, but it was waiting for me on the roadside when I came out. A black Mercedes. I got a good look at the driver. There's no mistaking that face. Not to worry, though." He swallowed. "I managed to shake him in the end."

"But how does he know your car?" Mara asked. "Julian, I *am* worried."

He considered the question. "Good point. Unless . . . I don't know. There was a sneaky little bloke who followed me to my van the day I was asking around after Kazim in Périgueux. Maybe he was one of Luca's boys."

"This isn't good," muttered Loulou. "If Serge knows your car, he probably knows a lot more about you. Where you live, for example. I'd say Serge was tailing you from the time you left your house yesterday morning."

Julian's eyebrows jerked upward. Had *both* Géraud and Serge been following him? It would have been comical, except that Serge did not look as if he had much of a sense of humor. Or—the thought struck him forcefully—had Géraud's unwelcome presence actually saved him from something more unpleasant than a cross-country chase?

"Well, no harm done," Julian said uneasily. He reached for another piece of bread and watched Paul hurry by, carrying platters of *steak-frites,* sizzling and mouth-wateringly appetizing, as only Mado could make them. "God, I'm ravenous." He had ordered the same thing, and this teaser—the smell of grilled meat and fried potatoes—was almost more than he could bear.

Mara gave him her news. As she told him about the *viager* and the information she had been able to pry out of Maître Joffre, Julian's eyes strayed to a neighboring table where a woman was breaking into a steaming pastry shell.

"Hmm." He stroked his beard thoughtfully. "I'd say that leaves both Christine and Donny well out of it. All the same, it might be worthwhile finding out who did purchase the *viager*—" He broke off in eager anticipation. At last Paul had come out of the kitchen and was heading their way. "Just because it's not Donny, it doesn't follow that someone else isn't interested in getting rid of Joseph to sell his land to Montfort-Izawa."

Loulou nodded. "*C'est logique.* A very good point."

Someone else? Mara recalled the *notaire*'s face as he told her that Donny was not the purchaser. His expression had been stony. Or stonewalling? The closed look of a man who shaves the truth very fine, of someone whose practiced answers hid as much as they revealed. Mara froze, her drink halfway to her lips. Suddenly she had a pretty good idea who the buyer was. Not Donny. Daisy. She was the one with the money, and she could have made the purchase in her own name. Which meant that the O'Connors had a stake in Joseph's life after all. All that feigned concern and the talk about getting him into care was so much eyewash. Then a horrible thought struck her. She jumped up, pulling Julian out of his chair just as Paul was placing their first course on the table.

"Hey, just a minute," Julian objected, indignant at having his meal snatched from him, or more precisely, him from it.

"Come on," she shouted, heedless that everyone in the restaurant was gawking at them. "Sorry Loulou, sorry Paul, this can't wait." She bellowed for the dogs and dragged Julian with her out the door.

"Do you mind telling me what this is all about?" Julian demanded as she started up the engine.

Mara said breathlessly, "It's about the fact that I'll bet the whole damned farm that Daisy owns the *viager*, and I stupidly told Donny that Joseph's live-in caregiver starts tomorrow. That's like saying they have until tonight to finish the old boy off!"

•

It was half past ten when they reached the house. Joseph was sitting in the kitchen watching television while eating a flan that Suzanne Portier had prepared for him. She had brought him vegetable soup and homemade bread, a slice of roast pork, boiled cabbage and potatoes, and the flan. The flan was stuffed with raisins. He had eaten half of it right after his dinner and saved the other half for a late-night movie he wanted to see. It had girls in it, and a certain amount of nudity. He had never been able to watch his choice of television when Amélie was alive. With her, it was always early to bed, early to rise, and she had closely controlled the programs they viewed.

"'Course I'm all right," he said in reply to Mara and Julian's question as they burst in on him. His eyes lingered on the television screen. A woman had just stepped out of a shower, letting a towel fall away from her. He seemed to have forgotten about his monsters. "Why shouldn't I be?"

37

It is a night of mist, with no wind and no moon. Even the stars are dead. Everything lies wrapped in the kind of absolute obscurity that only occurs deep in the countryside. Here, no lamps illuminate empty streets, no traffic signals flash their mindless red–green cycles, no stain of neon bleeds through the drifting darkness.

The house inside is dark, too, and silent, except for the heavy ticking of the grandfather clock, spelling out the hours in its corner of the front room.

Outside the house, something moves. A pencil beam of light wavers through the hazelnut grove, points momentarily at the black switches of the fuse box in the wood hangar. Now it glances off the concrete surface of the terrace, focuses on the lock fixture of the back door. When the door swings open, the pencil beam moves within, sliding like a sly finger over the flagstones of the kitchen floor, illuminating the leg of a table, the worn flooring of the hallway. It slips across the threadbare carpet of the front room, where the old clock stands, pauses before the dark bulk of the sofa. Now it points back down the hall and glimmers on the handle of the bedroom door. The handle turns, as if of its own accord. And then the pencil beam goes out.

Something has come into the bedroom. It makes its presence known by a slight disturbance of the air, by a blackness that is denser than the blackness that surrounds it. The room pulses with its entry, as if it has been waiting to enclose this moment.

The sleeper lies motionless. The thing has crossed the intervening space to stand so near that its breathing enjoins with the breathing coming from the bed. Another displacement of air betrays movement. Carefully, a hand searches out the sleeper's face, touches skin.

There is a muffled cry. A roundhouse swing catches the thing a stunning blow. It reels back amid sounds of struggling, of furniture being overturned, of things crashing to the ground.

"For God's sake, Mara," Julian shouts. "Give us a bloody light, will you?"

In the sudden flare of the flashlight beam, Mara sees Olivier Rafaillac sprawled on the floor. He is wearing his padded nylon jacket over pajamas and is wrestling with a pair of legs that kick and thrash beneath him. Julian is lying across an expanse of black rubber poncho that covers a large, writhing body. He scrambles to a kneeling position, shifts his hold to grab the front of the poncho and jerks the body upright.

"All right, you bastard," he yells, fetching Donny O'Connor a mighty sock to the jaw. "Just what the hell do you think you're up to!"

•

"He came here to murder Joseph," Mara declared, pointing an accusing finger at Donny.

The pair of gendarmes who had answered their call looked doubtful. Mara told them about the attacks on Joseph and the pivotal importance of the Gaillards' land to the Montfort-Izawa development, in which she was sure Donny had more of an interest than he admitted. Julian explained that he and Mara had anticipated that Donny would make another attempt on Joseph that night. They had therefore bundled Joseph off to Olivier Rafaillac's house. Then they had enlisted Olivier's help and returned with him to lie in wait for Donny.

Donny's story was that he had come to the house to check up on Joseph because he had heard the old fellow had been troubled by nighttime prowlers. Of course he had a key. Why shouldn't he? His wife had bought the Gaillards' property *en viager* years ago. ("I knew it," Mara growled at Julian.) The Gaillards were practically family. Mara also had a key, he pointed out. So did just about everyone else in the neighborhood.

"If I'm supposed to be the monster that's been scaring Joseph, shouldn't I have some kind of costume?" Donny argued. "A mask? Fake fangs? A gorilla suit? So where's my Halloween outfit?"

"You're wearing it," said Mara, pointing at his poncho. She recalled Joseph's description of his first intruder. Big and black, he had said, with loose, rubbery skin. "All you needed to do was pull that over your head. In the dark, you'd look like the Blob."

"Give me a break," snorted Donny, touching a reddening welt on his jaw. "I'm gonna have you charged with assault."

Olivier confirmed most of Mara and Julian's account but admitted that he knew nothing about any land deals, nor had he exactly witnessed Donny attacking Joseph—Mara—in the bed. It had been too dark to see. He had merely followed Julian's order to jump anyone who came into the room. Monsieur O'Connor, as it turned out. Yes, he could confirm the fact that Joseph thought he was being terrorized. However, no one had really taken him seriously.

One of the gendarmes went with Olivier to his house to take down his statement and to get Joseph's version of events. The remaining gendarme searched Donny. He found a wallet, a wadded-up handkerchief, loose change, keys, a slimline flashlight of American make. Nothing that could be construed as a weapon.

"There's your weapon." Mara waved at a cushion lying on the floor. "It's from the sofa in the front room. He was planning to smother Joseph—me—with it."

"You're nuts," sputtered Donny.

"What's this?" the gendarme asked, unfolding a piece of paper he had pulled out of Donny's jacket pocket. In the next moment, the officer became quite excited. He read it aloud:

Hee Hee Hee
Hah Hah Hah
Cherchez partout
Vous ne me trouverez pas

Translated, with a little poetic licence, it read

Hah Hah Hah
Hee Hee Hee
Look everywhere
You won't find me

The gendarme stiffened like a game dog on the scent. "Monsieur," he addressed Donny, "I'm afraid you'll have to come with me. There are a number of questions we would like to ask you."

•

At the local gendarmerie where their statements were formally recorded, Mara protested loudly to the brigade commander.

"Why won't you listen? Donny O'Connor isn't the rhyming burglar. He went to the house not to steal but to murder Joseph Gaillard. I think he planned to pass the crime off as a burglary gone wrong, and he was going to leave a bogus poem behind to throw you off the track."

"She's crazy," Donny denied. "I didn't write any goddamn poem, and if it wound up in my pocket, she planted it there to land me in it."

Mara threw up her hands. "Can't you see the MO is all wrong? The rhyming burglar is selective. He chooses unoccupied houses with things of value in them. Joseph's house is very much occupied and it has nothing worth stealing." She made a last desperate attempt to convince. "The poem. If Donny O'Connor really is the rhyming burglar, he would've come up with something a lot better, don't you think? The thing doesn't scan. It's inconsistent. Before the burglar used *tu.* Here he switches to *vous.* He spells *Hah Hah* and *Hee Hee* the English way. In French it would be *Ha Ha* and *Hi Hi.* Not only is this poem not up to usual standards, it's plain awful!"

"I've been set up," Donny insisted.

Nevertheless, he remained in custody. Officers hurried past the room where his ongoing interrogation was taking place. An excited buzz filled the hallways. The news spread quickly: the gendarmes had finally caught their man.

•

The sky was bright with morning by the time Mara and Julian's statements were complete and they were told they could go. Mara, with Julian hurrying in her wake, strode furiously out of the gendarmerie and plunged into the nearest café in search of a badly needed jolt of caffeine.

"He's going to get away with it," she fumed as they stumbled into an empty booth. They had not seen bed for twenty-four hours, and both looked drained. "The gendarmes can't see past their housebreaker, and the bastard is going to get away with it."

"It's because the case for Donny as burglar looks stronger than Donny as murderer." Julian leaned his head wearily against the padded wall of the booth. The atmosphere in the café was warm and comfortable, the smell of coffee strong on the air. A few early patrons paused over steaming bowls of café au lait to glance their way.

"Say the O'Connors work as a team," Julian went on. "They

get themselves invited to people's houses. Daisy knows antiques. She does the selecting—you saw the way she scoped your front room when she was there—Donny does the grunt work. Plus, she's a natural for moving the stolen articles." He yawned gustily. He recalled that he and Mara had agreed to go orchid hunting that day. At the moment, he wanted nothing more than to get horizontal for about ten hours.

Gloomily, Mara admitted the force of Julian's reasoning. She thought angrily of Prudence's bronze animal pieces, her Lalique lamps, her Degas statuette, probably sold by now to purchasers in New York, Philadelphia, London, and Paris.

"All right," she conceded. "Maybe the O'Connors are behind the robberies as well. But that doesn't change the fact that Donny went to the house last night to murder Joseph. The police just don't get it."

She had been repeating variations of this complaint for the last four hours. Fed up with it, Julian went to the bar for a newspaper. He had to settle for one of the regional weeklies, dating back a few days, but he did not mind. He had not had much chance to read the news of late.

"The problem is," he said, sitting down again and shaking the tabloid open, "we might have got him if you hadn't acted prematurely."

Mara stared at him. "If I hadn't *what?*"

"You clouted him too soon." Then he said, "I'll be damned." He folded the paper back to show Mara a photograph of a large woman standing on the deck of a boat. "That's her. Adelheid Besser. On board the Ropax *Bosporus I* on its maiden voyage to Istanbul. Says here it's the first of a new line of roll-on/roll-off vessels carrying freight as well as passengers and their vehicles between Marseille and Istanbul. Apparently it can do up to thirty knots an hour. So that's how she went."

Mara was not interested in Adelheid Besser or the Ropax *Bosporus I.*

"So what are you saying? I should have let him smother me?"

"At least given him a chance to attack you properly."

"Oh, thank you very much. Maybe you should have been the decoy. No doubt you would have done a better job."

"Hmm?" Julian had gone back to his reading. "Wouldn't have worked. My beard. Dead giveaway."

38

A few days later Daisy came to the house. Mara received her alone since Julian was out, still dealing with a client's hedge.

"Oh," said Mara a little nervously, as she opened the door. Was the woman going to scream at her? Attack her with well-manicured nails? Mara had, after all, accused her husband of attempted murder. No, she revised, as Daisy, in her perpetual cloud of scent, marched straight past her into the front room and sat down uninvited on the art deco sofa. She was dressed for the occasion: mid-heels, a tailored plum-colored linen suit, a blouse with a frilly collar—businesslike but conciliatory. She wanted something. Warily, Mara lowered herself into an armchair, one of a recently acquired pair of bergères.

"I came to tell you the police have released Donny." The Barbie doll fixed Mara with unblinking eyes that today had a cobalt hue. "Donny was absolutely out of the country during three of the break-ins. We both were, which puts him—and me, in case you were going there—out of the picture. And before you ask, the gendarmes have verified all this. I can also vouch for Donny being at home with me on the other four occasions."

"I'm more concerned about last Friday night and the other times he tried to frighten Joseph to death," Mara said, equally direct.

"Those incidents never happened," Daisy snapped. "These monsters you keep talking about don't exist. They're all in Joseph's head. Everyone knows he hallucinates. Look, I'm telling you Donny went over there simply to make sure Joseph was okay."

"At three o'clock in the morning?"

"He couldn't sleep. I was in New York, and he often can't sleep when I'm away. So he decided to go to the house and check things out. The police have cleared Donny of any suspicion of housebreaking."

"What about the poem the gendarmes found in his pocket?"

"He never wrote it, and the only way it got there is if you planted it. Look, I'm prepared to cut a deal with you. Drop your ridiculous accusation, and we won't have you prosecuted for trying to frame Donny. Tell the police you were mistaken. You know as well as I do that Donny would never try to harm Joseph."

It was as close as Daisy would ever get to pleading. Her makeup, Mara observed uncharitably, did not cover the age spots that were beginning to blotch her pale complexion. Papery skin stretched across jutting cheekbones to a narrow jaw. Her knees were knife-sharp and bloodless where they strained against her pantyhose, her wrists impossibly thin. She looked exhausted, as if she were held together by wires, but Mara did not feel sorry for her.

"Think again, Daisy. When scaring Joseph didn't work, and when your husband realized he was running out of time, he tried a more direct approach. He planned to make it look like a break-in, take whatever the Gaillards had of value, and leave the poem behind so the police could conclude it was a burglary turned violent. If we hadn't intervened, Joseph would be dead. There's a lot of land and money riding on Joseph's death, as I think you know."

"You're talking about the golf course? I know nothing about it. I don't get involved in Donny's business dealings. But I can tell you, if Donny needed the land, he'd get it, and he wouldn't have to kill Joseph for it. He'd find a way. Legally."

"No. The fact that Donny hasn't done so already tells me that he can't. You didn't have a *rachat de la rente* provision in your purchase contract, did you?"

"A what?"

"A clause allowing you to do a buyout. It would have let you pay Joseph off outright. Without it, you have to wait until Joseph dies before you can touch the land. Joseph has the right to stay where he is, and there's nothing either of you can do about it. He intends to take up raising sheep again, did he tell you?"

"That's ridiculous," Daisy snapped.

"Maybe, but it's his decision, and it's your tough luck. The Gaillards sold to you in 1985. That means you've been paying out annuities for over twenty years. You were probably wondering how much longer this was going to go on. Joseph is shaky and slow, but otherwise he's in good shape. And contrary to your belief, his heart is fine. He could last a long time. Easier and cheaper just to bump him off, don't you think?"

The blue eyes took on an arctic chill. Mara, a Canadian used to winter, discovered in that moment a new meaning of the term *cold burn.*

"I think you're despicable," Daisy said with a vehemence that made the tendons of her neck stand out like cords. "I care about Joseph almost as much as I cared about my father. I would never let any harm come to him. *Never,* do you understand?" Her sincerity was undeniable. Then she dispelled any growing sympathy Mara might have had for her by slapping the sofa seat.

"How much?"

"What?"

"This sofa. How much do you want for it? Name your price. Fifty? A hundred thousand?"

Mara's breath exploded from her in an incredulous laugh. "You think you can buy your way out of this?"

"I'm prepared to do what it takes to clear my husband of this outrageous charge. If I can't appeal to your common sense, what else can I do?"

"You can leave," Mara said, standing up abruptly. "I won't change my mind about Donny, and this conversation is over."

•

Mara was still feeling a little shaken over Daisy's visit when she met Sébastien Arnaud at Prudence's house later that afternoon. Their appointment was for two. She arrived on time. He was late, as usual.

"*Bonjour*," he hailed her as he climbed out of his car. "Have you been waiting long?"

One of his boys had been bitten by a dog, nothing more than a nip, but he'd had to catch the dog, find the owner, and then take the child for a tetanus shot. He looked as if he had been dragged backwards through the proverbial hedge. His hair seemed even more at odds with itself than usual, his jacket hung crookedly, his shirt was not quite tucked in. As he enveloped her hand in his big paw, Mara wondered how he managed to maintain his cheerfulness.

They inspected the repairs from the outside and then from the inside. The damaged pane had been replaced and the faulty shutters put right.

"Looks fine," said Sébastien, satisfied with the job.

"I heard," Mara said, choosing her words carefully, "that Assurimax is the insurer of all the houses that have been burgled. It must keep you busy."

"I'm always busy," Sébastien grinned. "But I'm the agent only for this and two of the other affected properties. The rest are out of my territory."

Mara breathed easier, but only a little. There was still Loulou's assertion that access to the company's databases was all the burglar needed to identify which houses had things worth stealing.

Sébastien went on to tell her that the claim settlements were a real headache because of the difficulty of valuing the objects that had been taken. Most, he suspected, were underinsured because they had appreciated over time, but that was the insuree's problem, except that the insurees generally tried to argue otherwise. Also, most of the owners were out of the country, which complicated matters. He was grateful that Mara was standing in for Prudence. It made his work easier.

"The burglar never takes paintings," she observed. "I wonder why."

Sébastien shrugged. "He never touches anything on the walls. Paintings, prints, tapestries, plaques, sconces. Some, like a couple of Picasso pencil sketches, were pretty valuable. Maybe he doesn't have a taste for them, or finds them hard to get rid of."

"And I don't see the point of the poems, apart from needling the police, do you?"

The agent chuckled. "The fellow has a sense of humor."

Something about the way he said it made Mara want to ask: "You don't by any chance like poetry, do you?"

But she did not.

•

Before they left, Mara checked the rest of the house. Everything was closed up tight. The refurbished Awful Wall stood bumpy and bare. She wondered what kind of covering Prudence was planning for it. A painting or anything rigid was impossible because of the uneven surface. A textile hanging might work, something that could be bracketed out at the top so that it would fall straight. Back home in Canada, modern handmade quilts were coming into their own as the new wall art. They cost a fortune. God forbid they should ever cover a bed. A quilt, she mused, would suit a country house like this. A motif of golds and browns would go well. The colors reminded her of something. She was thoughtful as they locked up behind them.

•

Toward the end of the day, Mara made a call to the Brames Gendarmerie. Adjudant Compagnon was warily interested in her question, but he did not have an answer. When he understood her reasons for asking, he agreed to have the matter looked into. It wasn't the kind of thing his officers would have necessarily noted. They, like the absent owners, were interested in what had been taken, not in what had been left. She got her answer two days later.

Then she called Prudence.

"Your repairs are done. Sébastien checked things out with me, and everything's fine."

"*Merci* a ton," said Prudence. "Nothing on my stolen goods?"

"Um, no." Her friend had obviously not heard that Donny had been charged and later cleared. "Prudence, what exactly are you planning to do with the Awful Wall?"

"The wall? Oh that," said Prudence. "I've commissioned a tapestry. I had someone in last fall to take measurements and talk about colors. It should be ready by the time I come back in June. Why do you want to know?"

39

The farm looked almost deserted when she arrived. She parked in the courtyard, told Jazz to stay, got out of the car, and went to knock on the door of the house. She waited. She banged harder. Everything was very quiet. The sheep were nowhere in view. Had Christine and Alice taken them to market? But a dusty, green van was parked alongside the barn. Or maybe they were out in the fields shearing the animals, or whatever people did with sheep in this season.

It did not surprise her to find the door unlocked when she tried it. People in the countryside rarely locked their doors.

"*Allo?* Anyone home?" she called as she entered. She stood once more in their sunny kitchen. Considerable progress had been made on the rust and ocher weaving. The day was hot. Mara felt thirsty from her drive so she helped herself to a drink of water at the sink, where dishes had been washed and neatly stacked to drain. Then, after a quick look into the courtyard, she began to snoop.

First, she snooped in the kitchen, and then in the room adjoining the kitchen, a kind of parlor-cum-office. There were shelves full of books and magazines. There was a desk, its drawers crammed with accounts ledgers that Mara scanned quickly. A cat lay on a daybed, regarding her with huge dilated eyes. Behind it, a yellow and green abstract tapestry decorated the wall. The woven signature at the bottom read *A. Lescuras.* Mara had already guessed that Alice would be the weaver. The colors suited her.

Next, she snooped in the rooms leading off a central hallway. The first held a television and a shabby sofa covered by a knitted throw. A variant of the *cache-misère.* The second was a bathroom with an adjoining toilet. The third was a bedroom. Mara liked the neat simplicity of it: more whitewashed walls, minimal furniture: a dresser, a chair, an armoire, and—the only touch of luxury—a brass queen-sized bed stacked with cushions and spread with a colorful tie-dyed cloth. A sunburst weaving hung over the head of the bed.

It was the shoes, organized on two slanted shelves, that made Mara suddenly and acutely conscious of her intrusion. They stood in pairs, worn and shaped to their wearers' feet—big, wide, serviceable (Christine's, Mara judged); narrower, more fanciful (Alice's). Mara had often thought that there was something terribly honest about shoes, and ultimately vulnerable, as if scuffed toes revealed some personal sadness, unevenly worn heels an imbalance of character.

She pulled open the dresser drawers. They gave off a scent of lavender. The armoire told her that Christine, whose larger, heavier garments hung to the left, preferred blues and greens, while Alice, on the right, favored brighter tones: yellow, magenta, orange. At the bottom of the armoire was a canvas tote. Mara unzipped it. What she found inside made her take a deep breath.

There was a stag, a hare, a wild boar, a prancing horse, and a greyhound. All in bronze, none bigger than her hand, each individually wrapped in tissue paper. She knew each piece well. They were Prudence's collection of eighteenth-century bronze *animalier.*

She sat back on her heels feeling very sorry for what she was about to do. The distant bleating of sheep alerted her. She zipped up the tote, tucked it under her arm, and ran. A moment later, she was speeding away down the road.

•

Mara's dilemma was that she liked them. In the space of thirty minutes, she had delved into their intimate life and had taken kindly to what she had seen. Except, of course, for the purloined bronzes.

Julian was out, so there was no one to talk to about her discovery, and for this problem she needed more than imagined emails from Patsy. Mara poured herself a large glass of red wine and sat down to work out what she should do.

An hour later, she made a telephone call.

"Christine?" she said when the Gaillards' daughter answered. "Mara Dunn. I want you to listen to me very carefully because I have something important to say. I've been to your house. I found what you had hidden in the bag in your armoire and—I took them. If you don't believe me, go and look." She paused, then plunged. "I know that you and Alice are the rhyming burglar."

As reply she got a brief silence, then snatches of muffled conversation, the scraping of a chair. Several moments later, Christine said, "All right." Her tone was interrogatory. *What now?* it seemed to say.

"Why did you hang on to them?" Mara felt both aggrieved and sorry. Aggrieved that the bronzes had been there for her to find, sorry that she now had to do something about her discovery.

"Are you recording this conversation or something?"

"Of course not. This is just between you and me."

Christine breathed deeply. "We didn't want to break them up. They're more valuable as a set, but the person we deal with wouldn't settle on a price."

"Who's the poet, you or Alice?"

Christine's laugh was deep. "Alice, of course. The game was getting too easy. She wanted to liven things up. She's a great one for livening things up, is Alice."

"Game? This was a game?"

"No," Christine responded heavily. "A necessity. We were in debt. We stood to lose the farm, our sheep, everything."

"And now?"

"We're not clear, but our financial profile is, shall we say, improving. Look," she broke off impatiently, "why are you calling? What do you intend to do?"

In fact, Mara was not sure. "I don't know. I should take this to the police. I haven't made up my mind."

"If you want money to keep quiet, we can't pay you. Unless, of course, we do a few more burglaries." Christine spoke with a bitter humor.

"*Bon Dieu,* I'm not trying to blackmail you." Mara was appalled that Christine would even think it. "I—I just wanted to let you know how things stand."

There was a silence. "I see." There was another interval of muffled conversation at the other end of the line.

"*Allo?*" Alice was suddenly on the phone. Her voice was teasing. "So you found the *animalier?* Good for you. But let me tell you something, *ma petite beezee-boddee*"—she said the word in a laughing parody of bad English—"the bag of bronzes, it is now with you. If you tell the gendarmes where you found them, it will be your word against ours. We will deny everything, of course. You won't be able to prove a thing. Fingerprints? I always wear gloves. If you handled them, the only fingerprints will be yours."

"Alice," Mara said wearily, "it's not just the bronzes. Once the police know who you are, they'll pry into every corner of your lives. They'll find someone who saw your vehicle near the burgled houses, they'll find who you use as a fence for the stolen property, and they'll follow up the critical link that they overlooked."

"What link?" Alice's voice for once lost its mocking assurance.

"Your tapestries. You've been in every one of the houses you and Christine burgled because you either did a wall hanging for the owner or discussed one. You work to commission, so you always go in to take measurements, talk about design and color, that kind of thing. You spotted the bronzes and the Laliques and the Degas dancer at Prudence Chang's house. And don't tell me you don't know Prudence, because you went to see her last September. I think the reason that you never took any paintings, even though some of them were quite valuable, was because you didn't want to call attention to the walls and the fact that five of the seven houses you robbed have an Alice Lescuras tapestry in them. The owner of the sixth house ordered something from you but in the end changed her mind. And you're weaving a tapestry for Prudence right now. I saw it on your loom."

•

Loulou's face, normally cheerful, darkened when he unzipped the tote and saw what was in it.

"Is this what I think it is? Where did you get them?"

Mara told him. They were sitting in the kitchen of his little house in Duras. She gulped the coffee he had made her. It was how she needed it: black and strong.

"They're all there, all the stolen bronzes. I don't know about the rest of Prudence's things. I assume Christine and Alice have sold them." Mara stared into the depths of her cup. "I'm in an awful fix, Loulou. If I tell the police, Christine and Alice will go to prison."

"*Mais oui,* that is the idea, usually."

"I can't bring myself to do it."

"You have to. If you don't, you'll be an accessory to the crime."

She shook her head. "Christine's had a rough life. I'm sure she and Alice did it out of desperation. They were in debt, the sheep farm wasn't paying, and the only extra money they brought in was from Alice's weaving. How many tapestries can she make in a year?"

Loulou knuckled his nose. He crossed his arms and looked up at the ceiling. He wagged his head from side to side.

"All right," he said finally. "Leave it with me. *On se débrouille.*"

Se débrouiller, to manage, to sort out, was a very useful verb in French. It was what Mara often said when she was landed with an impossible decorating problem and had somehow to reassure herself and her clients that she could make it all come right. In this case, it was Loulou who was offering to fix things for her. Gratefully, she gave the tote to him.

"And not a word to Julian, please."

"Ah. You don't want to look like—how do you say it?—the piece of fruit?"

"Fruitcake," Mara corrected in English. The translation did not work at all in French.

40

The Ropax *Bosporus I* completed its voyage from Istanbul to Marseille, docking at 13:10 on Friday. It arrived loaded with vehicles and freight designated as *marchandises diverses:* textiles, clothing, foodstuffs, rolls of carpets, ceramics packed in straw, hammered metalware. In addition to carrying cargo, the *Bosporus I* also provided limited cabin space for a handful of passengers, one of whom was Adelheid Besser.

Twelve days earlier, Adelheid had made the outbound crossing from Marseille to Istanbul, taking on board her specially adapted van. She had spent three days in Istanbul talking about salep, its use in Turkish ice cream, drinks, and health products, and the imperilled state of Turkish orchids. Then she had made trips into the field and to research stations with fellow conferencees, and now she was returning, bearing with her many flats of immature plants, individually potted. They had lived with her during the sea crossing, taking up most of the space in her cabin. Now, as the *Bosporus I* approached its destination, she had loaded them into the cargo space of her Kangoo preparatory to disembarkation and inspection.

•

"They are seedlings of the *Ophrys* and *Orchis* genera," Adelheid said grandly to the customs officer who poked his head into the back of her van. "I am bringing the plants in for scientific purposes."

The man held her passport. She shoved more documentation at him. "Here are their phytosanitary papers and CITES permits, duly issued by the appropriate Turkish authorities. It is all quite in order, as you can see."

"I have to refer this," said the customs officer. The matter was outside his area. "Please pull your vehicle to the side and wait."

"*Natürlich,*" muttered Adelheid between tightly gritted teeth.

•

At roughly the same time, a five-year old Rottweiler named Zaza was growing very agitated. She circled and scratched at a wooden crate, one of many that had been off-loaded from the *Bosporus I.* Zaza whined, gazed intently at her handler, and then sat down panting by the crate. The handler called over a colleague, and together the two men checked the origin and destination of the merchandise. Prying open the crate very carefully, they ascertained that it contained six dozen tins of olives. Just as carefully, the customs agents nailed the crate shut again.

"Okay. *Ça va,*" said the first agent, giving the crate a slap. "This can go."

•

Adelheid sat in her van. Then she got out and stood beside it, tapping her foot impatiently. After a very long wait, another officer appeared. He was a bright young man attached to the Port of Marseille *Bureau à Compétence W,* responsible for the import and export control of live and dead specimens of wild flora and fauna and endangered species.

"These are orchids of the *Ophrys* and *Orchis* genera," Adelheid repeated with slightly less aplomb than the first time she had made this announcement. "I have here all the necessary papers. Everything is in order. My purpose for bringing these plants in is scientific. I am doing research on root regeneration in co-operation with Turkish colleagues related to the sustainable harvesting of salep orchids."

"*Ah oui?*" said the *Compétence W* man. He scanned the flats of orchids, read the documentation, and turned doubtfully to her. There was something about this large woman that—well—stuck out. The plants themselves were immature, none of them in flower, which made their identification difficult. And that was precisely the problem. There were so many kinds of orchids, and in their early developmental stages they were hard to tell apart. It would be easy to slip another kind of orchid in among the mix—say, something extremely rare that had not been cleared for export, although what this might be the officer had no idea. It required considerable expertise to identify different orchid species correctly. In fact, molecular analysis was really the only certain way of avoiding species confusion. He had not the means of subjecting the plants to anything more sophisticated than a visual examination, and everything appeared straightforward. But he sensed that all was not well.

Madame Besser gazed off into the distance, looking bored while the officer studied the plants, flipping occasionally through a reference manual. She began to tap the toe of her shoe on the ground. The noise got on his nerves, and he raised his head sharply. It was then that he noticed the thin film of perspiration gathering on her upper lip. It was a warm day, and it could be that she was simply feeling the heat, but it set more alarm bells ringing in his head.

The officer smiled. "I'm afraid, madame," he said pleasantly, closing his manual, "that I will have to ask you to remove the orchids from your vehicle for closer inspection. And it would be helpful if we could go over the origin of these plants and your reasons for bringing them in once more."

•

Later that same day, in another part of the country, Julian and Mara were returning home after a wearying day of tramping the forested slopes of Aurillac Ridge, looking for *Cypripedium incognitum.* It was Madame Audebert's day in again, and neither Julian nor Mara had needed to think twice about leaving the house to her. This time they did not encounter Géraud on their trek, or Serge, for that matter. They did see plenty of flora. The fields and woodlands, the verges of the roads clamored with orchids. Bell-like Helleborine and tightly braided spires of *Limodorum* were beginning to open in the shelter of the trees. Green-winged and Tongue orchids were just coming into evidence. Sun-loving pink Pyramidals, Lady and Military orchids, those sturdy inhabitants of open meadows, now lent their colors to the grass. They also found numerous Aconite bushes, growing along stream beds. They did not find anything that resembled Julian's mystery Lady's Slipper.

As they drove, Mara gave vent again to her frustrations, which had nothing to do with flowers. The gendarmes were continuing to ignore the fact that Donny had tried to smother Joseph in his bed. Now that Donny had proved not to be their burglar, he was out free. She imagined the Barbie doll's eyes, full of gloat.

"He's getting away with it," she grumbled. "If there were only some way we could prove our case."

"Seems to me we've exhausted our case," said Julian. "I ran into Jacqueline Godet at the supermarket yesterday, and she told me Donny and Daisy are returning to Florida next week."

"Damn! It gives us no time at all. Once they go, the gendarmes will never pursue the matter."

"Look on the bright side. With Donny no longer around, maybe the Montfort-Izawa project won't go through. At least not until they can get hold of Joseph's land legally. And Joseph won't have any more night visitors. Jacqueline said Madame Tisseuil, his new live-in help, is working out well, by the way. Apparently the woman's only shortcomings are that she talks a lot and knows nothing about sheep."

Julian's own preoccupations lay elsewhere. Osman had been beaten up (he still couldn't decide if the Turk was as innocent as he claimed), Betul was worried out of her wits, and Ton-and-a-Half was having him, Julian, followed. The fact that Adjudant Compagnon had warned him to stay away from Lokum only raised his suspicions. However, he yearned for Betul's pastries.

Therefore, on the way home he drove via Brames, parked down the road from the store, and sent Mara in to find out how things were going. While she was there, he said she might as well stock up on a few things: some *borek,* preferably the spinach and eggplant kinds. Then there was a cardamom-spiced flatbread filled with sweet potato that he liked. Oh, and some baklava.

Mara returned to the car a very short time later with no *borek,* no flatbread, and no baklava. She told him that Betul had been trying to get hold of him all day. She was very upset. Mara switched on her cellphone and handed it to him.

"She's going to call you."

"What? Now?"

Julian then had the peculiar experience of watching Betul leave the store and walk in their direction to an outdoor pay phone almost opposite where they were parked.

"I can't talk from the store or house," Betul said when he answered. "Osman is sure our line is being tapped. He only uses our phones for business. Everything else, he goes out to pay phones. He even drives to different public phones to make sure no one listens in."

"What's happened?" Julian demanded. He knew from her hunched, defensive posture, which he could plainly see, that it was something serious.

"I think Osman has found out where Kazim's girlfriend, Nadia, is hiding. You know she's been missing since Kazim's death? Last night Osman went out. I followed him. He made a call from this phone I'm using now. I heard him say 'Nadia' several times, and then he said something about a place called Le Clos de Jacques or Jacquot, something like that. I didn't hear any more because he stopped talking as soon as he realized I was there. He was very angry."

"And you think this Le Clos de Something is where Nadia is?" Julian asked.

"Yes." Betul shifted the receiver to her other hand and turned to look directly at him. "He drove off in the truck very early this morning. He wouldn't tell me where he was going, and he hasn't been back since. You know he believes Nadia was responsible for getting Kazim into drugs. I'm afraid"—her voice broke—"he has gone to do something stupid. Oh, Monsieur Wood"—her free hand rose in appeal—"how can I stop him?"

Julian knew the question she really was asking.

"Call the gendarmes," he suggested without much hope.

"They will send him to prison."

They would, if Osman had really done the stupid thing that Betul feared. Julian sighed.

"I'll see what I can do," he said.

•

The Brames gendarmes, at that moment, had their hands full. Earlier in the day, Loulou La Pouge had communicated something of great importance to Laurent. He had also left a tote bag with his grandnephew. Laurent took one look at the contents of the tote bag and went immediately to inform his commanding officer.

For the first time in months, Jacques Compagnon's unlovely face broke into a smile. He uttered a string of epithets, briefly (and mildly) translated as: "Well, I'll be a monkey's uncle!"

And then the gendarme on duty passed a call through to him.

"Osman Ismet did what?" roared Compagnon.

•

"Have you ever heard of it?" Julian asked Mara as they drove out of Brames.

Mara shook her head.

"She's expecting me to head him off somehow."

"It's a bit late," said Mara. "He's had all day to get to Nadia, if that's what he was planning to do."

"I know."

"It sounds like a *gîte* or a *chambre d'hôte,*" Mara said a moment later as they drove through gentle hills lit by a late afternoon light. "They're often called Le Clos de something. A campsite, maybe."

"But where is it? We don't even know where to begin. We can't comb through the phone book searching for every Le Clos de something. It'll take ages."

Mara gave him a look. "Of course not, silly. There's a much faster way of finding out."

•

When they returned to the house, they went straight to Mara's studio. She sat down at her computer and logged onto the Internet.

"If it *is* a holiday spot, they probably have a website." She squinted at the screen, not even bothering with her glasses.

"Right," said Julian, who was Internet-illiterate and wished to stay that way.

While she worked, he walked around her studio, hands in pockets, taking in the disorder. There were large chunks of plaster molding stacked in one corner, an ancient stone sink in another. Rolls of material leaned against the walls. Her drafting table was piled high with client files loosely stored in cardboard boxes. She'd had to clear a litter of loose paper from her desk before she could even find her keyboard. He wondered how she managed to work in such an environment. It was significant that Mara did not let Madame Audebert in her studio. Maliciously, he imagined the cleaning woman suffering a terminal *syncope* in these surroundings.

After about fifteen minutes, Mara came up with three possibilities. There was Le Clos du Jacquot near Montferrand; Le Clos de la Jaconde outside Les Eyzies; and a place called Le Clos de Jeannot southwest of Issigeac. Each website showed photographs and gave details and coordinates. The first was a cluster of *gîtes,* self-catered cottages, that offered a swimming pool, a play area for children, and barbecue facilities. The second was a bed and breakfast. The third was a couple of rather tatty-looking holiday chalets near the river. Mara called the numbers given. The owner of Le Clos du Jacquot told her that none of the *gîtes* was rented at the moment but all were spoken for as of the end of May. A call to Le Clos de la Jaconde activated a bilingual recorded message asking Mara to leave a name and number; the owners, Beth and Didi, would call her back as soon as possible. The number for the chalets was answered by a very deaf old woman who shouted at her and eventually gave her to understand that the chalets were available but that she would have to speak to her son who was not there at the moment and could she call back?

They put Beth and Didi's establishment lowest on the list because Julian said he couldn't see Nadia holing up in a B & B. They decided to drive out to the other two places. Le Clos du Jacquot was nearest, so they went there first. The *gîtes,* three of them, stood on a wooded rise overlooking farming country. There was a chain across the access road. Julian parked in front of it, and they went the rest of the way on foot. Jazz and Bismuth ran ahead, marking every upright object with abandon.

All of the *gîtes* were shuttered. The owner did not live on the property or anywhere adjacent that they could see. Perhaps he was one of the local farmers. In the distance, a man on a tractor was harrowing a field. The puttering of the tractor sounded small and lost in the early evening silence.

They walked around the property, rattling the door handles, trying to see through gaps between the shutters. Dimly they made out plastic deck furniture stacked inside the front rooms, iron bedsteads with bare mattresses. The pool stood half drained and covered; the brick barbecue was in bad repair; the sandy play area was overgrown with weeds. If Nadia were hiding out here, it would be a pretty cheerless existence, Mara observed. Julian shrugged and said it was easily as good as what she'd been used to in Périgueux.

When they returned to the van, Julian walked down the road a bit. Apart from their own tracks, the grass was upright and unbroken. No other vehicle had come that way recently.

It was growing dark by the time they reached Le Clos de Jeannot, a waterfront property that stood on the north shore of the River Dropt, just on the border between the departments of the Dordogne and Lot-et-Garonne. The chalets were nothing more than a pair of weathered pine cabins with identical cookie-cutter design facades, suggesting that they aspired to an alpine setting. They, too, were locked and shuttered, although the sandy road running past them had seen recent traffic. The site offered no special amenities. Perhaps guests were meant to swim in the river, for there was a patch of shingle that could pass as a minute beach on which a picnic table stood lopsidedly, like a piece of jetsam abandoned by the sluggish, green current.

The dogs were running back and forth, tongues out, tails up. Bismuth found a plastic bag of garbage along the side of the first cabin. Julian chased him off before he could rip into it. Then, frowning, he squatted down and opened the bag. It was full of greasy food wrappers, plastic milk bottles, chicken bones. He stood up, signaled Mara to stay where she was, and slipped quietly around the rear of the cabin. Everything was utterly still. A loose shutter gave him a view of the interior. He made out nothing but the dark shapes of furniture upended against a wall. He was moving toward the second chalet when Mara was suddenly beside him.

"I think there's someone in there," she said in a low voice. "Bismuth is scratching at the door."

Together they crouched behind a screen of bushes. The other cabin was set downstream and a little further back from the river in a copse of trees. Bismuth was on the porch, looking up expectantly. He whined softly and clawed at the bottom of the door. Jazz, on the pathway leading up to the porch, gave a sharp bark. Bismuth continued whining.

The door opened cautiously. Bismuth wagged hopefully. A booted foot shot out to drive the dog off. With a yelp, Bismuth shied away, tail between his legs. A trusting animal, Bismuth was sure this human had not meant to kick him, so he edged back cautiously to try another friendly approach. From his position on the path, Jazz barked again. The door opened wider and a head poked out. It was bound in a print scarf tied at the back. In the dying light, Julian made out dark curls springing out from the front of the scarf, thick eyebrows that curved over two large eyes. The nose was long, the cheeks fat with the fullness of childhood not yet outgrown. Somehow Julian felt he knew the face; it was enough for him to realize that the person in the doorway was not Nadia.

"*Va-t-en! File!*" a voice yelled. The door slammed shut.

"Wait," Julian said, putting a restraining hand on Mara, who was already on the move. "Until it gets dark."

"It's not that," she whispered. "I just remembered it's Friday. We've forgotten about Loulou again. He's probably waiting for us right now at Chez Nous. I left my phone in the van."

Julian swore. "Leave it. He'll forgive us."

A half-hour later, as night closed in around them, thin lines of light became apparent between the shutters of the second chalet. Julian and Mara made their way toward it and stepped quietly onto the porch. Julian reached down and scratched at the door. Jazz and Bismuth, attracted by this dog-like behavior, trotted up to investigate. Julian went on scratching. Jazz, intensely interested, barked. Julian heard footsteps. The instant the door was jerked open, he was through it, followed by Mara and the dogs.

"You're supposed to be dead, you little bastard!" Julian roared, flinging himself onto the figure that tried to squirm away. "Maybe you'd like to tell me what the bloody hell is going on?"

• 41 •

"Who are you?" the young man said. He was lying flat on his back, looking very frightened.

"Julian Wood," said Julian, stooping over him. "You called me, remember?"

"This is Kazim?" Mara was so startled that she nearly dropped the length of wood that she gripped like a club.

"Leave me alone!" Kazim cried out shrilly, but he seemed to have no real fight in him. "And get those dogs out of here. I don't like dogs." Jazz and Bismuth were circling around, toenails clicking on the wooden floor.

Julian grabbed Kazim by the shoulder, flopped him over onto his stomach, and kneeled on him. "You're in no position to be picky about your company." He yanked the scarf off the young man's head and bound his wrists behind his back. Then he leaned down to address Kazim's left ear.

"You really are a piece of shit, aren't you. Do you know your mother is crying her heart out because she thinks you're dead?"

"Well, I'm not," Kazim retorted sulkily. "All right?"

"Not all right, you little *merdeux.* If you're not dead, whose body was it they found in the skip?"

"I'm not saying anything to you."

Julian yanked the curly head back sharply and let it free-fall to the floor. Mara winced.

"Let's get something straight. I will ask you questions. You will give me answers. Otherwise I will beat them out of you. Clear?"

"Okay, okay," Kazim gave in.

"So talk."

Kazim talked, punctuating his sentences with the meaningless *quoi* that seemed nowadays to be the inevitable tag to everyone's speech.

"It was Peter, *quoi.* The English guy living with Nadia. He stole the caps I gave her. He overdosed. He was a jerk, a *zéro.* And before you go on about my mother, my father knows I'm alive. Who do you think has been bringing me food, *quoi?*"

"Your father knew all along? He purposely identified Peter as you? Why?"

"Oh, *merde.* Do you need everything spelled out? The Ton was after me, *quoi.* It was the only way I could shake him."

"You were selling drugs?" Mara asked.

"Nadia did the pushing, not me."

"Speaking of Nadia"—Mara looked around her—"where is she?"

"That little bitch? How should I know?"

"She's not staying here? The police are looking for her, you know."

"So's my old man."

"Wait a minute." Mara exchanged looks with Julian. "Did you happen to talk to your father about her on the phone last night?"

"Might have done. What's it to you? He blames her, all right?" Kazim burst out. "He thinks what happened is all her fault. He wants her punished. What"—Kazim broke off as Julian stood up and hauled him to his feet—"what are you going to do with me?"

"Personally, I'd like to kick the crap out of you." Julian shoved him toward the door. "But first I'm taking you home."

"Then what?"

"Then I'm going to drop you in it."

•

Julian made Kazim lie on the floor of the van and tied his ankles with a length of nylon cord. Mara drove, and Julian sat in the back with the Ismets' errant son, riding shotgun, so to speak. Far from being silent, Kazim talked volumes on the drive to Brames. He seemed relieved at being found and did not object even when the dogs nosed him.

"It was my cousin in Istanbul who started it, *quoi,*" he said, as if to exonerate himself. "He'd bury maybe 50 grams of H in with our supplies for the store. I'd cut and sell it here through Nadia. She uses, and she knows her way around. Then I'd send my cousin a share of the profits, and he'd send more stuff. But I want one thing straight. My parents never knew a thing, okay?"

"How did Ton-and-a-Half come into it?" Mara asked over her shoulder. "Were you dealing for him as well?"

"No way," said Kazim vehemently. "Oh, I knew who he was, *quoi.* Him and that axeman of his. But the last thing I wanted was to get mixed up with either of them. And that was my problem. The Ton got word someone was working locally, and he didn't like it, *quoi.*"

"So you were competing on his turf?"

"*Merde,* you just don't get it, do you? He's got his own pipeline, I mean big volume, and he didn't want my chicken-piss action bringing in the cops. So he put the word out, *quoi.* He wanted my ass!"

Julian intoned grimly, "I'll bet he did."

"Yeah. So Nadia tells me I have to cool it, *quoi.* But then my father gets this stupid idea about Elan and me dressing up as a *salepar.* I don't want to, but he makes me do it. So here's me, working the markets dressed up in this fairy Turk outfit, fucking slippers on my feet, great stinking jug on my back"—Kazim's voice cracked slightly—"and who should I see one day but the

Ton and Serge coming toward me in the crowd. I nearly crapped my pants, *quoi.*"

"So you started a fight to get yourself arrested," Julian cut in. "And then you disappeared. You think fast, I'll give you that."

"Yeah." Kazim gave a hoarse laugh. "But the funny thing of it was, turned out the Ton hadn't even figured out who I was yet, *quoi.* Not until *you* started asking around for me, *quoi!*"

"For Christ's sake, stop saying *quoi,*" Julian snapped in irritation.

"Then what happened?" Mara asked, barely able to keep her eyes on the road.

"I hung out at Nadia's. But I was running low on cash, and she was leaning on me for rent, *quoi.* I knew my cousin was due to send another shipment, so one night I went back to the store for it. I let myself in, and I had to go through all the new foodstuffs before I found it in a bag of spices. But I saw right away I couldn't leave things like they were, boxes broken open, bags torn apart. So I had to make it look like a trashing, *quoi.* And I had to be quiet about it, with my parents sleeping upstairs. You ever try trashing a place without making a sound? I didn't break anything except the glass in the door, just made a mess, *quoi.*"

"You really are a toe rag," snarled Julian.

"At least I didn't take the cash." Kazim sounded huffy. "And I couldn't bring myself to write racist shit on the walls the way some would have done."

"Oh, good of you."

"What else could I do? I couldn't tell them. They'd have gone straight to the cops, *quoi.*"

At this point Kazim seemed to dry up. Maybe he was thinking of his parents. More likely, Julian thought, of the trouble he had landed himself in. If his imagination stretched to it, he might also have wondered about what would happen to his father for having falsely identified Peter and burying him as his own. What kind of penalty did that carry?

Julian nudged him with his foot. "Go on. What happened next?"

"You happened," said Kazim sullenly. "You spread the word on who I was and that I rode a red Honda Bol d'Or. It was easy for the Ton's men to spot me after that, *quoi.* A junkie named Deep Freddy told Serge you were after me, and the Ton sent Serge to get to me before you did because he figured you were a narc."

"You should have gone straight to the police." Mara glared at Kazim's prone form in the rear-view mirror and immediately found herself swerving to avoid dropping them in a ditch.

"Are you crazy? And put myself in it? I would have been all right, but that *vache* Nadia sold me. Serge caught up with me outside her place. He sticks this fucking gun in my ear, and says, 'The Ton wants a word.'

"So then he ties my hands and blindfolds me and dumps me in the trunk of his car, and we drive. When we get to where we're going, he drags me out, and I'm shitting myself because I'm pretty sure he's going to waste me, *quoi.* But he pushes me ahead of him and pulls the blindfold off. I'm in some kind of room full of ferns and stuff, *quoi,* and I see the Ton and a woman, and the Ton says, 'Welcome to the party, son.' He says, 'You hungry? You want something to eat?' And I start to feel better because why feed me if he plans to bump me off, *quoi?* He says, 'Open your mouth, kid,' and I open my mouth, and Serge jams the barrel of his gun in it. It nearly broke my front teeth, and it cut the back of my throat. I'm choking on my own blood, and the bastard keeps shoving the thing in. 'This is the *amuse-gueule,*' Serge says, and you can tell the *salaud*'s enjoying himself by the way he says it. Then the Ton says he's a businessman and he's interested in my little pipeline. He says, 'Who'd've thought a snot-nosed kid like you could think up such a sweet set-up?' Which I guess was a kind of compliment, except I wasn't feeling all that good about it, *quoi.* He says he's got a proposition for me. I go home, do business as usual, only now it's his associates in Istanbul at the other end, and the shipments are in kilos, not grams. As long as I do my job, he says, I'll be okay, my parents will be okay, and there'll be a year-end bonus for me, *quoi.* I tell him I don't know what he's talking about, I don't do drugs, and he laughs and says, 'Dunk him.'

"So Serge grabs me and dumps me in a tub of water, a Jacuzzi, *quoi.* They turn the jets on and he shoves my head under and keeps it there until I think I'm going to burst. Then he pulls me up for a bit and the Ton asks if I've changed my mind, and when I say no, Serge pushes me under again and keeps on doing it until I've pretty much swallowed the whole fucking tub, *quoi.* On one of my times up I hear the woman say they should be careful not to drown me, but Serge keeps on shoving me under and pulling me up until I crack, *quoi.* I say, 'Okay, okay, I'll do it.' So then the Ton says, 'Lift him.' So Serge pulls me out and dumps me on the ground, and I'm puking my guts out in a fucking flower bed. And the Ton says, 'Okay, we got a deal.' And he says to Serge, 'Get him out of here and lose him.'"

"That was it?" Mara broke in, incredulous. "Luca let you go like that?"

"Well, he got what he wanted." Kazim sounded aggrieved. "He knew I'd keep my end of the bargain, because if I didn't, he'd fix me, and not just me, my parents, too, *quoi.* But I told him, no way. They had to drive me back to Périgueux because I didn't know where the fuck I was, and I had to get my bike, *quoi.*"

"*Zut!*" Julian had to admire the kid's crazy nerve.

"So Serge took me back to Nadia's, but my bike wasn't where I left it. I figured, *merde,* some shithead's stolen it. I went up.

Nadia looked like she'd seen a ghost. Then I knew my bike hadn't been stolen, the bitch had sold it. I hadn't been gone more than a few hours, and she'd already sold my bike, *quoi!* She said she thought I was history, so why would I need it?

"But she had a bigger problem than me on her hands. Peter had been into her fanny pack and took the H she had off me. He'd overdosed, and now he was out cold. I had a look at him. 'He's not out,' I told her. 'He's meat.' She knew it, just didn't want to believe it, *quoi.* Brigitte had taken off by then, and Nadia was in a real sweat. She didn't want a dead junkie on her hands. So I told her I'd take care of it, but she had to give me the money she got for my bike. She said she only got a thousand euros, but I said, 'Don't con me, bitch. That bike was worth ten thousand new,' and she coughed up another two thousand. I figure she still kept most of it back. Junkies are like that, *quoi.*"

"So that's when you got the idea to put Peter's body in the skip? You put your ID on the body so it would be identified as you?"

"Yeah. Nothing with a photo on it and enough cash to make it look right. Nadia helped me carry Peter down. I wanted to leave him in the street, where he'd be found right away, but she insisted on putting him in the skip and covering him up with junk."

"You're a right piece of work," Julian informed him. "I don't suppose it ever occurred to you that Peter has family who should have been informed of his death, who still need to be told?"

"It was a way out of my problem, all right?" Kazim said, with the heartlessness of youth. "Anyway, I told Nadia she had to lose herself, and if she got picked up by the cops she had to swear the body was mine, *quoi.* She said she'd do it, and I knew she would because with the Ton thinking I was dead, the heat'd be off her, *quoi.* That's how her mind works. But now I had another problem, because my parents were going to think I was dead."

"Good of you to consider it."

Kazim said defensively, "Look, I called my father, okay? I told him, I'm alive, but tomorrow they're going to find a body with my ID on it, *quoi.* I said if he wanted me to go on breathing he had to identify the body as mine, not to ask questions, and not to tell my mother. That was the hard part"—Julian was surprised to hear Kazim's voice catch slightly—"letting my mother go on thinking I was dead. But I knew she'd tell the cops if she found out the truth. I figured once the Ton heard I was history, he'd leave my parents alone. But it didn't work like that. He never really needed me, just the shop as a front, and he could deal with my father just as well as me, *quoi.* Except my father wouldn't go along with it."

"And that's why Luca had him beaten up," Julian concluded.

"Yeah," said the Ismets' son, after which he fell silent. By then, they were entering Brames. Julian wanted to believe that Kazim was thinking about what he would say to his mother when she discovered that he had faked his own death. He wondered what Osman would say to Betul, for that matter.

Kazim insisted that they take him in through the back. He was terrified of being seen by Luca's goons, who might be watching the shop. Julian could understand his fear, since the lad was supposed to be dead, but it was half past nine at night, and there was no one in the streets. All the same, he obliged. The alley, as they nosed into it, was empty. Julian pulled up behind the shop. The downstairs of the Ismets' building was dark. Only a single light showed in an upper window.

"Get out," Julian said, opening the rear door of the van and dragging Kazim out by his feet.

"Hey, untie me. How do you expect me to walk, *quoi?*"

"Hop." Julian was taking no chances with the Ismets' slippery son. "You have a key, or do you knock?"

"I got a key," said Kazim sulkily. He indicated his jeans pocket. Mara dug it out. It came on a ring attached to a metal disk stamped with a death's head. However, she found that the door had been left unlocked.

"That's funny," said Kazim. "My parents always lock up at night."

Mara turned back. "I don't like this."

"Neither do I," muttered Julian. Nervously he pushed the door open and listened. Silence. "You'd better be playing straight with us, Kazim," he hissed and maneuvered the boy through the doorway first, securing him by the belt. They stepped inside.

In that instant several things happened. The door slammed shut behind them, there was a rush of movement, the darkness was suddenly bulky with bodies, and a gruff voice that Mara and Julian both recognized shouted: "Freeze! You're surrounded!" Kazim pitched forward, pulling Julian with him to the ground. Then the lights went on.

42

Jacques Compagnon was furious.

"*Imbéciles!*" he roared. "You have compromised our only chance of catching Rocco Luca in flagrante. You are obstructing the law in the exercise of its functions—"

Julian sat up to reveal the prone form beneath him.

"This," he said, cutting through the stream of the adjudant's invective, "is Kazim Ismet."

Compagnon's prominent eyes bulged. "What?"

"I think he has a lot to tell you." Tenderly, Julian fingered his left elbow where it had struck the floor.

"*Bordel!*" spat the adjudant. "I'll wager he does."

"I'm not saying anything until I've seen a lawyer," said Kazim. "It's my right. What have you done with my parents?"

Compagnon smiled unpleasantly. "Your mother is upstairs. Keeping company with Gendarme Sauret. Your father"—the veins in the adjudant's neck swelled—"is being entertained by the drug squad in Marseille. Earlier today he took delivery of a crate of six dozen cans of olives laced with heroin, my lad. Two kilograms of the stuff. It was tagged by a sniffer dog at the port."

"A dog can smell through cans?" Mara marveled.

"Easily."

Kazim made a strangled noise. "You're crazy. My father wouldn't get involved in something like this."

"I've got news for you, *mon gars.* He is involved. Our telephone surveillance logged a call to your father at 11:03 last night ordering him to meet a shipment due to arrive at Marseille port at thirteen hundred hours this afternoon. He doesn't normally drive all the way to Marseille for a crate of olives, does he? We couldn't trace the call back to Luca—the bastard uses throwaways—but we know the word came from him all right. Your father's *linked*, Kazim. The only thing that will go in his favor is that he turned himself in."

"What?" said Julian.

"That's right," said Compagnon, and he sounded more outraged than pleased. "Customs let the crate pass in the expectation that whoever came for it would lead us to Luca. Unfortunately, it was Osman Ismet, and he gave himself up voluntarily on the spot." The brigade leader's features shaped into a horrible grimace. "He told a customs officer he *thought* there *might* be something funny with the olives. God in heaven! We could have landed Luca in it, but Ismet short-circuits the whole operation by singing like a choirboy! After that, our only hope was that Ismet was supposed to bring the shipment back to the store. He was to set the crate inside the rear door and leave it unlocked. He only thought to inform the drug squad of this when he realized his wife would be in for it if Luca's goons came and found no olives. The drug squad informed us. We were waiting for Luca to take delivery"—Compagnon's face turned nearly purple—"when *you* turned up."

"Look," pleaded Kazim, and for the first time Julian had the impression that he was worried about someone other than himself. "You've got it all wrong. The heroin was me, okay? I mean, before this. I was doing a little business on the side, *quoi*, but my parents knew nothing about it. First of all, they would never deal drugs. Second, they'd never order that many olives at one time. Besides, two kilos of H? That's chicken piss. It's more than I ever handled, but way less than Ton-and-a-Half would even bother with. He's expecting a big shipment, I mean *une grosse affaire, quoi,* but it has nothing to do with us."

"A big shipment?" Compagnon demanded hoarsely, "How big?"

"He didn't say."

"How do you know all this?"

Kazim recounted his experience in the Jacuzzi. "After they hauled me out, I heard him talking about it."

"Luca?" Compagnon wanted to be certain. "You're positive it was Luca?"

Kazim shrugged. "Sure. I saw him, *quoi.* He said a mom-and-pop outfit like Lokum had its uses, but he wouldn't risk using us for something really heavy. Anyway, why would the Ton even want to touch us? He must have figured you were already all over the shop because of me. I think he just wanted a front." Kazim looked resentful. "I heard him say something about a *passe-passe.*"

"*Passe-passe?*" Compagnon said sharply. A conjuring trick. His color went from white to red with shock and anger.

"Now you see it, now you don't," murmured Julian.

"*Putain!*" roared the adjudant, and expelled a volley of even stronger curses. He looked as if he would explode. "Are you telling me while the sniffer dogs were occupied with a crate of *maudits* olives, something else came in on that Ropax?"

"Ropax?" Julian stiffened. "Are you talking about the *Bosporus I?*"

"Exactly."

"What day is it?" Julian asked urgently.

"The sixth," said Mara. "Why?"

"You," Julian addressed himself to Kazim. "The woman you said you saw with Luca. What did she look like?"

"Don't know. I just got a glimpse of her, *quoi.* They were trying to drown me, remember?" Kazim's tone was petulant.

"Think, you little prick," Julian said in a barely contained voice.

"Okay. Okay." Kazim spoke very quickly. "She had crazy red hair, *quoi,* and big bazookas."

Julian swung around to the brigade head. "What time did the *Bosporus I* dock?"

"A little past one."

Julian checked his watch. Ten past ten.

He said, "She was bringing back a load of orchids. Adjudant Compagnon, I think I know how the drugs came in. Trouble is, by now we may be too late to catch her."

43

"Her name is Adelheid Besser," Julian told the gendarmes. "She's an orchid collector and breeder. She went to Turkey for a conference. She traveled out on the *Bosporus I.* She was due back today, and that's probably how she returned."

"And you think the drugs are coming in with the plants?"

"If she was the one Kazim saw, then she's clearly involved with Luca, and it's a good bet that's how they're doing it. The orchids make a good cover. Customs focuses on the plants. Their interest would be on spotting a rare species she might be trying to smuggle in, not on drugs. But, of course, she'd have all the necessary import documentation because the orchids are for scientific purposes. She's got some kind of research project going with people in Turkey. The plants would have cleared easily."

Compagnon ordered two officers to remain at Lokum and called the gendarmes staking out Luca's residence.

"He's not here, sir," said the officer who responded. "Do you want us to remain?"

"Damn right," barked the adjudant. He then called Brames for reinforcements to join the team at Luca's.

Compagnon, Laurent, and Julian jumped into a police car that Albert brought to a squealing halt in front of the store. Four more gendarmes piled into a second vehicle. Mara wanted to pile in as well, but Compagnon told her irritably to return to the store and give her statement to Lucie Sauret who, with her partner, was remaining to guard Betul and Kazim. Before Mara could protest, he slammed the car door in her face. Julian powered down his window.

"Be reasonable, Mara. Do what the adjudant said. I'll see you back at the house." He tossed her the keys to his van.

He directed them out of the town, onto the D660, then north toward Queyssac. The village was dark and silent as they sped through it. After continuing for another few kilometers, Julian realized that he had missed the turnoff. He told Albert to go back. Albert braked hard and swung around sharply, nearly sideswiping the gendarmes following them.

"*Bordel!*" roared Compagnon as Albert veered wildly. They bounced over the rough shoulder, teetered on the brink of a ditch, regained the road, nearly hit another oncoming vehicle, and shot back down the way they had come. The second car of gendarmes completed an equally reckless U-turn and came roaring up behind them.

"For pity's sake!" Julian exclaimed. "Slow down. It's somewhere around here."

"It had better be," Compagnon growled dangerously.

Eventually their headlights caught the wink of a reflector on a signpost ahead of them on the left.

"That's it." Julian pointed. "Turn there. Her house is at the top of the hill."

"Pull off," Compagnon ordered Albert. "We'll go on foot from here. Don't want to give the game away."

Julian added silently, *If there's anyone there to give the game away to.* He had no reason to believe there would be. Grimly, he put the probability of coming up empty-handed against the probability of success at ninety to ten. Too much time had elapsed. Compagnon's growl was a pale forewarning of terrible things to come if the entire operation proved fruitless.

They left the cars at the roadside and went at a trot up the long, steep lane leading to the house. A bright moon made it possible for them to find their way without the use of flashlights. At the gate set into the high stone wall surrounding the property, Compagnon called a halt.

"The entry is remote-controlled," Julian informed him. "You have to ring the bell. She likes security."

Compagnon said, "Security, eh? Do you know if the wall is wired? And if the grounds are equipped with motion sensors?"

"Er—no. I don't know, that is," said Julian lamely.

Laurent was shining his light along the top of the wall. "Looks clear, sir."

Compagnon and his men were fit and well trained. Swiftly and silently they were up and over the barrier, which proved not to be wired, but their movement on the other side as they ran toward the house triggered a flood of outdoor lights. Julian, who was left hopping about on the outside, heard Compagnon swear.

Julian tried to scale the wall as the gendarmes had done, scrambling for hand- and footholds. Unfortunately, his repertoire did not run to vertical assaults. A second attempt was equally unsuccessful. The third time, he found a toehold, but it crumbled under his weight just as he flung an arm over the top. He hung in limbo for a moment, then slithered down painfully, scraping his hands and nose.

"You need a boost," said a voice behind him.

He whirled around and stared into the shadows. "Mara? What the hell? What are you doing here? Christ, Compagnon will explode when he finds out you followed us."

"Good. I'd like to see him all over in little bitty pieces. You came damned close to hitting me back there on the road, you know. Where did Albert learn to drive? Montreal?"

"Ah," said Julian. "That was you."

"Of course it was me. That was a rotten thing you did, leaving me behind."

"I'm sorry, but you really shouldn't be here."

"And you should? Oh, forget it. Come on. Leg up."

She made a platform with her hands, and Julian used it. This time, with a few additional shoves from Mara, he made it all the way to the top. From where he sat, straddling the crown of the wall, he saw lights coming on in room after room of the house. He glimpsed shadowy forms moving swiftly past the windows. Ever direct in his methods, Compagnon must have gained entry by knocking on the front door. So someone was at home, and the gendarmes had been admitted to search the premises.

"Hey, what about me?" Mara called up to him.

"Look," Julian said. "You'd better stay where you are. You don't know what they're going to find in there. Ow! Let go, will you!"

"Like hell I will." She was hauling herself up with the aid of his right leg. If he wasn't going to help her, she would help herself. Julian had no choice, if he wanted his knee to remain intact, but to pull her the rest of the way.

"Do you mind telling me what this is all about?" Mara demanded once she was perched rather breathlessly beside him.

"Drugs. And orchids." Briefly, he explained.

They jumped down together, landing on soft earth on the other side. The house went suddenly dark. Then the exterior lights went out.

"The greenhouse is at the back," Julian said. "That's where the action will be. If there *is* any action," he added, revisiting the bad feeling he was having about the operation.

He led the way. Rounding the corner of the house, they nearly collided with Compagnon. Behind him were Albert and two other gendarmes.

"We've been over the entire property," the brigade head told

Julian ominously. "No one's here but a woman who says she's the live-in plant assistant. She said she was expecting her employer back sometime this evening, but she hasn't seen or heard from her. So where is Adelheid Besser, eh?"

"Ah," said Julian stupidly.

"And what's *she* doing here?" Compagnon flared, realizing who was with him. Then he said wearily, "Don't tell me. I don't want to know. In fact, the real question is what the devil are *we* doing here?"

Julian heard movement behind him. Laurent's long shape appeared.

"Exterior sensor lights deactivated, sir," said Laurent. "Jean-Louis is with the employee to make sure she doesn't take off or make any phone calls."

"This is nothing but a wild goose chase," Compagnon sputtered at Julian. "A complete waste of police time. To say nothing of the hot water you'll land me in if Madame Besser chooses to lodge a complaint. I'm treading a fine line here, making a night search based only on a hunch—a foreigner's hunch, at that!"

Julian could feel the adjudant's anger blasting him like heat from a furnace. The ninety–ten odds he had given himself collapsed completely. It had been his intuition, the gut level understanding one orchid freak has of another, that had brought them there. He had reasoned that Adelheid would want to get her plants bedded down as soon as possible after their stressful journey. But he had thought simplistically. There was no reason why she had to bring them back here. What was to prevent her from bedding them down in Marseille itself, or Montpellier, or Nice, or Cannes, or Zurich, for that matter? Except, the tiny intuitive voice in his head reasserted itself, she was fussy about her orchids, and they would take precedence over any non-botanical cargo she might be carrying. She would be especially fussy if she were trying to smuggle in something rare. Her priority would be to get it into an optimum environment, and where better than here?

Then where, as Adjudant Compagnon had asked, was she? It was now twenty to twelve. The *Bosporus I* had docked almost eleven hours ago. The trip from Marseille took seven, maybe eight hours. There were many reasonable explanations for her delay. Traffic, car trouble, an accident. Or, if there had been some problem with her documentation, if she had encountered a very thorough inspector who had wanted to examine each plant, she could have been held up for any amount of time.

"Adjudant Compagnon," Julian said. "I think you should wait."

"For what?" snapped the seething brigade commander.

"I think Adelheid Besser isn't here because she's still on her way."

"*Pah!* The woman's had plenty of time to arrive. Plenty of time to go anywhere. She could be in Paris by now."

"No, she's coming here," Julian said stubbornly. He was growing more certain of his conclusions by the second. "She needs to. For the orchids. Besides, she'd figure there's no risk. They think you've fallen for the *passe-passe*."

Compagnon's scowl lunged at him out of the semi-darkness. "All right," he said reluctantly. "But you'd better be right."

Mara spoke up: "If you're planning on taking anyone by surprise, shouldn't you do something about your vehicles, adjudant? They're sitting on the roadside like beacons."

"*Merde!*" exclaimed Compagnon. "Albert, Roussel, on the double. Get them out of view. And take this—take her—with you!"

44

At a little past midnight, headlights flared among the trees lining the long approach to the house. A few minutes later, the automatic gate swung inward, and a vehicle passed through. Its tires crunched quietly over the gravel of the drive leading around to the greenhouse. The gate remained ajar.

Adelheid parked the Kangoo. She sat for a long moment, staring at the play of moonlight on the glass panels of the greenhouse. Briefly, she wondered why the motion sensor lights had not come on but concluded that the system had short-circuited again. It was always happening. She was too weary after a long day, a long drive, to give the matter much thought. She had gone through a very tense time with that damned *Compétence W* agent, who had wanted to impound her orchids. However, she had held her ground, had even threatened to lodge a formal complaint with his superiors, naming people on whose favors she knew she could not call. In the end, she had outlasted and outargued him.

She climbed stiffly out of the van and, with a jingle of keys, unlocked a side door leading into the anteroom of the greenhouse. She returned and opened the rear of the van. She reached inside, partly disappearing from view. As she reappeared, bearing a flat of plants covered by a clear, rigid plastic top, another car, its lights extinguished, pulled up alongside her. Serge lowered the driver's window.

"Ah," she said, "*c'est vous.* You came quickly. I haven't unloaded yet."

The doors of the Mercedes swung open. Serge's thin form emerged from one side, the bulky figure of Ton-and-a-Half from the other.

"Forget it. We'll take over from here," the Ton said.

"No," she said firmly. "You must wait until I unload."

"I said, we'll take over from here."

"Wrong," said Adjudant Compagnon, stepping out from the side of the greenhouse as the floodlights came on. "*We'll* take over from here." Gendarmes moved in swiftly from all directions. "If you would oblige us, Monsieur Luca?"

"What the hell?" snarled the Ton as Roussel and Albert pushed him and Serge against the Kangoo to frisk them. Laurent clamped a restraining hand on Adelheid.

Another gendarme, one Hubert Chauvin, checked the interior of the Mercedes. "Clear, *mon adjudant*."

Adelheid stared about her, open-mouthed with shock.

"You!" she exclaimed, spotting Julian.

"Afraid so," Julian said with some satisfaction.

"Funny time of night to be paying a visit," Compagnon observed to Rocco Luca.

The Ton said coolly, "What's funny about it? I ordered some plants. I'm collecting them. When I do it is my business."

"You, a plant lover?" Compagnon snorted.

Luca shrugged. "Well, sergeant, you know how it is—"

"*Ad-ju-dant*," Compagnon corrected, biting the word out in three syllables.

"Whatever. You got a conservatory, you fill it."

"What's in there?" Compagnon demanded of Adelheid, thrusting his chin in the direction of the van.

"Plants," said Adelheid.

Laurent played the beam of his flashlight around the interior of the cargo area. Julian peered in. The shelves of the Kangoo were crammed. Roughly twenty pots to a flat, ten flats in all, he counted swiftly, including the one Adelheid held.

"Orchids," he corrected. He turned to her unbelievingly. "You supply *him* with orchids?"

"You got something against it?" said the Ton. "I'm not supposed to like flowers?"

"Orchids and what else?" demanded Compagnon. "All right," he barked at Julian. "Don't just stand there. Get on with it."

Julian approached Adelheid. "Let's start with these," he grinned. He had to pry the flat from her fingers.

The plants were young, not in flower, and exhibited none of the uniformity of nursery-cultivated specimens. At this stage they consisted of rosettes of leaves, many blotched and lanceolate (some kind of *Orchis,* he guessed), others rounder and unmarked (probably a species of *Ophrys*). The fact that most were in terrible condition, limp and bruised from the jostling they had experienced in transport over many days, confirmed all of his suspicions: the orchids themselves were not the objective of the exercise. Moreover, if the objective was to carry out—what had she said?—root regeneration trials, why do it in France? Why not in Turkey? Or if it was necessary to run the trials in Adelheid's laboratory, why subject the plants to the stress of a long sea and land journey when it would have been so much better to air freight them? Most significantly, why now? Why not wait until the plants were dormant and simply ship the tubers? None of this added up from a botanical perspective.

Julian set the flat on the ground, squatted down, and removed the pot closest to hand. He squeezed the flexible plastic sides and eased the single plant out into the palm of his hand. Gently, he probed with his finger. He saw nothing but soil and moss surrounding an immature root structure. He restored the orchid to its container, carefully tamping down the bedding around it.

Luca, who had been watching the proceedings with an expression of disdain mixed with puzzlement, said, "I'm leaving. You have no right to detain me. I'll have the skin off your backside for this. I have friends who could have you busted down to *gendarme auxiliaire, ad-ju-dant.*" He stressed the title with muscular antagonism. He straightened his clothing and started to walk away.

Compagnon said sharply, "I suggest you remain where you are, monsieur." To Julian, he snarled, "Speed it up, will you?"

Julian pulled out the next container. Again he turned up nothing more suspicious than potting soil. Behind him, Compagnon breathed with heavy impatience. When Luca asked sarcastically if this was going to take all night, Julian had to suppress an almost hysterical desire to giggle. Then he realized that it was a case of hiding the trees in the forest. *Go for the plants in the middle.* His hand hovered over a pot in the very center of the flat.

"Wait," Adelheid broke in. For the first time, her voice sounded slightly shrill. "If you must, I will do it."

Aha! The hairs on the back of Julian's neck rose up like tiny antennae. He was about to make Adjudant Compagnon a happy man. Unless . . . his orchid freak's mind neatly sidestepped the matter at hand to pursue a mystery of its own. Her sudden desire to be helpful could also mean that there was something more than drugs in there, something that she wanted handled very carefully. An orchid, but not just any orchid. She had brought it in, slipping it past the eye of the inspecting agent. Maybe there was more than one, mixed in with the common specimens he saw before him. He took the flashlight from Laurent and directed it at the plant he had been about to pick up. There was nothing really unusual about it, except—yes—its leaves were slightly wider and more strongly veined than those of its neighbors. It was also in considerably better health, as if it had received more careful treatment. And there, if he was not mistaken, was another like it. And another. So what were these little beauties that Adelheid had managed to smuggle in? Turkey, he knew, had orchids that grew nowhere else. Julian felt the woman stiffen as he lifted out the pot. Her tension communicated itself to the gendarmes. All of the officers watched mesmerized as Julian held his prize up. Suddenly, he paused.

But it did not make sense! His mind switched back to what he was supposed to be looking for. The orchid was something he could turn over to the proper authorities later. For now, Compagnon was waiting. Kazim had said *une grosse affaire,* a big shipment. By his reckoning, Adelheid had brought back some two hundred plants. If the drugs were hidden in the pots, as he had surmised, that would mean each plant, each pot, had to conceal a certain amount of heroin. But the containers were small, scarcely holding two cups of soil, and so far he had found nothing that should not have been there. Perhaps the shipment was a lot smaller than Kazim had thought. Say, 5 to 10 kilos, 25 to 50 grams a pot, that was possible. But would a man like Rocco Luca even bother with something that insignificant? *Or*—slowly, he turned the container about on his palm—*perhaps the orchids were not the medium at all, and they were dealing with a double conjuring trick.*

He put the plant down and stood up. "It's not in the pots," he said decisively. It was what he should have realized from the beginning. "It's in the van itself."

For a big man, Luca's movement was as swift and fluid as running water. He was around the front of the Kangoo and into the Mercedes before any of the gendarmes could react. Serge turned to run as well, but Albert brought him down in a neat tackle.

"Halt!" ordered Compagnon as the Ton spun the Mercedes around, its tires spewing gravel. Compagnon pulled out his

Beretta and fired. Laurent fired. Compagnon's shot struck the right rear fender of the car just centimeters above the tire. Laurent's bullet nicked the corner of the house as the Mercedes swung around it and out through the open gate.

"*Merde! Putain! Bordel!*" bellowed Compagnon, unleashing his armory of expletives. "Laurent, Roussel, after him, dammit!" Then he was on the phone.

"No sign of Luca this end, sir," a voice answered crisply.

"That's because he's here," Compagnon shouted. "He's on the run. Stay there in case he returns. I'm ordering blocks on every road leading away from the Besser woman's place. We've got to stop the *salaud*."

It had taken Roussel a moment to wrest the Kangoo's keys from Adelheid, but he and Laurent were now in the van and bucketing through the gate and down the lane after the fast-disappearing tail lights of the Mercedes. Once the Ton reached the main road, the Kangoo would be no match for the powerful Merc. Luca would be away. As for Compagnon's road block, they both knew that there were as many byways threading the area as there were capillaries supplying the human body.

The Kangoo bounced over the deeply rutted lane, its cargo of plants shifting crazily, its rear door swinging wildly. As it lurched around a bend, the door caught a tree and crashed shut with a noise of breaking glass. The impact was enough to cause the van to slew sideways. Roussel gunned the motor and pulled back onto the lane, but it was precious seconds lost, and the Merc was gaining distance, accelerating toward the bottom of the hill, with fifty, now twenty-five meters to go before it met the junction with the road.

"*Merde!*" Laurent shouted. "We're going to lose the bastard."

Suddenly, as if he had willed it, a wall of white shot across the Mercedes' path. The Ton, with the momentum of his downhill escape, had no time to brake. He smashed headlong into it with a sickening thud followed by the endless blaring of a horn.

•

The horn wailed, an alien sound, through the woods. Adjudant Compagnon set off at a run, Julian behind him. Albert and Chauvin remained behind to handcuff Adelheid and Serge to the wrought-iron gate and ensure that they stayed that way.

"*Mon Dieu!*" shouted Julian when he saw the wreckage.

The nose of the Mercedes was buried in the right side of a van—Julian's van—which was folded at a crazy angle. Rocco Luca was slumped forward against the steering wheel, his groans muffled by the deflated airbag. His head rolled sideways, and the horn stopped, leaving an almost jarring silence.

Laurent backed out of the Mercedes.

"What?" demanded Compagnon, breathing hard.

"He's alive, sir," Laurent called over his shoulder. "I've called SAMU. An ambulance is on its way."

It took Julian a moment to realize what must have happened. When he did, he felt sick.

"Mara!" he cried out as Roussel appeared around the front of the van. In the illumination of the headlights the gendarme looked white and shaken.

"She—she's not there," he stammered. "The driver's door is sprung open. She must have been thrown out on impact. But I can't find her." He waved his flashlight around him, as if to prove his point.

Julian snatched it from him. "Mara!" He ran forward, sweeping the beam across the ground. He saw nothing but empty asphalt and broken glass.

Roussel, Laurent, and Compagnon joined him in the middle of the road.

"Mara!" four voices called together.

Their ringing cry elicited only silence.

A dense wall of shrubbery rose up on the other side of the road. Julian stumbled toward it. Could she have been thrown that far? Her injuries would be terrible. And then, in the tall grass, lying at the base of a tree, he saw something that nearly broke his heart.

"Mara!" he shouted in anguish, dropping to his knees beside a limp form, sprawled face down, that was frighteningly still.

•

"She's alive," said Compagnon.

"Don't move," Julian ordered gruffly as she tried to raise her head. In the illumination of three flashlights, he was relieved to see no serious bleeding. She must have jumped at the point of collision and rolled, finishing up on the other side of the road. Only the thick grass had saved her from major injury. She was stunned, bruised, badly scratched, and winded, but otherwise intact.

"The ambulance will be here any minute," said Laurent.

A few minutes later, when Mara had recovered enough to speak, she told Compagnon rather jerkily: "He told me to go home"—indicating Roussel—"but I decided to hang around. I drove the van down the road and left it. Came back on foot. Then I saw a Kangoo go up the lane. Then a Mercedes. So I went back for the van. I thought if any of them tried to get away, there the lot of you'd be. Up a hill with no vehicle."

"Up a hill—?" the genuine concern in Compagnon's face flushed into embarrassment.

"Well, I was right, wasn't I? I was driving back when I heard gunfire. Then I saw headlights coming down the hill. Fast. I knew someone was making an escape. That's when I got the idea of blocking off the lane. I—I'm sorry about your van, Julian."

"The van? The van? Forget the sodding van!" cried Julian with feeling, not knowing where to touch her, how to hold her.

• 45 •

The Two Sisters Restaurant was full for lunch as usual that day. They had not been to bed, but Mara, too keyed up for sleep by the night's wild events, had downed two painkillers and insisted on celebrating. She had wanted a table on the porch, where patrons were sitting happily in the sunshine. However, it was market day, and the only spot available was the same one they had sat at the last time they had eaten there. It was, Julian decided, a placement of last resort. The rush of waiters past them created, as before, a constant stirring of air, and the clanging of the elevator door disturbed their conversation.

They had a lot to talk about. Eleven hours earlier, Jacques Compagnon and his officers had lifted a false floor in the cargo area of the Kangoo to discover 200 kilograms of very good-quality white, sealed in zip-lock bags, worth an estimated forty million euros, street value. The adjudant was crowing like a morning cock. His *flair* about Rocco Luca had proved right, and he had just pulled off one of the biggest drug busts in French history. As for Yvan Bordas, Compagnon was confident that this was the important shipment the narc had got wind of, that Kazim's testimony established an MO linking Luca and Serge to the undercover agent's murder. The chlorinated water found in Yvan's lungs was consistent with his having been drowned in Luca's hot tub. The potting material found in his nostrils could have got there if he had been dumped or pushed face down into one of Luca's flower beds. Samples found on the dead man were being compared with samples from the Ton's conservatory.

It was the best day in Compagnon's life, and for the Brames Gendarmerie. All of the gendarmes attached to it shared in their commanding officer's glory. If the adjudant forgot to acknowledge the role that Mara and Julian had played in his success, it was no doubt because he had many other things to occupy him. Congratulations rained down on him from his peers and superiors. Judge Bouchillou, the *juge d'instruction* heading up the case, had commended him. Praise had come direct from the Procureur de la République himself. Promotion was sure to follow.

Rocco Luca was in a closely guarded hospital room, recovering from a fractured jaw, a broken nose, and major facial burns from the airbag. Serge Taussat was in custody being questioned about the murder of Yvan Bordas, along with a string of other unsolved gangland assassinations.

Adelheid had been charged with possession and trafficking of illegal drugs. She vehemently denied all involvement, claiming to know nothing about the cargo of heroin and admitting only to agreeing to leave her Kangoo, while in Istanbul, in the care of a man named Mustafa for the space of three days. She had done this at the explicit request of Rocco Luca, to whom she sometimes supplied orchids. The greenhouse assistant confirmed that her employer often traveled with the Kangoo on orchid-related business. It was equipped for the transportation of plants, and Madame Besser had planned to bring back a load of orchids from Turkey for research purposes. She was certain her employer would never have anything to do with drugs. However, Kazim had positively identified Adelheid as the woman he had seen in the conservatory at the time of his dunking, making her an accomplice to the plan.

It was clear now how Luca's mind had worked. Seeing his Toulouse base compromised, he had hit on his orchid supplier as a fallback. She was, providentially, planning to attend a conference in Istanbul. Kazim's little sideshow had given the Ton the idea of diverting the police's attention to Lokum. He knew a tap would be ordered on the Ismets' line, enabling the gendarmes to hear what they were meant to hear, and he had ordered Osman beaten up to make things look convincing. It was a cunning scheme, worthy of the Ton, but not clever enough, everyone was saying, for Jacques Compagnon. The adjudant was almost convinced of it himself.

That morning, Julian had the pleasant experience of informing Géraud that he could kiss goodbye any expectations, botanical or monetary, where Adelheid was concerned.

"*Bah,*" Géraud had scoffed. "I never needed her."

"Oh, and by the way, I happened to mention to the gendarmes that you are a business associate of hers," said Julian happily. "They'll be round to talk to you. In due course."

"What?" said Géraud, badly shaken.

That, Julian thought with satisfaction, *should take the wind out of the old goat's sails. Just long enough,* he prayed, *to let me find* Cypripedium incognitum *first.*

Mara had come through her ordeal with nothing worse than bruises and loss of skin. Her elbows and forearms were bandanged, she showed a purple welt on her forehead, and the palm of her right hand was heavily gauzed and taped. Since she was left-handed, it did not impede her lifting a glass to Julian.

"Congratulations," she said.

"And to you." He toasted her. "We deserve this."

•

Kazim had had his time with a lawyer and was now sitting on one side of a table in an interview room at the Brames Gendarmerie. He had been there since ten o'clock that morning. His posture, at first cocky, had sagged as his interrogation proceeded. Now he was slumped sideways, legs splayed, in an attitude of sullen antagonism. Opposite him sat Laurent and Adjudant Compagnon.

"I need to take a piss," said Kazim.

"You just had a piss," said Compagnon. His bulging eyes were bloodshot. His carrot-colored hair stood on end. His uniform was rumpled and he was running on nothing but coffee, but elation over his success buoyed him above bodily considerations.

Kazim shifted his legs in the other direction. His eyes followed the flight of a hornet thumping senselessly against a window.

"Let's go over this again," said Compagnon.

"Look, I keep telling you. My parents had nothing to do with any of this. They knew *rien, nada, niente.* Got it? And you might remember, this is my first offense, *quoi.*"

"So you keep telling me."

"Plus, I've co-operated. I've spilled my guts, haven't I? You're supposed to go easy on me."

Compagnon barked out a laugh. He leaned in. "Come on, Kazim." His tone was as heavy as the fall of an axe. "Face it. You're in it up to your neck, and so are your parents. You've been bringing in drugs with their knowledge and acquiescence for months. It doesn't get more serious than that, even if you and your father turned co-operative in the end. And don't count on Luca to help you out. Once he's able to talk, he'll be fighting to save his ass."

Kazim's eyes returned to the hornet.

"All right," he said finally. "Maybe we can do a deal."

Compagnon's mouth stretched into a terrible grin. "What do you have to deal with? Like you say, you've spilled your guts."

"Yeah, well, there's something else. You drop all charges against me, leave my parents out of it, and I'll give you something you don't have."

The adjudant's prominent eyes grew wary. "I'm listening."

"Are we on?"

"What have you got?"

"I know what happened to the old woman."

"What old woman?" asked Compagnon, frowning.

"*Merde.*" Kazim threw up his arms. "The one who fell down the stairs, *quoi!*"

•

Their lunch was long in coming. By the time it arrived, they were both starving.

"How is it?" Julian asked. She had ordered braised lamb shanks that he had insisted on cutting up for her. He himself was tucking into an ample, straightforward serving of steak and fries, the meal he had been denied at Chez Nous the night Mara had dragged him away to save Joseph.

"Mmm," she said with her mouth full.

The waiter Emile gave them a nod of recognition as he hurried by.

And there was more than a Kangoo full of heroin to talk about. The morning's *Sud Ouest* had carried the story, not of the drug bust—that news was still breaking—but of the arrest of the rhyming burglar. Loulou had "*débrouiller*-ed" the matter. The gendarmes had paid Christine and Alice a visit, the bronze *animalier* were being held as evidence but would eventually be returned to Prudence, and Adjudant Compagnon, another major triumph to his name, was full of himself. Interestingly, Alice had claimed all responsibility for planning and executing the robberies, including the doggerel. Christine, Alice maintained emphatically, was innocent in knowledge and deed.

"It's the only thing I don't understand," said Mara. "Why is she doing it? Why shoulder the blame? They were both involved. They had to be." In fact, she thought that of the two women, large, stolid Christine was the more likely to take everything onto herself, to do the sacrificing. She seemed to love more.

"Pragmatics," Julian said around a mouthful of very rare steak. "They probably worked it out between them. Alice's weavings necessarily link her with the targeted houses, so she took the rap." He swallowed and followed up with a sip of wine. "Someone's got to look after the sheep. Besides, Alice will probably get a short sentence, with time off for good behavior. And they'll probably let her go on weaving while she's inside. She'll have an exhibition, to a lot of fanfare, when she comes out, and everything's brilliant."

Pragmatics. With a splash of tease, for dashing Alice was enjoying her moment of celebrity. Indeed, she competed with Adjudant Compagnon, the man she had so sorely twitted, for media space. The *Sud Ouest* had devoted its entire center section to the case. Why had she written the poems? For the fun of it, *mon cher.* Why had she made a target of Jacques Compagnon? "Oh," she had replied unrepentantly, "the world is too full of people who take themselves so seriously. We need a little fun in our lives, *n'est-ce pas?*"

A few minutes later, Mara said, "The only person we can't sew up is Donny O'Connor. He's getting away with attempted murder, and he and Daisy are returning to Florida the day after tomorrow."

"There's not much we can do about it."

"Bastard. I never liked him."

"You never liked *her.*"

"Or her," Mara admitted. "But for different reasons."

"Maybe it's because the two of you are alike in some ways," Julian risked observing.

"Alike?" Mara jerked her head up sharply. "Alike? Is that how you see me?" She was shocked.

"I mean, deep down." He wished he had not said it. "You both have that core, go-for-it disposition."

Emile, on his way past their table to the kitchen, interrupted them to say quickly: "You were asking about that third party?"

"Who?" glowered Mara, still affronted.

"The one who was supposed to have lunch with Monsieur Luca last month."

They both looked at him expectantly.

"Well, that's him. I thought he seemed familiar when he came in, but it wasn't until he sat down at the same table that I realized who he was. Monsieur Luca has a reservation today, you see. It jogged my memory because that fellow was the first to arrive the last time as well. I recollect he hung around for a bit, and then he left."

Mara and Julian stood up to see over the crowd.

"Wait here, Julian," she said.

"No." He tossed down his napkin. "We'll both go."

•

They approached the window table casually.

"Business lunch?" Mara inquired.

"What's it to you?"

Mara shook her head. She sat down on one side of the American. "He's not coming, Donny."

"He was arrested last night," said Julian, taking the chair on the other side. "He and Serge Taussat. It'll be top story on the eight o'clock news tonight."

Donny looked from one to the other.

"What are you talking about?"

"Big drug bust. Rocco Luca. The cops will be looking into all his dealings. That includes associates."

"Nothing to do with me," Donny shrugged. "Never heard of the guy."

"Oh, come on, Donny," said Julian. "Why are you here? At this table? I'm sure the police will be very interested in Montfort-Izawa. I take it Luca is the Montfort part?"

"I told you. Never heard of him."

Mara smiled, not very nicely. "You should choose your business partners more wisely. Did you know you'd be laundering drug money? Or perhaps you didn't care?"

Donny's face went hard and red. "Look, you two. I don't want to be rude, but I've had just about all I'm fucking well going to take from you. You've got nothing on me, you never will. So get out of my face. Get out and stay out, you hear?"

He pushed away from the table and left them, just as Adjudant Compagnon, accompanied by Laurent and Albert, entered the restaurant. They spoke with a waiter who said something and looking uncertainly about him. Heads turned curiously in the gendarmes' direction. Donny was halfway across the floor, walking quickly, bum tucked under. Then he was past the gendarmes and nearly through the double glass doors when Julian realized what he was seeing: the guilty waggle. He stood up abruptly, knocking over his chair.

"Oi!" he yelled, skipping around a busboy. "Oi!"

· 46 ·

"I know you've never liked me."

Mara did not try to deny it.

Daisy looked around her, gravitated toward the art deco sofa once again, and sat down. As always, she was well groomed, but she looked tired and pale.

"I've never liked you much, either, to tell the truth. I've always found you so—I don't know—so earnestly Canadian."

Mara's eyes flashed dangerously. "What's that supposed to mean?"

Daisy sighed. "Forget I said it. I'm not here to pick a fight."

"Then what are you here for?"

"I've come," said Daisy without a trace of embarrassment, "to ask something of you."

Thrown off balance, Mara stared at her visitor. Then she did something that surprised even herself. She laughed. Her laughter started small and grew until she was coughing out breathless, slightly hysterical salvos. It was as if she were expelling all of the tensions of the past month. Daisy smiled, not her bright red elastic smile but a tight, bitter thinning of the lips, waiting for Mara to compose herself.

"What?" Mara leaned back in her chair, regarding the Barbie doll with something like complacence now.

"I had nothing to do with Amélie or Joseph. And I had no idea what Donny was up to. I want you to believe that."

"I suppose I do," Mara admitted reluctantly. "If you'd wanted to kill Joseph, you would have succeeded. And you wouldn't have relied on a chance encounter to push Amélie down the stairs."

"Thanks very much," said Daisy ironically. "But that *is* how it happened, you know. Donny had come to France—"

"Yes. You covered for him well. You let everyone think the two of you had arrived only in time for the funeral."

"*I* arrived in time for the funeral. I can't help what you assumed. As I was saying, Donny had come out earlier to get things going on the golf course project."

"His business partner was Rocco Luca. One of France's biggest drug barons."

Daisy lifted thin shoulders in the hint of a shrug. "Donny never was a good judge of character. Of anything. Luca was pressuring him to bring off the Montfort-Izawa deal. It's been pending for years because it was pinned on the Gaillards' land. I knew nothing about it. It's God's truth. I did the *viager* simply to help Amélie and Joseph out financially. They really were struggling. But Donny, being who he is, saw it as a development opportunity. He bought up the surrounding land with the idea of creating a golf–condo complex, and he made the mistake of borrowing from Rocco Luca to pay for it. When he couldn't make good on the loan, because he's always overextended and I wasn't willing to go on bankrolling him, he gave Luca shares in the scheme in lieu of. He never expected either of the Gaillards to live so long." Daisy pushed back a loose strand of hair.

"So he murdered Amélie and tried to bump off Joseph."

Daisy's face stiffened. "That's not how it happened. That Saturday, Donny was supposed to meet Luca at the Two Sisters. He got to the restaurant early. He was crossing the porch to use the men's when he saw Amélie starting up the stairs. She'd lost Joseph in the market, and she thought she could get a better view of the crowd from the porch, so he went down and helped her up the rest of the way."

"And helped her down," Mara said harshly. "He gave her a murderous shove and coolly went back into the restaurant and out the back way using the elevator."

Daisy shook her head. "He swears he didn't plan it, and I believe him. They were up there on the porch alone, no one could see them, and it suddenly came to him that with Joseph ill, if he could get Amélie out of the way, he could probably persuade Joseph to settle up and move off the land. Luca was leaning on him hard, and he really was desperate. So"—she took a deep breath—"he pushed her. Like a little kid who shoves another out of the way to get a toy he wants."

"And then he set to work on Joseph. First, he tried to get him into a nursing home. You gave him his lead there. But Joseph insisted on dying in his own bed, so your husband decided to speed things up for him by frightening him into a heart attack. And when that didn't work, by smothering him. Donny's not a toddler, Daisy. He's a vicious, murdering bastard."

The porcelain-blue eyes went dull. "He's weak. He always means well, but he's weak. Do you know what my daddy said when I told him I was going to marry Donny? He said, 'He's a bad planner, baby. He's a gambler who'll spend his life and your money dreaming up big deals he can't pull off because he hasn't a clue how to get to where he wants to go, and he'll always try to take a shortcut without seeing where it will land him.'"

A silence fell between them. Daisy studied the Aubusson rug without seeming to recognize its value. With a sense of mild surprise, Mara realized that she wore no perfume. Her clothing was unusually casual: jeans and a cotton shirt. Was this a purposeful performance, calculated to win her sympathy? Or was this the stripped-down Daisy, someone whom Mara found she could not dislike quite as much as she thought?

"What will you do now?" she asked.

Daisy surfaced from her thoughts. "I have two choices. It's the other reason I came to see you. I'm thinking of selling up and leaving France. That includes the *viager.* But I want to be sure the person who buys it won't try to take advantage of Joseph. That's why I thought of you. I know you'd never do anything to hurt him. Are you interested?"

"Me?" For the second time, the Barbie doll had thrown her off center. It had never occurred to Mara to acquire more property. She already had more than she could manage. But on the other hand, it might be the only way she could ensure that she would not eventually be encircled by something she did not like. She pondered. Why not? And then she wondered, how much?

"I—I don't know," she said faintly. "It's a big property."

"I suppose you'll want to talk to Julian?" This time Daisy had no trouble with Julian's name.

"Well, yes. I suppose I do." The two of them together? Maybe they could swing it.

"If you don't buy it," said Daisy with calculation, "I'll have to find someone else who will. No telling what they'll do with the land."

Mara sensed the arm-twisting and set her chin stubbornly.

Daisy saw the chin. "There is an alternative." She fixed her gaze on Mara. "You know Joseph has someone living in?"

"Yes. Madame Tisseuil."

"Well, I heard from Jacqueline that she's not working out as well as they'd hoped. She's starting to get a little sloppy about his care. I know what you think of me, Mara. You think I'm aggressive and grabby and pushy." She shrugged off any denial on Mara's part. "You don't have to be polite. And maybe I am all those things. But that aside, I really do care about Joseph. And, like you, I want him happy and well looked after."

"I know that," Mara said sincerely. "Although we differ on how that should happen."

"No, I accept now that he really does want to remain in his home. So I've talked with him, and with Jacqueline. If I can't find a suitable buyer for the *viager,* he's going to get rid of Madame Tisseuil and I'll move in to look after him myself. The place will take some fixing up, but it's mine anyway when he dies. You'll have me"—Daisy's wide, red smile was back—"for a neighbor."

Mara swallowed involuntarily and choked.

"Joseph has agreed to that?" she gasped.

"Why not? He likes me. And I've had plenty of experience with my daddy."

"But"—Mara's mind marshaled objections—"your work. Your travel. And you're not here year-round."

"I can be, and I'll hire in temporary care when I'm on the road."

"But"—for the first time, Mara felt genuine concern for the woman before her—"how will you deal with the neighbors? I mean, even if they believe you're blameless in all of this, you'd still be seen as the wife of a murderer. It's a small community. They'll never accept you, Daisy." She pictured Suzanne Portier, Francine Boyer, Huguette Roche, to say nothing of the men and the other commune residents, all of them standing stony-faced, like a human barrier. Community ill will could be a long-enduring thing, as Christine Gaillard could attest.

Daisy's face took on a set expression. "I'm not one to run from things, Mara. It's what I don't like about backing out of France. Part of me would rather stay and meet things head on. For my own sake, if not for Donny's."

"So . . . are you saying the choice is somehow up to me? If I accept to buy the *viager,* you'll leave? If I don't, someone else will get it or you'll stay and—and be here?"

Daisy grinned. "Interesting prospect, isn't it?"

•

Dinner was not at Chez Nous that Friday but chez Mara and

Julian on Monday night, when the bistro was closed and Paul and Mado could join them. It was a joyful celebration that included not only Loulou (who had forgiven Mara and Julian for standing him up the previous week), but also Joseph and Jacqueline Godet. Paul was in an excellent mood, and Mado, looking gorgeous, shared wonderful news. She was expecting again. The couple had brought champagne, and everyone drank to the mother's (and the baby's) health. Mado joined in the toast with an unaccustomed glass of milk. Julian put out a tray of Betul's savory snacks to go with the bubbly.

"What is this?" murmured Joseph, staring at the cocktail-sized dolmas before him.

"Grape leaves and spiced rice," said Paul.

At this point, they were joined by Laurent and his girlfriend, Stéphanie, a tall young woman with freckles and corn-colored hair, so they did the toast all over again. The pair seemed shy in the presence of others, especially since Loulou could not refrain from firing broad hints about June weddings at his grandnephew. Perhaps that was why the young couple spent most of the evening exchanging bashful glances. Mara, reading symptoms of the tender, silly first throes of love, felt warmly toward the two and wistfully envious.

"*Tout est bien qui finit bien,*" beamed Loulou. All's well that ends well. "Monsieur O'Connor and the Besser woman have been charged, and Luca and Serge won't be troubling us for a long time to come."

"That's a relief," Julian said. "Serge was tailing me, you know."

Laurent shook his head. "He wasn't. He was on his way to Madame Besser's to return some orchids that Ton-and-a-Half's girlfriend complained weren't blooming. Serge just happened to fall in behind you, and when he saw you turn up the lane, he waited at the roadside until you went away. He never even realized who you were."

"Really?" said Julian, feeling oddly let down.

But the best news that Laurent had to impart was that Betul and Osman Ismet had been cleared of any involvement in smuggling or possessing drugs. Osman, however, would have to answer for concealing Peter's death and burying a British national under a false identity. Kazim faced charges, but his punishment was likely to be lenient, given his youth, his clean record, and his co-operation with the police.

The meal was excellent. Julian's starter of cold poached asparagus (fresh green sprigs, not white) and quail eggs in a tasty *sauce béarnaise* was much appreciated. Mara surprised everyone with a succulent veal roast (bought rolled, seasoned, and ready to cook from the butcher).

"Better than that dog food you made me," Joseph grinned.

"What dog food?" asked Jacqueline, startled.

Mara also served up an entirely successful version of her mother's recipe for oven-browned creamed potatoes. *Gratin dauphinois* sans tears, she confided to Julian. Loulou provided a selection of cheeses. Dessert was Betul's *mulhallebi.*

"So what do you think, Paul?" Julian asked as the bistro owner dug into the sweet, pistachio-sprinkled pudding.

Paul swallowed. "Not bad," he said. "Still doesn't beat a crème brûlée. But I guess the customers will get used to it."

"The customers—?" Julian looked bewildered.

"Lokum," Mado laughed. "Paul's done a deal with Monsieur and Madame Ismet. They're supplying us with a whole line of Turkish foods."

"Paul?" Julian turned to his friend in astonishment. "I thought you said—"

The bistro owner cut him off. "Their stuff's not bad. Not to my taste, mind, but we're giving it a try. Mado needs to take things easier." He pulled a folded menu from his jacket pocket, smoothed it open, pushed it in front of Julian, and pointed to the newly worded script.

"'International Cuisine'?" Julian read and marveled. "You're billing yourself as offering international cuisine?"

"Why not?" said Paul, assuming an offended air. "You got something against foreigners?"

EPILOGUE

"Are you sure you want to do this, Julian?" Mara asked as they walked down the rutted road that led to the forest at the side of Mara's land. The dogs galloped ahead of them. It was getting on for the middle of May, and the sweetness of robinias had replaced the lilacs on the breeze. "We'd have the Gaillards' property, but all of this, the woods and the fields below, would still be open for whatever Montfort-Izawa wants to put on it."

"We can't shut out the world, Mara." He stood looking up at the trees, the cloudless blue sky above them. "But since Donny and Luca are two of the moving forces behind Montfort-Izawa, and since neither of them will be thinking much about golf at the moment, I'd say we're safe. For a while, at least."

"But your cottage. You'd have to sell your cottage." Her voice rang with hope and an after-peal of mourning. Hope for them together, for the bigger thing his decision seemed to suggest. Mourning for what she knew he would lose.

My cottage, he thought. *My retreat, my own little haven where I can leave my socks and books lying about, my dishes unwashed.* The wildflower garden that he had built up lovingly over the years. The chimney that never drew well, the roof that leaked. The poky back rooms that offered more damp than cheer. But his own thing, his safety net, his private space.

There came a time when one had to make big decisions, and this was one of them. Julian turned to face her.

"You know, when Luca crashed into my van, I thought I'd lost you." His voice caught in his throat. "I don't think I could have stood it."

"Oh, Julian," Mara whispered.

He took a deep breath. "So. I'm going in with you on the *viager*. But I have two conditions."

"Name them!"

"One, starting tomorrow you help me do a serious search for my orchid. I'm not talking about an occasional tramp through the fields. I mean a thorough, methodical scan of every possible habitat until we find it. It will mean days of rough walking, rain or shine, for the next three weeks. And the same thing next spring, and the one after, and after that until we find it. You'll get scratched and muddy. Your feet will hurt, your back will ache. You will end up hating me. Don't agree until you've thought this through."

"Done," she said without hesitation. "And two?"

He gave her a long, searching look.

"What?" she said, her heart beginning to beat very fast.

He grinned, drew her close, kissed her, and whispered three words in her ear: "Dump Madame Audebert."

"Dump—?"

>*Patsy*, Mara fired a message into the ether, *you're not going to believe this!*<